KAT & MOUSE

KAT & MOUSE

A CROSSCANNON ROLLER DERBY ROMANCE

JACQUELYN HEAT

Jacquelyn Heat

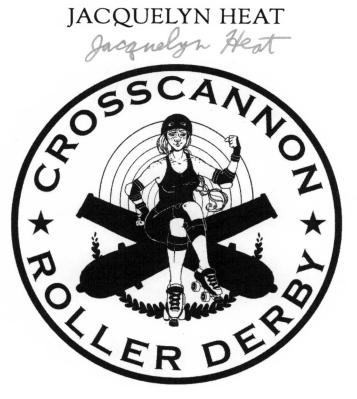

METAL HEART PRESS

CRD logo illustration © 2019 by Arthur Oak Padelsky

ISBN 978-1-7339402-0-7 (paperback)
ISBN 978-1-7339402-1-4 (ebook)
Library of Congress Control Number: 2019905400

Published by Metal Heart Press
Downingtown, PA
www.metalheartpress.com

For my #1 fan
and motivator.
Thanks, Poppo.

Contents

What is Crosscannon Roller Derby?

Welcome to historic Crosscannon, Pennsylvania! Located roughly an hour outside Philadelphia, this vibrant suburban town is home to the Crosscannon Roller Derby league (CRD).

CRD plays modern flat track roller derby. This version of the sport was invented in 2001 and has been growing rapidly ever since. Today, flat track derby is played internationally, with leagues participating across the globe. While there exist multiple variations on the rules, CRD follows those developed by the International Federation of Flat Track Derby (IFFTD)—a fictionalized parallel of the real-world Women's Flat Track Derby Association (WFTDA).

Crosscannon fiction is romance set in and around the derby world. Occasional gameplay sequences take place in the story, and these scenes aim to feel authentic to those who know the game. However, for those readers who are less familiar with roller derby rules and terminology, a "New Recruit FAQ" is provided on page 387. The FAQ serves as an on-hand reference, explaining the basics of derby in lay terms.

If indeed you are new to derby, I hope you find *Kat & Mouse* an enjoyable introduction to our sport, our culture, and our community!

CHAPTER 1

Pinned

Jet rolled up to the jammer line with an air of casual indifference. Short, pastel purple hair protruded from beneath her helmet. The back of her white jersey displayed the name "Polly Rocket" above the number ninety-seven. Tall and thin, she appeared downright waifish next to her opponent.

Geneva Convulsion, who answered to "Vee" both on and off the track, was already set just to Jet's left—crouched, focused, and itching for the whistle to start the jam. Her long, blonde ponytail cascaded across her back, momentarily obscuring the name and number on her black tank top.

The jam timer called, "Five seconds!"

Blockers for both teams steadied one another in their respective formations. Dorothy Mauser planted herself on the inside line, just ahead of Vee. Dot, as they called her, went by the derby name Dreadmau5—or "Mouse" for short, though she was anything but. Dot was five feet, six inches of pure ferocity with the brute strength to back it up.

Blood Siren, wearing white, occupied the space directly in front of Dot. It would be Dot's job to move her out of the way and make a path for Vee. Not a terrible challenge, provided she could find an angle. A little teamwork could make that happen. Dot dropped her left arm and signaled to Vee with a hand gesture.

TWEEET!

The whistle blared.

Dot stepped aside, allowing Vee to skate past her and approach the white defense. Vee juked to the right. The white team shifted with her, which resulted in Siren leaving the inside line briefly unguarded. Dot skated into that vacant position and plowed into Siren's flank, prying the gap open further. Vee cut back to the inside and slipped through the space Dot had created.

But Lynn, or Lizzy Clementine, had seen this coming. She'd been up front, acting as a support for her white teammates—and keeping an eye on the black jammer. Now she rolled to the inside and boxed Vee in, halting her progress.

Meanwhile, some distance back, Jet was getting the better of the black team's defenders. She faked to the left, then twirled to the right, spinning around MasKara Crush. Before the blockers could react, she'd blown past them like a leaf on the wind.

"Mouse! Jammer out!" Kara cried.

At her teammate's call, Dot shifted her attention away from Lynn and Vee. The pack was entering turn one. Jet came rocketing up the outside, and only Dot could stop her now.

With three powerful strides, Dot hurled herself across the track on an intercept course. Jet saw her coming just in time and stopped short, wheels screeching against the wooden rink floor. Dot adjusted. She leaned hard right and curved her trajectory toward Jet.

"RRRAAHHH!" With a roar, Dot swung her hip and shoulder into Jet. The impact knocked the white jammer clear off the track and left her sprawled on the floor.

A cheer erupted from the black team's bench. Dot's adrenaline surged. These were the moments she lived for. It was pure elation.

TWEEET!

But it was not to last.

"Black five, direction!" The penalty was called by referee Katrina "Katbot" Brooks. Kat gestured the direction-of-gameplay hand signal, followed by the signal to leave the track.

"What?" Dot turned to face Kat with fire in her eyes. "That's such bull! There's no way!" She was indignant, certain that hit had been flawless.

"Black *five*, direction!" Kat's delivery remained calm and composed. Her expression betrayed no reaction to Dot's outburst. She performed the hand signals again.

"Mouse!" Coach Rex's voice came from behind. "Don't get an insubordination! Just go!"

"Ghaaa!" Dot huffed in frustration, but she left the track and headed for the penalty box.

This was far from the first time Dot had butted heads with Kat. She was up to six penalties in tonight's scrimmage. Kat had called four of them.

Dot sat in the box and fumed. She needed to avoid getting another penalty. Seven would be enough to foul out of an actual bout, and she really didn't want to see the look of disappointment Coach would give her if she "fouled out" at Tuesday night scrim. Dot had seen it once before. Once was enough.

* * *

"Problem is, I feel like I have to walk on eggshells or I end up getting some bullshit call. I can't play my best derby like that!" Twenty minutes later, Dot was getting her chance to vent.

Lynn sat next to her, listening patiently while unstrapping her elbow and knee pads. Lynn was taller and leaner than Dot, with well-defined musculature and a wavy, platinum-blonde fauxhawk.

"What's goin' on?" Jet was late to the conversation. She took a seat on the other side of Lynn, who answered her with a bored look.

"Mouse thinks the refs are out to get her."

"Again with this?"

"Look, it's true." Dot lifted her helmet off. She shook out her wild mane of electric blue hair and brushed it back with her fingers. "It makes sense. Think about it. They know I'm always penalty-heavy, so they watch me like a hawk, already *expecting* me to fuck up. Then of course they call a penalty at the slightest glimmer that I might have done something wrong. And that's how I end up penalty-heavy *again*. It's a self-perpetuating cycle!"

"Uh-huh." Jet was only half listening, her attention focused on untying her double-knotted skate laces.

"Meanwhile, look at all the forearms and multiplayers that were happening tonight. And none of that shit got called. Why? Because they're fixated on me! And Kat's the worst of them. I don't know what *her* deal is."

"Maybe she likes you," Jet teased. Lynn snickered.

"For real, though. It's ridiculous." There wasn't an ounce of humor in Dot's tone.

"So what're you gonna do?" Lynn shot her an expectant stare. "Have you thought about talking to Kat?"

Dot fired back a sideways look. "Are you serious? Honestly. How do you think that conversa—"

"Ladies and gentlepersons!" Coach's voice boomed from several yards away. Dot, Lynn, and Jet turned to find her literally standing on a soapbox. Yes, Coach Train Rex had a wooden crate with the word "SOAP" painted on it, just for occasions like this. "Our next bout is seven weeks from now!" She paused and bent down as Vee muttered something in her ear. Then she straightened up again. "Make that *six and a half* weeks!"

Coach folded her arms and waited a moment longer to be sure she had everyone's attention. "I know that seems like a long time, but we can't afford to get complacent. This is *the* bout, people. Right now our ranking doesn't qualify us for playoffs, but if we beat the spread against Second Bridge we can still make it in." At that, the few remaining side conversations fell silent. Every ear in the room perked up. "We have a real shot here. We played well on Saturday, and I want us to build on that momentum. That means showing up for practice ready to work these next six weeks. This is not a break for us. Everybody with me?" Coach scanned the room. Heads nodded. Eyes watched her attentively. She continued, "Also, *please* make sure you're meeting all the league requirements so you're eligible to be rostered. Pay your dues for June, and get your community event participation if you still need it. If you missed the First Friday event, you can still sign up to help with Pridefest, which is on June second. And again, come to practice! I cannot stress that enough!"

Vee added, in her thick Irish brogue, "That means no skippin' Sunday mornings, Miss Polly!"

Jet shrank in her chair, face screwed up in a guilty grimace.

"Alright . . ." Coach jumped down from her box. "Everyone finish gearing down, and let's get outta here before they kick us out."

Lynn zipped up her now-full skate bag, then fastened her helmet to an outside strap. She stood and slung the bag over her shoulder. Jet was nearly finished packing her things as well. Dot, who'd been preoccupied griping about the refs, still had half her gear on.

Lynn addressed Jet over her shoulder. "I'm gonna put my things in the car, babe."

"Okay, I'll be out in a sec." As Lynn walked to the door, Jet turned her attention to Dot. "You coming to the diner with us?"

"I don't know." Dot was hastily removing her knee pads. "I kinda just wanna go home, have a beer, and go to bed."

"Aw, come on. You know you'd rather have a milkshake than a beer." Jet closed her eyes and moaned. "*Mmm*, Maggie's double chocolate milkshake."

"Sorry, Pol. Not tonight."

"Alright, suit yourself." Jet stood and extended the handle on her rolling skate bag. "We'll be there if you change your mind." She offered Dot a sympathetic smile and then followed after Lynn.

The rink cleared out quickly after that. Dot hurried to cram her things into her own bag—the same kind as Jet's, but in black instead of Jet's turquoise. She zipped it shut, slipped her shoes on, grabbed the green canvas bag she called a purse, and strode toward the exit. Looked like she'd be the last one out.

As Dot approached the door, something caught her eye. A metallic glimmer on the floor. A pin? She picked it up and inspected it. Yes, it was an enamel pin—a green leaf outlined in gold. It had sort of an oblong heart shape to it, or maybe a spearhead, with serrated edges. Could be a mint leaf. The backing was missing. Dot scanned the carpet, but the little piece wasn't to be found. In any case, this thing probably belonged to someone in the league.

She put the pin in one of the side pockets of her bag. Finding the owner could wait until Thursday night practice. Right now, it was beer and bed time.

* * *

Mid-afternoon the next day, Dot sat at an old, heavy wooden table. Years of abuse could be seen on its uneven surface—dents, scratches, paint flecks of all colors.

Deafening electronic dance music filled the large, open room. Progressive house music, to be precise. It was so loud as to drown out all other sound.

Dot's foot tapped with the beat. Her attention was focused unwaveringly on the task in front of her. Fine-tip Sharpie in one hand, ruler in the other, she measured and made markings on a thin sheet of aluminum.

On the table, to Dot's left, lay a pile of such aluminum sheets. Each sheet bore the Coca-Cola logo and vivid red background on one side.

A cardboard box several feet away held the tops and bottoms of the former cans.

To Dot's right was strewn an assortment of tools and accessories—heavy-duty scissors, a few more markers, a rotary tool and several bits, a tube of industrial craft adhesive, a small hammer, and a box of metal stamps in various shapes and sizes.

Set back from Dot, in the center of the table, stood a roughly three-foot-tall sculpture in the shape of a dragon. Held up by a rod attached to a metal base, it looked to be in the process of taking flight—positioned upright, wings halfway unfolded, hind legs extended as though they'd just pushed off the ground, and tail still dragging behind.

Every inch of the dragon was built out of these aluminum sheets, which Dot had cut, shaped, filed, sanded, and connected together. Large portions of the beast's metal skin had been stamped into patterns resembling reptilian scales, in both appearance and texture.

The sculpture remained unfinished, however. The jaw and most of the two front legs had yet to be added, among other small pieces and fine details.

Dot finished cutting along the markings she had made. Then, with her hammer and a diamond-shaped stamp, she started tapping the scale pattern into the sheet, one tiny diamond at a time, in rhythm with the music.

Tap . . . tap . . . tap . . . tap . . . tap . . .

Silence. Huh?

The music had stopped. Dot lifted her safety glasses. She twisted around and craned her head back to find Lynn standing by the computer desk, squinting and covering her nose and mouth.

"Oh my *god*, Dot! Open a window!"

The fumes from Dot's adhesive had filled the room. It stank like chemicals. Dot had grown used to the smell over the past few weeks, in the course of building her creature. She must have forgotten to open up some ventilation today.

"Shhhit! Sorry, my bad!" Dot jumped out of her chair. "I *wondered* why my eyes were burning. Mystery solved!" She rushed across the room and began opening the three windows on the far wall.

Back at the entryway, Lynn turned the ceiling fans to max speed. "You're gonna give yourself brain damage with that stuff. How long have you been in here?"

"Uh, since noon. What time is it now?"

"A few minutes past three."

"Yeesh." Dot had noticed she was feeling a little dizzy upon standing up. "I'm just gonna stay over here, then, and breathe some actual air for a while." She sat back against the window sill. "So what are you working on?"

Lynn dropped her sketchbook onto the desk. "I'm hoping to finish the new Burger Life design, so I can get it scanned into Photoshop and start coloring."

"Ooh, I'm excited for this one. Can I see what you have?"

"Of course! One sec." Lynn opened her sketchbook and flipped through it with a delicate hand. Then she carried it over to Dot and presented the showing page.

The sketch portrayed a derby skater in full gear. She appeared to be jumping, soaring through the air with her arms out. Her pose was more comic book superhero than realistic skater, but it made for a great tee shirt design. The standout aspect of the picture, though, was the fact that she had a cheeseburger crammed in her mouth, a box of french fries clutched in one hand, and an overflowing cup of soda in the other. To the left of the skater appeared the words "WILL SKATE FOR BURGERS."

Dot's eyes lit up. "That's fantastic!"

"I wanna redo the liquid spilling and add some more fries flying out of the box. Otherwise I'm pretty happy with it." Lynn turned the book around and inspected the sketch herself. "If I get it into Photoshop today, hopefully I can have transparencies ready by Friday and we can make the screens."

Lynn and Dot did a lot of screen printing. Dot was the real expert on that end, while Lynn provided the original art. They ran an online shop—Lizard & Mouse—where they sold their creations.

This room, a converted three-car garage, comprised their studio space. The wall with the three windows stood in place of the original garage doors. The interior was painted entirely in matte white, and fluorescent track lighting on the ceiling provided brilliant illumination. The computer desk stood against one wall, next to Lynn's drawing table. A multi-basin steel sink and counter took up most of the opposite wall.

Besides their screen printing equipment, the studio was littered with art projects. Lynn's sketches and full-color drawings adorned the walls, some framed. Dot's sculptures filled the corners of the room, except for a few wall-mounted pieces interspersed among Lynn's art. But these items had all become background noise to Lynn and Dot, who worked in this studio on a near-daily basis.

These side projects represented their passions as artists, but screen-printing was their bread and butter. Tee shirts, pillows, tote bags, and patches were the big sellers on Lizard & Mouse. The artwork generally catered to the derby community. That's where L&M got the most exposure, thanks to Lynn and Dot's expansive social media networks.

Lynn laid her sketchbook on the drawing table, then plopped herself into the cushioned office chair in front of the computer. She entered her login and password and sat back while it loaded her settings.

"How'd you sleep last night?" Lynn asked without turning away from the screen.

Dot heaved a sigh. "Crappily. I was too keyed up after scrim."

"I figured. Every week." Lynn smirked. "You should just come to the diner on Tuesdays and get some food in you. You'd sleep like a baby."

"Yeah, probably." Dot pushed off the window sill and ambled lazily back toward her work table.

"Anything exciting happen after we left? Did Coach chew you out again?"

"Pfft. No, I just took forever getting changed, and I was the last one there." Dot paused and pursed her lips in thought. "You know what . . . I found something on the floor as I was leaving. Maybe you know who it belongs to." She turned to face Lynn. "It was a pin, like"—she motioned with her fingers to indicate the size—"you know, one of those enamel pins. Shaped like a mint leaf."

Lynn swiveled the chair around to face Dot. "A mint leaf?"

"Yeah, sort of an oval spearhead shape, with jagged edges. I'm guessing it belongs to someone in the league. Probably fell off on their way out the door."

Lynn leaned forward, elbows on her knees and hands folded. "Mint leaf. Where have I seen that before?" Her brow furrowed for a few seconds. Then she inhaled sharply. "Oh! I know that pin. It's not a mint leaf. At least, not like a regular mint leaf."

Dot raised an eyebrow. "No?"

"No. You're not gonna like this."

"Try me."

Lynn hesitated for a moment. Then she said, "If it's the pin I'm thinking of . . . it's a catnip leaf."

Dot's other eyebrow rose. "You're kidding me."

"Not kidding. And I know what you're thinking. And you're right. It's Kat's."

Dot closed her eyes and exhaled. "Of course it is."

"Wait." Lynn held up a finger. "Let's just make sure it's the same pin."

She swiveled back to the computer and opened a browser window. Dot could tell she'd gone to Facebook, but couldn't see what page. Lynn typed something in a search bar, then scrolled past a number of posts. Finally she clicked on an image, which opened larger on the screen. A photo of the pin.

"Is that it?"

Dot moved closer, peering over Lynn's shoulder. "Yup, that's it alright. Where is this pic posted?"

"One of the visual art groups I'm in. It's all local people. Kat's in it too." Lynn glanced back at Dot. "This pic is the only reason I knew what kind of leaf it was." She pointed to the image description. "Check it out. Hashtag 'catnip.'"

"Okay, right. But what's Kat even doing in that group? Is she an artist?"

"She's a photographer."

"Oh?" Dot's eyes narrowed.

"Yeah, fine art photography. And she's got serious skills. Here, hold on." Lynn clicked a link that took her to Instagram—Kat's profile.

As Lynn scrolled down through Kat's gallery, Dot noticed there were very few selfies or impromptu shots. Nearly every image appeared to have been carefully composed.

Lynn clicked on a photo taken inside an old, abandoned building. "See? She's really good. Look at the way she caught the beams of light streaking in through holes in the ceiling. How cool is that? And I love how she plays with focus in a lot of these." She cycled through a few more photos.

Dot gave each image a cursory glance as it appeared on the screen. "Yeah, she's okay."

Lynn snickered. "Come on. I know you're not fond of her, but you can at least give credit where it's due."

"*Okay*, okay! She's a really good photographer." Dot sighed. "Crap ref, but good photographer. Does that make you happy?"

"Yes, very." Lynn grinned. "I knew you had it in you."

"Alright, so what am I gonna do with this pin?"

Lynn turned around to face Dot. "Uh, give it back to her."

"Right, but I mean . . ." Dot bit her lip. "What if I give it to *you*, and *you* give it to her? You seem to have a rapport with her."

"Dot. Really?" Lynn gave her a dead-eyed stare. "For one, just because we're in the same Facebook group, that doesn't mean we're best buds. And that's beside the point anyway! Just give her the pin!"

Dot looked down at her feet and blew out a breath.

"What are you afraid of?"

"It's not that I'm afraid! It's just . . ." Dot folded her arms. "Look, you know I hate confrontation."

"Ha! It didn't look that way when you yelled at her on the track last night."

"That was different. It was in the heat of the moment. I don't know what to say to her, just face to face."

Lynn rolled her eyes. "Say, 'Here's your pin back.'"

"Ugh, you make it sound so easy."

"You can do it." Lynn put a hand on Dot's arm. "I believe in you."

Dot groaned.

"Alright." Lynn focused her attention back on the screen. "Now that that's settled, I'm gonna check email and sales, and then I wanna get that drawing done."

Dot pivoted on the ball of her foot and returned to the old wooden table. She stood behind the chair and stared at the dragon's face. But she wasn't really looking at it. Her mind was elsewhere.

So the pin belonged to Kat. Certainly Dot could get it back to her without having to talk to her. She'd leave it on top of Kat's skate bag next scrim. No big deal. Kat wouldn't even know who'd returned it.

There. Problem solved. Satisfied, Dot sat down at the table and picked up her little hammer. Something else was missing though . . . Oh!

"Hey, Lynn, you mind turning the music back on?"

"You got it."

With a couple of mouse clicks, the heavy beats resumed—at half the volume they had been, but Dot could work with that. Her foot found its rhythm, and soon her hammer was tapping away once again.

* * *

That night, Dot was sitting up in her bed, scrolling through Facebook on her tablet. She'd already checked all of her notifications. Not that there had been many. She'd also read all of her email and looked for updates on her favorite blogs. And swiped left until she'd run out of faces to swipe. There really wasn't anything left to do but go to sleep.

Yet there she was, scrolling past post after post, not really absorbing what she was looking at anymore. She was wasting time, avoiding a little seed of curiosity that had been germinating since that afternoon. Of course, this was getting her nowhere. But then, if she tried to go to sleep she'd just be lying there thinking about it. Hmm. *Fine.* Maybe if she just satisfied her curiosity it would leave her alone. That's what she told herself.

Dot returned to the home screen and opened the Instagram app. She was hard pressed to remember her password, but with a few educated guesses she figured it out.

Her own account displayed all of a dozen pictures—random memories from years ago. She tapped the magnifying glass icon and in the search bar entered "Katrina Brooks." Then with one more touch, there was Kat's page.

It was no wonder Dot had felt compelled to return to this gallery. Each photograph had a way of standing out on the screen. Each one drew the eye to explore it further. Side by side like this, they seemed to compete for attention.

Dot found the first photo Lynn had shown her—the one in the abandoned building—and opened it full-screen. Those sunbeams shone down from above, reflecting off the dust in the air. The light seemed to create a sanctuary of warmth in the center of the shot. Outside of it, deep shadows filled every crevice, and surfaces were illuminated only in a pale blue. The floor was blanketed with chunks of broken concrete, steel rebar protruding from many of them. In the background, a decaying wooden staircase rose out of the rubble. There was a loneliness to the scene. A kind of sorrow. Maybe even a sense of fear.

Dot returned to the gallery and opened the next photo. This one depicted a statue of Lady Godiva, as noted in the caption. A replica, actually—not that it was important. The shot had been taken from the front, with light coming from the right. It was the deep red-orange light of a sunset. The contrast it created on the surface of the statue was brilliant. The warmth of the sun and the chill of the shade were almost palpable. What's more, the background wasn't just out of focus. There was something about the *way* it was out of focus. Something that made the lady and her horse seem to come forward, right off the screen. They seemed *alive*. Dot was impressed.

She continued through a few more photos, each one as alluring and unique as the last. Kat hadn't left lengthy descriptions—just a hashtag, or a short note at the most. However, what did appear in her bio was a link to a website. By the eighth photo, Dot was invested enough that she had to know where this link led. She touched it.

What opened in front of her was Kat's own fine art photography site. Here, the photos were presented in high resolution and organized into several themed galleries. There was the gallery of abandoned buildings, and one of statues and figures. The other themes included disassembled objects, antique medical equipment, and miscellaneous. The site itself had a professional-looking layout.

Dot began exploring. The medical equipment drew her attention first—vintage syringes and surgical tools, bloodletting equipment, apothecary jars and the like. Around each object, a scene had been constructed which gave it relevance and dimension. Photo after photo, Dot was fascinated by the way this still frame world came to life. She took her time with each picture, marveling at Kat's ingenious composition. And when she finished that gallery, she moved on to another.

By the time she'd made it halfway through the fourth gallery, Dot was struggling to stay awake. She had become so thoroughly immersed that she'd lost her sense of time. How long had she been at this? A glance at the clock showed it to be . . . *1:00 AM?* That would mean she'd just spent two hours going through Kat's photos!

Dot rubbed her eyes. How had two hours gone by so fast? She'd fallen down a rabbit hole of Kat's creation. *Kat*, of all people! Of course, Dot had always known there had to be some kind of depth to Kat beneath that robotic facade. But this? This was . . . unexpected.

She plugged the tablet into its charger and set it on the nightstand, then turned off her little bedside lamp. Sleep came soon after her head touched the pillow. That night, Dot dreamt she was skating through a derelict Victorian hospital, where statues moved and nothing was as it seemed.

CHAPTER 2

Pawed

Kat whipped around the curve of the track, leaning deep into the turn and taking long, slow strides. The wind rushing against her skin gave the sensation of flying. There was something so serene about having the entire rink floor to herself.

Refs didn't usually attend Thursday practice, but Coach Rex had requested Kat's presence. Not entirely knowing what to expect, Kat had arrived early. She'd been the first to gear up and was out doing laps while skaters were still trickling in.

Before long, Vee came onto the floor and began her warmup laps. Then Siren—or Leah Dietrich, as Kat also knew her—followed by Fiend Ish and Princess Peaches. As more skaters entered the track, Kat found herself feeling out of place. On a Tuesday night, other refs would have been out there with her, but tonight she was on her own. At least she wasn't wearing stripes. Her tank top from last year's Mid-Atlantic Derbycon blended in well with everyone else's practicewear.

"Hey! Fancy seeing you here!"

That was Jet's voice! Of all the skaters in the league, she and her girlfriend, Lynn, were the only ones Kat really hung out with. Jet caught up with Kat and matched pace with her.

"Yeah, it's a little weird." Uneasiness weighed on Kat. "I feel like an outsider tonight."

"Nonsense!" Jet put a hand on her shoulder. "You're one of us. We're all CRD, refs included."

"Heh. Thanks. I wish everyone felt that way." Kat scanned the changing area, where skaters were still putting on gear.

Jet followed her gaze. "You mean you wish *she* felt that way. And yes, she's here. In the middle there, sitting down behind Lizzy."

Lynn was standing, facing away from the track. She moved to the right, and then Kat saw a familiar shock of blue hair. There was Dot, looking down at something in her hand. Kat watched her for a moment. The way that hair contrasted with her olive skin and fell over those dark eyes—it was magnetic. Why was Kat so drawn to her, of all people? Dot raised her head, and Kat looked away.

Butterflies fluttered in Kat's stomach. She took a deep breath and exhaled.

"Hey, it's gonna be fine," Jet said. "She's not gonna pick a fight with you or anything."

"I know. I'm just afraid it's gonna be tense all practice."

Jet looked around at the other skaters on the track. "Well, you two are hardly the only ones with tension."

Kat gave her a quizzical glance.

"There are skaters here tonight who can't stand each other," Jet went on. "Clashing egos, mostly. Just try to focus on what you're doing, and you won't think about it so much. And trust me, Coach will keep us busy the whole time."

"Alright . . . I'll try not to stress."

"Good. Now, lemme get in a few speed laps before things get started." With three quick steps, Jet took off and left Kat in the dust. Damn, she was fast.

She'd been right about keeping busy. The first hour of practice focused on endurance and agility. They started with a familiar pace line exercise that Kat had seen done on Tuesdays. As she weaved in and out between skaters, some of them gave words of encouragement—"Nice, Kat! Way to keep it tight!"—or offered tips—"Remember to stay low! Don't pop up!"

These comments weren't limited to her. Other skaters were receiving similar feedback. They were treating Kat the way they treated each other, which was comforting. She began to feel less like an outsider and more like a welcome guest. Even so, she couldn't help but notice that Dot remained silent throughout the exercise.

Over the course of that first hour, Coach Rex put the group through the ringer with a series of intense footwork drills—lateral movement, hard stops, quick transitions, the works. They spent several minutes on each skill before moving on to the next. With only brief breaks to rehydrate, it was all Kat could do to keep up.

Still, she found herself subconsciously keeping track of Dot's location. Every now and then, Kat would glance across the way and catch sight of her. Always on the opposite side of the track. Was that intentional? It had to be.

To be actively avoided like that . . . it stung. Kat figured it was better than getting yelled at, but she rather wished Dot would just talk to her. Not that Kat had tried initiating conversation herself. She feared Dot would be less than receptive.

Dot turned her head and made direct eye contact with Kat. *Shit.* Caught staring again. Kat tried to play it off by looking around at other skaters too, but it couldn't have been a very convincing cover. Ugh. That was the second time tonight Dot had caught her watching. Kat needed to focus and stop letting her eyes wander.

The drills continued until Kat's quads and calves were burning and her hip flexors were aching. Relief finally came at the end of the hour, when Coach Rex called everyone into the center.

"Alright, rest for a minute and get a drink," Coach said. "Go piddle if you have to. What we're gonna do next is get into some strategy."

Roughly half the skaters scattered in different directions. The rest remained nearby, talking amongst themselves.

Coach turned to Kat. "How are you holding up?"

"Good! I'm good." Kat wiped sweat from her brow with her forearm. "That was intense. Definitely not what I'm used to."

Coach patted her on the arm. "I wasn't sure you'd join us for the first hour. I'm glad you did. You know you're welcome any time, right? You'd just have to sit out when we do full contact drills."

"Yeah, I'll keep it in mind." Kat smiled. She'd known refs were technically allowed to join in skater practices, but she'd always imagined she'd feel like the odd one out. Tonight was defying expectations. For the most part.

As the skaters finished reconvening, Coach addressed everyone again. "Now, talking strategy, I want to try some new things with you guys. Some of this is stuff we've seen from other high level teams this season, and some of it will be totally new. I asked Kat to be here tonight so she can watch what we're doing and make sure it's executed cleanly." All eyes turned to Kat. Coach went on, "We don't want to develop bad habits that come back to bite us. So she's gonna let us know if she sees any issues from a ref's point of view. When she gives us feedback, we're going to accept it graciously and make corrections, yes?"

Heads nodded in response—Dot's included. Jet beamed a smile at Kat.

Kat looked to Coach Rex. "Ready when you are."

Coach put her hands on her hips. "Okay, I need two teams of four on the track. Set up like you would for a jam start."

In short order, eight skaters volunteered themselves and took up positions.

"The first thing we're gonna talk about is how we can provide offense from the front. Let's get a jammer out there too."

Jet jumped at the opportunity. Coach Rex proceeded to explain various strategies by which the front blockers could help their jammer get past the back wall. Offense was typically more straightforward when coming from behind. From the front, it could be tricky. Coach walked the skaters through each maneuver step by step.

"This requires everyone to be on the same page and act as a unit. And communicate to your jammer what you're doing. Let's give this a shot."

The skaters returned to their starting positions. Coach raised her whistle to her lips.

TWEEET!

The mock jam was on. The jammer hit the pack. Blockers collided. The action ebbed and flowed. Kat's eyes jumped from skater to skater, maintaining a keen awareness of the entire scene. She knew instinctively when and where to focus her attention.

Kat was now totally in her element. When she was reffing, the world was simple. Black-and-white. Governed by the rules of the game, which she knew inside and out. Over years of practice, her skill at enforcing those rules had been honed to near-robotic precision. Not only did she take pride in that, but she found comfort as well. A sense of purpose.

Finally, Jet emerged from the front of the pack, and Coach whistled for play to stop.

"That was . . . interesting." Coach eyed each of the skaters that had been playing offense. "It took you a while to get your jammer out. Does anyone know what went wrong?"

Vee chimed in with an answer, and a short discussion ensued. Meanwhile, Kat was replaying the jam in her head. Her eyes continued to wander from one skater to the next, but her mind was busy making notes about what she'd just seen. That is, until she happened upon another pair of eyes looking back at her. Deep-set, brown eyes . . . olive cheeks . . . strong jaw . . . soft, full lips . . . wait—Dot?

As quickly as Kat realized it, Dot looked away. Kat lost her train of thought. Had she just caught Dot staring at her?

"Kat, did you notice anything?" Coach's voice snapped her back to the present.

"Huh? Oh . . . no, everything looked clean."

"Okay, let's reset and run it again with the same people." Coach motioned for the skaters to take the track once more.

TWEEET!

The sound of that whistle put Kat back on her game. She quickly centered herself and resumed her duty.

As the night went on, Kat called the occasional penalty and fielded questions about some of the trickier rules. Coach Rex introduced two more strategy exercises. Once the skaters found their collective groove, they were quicker to reset following each mock jam. That meant less downtime and more action. The last hour of practice seemed to fly by.

Before Kat knew it, Coach was glancing at the clock and called everyone together. After a final review of the key points and areas for improvement, she wrapped things up.

"We're gonna work on these again on Sunday. I want everyone to feel comfortable enough to start using these strategies in scrimmage next week. That's all for tonight, so let's go, hands in."

All of the skaters joined Coach Rex in a circle, each with one hand in the center. Kat stood by and watched.

"Come on, Kat." Coach motioned for her to join in. "You're part of this."

"Oh!" Kat had never done this team cheer thing before. She squeezed into the circle and added her hand to the stack.

"What should we say?" asked Vee.

Jet offered, "'Thank you, Kat!' We always thank our officials!"

Kat blushed. It felt good to be appreciated. She just wasn't used to this kind of attention.

"Sounds good to me!" Vee said. "'Thank you, Kat' on three. One. Two. Three."

In unison, the skaters shouted, "THANK YOU, KAT!" Then the circle broke. Stray water bottles were gathered up, and everyone headed off the rink floor.

Kat returned to where she'd left her things, in the refs' usual changing area. She hurriedly removed her gear, leaving it in a pile on the carpet, then slipped her shoes on and headed for the restroom. On the way there, she received high-fives and pats on the back from several skaters.

"Hey, Kat! Great work tonight!" Kara said as she passed.

"Thanks for coming!" added Leah.

So that was it. Kat had survived a Thursday night practice with the skaters. To think she'd been dreading this night ever since Coach had asked her to come. Seemed she'd been worried over nothing.

She spent a few minutes at the sink, scrubbing the wristguard stink off of her hands and forearms. Then she attempted to do something with her sweaty mop of chin-length, dark brown hair. She pulled it all to the right, exposing the shaved left side of her head. It just laid flat and hung over her blue eyes, so she brushed it toward the back. Oh well, good enough. She was only going to the diner.

On her way back from the restroom, Kat saw something on top of her skate bag that hadn't been there before. When she got closer, she found it to be a small, rectangular, plain cardboard box, maybe three inches long. There was no note attached. She picked it up and inspected it. The corners were beat-up, and the sides dented and scuffed. Nothing was written on it, but something rattled inside.

Who had put it there? Kat glanced around the place, half expecting someone to claim responsibility. But no one was looking her way. Maybe the contents would provide an answer. She carefully pulled open one end of the box and peeked inside.

"*What!*" She went wide-eyed. *Now* people were looking at her.

"What's wrong?" Kara asked with urgency.

"Nothing! Look!" Grinning ear to ear, Kat dumped the contents of the box into her hand and held it up. "My catnip pin!"

"Is that all? You startled the crap outta me, yelling like that."

"Well, I thought I'd lost it. I love this pin. My nephew made it."

"Ahh, important pin. Got it." Kara returned to the business of packing her things. Then she paused, her brow creased. She looked up at Kat again. "So why so surprised? Didn't Mouse tell you she had it?"

"Whowhatnow?" Kat's grin disappeared, replaced with a gape of disbelief. "Mouse?"

"Yeah, she left it on your bag while you were in the bathroom."

Kat immediately looked to the seat where she'd seen Dot sitting earlier. It was empty. Dot's things were gone. She scanned the area, but that wild blue hair was nowhere to be found.

So *Dot* had had it? And she hadn't said anything? Of course she hadn't said anything. But she'd returned it. In a nice little box, no less. What did this *mean?* And had she left already? Kat would feel terrible not saying thank you.

She dashed over to Lynn and Jet, almost skidding to a stop in front of them.

"Hey, you two! Um—" She found herself a little short of breath. Her heart was racing. "Where'd Mouse go?"

Jet smiled widely. "You just missed her. You can probably catch her in the parking lot."

"Thanks!"

As Kat ran to the door, Jet grabbed Lynn's arm and whispered excitedly, "There she goes! This is it!"

* * *

Dot slid open the side door of her old, gray van—though to call it *gray* wasn't entirely accurate. At this point in its life, it had achieved a *multicolored* state, thanks to a smattering of paint speckles and smears, graffiti, and rust spots. But it still ran, and that was the important thing.

She heaved her skate bag into the van and plopped her purse down beside it. Keys in hand, she pulled the door shut with a *thud.*

"Mouse!"

Oh great. There was no mistaking that voice. Somebody must have told her who'd left the box. Fine, then. Here we go.

Dot turned around. Kat was halfway across the parking lot, running toward her. She'd gotten her pin back. What else could she want?

Kat stopped about ten feet away, panting. "You found it!" She held the pin out in front of her. It shimmered in the moonlight. "Thank you."

Dot waited for a *but*. Kat just watched her expectantly. Was that it?

"Uh. Sure, no problem." Dot was hesitant. Her voice barely carried over the distance between them.

They stood briefly in silence. The air was still. Kat's hand trembled slightly.

"It was a gift," she said. "My nephew made it for me. It's . . . it's irreplaceable. I was really scared I'd lost it."

Was Kat getting sentimental? Dot swallowed. She hadn't seen this coming. She wasn't sure what to say next.

Kat looked down at the pin and closed her fingers around it. "So, um . . . that's all. I just wanted to say thanks, Mouse. Have a . . . a good night." She backed away, offering a little wave, then turned and started walking.

Dot felt she should say something. She remembered Lynn's words from the day before. *Give credit where it's due.*

"Hey."

Kat stopped and half-turned, looking back at Dot. "Yeah?"

"I . . . really like your photography. You're really good."

Kat's mouth hung open for a second. "Uh—thanks," she managed. "That . . . that means a lot, coming from you."

Coming from you? Was she being sincere? Dot couldn't tell. They barely knew each other, so how could that . . . ? Whatever. Dot had made an effort. This was a strange ending to a strange night, and she was ready for it to be over.

"Okay. I'm gonna get going." She opened the front door of the van.

"Right. Of course. See you at scrim."

"Yep." Dot climbed into the driver's seat and shut the door. As she turned the key, she glanced out the window. Kat was still standing there. When the engine started, she turned away again and headed for the rink doors.

* * *

"She *said* that? To your face?" Jet gawked at Kat in amazement. Jet and Lynn occupied one side of the diner booth. Kat sat across from them.

"Yeah, it just sorta came outta the blue!"

"She straight up told you she likes your photography." Lynn nibbled on a french fry. "Unprompted? That's impressive. Talk about a one-eighty."

Kat fidgeted in her seat. "I don't know about a one-eighty. She seemed a little standoffish, even when she said it."

"Dude. You clearly don't understand how stubborn she is."

"And regardless," added Jet, "I'm really proud of you for doing what you did."

Kat looked down at the table. She could feel a blush rising.

Jet continued, "You started a dialogue. That's huge! You've got a foot in the door now!" She took a long pull from her milkshake.

"I suppose."

"Seriously," Lynn said. "She had this false idea of who you are, and now there are cracks in that idea. You just need to keep chipping away."

"Yeah, well"—Kat absentmindedly played with her straw—"how do I chip away when she keeps avoiding me?"

"Okay." Jet leaned forward and put her elbows on the table. "When we were leaving the rink, what was the thing you said about tonight's practice? About not feeling like an outsider."

"It defied my expectations?"

"Yes, that!" Jet pointed at Kat. "That's exactly what *you* did tonight. You defied Mouse's expectations."

Kat raised an eyebrow. "By thanking her?"

"Ha! No—well, yes, but—by running out there to do it. You could have waited, sent her a thank-you online or something low-key like that. But you ran after her in the parking lot, like the ending to some romantic movie. You think she saw that coming?"

A smirk forced its way onto Kat's face. "Probably not."

"And that was all you. You chose that route because you wanted to talk to her, face to face, seize the moment, right?"

Now Kat could definitely feel her cheeks flushing.

"That's a side of you she doesn't normally get to see. But she saw it tonight, and she responded to it. So keep showing her that side."

Kat considered this. "Yeah, but . . . I mean, opportunities like that don't come along very often."

"Well, that was a big one," Lynn said, "but you've gotta seize the little ones too. You know, smile at her, say hi. Don't shy away just because she *thinks* you don't like her. Like Polly said, defy her expectations."

"I don't know. What if I keep putting myself out there and she's still standoffish?"

"You mean what if she rejects you?" Jet asked.

Kat turned bright red. "Well . . . yeah."

Jet shrugged and leaned back in her seat. "I dunno, life goes on?"

"Sometimes you just gotta take that chance," Lynn added. "You either live with the status quo, or you change it and hope for the best."

Kat sighed. "That's easy for you two to say. It worked out great for you."

"*So far.* But who knows? We could crash and burn any day now!"

Jet glared at Lynn. "Thank you, darling. You're helping."

Lynn snickered. Jet backhanded her in the arm.

"Ow . . . But in all seriousness," Lynn went on, "the current status quo sucks, right? So what do you have to lose?"

Kat bowed her head slightly. "Fair point."

"Plus, it's a two way street, and it sounds like she extended an olive branch tonight."

Kat grinned, her eyes shining. "I guess she did, didn't she? I have to admit, it felt pretty amazing to get a compliment from her." Her grin started to fade, though. "I was taken so off guard, I froze up. I hope I didn't come off as dismissive."

"Stop." Jet caught her with an assertive stare. "I'm sure you were fine. And you can't go back and change it anyway, so there's no point in dwelling on it. How did you leave things? What was the last thing you said?"

"'See you at scrim.' And she said, 'Yep.'"

"Perfect!" Jet sat up straight. "That's perfect!"

"She sounded kind of curt, though."

"It doesn't matter. You couldn't have ended it better."

"You think?"

"I *know*," said Jet.

Lynn leaned forward. "That's gonna echo in her brain from now 'til Tuesday. 'See you at scrim'... 'see you at scrim'... 'see you at scrim'..."

Kat buried her face in her hands. "Oh jeez."

"What? That's a good thing! Means she's gonna be thinking about you. Oh man, this is exciting. I can't wait to hear her side of this when I see her tomorrow."

Kat slid her hands down, uncovering her eyes. "Ugh. Tomorrow's gonna be a long day. I have a wedding to shoot, out in Carlisle."

"Wow, that's a hike," said Jet.

"I know, but it's money." Kat took a fry from the basket.

"The art photos aren't selling?" Lynn asked.

"They are, a little. I sell a few stock photos here and there, but I barely make anything off that. And nobody's ordering prints."

"I'm telling you," Lynn said, "if more people knew about your work and where to find it, you could make a mint. You just need to get it in front of the right eyes."

"Well, I got a vendor space at Pridefest. Maybe I'll sell some prints there."

Jet lit up. "That's a great idea!"

"Yeah, fingers crossed." Kat unzipped her little black purse and dug around in it. "The space isn't free, so hopefully I sell enough that it pays for itself." She laid a ten dollar bill on the table. "That should cover me."

"You heading out?"

"Yeah, it's late." Kat stood up and strapped her purse across her body.

"Alright, well come 'ere." Jet nudged Lynn, and the two of them slid out of the booth. Jet threw her arms around Kat. "Good job tonight. On all counts."

"Thanks. Both of you."

Kat hugged Lynn as well, then made her way to the exit.

Once Kat was out of sight, Jet sat down opposite Lynn. "Now . . . if only we could get both of them to come out like this on the same night."

* * *

Kat didn't sleep well that night. She kept thinking about the exchange in the parking lot. Dot had gone out of her way to avoid Kat all through practice and then complimented her—seemingly out of nowhere—at the very last second. Why? Why then?

What's more, Dot was apparently a fan of Kat's photography? Kat was shocked that Dot had even seen it. She felt exposed, as though Dot had seen a piece of her soul. Of course, she had put her work out there for anyone to see, but somehow it was different knowing *Dot* had seen it. At least Kat now knew there was something about her that Dot liked. That was reassuring.

Come morning, Kat allowed herself to sleep a bit later than she'd planned to. Though it wasn't enough to make up for a restless night, she'd take every minute she could get. When she did finally roll out of bed, there was no time to relax. But before anything could be done, step one was to locate coffee.

Kat rented a room in a house, where she shared the third floor with Lonnie. He and Kat tended to be the late-risers. The two second-floor folks worked regular nine-to-fives, and Kat rarely bumped into them. She did, however, often bump into their leftover coffee in the communal kitchen. Today she found a quarter pot waiting for her—cold, but it would get the job done. She filled a tall mug, added a spoonful of sugar, and hastened back up the stairs with her prize. Now she could get down to business.

Her backpack camera bag lay open on the floor of her room,

surrounded by some of the less-delicate pieces of equipment in her collection. These included a tripod, backup batteries, flashes, memory cards, and a few other accessories. Kat surveyed the scene, checking off a mental list while sipping from her mug.

It should be noted that Kat was not a wedding photographer by trade. She was able to land gigs like this because she came cheap. Relatively so, anyway. Most of her gear had been acquired second-hand and wasn't necessarily perfect for wedding work. But she did her best with what she had, and Kat's best was nothing to sneeze at.

When she'd finished her coffee, Kat put the mug on her dresser. She approached a black footlocker that sat under a shelf along the wall. Kneeling in front of it, she opened the lid. The inside was lined with foam and organized with soft dividers. Stored in here were several lenses, of varying lengths and purposes, as well as Kat's two babies—her Nikon D750 camera and her old D90, which still served as a formidable backup.

She retrieved the cameras first and fit them into their compartments in the backpack. Then she looked over her collection of lenses. She had seven. The macro lenses were some of her favorites to work with, and she would need one of those today. She also picked out a wide angle lens and—did she have room for both short- and medium-range telephoto lenses? Prrrobably? Yes. If she moved some things around, she could squeeze them in.

With the bag packed, it was time to make herself presentable. For a wedding, that meant a fair amount of prep beyond the usual. After a quick shower, she blew out and styled her hair. A little product would hold it back, out of her eyes. For makeup, she added some shadow to her standard black eyeliner and put the faintest touch of rouge on her normally pale cheeks. Her favorite dark red lip color finished the look—dramatic, perhaps, but signature Kat. She left out mascara on purpose, as it always seemed to become a mess when shooting through the viewfinder. When in doubt, work before lashes.

Her outfit consisted of black suit pants and a simple white dress

shirt. Tie or no? No, she decided just to leave the top two buttons
open. Casually formal. She hated feeling constricted while shooting.
The event was to be outdoors, so she opted for her flat, rugged, black
ankle boots. They'd already been cleaned well since their last use, but
she added a bit of polish and shined them up.

And that was everything. Five minutes later, her camera bag was
buckled in the back seat of her red 2005 Toyota Corolla, and Kat was
ready to roll.

It was a warm spring day with clear skies, and due to stay that way
into the night. Perfect for an evening backyard wedding. Kat didn't love
shooting weddings, but good natural lighting was a gift she wouldn't
take for granted.

Still, it was going to be a *long* warm spring day, and sleep deprivation
wasn't about to make it any easier. On top of which, her stomach was
reminding her she hadn't eaten yet. She made one last stop, to pick up a
wrap and a fresh cup of coffee.

It was an almost two hour drive from Crosscannon to Carlisle. Kat
spent it running through the day's timeline while listening to seventies
punk rock. It was tempting to put on a podcast. She'd been saving
one—an interview with Patti Smith—for a long ride like this. But she
wanted her mind to stay on the coming task. She hadn't done enough
weddings for this to be second nature yet.

From the moment she arrived on location, the action was non-stop.
People were constantly buzzing about, fretting over this or that. Kat
found that her reffing mindset translated well to this environment. She
was able to tune out the noise and focus on what she'd come to do.

The whole affair was relatively small—roughly fifty guests. The
budget had been kept very tight. The bride's parents' one-acre property
hosted both the ceremony and reception.

While it was a long day for Kat, it remained a pleasant one. The
night's festivities were mercifully devoid of rowdily drunken
groomsmen, there was free coffee, and the DJ even played The Clash for
her.

By the time her job was done and she was packing up, midnight had come and gone. She used her last reserves of professional cheer to bid a fond farewell to her clients.

The drive home felt torturously long. She put on that podcast. Though she lacked the mental energy to really follow and enjoy it, it kept her engaged and awake until she made it home.

Once back in her room, Kat left the camera bag next to the foot locker and fell into bed fully dressed. Tonight, she didn't have much trouble sleeping.

* * *

Knock-knock.

"Yeah?"

"Hey, sis, you gonna sleep all day or what?"

"You can come in. I promise I'm decent."

Lonnie opened Kat's door and stood leaning against the frame. Kat was sitting at her desk, which faced the wall just beside the doorway. It was a rainy Saturday afternoon. She'd been working on her laptop since morning and had barely left her room.

"So you *are* up. Oh . . ." Lonnie froze. "You look busy. I can come back."

"No, it's okay. My eyes could use a break."

"Ah, well perfect! That's what you have *me* for, isn't it?" Lonnie put a hand on his hip and ran the other through his hair, striking his best seductive pose. He wasn't a bad looking dude, with his dark, bedroom eyes and tall, toned physique. If Kat were into guys, the sight might even have been enticing.

"I said they could use a *break*, Lon. Don't excite them further." Kat's tone was playfully sarcastic. "What can I do for you?"

"See, you tell me to stop, and then you ask questions like that."

Kat narrowed her eyes at him. He stuck his tongue out at her.

"Actually, I was wondering if you had rent money," he said. "I hate to bug you about it, but we're due in a week."

"I will. That's why I've been in here, working." Kat motioned to the screen in front of her. "Once I get these proofs to the client, I'll get the rest of my fee."

Lonnie stepped into the room and looked over her shoulder. She was editing a photo of the previous day's bride.

His brow creased. "They didn't pay you yet? My sister had to pay her photographer in full, like a month before the wedding."

"Yeah, well, if I were a real wedding photographer, I could do that too."

"What . . . ?" Lonnie screwed up his face. "How are you not a real wedding photog? You photograph real weddings! You're a pro at it!"

"I've shot, like, three weddings, Lon." Kat turned to face him. "Four, counting this one. If I really wanted to make a business outta this—"

"I know. You don't have the gear, and it's not what you wanna do with your life." Lonnie folded his arms. "I still think you should. It's good money, and you're good *at* it."

Kat sighed. "Well, that's why I end up doing it at all. But if I wanna make something outta my art photography, I need to stay dedicated to that."

"Yeah, fine. As long as you keep making rent." Lonnie eyed her sympathetically. "I don't want you to have to move out and let some other yahoo move in here next to me."

Kat laughed. "Don't worry, sweetcheeks. I'm not leaving you any time soon. I already have jobs lined up to get me through the next few months."

"Alright, good."

Lonnie's stance visibly relaxed. Wow, he really was concerned. Kat made a mental note to keep him updated when she landed new gigs. Lonnie put up a carefree facade, but every once in a while Kat saw through the cracks. He looked out for her like a brother, and she didn't like having him worry.

"So, change of subject." Kat rested an arm over the back of the chair. "We're hitting the market next week, right?"

Third Saturday Market was a massive flea market located about thirty minutes north of Crosscannon. Kat and Lonnie had a tradition of making the monthly pilgrimage together. It was a great place to find new subjects and inspiration for Kat's photography.

"Oh shit." Lonnie cringed and rubbed the back of his neck. "Sorry, sis, I forgot to tell you ... that's the same day as my family reunion. I have to be in Jersey by noon."

"Aw, Lonnie!"

"I know! I'm sorry!"

"You know I hate going alone."

Lonnie shrugged. "So? Bring someone else this time. I'm sure one of your derby friends would go."

"Hmm." Kat looked away in thought. "I think Lynn and Jet are away next Saturday. Going to Lynn's parents' or something."

"What about the blue-haired girl you like? The mouse."

Kat's heart skipped a beat. "It's um ... it's just Mouse." Her voice shook a little.

Lonnie frowned. "You're not feeling that suggestion?"

"No ... I mean, yeah, I'd love to spend the day with her. It's just ... that situation is still, uh ..."

"Still complicated."

Kat nodded.

"Are you ever gonna uncomplicate it?"

"I'm working on it. She might be starting to come around, actually. She did say she likes my photos."

Lonnie's eyebrows rose. "Well there's a start!"

"But that's way too big a step, asking her out like that! To the market, I mean. There's no way she'd say yes." No way she'd say yes? The question alone would totally blindside her. Talk about defying her expectations, jeez.

"Well there's gotta be somebody who'd want to go." Concern etched Lonnie's face. "Maybe one of the other refs?"

"I don't know." Kat tilted her head dismissively. "Don't worry about it. I'll figure something out when I'm done with this wedding stuff."

"Alright. Sorry about the short notice."

"It's okay. It's a week away. That's not exactly short. And it's just the market anyway. I'll be fine." She gave him her best unconcerned smile. "Now, I do want to get back to this." She pointed her thumb at the laptop.

"Okay, you got it." On his way out, Lonnie stopped in the doorway. "I got vegan pizza if you want some later. And a new case of beer."

"It's not another IPA, is it?"

"It's a variety pack from Upstarts."

Upstarts was the local microbrewery, and a sponsor of CRD.

"Oh fun! You're on!"

"Cool." Lonnie smiled and pulled the door shut as he left.

CHAPTER 3

Hemmed

TWEEET!

"Black five, out of play block!" Agent Smithereens made the call.

"God—! Nnngghh." It took all of her will, but Dot held her tongue. The last thing she needed was an insubordination call on top of this penalty. Without another word, she exited the track and skated to the box.

After she sat down, Dot twisted around to address Pixie, who was timing her.

"Do you know how many I have?"

Pixie checked her clipboard and did a quick count. "Looks like this is your fourth."

"Dammit," Dot muttered. She checked the scoreboard. Seven minutes remained in the first half of scrimmage.

"Black five, stand."

Dot stood up and glanced back. "Thanks."

Pixie nodded. "Black five, done."

TWEET-TWEET-TWEET-TWEET!

End of the jam. Dot had been released just in time. She rolled away and headed toward Lynn, who waited on the sidelines.

"Eggshells, Lynn!"

"I know, but you gotta take it easy. We're not even at the half yet."

"You think I don't *know that?*" Dot gave her a death glare . . . briefly. Then closed her eyes and exhaled. "Sorry, I . . ."

"It's okay."

Lynn put a hand on Dot's back. Dot folded her arms. The two of them stood side by side in their black jerseys, watching the action on the track.

After a beat, Lynn continued, "You still think the refs unfairly target you."

"I know, you think it's a bullshit excuse."

"I never said that."

Vee was jamming. Dot watched as she approached the pack. She juked out, then charged in and jumped the apex. Four points. Like magic. She made it look effortless.

"But in all seriousness," Lynn said, "I do think—"

"I'm not gonna confront them about it, Lynn."

"I'm not saying confront them. I'm just saying talk to them. Get their perspective."

Dot sighed.

"You *could*"—Lynn smirked—"talk to *Kat.* You seem to have a *rapport* with her."

Dot rolled her eyes.

Lynn tried to stifle a snicker and ended up snorting.

Dot remained stony. "I'm glad you amuse yourself."

"Hey, turnabout is fair play."

TWEET-TWEET-TWEET-TWEET!

Another jam finished. Time to line up for the next.

Lynn turned to Dot. "Let's go in this one."

Jet, coming off the track, handed Lynn the black star. Lynn skated away, motioning for Dot to come. Dot watched her for a second, frowning. She inhaled sharply through her nose, then followed Lynn onto the track.

Dot lined up with the other black blockers. She took the brace position, facing backwards—facing her teammates, who would use her for support.

Siren took the role of pivot, pulling the striped cover onto her helmet. Dot was grateful for that. She didn't want to risk having the star passed to her. Dot jamming usually spelled disaster.

Vee came onto the track to jam against Lynn. The two of them were well-matched. Both were in the primary jammer rotation on CRD's all-star team, the Heavy Metal.

"Five seconds!"

Here we go. Easy, Dot. Trust your teammates. Don't go rogue.

TWEEET!

Right off the bat, Vee got aggressive with Lynn and forced her into the white team's waiting defense. Dot monitored what was happening back there. Lynn appeared to be hung up. Meanwhile, Vee ducked behind one of her own blockers, and Dot lost sight of her. Then she reappeared, coming up the outside line.

Vee was already too close. The black wall wouldn't be able to move laterally fast enough to block her. But there was another option. Wordlessly, Dot directed her teammates to rotate their formation, sending her right into Vee's path.

Vee plowed into Dot. It was a solid hit with a lot of strength behind it. Fortunately, Dot had turned her side to Vee, but the impact still left her reeling.

Dot regained her footing. Vee advanced again, but Dot crouched lower, getting under Vee's center of gravity. This time, when Vee got close, Dot thrust a shoulder up and caught her in the chest.

The hit lifted Vee and put her off-balance. She staggered and fell to a knee before quickly recovering.

TWEEET!

"Black five, stop block!" That was Kat.

"God dammit!"

Dot turned to Kat, brow creased and face screwed up in a scowl. Then she froze. Kat was holding her whistle near her mouth, but her eyes were . . . pleading? That sight deflated Dot's rage a bit.

"Mmhh!" Dot pressed her lips together. She tore her gaze away from Kat and left the track, headed for the box once again.

Five fucking penalties in one period. Coach would have her head. In the box, Dot didn't even look at Pixie. In fact, she looked at the floor.

When her thirty seconds ended, Dot wasn't especially keen to get back on the track. She rolled away from the box at a languid pace.

Siren called to her, "Come on, Mouse! We need you!"

Fine. Dot huffed. She sped onto the track and took her place in the front of the black defensive formation.

Vee came speeding around for another pass. Dot directed the black blockers to rotate again, putting her back in Vee's path. But her heart wasn't in it this time. Vee charged forward, ducked low, and came up as she connected with Dot's side.

Dot twisted as her feet left the ground. She hit the floor backwards. Hard.

Seconds passed. She didn't get up. She couldn't catch her breath. The wind had been knocked out of her, and she was struggling not to give in to that initial rush of panic.

TWEET-TWEET-TWEET-TWEET!

Kat's face appeared overhead. "How many fingers?" She held up three.

"Th . . . th . . . three," Dot gasped, voiceless.

Coach and Vee arrived, kneeling on either side.

"Did you hit your head?" Coach asked.

"Don't . . . know."

"Try to relax. Bring your knees up."

Coach Rex put a hand behind one of Dot's thighs and directed Vee to do the same. They gently pulled Dot's knees toward her chest.

Kat hovered over Dot with a worried look. Dot focused on those sapphire blue eyes. There was something calming about them. Comforting. Something extending beyond this fleeting moment of shock and fear. Like ancient wells that ran deep into the cool earth.

Air was slowly starting to come back.

"Huhh," Dot vocalized. She tried a tentative deep breath. With careful control, she managed to draw air in and blow it out. "Okay . . . okay . . . breathing."

"Good," Coach said. "Your head. How's your head?"

"It doesn't hurt."

"What day is it?"

"Tuesday . . . the fifteenth."

"How about the rest of you?"

"Uh . . . my ass hurts."

Coach addressed Kat. "Would you be able to grab an ice pack? Do you know where they are?"

"Yes! Of course!" Kat zipped away without a moment's hesitation. Dot's eyes followed her across the rink.

Coach turned back to Dot. "Okay, come on. Up slowly."

Coach and Vee guided Dot up to a sitting position. From there, she got to a knee and was easily standing soon after.

The rink echoed with applause as Dot rolled back to the sidelines. She found a spot to rest on the floor, away from the other skaters. Sitting proved rather painful, so she lay down, parallel to the wall. She took her helmet off and removed her mouthguard, tucking it behind the strap of her sports bra.

Then Dot heard the rumble of wheels approaching on the wood floor. Kat appeared, kneeling beside her, ice pack in hand.

"Hey, how're you feeling?" Kat popped the instant ice pack and shook it up. She wore a slight frown, that look of concern still wrinkling her brow. The rink rang with the sounds of a jam in progress. They'd started up again without her.

"Shouldn't you be out there?" Dot shifted her gaze toward the track.

"They'll manage. I wanted to make sure you're okay."

Kat handed the pack to Dot, who placed it underneath her butt and gingerly lowered her weight onto it.

"Well, my right butt cheek is throbbing, but otherwise I'm fine."

"I have Motrin in my bag, if you want some." Kat motioned in the direction of her things.

"Nah, that's okay."

Kat delayed for a moment, watching Dot's expression, before speaking again. "I'm . . . gonna get back to it, then."

Dot was curt. "Yeah, go. I'm good."

Kat stood up and rolled away backwards, her eyes still on Dot's. She started to turn.

"Thanks," Dot said.

Kat glanced back and smiled at her, then sped off.

She had a cute smile, Kat. And there was something majestic about her—the way she held her square shoulders back and crossed one long, tattooed leg over the other with each stride. And those eyes . . .

"What'cha lookin' at?" Lynn rolled around into Dot's field of view.

"Nothin'."

"Uh-huh." She sat down cross-legged in front of Dot. "That's the most you two have said to each other in—I dunno—ever?"

"Probably."

"I gotta say, if your goal was to talk to her, you really went about it the hard way."

"Ha ha." Dot was not in the mood for Lynn's lighthearted banter.

"How's your ass?"

Or her genuine concern, for that matter.

"It's fine. It just hurts." Annoyance tinged Dot's voice. "No, I don't want Motrin. Or Tylenol."

Lynn frowned. She repositioned herself to the side so both she and Dot could watch the track. She waited until the current jam ended before trying again.

"Do you want to be distracted? I have good news."

Dot sighed. "Okay, what?"

"We got orders for five more Burger Life prints."

"That's good. I was thinking of doing a run tomorrow, if we have enough to warrant it."

"Ehh," Lynn stalled, "you, uh, might want to wait until the weekend."

"Yeah?"

"Yeah. The orders are sort of . . . trickling in." Lynn turned to look at Dot. "Steadily, I mean! But, ya know, slowly."

"Right. So, how many total so far?"

"Erm . . . eleven."

Dot exhaled audibly. Eleven wasn't much, considering the design had gone live on Saturday. She'd expected a bigger initial rush.

Lynn continued, "Keep in mind, we haven't done much promotion yet. I'm gonna set up ad campaigns Thursday night, to run through this weekend. We missed Friday last week. That's when people get paid—and when we usually get our first rush."

"Okay . . ." Dot looked up at Lynn, trying to gauge her confidence in that assessment. "You're probably right. You know that end of things better than I do."

She did her best to sound optimistic, but she was worried. If Lynn was wrong . . . They were counting on that income. They had overhead to pay. Utilities. Insurance. They needed to eat. They needed to pay dues for derby.

Dot hated feeling like a starving artist, scraping by with just enough. And she especially did not want to ask her dad for money again. She *needed* L&M to succeed.

"You should go play," Dot said. Lynn had been sitting with her instead of being on the track.

"It's almost halftime anyway."

So it was. Dot could see the scoreboard from where she lay. Eleven seconds left in the period. It felt like the clock was mocking her.

She watched the final jam play out. Fiend and Kara were jamming. Fiend had gotten lead status, but she'd just been called on a track cut.

While she made her way to the box, Kara broke out of the pack on her
initial pass.

Most of the skaters in this jam played for CRD's B-team—the Powder
Kegs. Their play tended not to feel as fast-paced as the Heavy Metal
jams Dot was used to. It was a bit like watching derby in slow-motion.

Kara came around on her first scoring pass. She juked around
Peaches, picking up a point for white. Nice going, Kara! But then she
tried to take the outside line. Dot could see that it was a trap. Don't
do it. Don't . . . Yup, she did it, and Jocelyn Ruffly knocked her out of
bounds. Jocelyn skated backwards, forcing Kara to skate back with her,
and joined up with Peaches. Oh, this was gonna be painful to watch.

Dot turned her attention away from the action to check the clock.
Fifty-three seconds remained in the jam, and then the period would be
over.

She raised her hip and felt the spot where she'd landed on her butt.
The ice had been doing its job. The pain had been numbed somewhat.
It would definitely bruise, though, and probably hurt for a few days.

Dot rolled over and got up to a kneeling position. Ow. She pushed
up and stood. Oww. Yeah, that smarted. Every flex of that glute muscle
resulted in sharp pain.

She lowered herself to the floor again and propped herself against the
wall, careful to keep the weight on her left side. She started to untie her
skates.

"Let me help." Lynn knelt in front of her. She remained quiet as she
removed Dot's skates and set them on the floor. "Here, give me your
helmet. I'll take this stuff. Just grab the ice pack."

The period whistle sounded as Dot limped along behind Lynn,
following her around the track and off the rink floor.

Along the way, skaters approached to check on Dot. "Are you okay?"
"How's yer butt?" "Do you need anything?"

She barely glanced at them as she replied curtly. "Yeah, I'll be fine."
"It hurts." "No."

Dot returned to the seat where she'd left her things. She sat down, gritting her teeth through the initial twinge of pain. After a few seconds, it faded to a dull throb.

There were skaters all around—chatting, adjusting their skates, checking their phones. The noise barely registered. Almost mechanically, Dot removed her wristguards, her elbow pads, her knee pads.

She tucked her skates into the bottom of her bag and took her time arranging her gear neatly on top of them. Then she sat and admired her work. Lo and behold, everything *did* fit in there.

Dot could feel Lynn's eyes on her. She turned to meet them. Lynn had both eyebrows raised as she looked from Dot to the skate bag and back again.

Dot's expression was unreadable. Indifferent. Though her ass hurt, she was feeling rather numb on the inside. Whether consciously or not, she was trying to avoid thinking about the past half hour—or the next half hour, for that matter. She'd be sitting idly by, watching instead of skating. That was not an appealing prospect.

Okay, so maybe she wasn't exactly numb. She just wasn't sure *what* she was feeling, other than a hollowness in the pit of her stomach. She didn't really want to be around people right now, even her teammates.

"I'm gonna go," she said under her breath, just loud enough for Lynn to hear. Upon speaking, she realized there was a lump forming in her throat.

"You sure?" But Lynn only needed to look in Dot's eyes for the answer. They weren't so stoic as they had been a moment prior. "Okay. You call me if you need anything." She hugged Dot. "Love you."

Dot tried to say it back but choked on the words. She looked away, zipped her bag shut, and extended the handle as she stood up. She glanced around the room to see if anyone was watching her. She was hoping to slip out unnoticed. If anyone had been paying attention, they didn't say anything as she grabbed her stuff and headed for the exit.

Dot marched across the parking lot to her van, jaw clenched. She pulled the side door open and heaved her skate bag inside, then plopped her purse down next to it. She reached for the door handle again but didn't pull it shut. She just stood there, half leaning on the van.

Five penalties in twenty-four minutes. Five! That was fucking embarrassing. And then . . . then she'd gotten careless. She'd known how hard Vee would be coming at her. She'd just stopped giving a shit at that point. She couldn't even pretend to blame that on anyone else.

She was angry at herself for that. Frustrated with herself. She felt so stupid. So *worthless*. She jerked a fist back and punched the van door—*thnk!*

Fuck, that hurt!

"Ahhh, god dammit!" she cried, immediately hoping no one had heard her.

She didn't know where to put this. These feelings. Forget the injury. She was paying for that in pain. But the penalties. She was just . . . It was just . . . She was pissed off! She *wanted* to be pissed off! But most of all, she was embarrassed, and that was worse.

She wanted to put this on the refs. She wanted to be mad at Kat—or *would* have been mad at Kat—but she couldn't bring herself to be. At this point, Dot had no idea where she stood with that woman. She just kept seeing those eyes, looking down at her when she couldn't breathe, easing her panic. In that whole shitshow—in the worst moment of it, in fact—her one bit of comfort had been Kat.

Tears dripped from Dot's chin onto the pavement. Her knuckles throbbed now, in time with her ass. The immediacy of the rhythmic, pulsing pain was beginning to center her. She turned around and sat down on the floor of the van, cradling her hand, and tried to focus on the present. What was she going to do *right now*?

She didn't want to go home. She didn't actually want to be alone, but neither did she want anyone to see her like this. Maybe she'd just sit here for a while, then, in the parking lot. In her crappy old van. Choking back sobs. God, she hated crying.

* * *

TWEET-TWEET-TWEET-TWEET!

The final jam of the night ended. Kat let her whistle fall from her lips and dangle from the lanyard around her neck. She held four fingers high above her head. Vee glanced at Kat's signal and pumped her fist victoriously.

Lynn came off the track, into the infield. "She got those points? I thought she wiped out on the landing."

"She did." Kat swiveled her head to look at Lynn. "But she got one foot down, in-bounds before anything else touched the floor."

"That's all she needs?"

"That's it."

"Hmm. Learn something new every day." Lynn circled around Kat and headed back to her teammates on the sidelines.

Kat plucked her water bottle from the floor in the center of the infield and took a swig. Agent Smithereens rolled by and high-fived her other hand, their wristguards clacking against one another.

The skaters gathered into their hands-in circle and cheered, "TOGETHER WE RISE!" After a beat, they did another one—"THANK YOU, OFFICIALS!" Then the circle broke.

As Lynn made her way back across the rink, Kat rolled up alongside her.

"She left at the half, didn't she?" Kat's tone was heavy with concern.

"Yeah. She needed some alone time."

"How did she seem?"

"Well . . ." Lynn glanced around to see who else was in earshot. "She didn't seem great. I think her pride was hurting more than her ass."

"Shit," Kat said under her breath. She looked down.

Lynn put a hand on Kat's back. "You know she brings this on herself. There's nothing you could have done differently."

"I know. It just sucks."

"I've known her a long time." Lynn looked Kat in the eye. "She'll bounce back. I promise."

They parted ways as they left the rink floor. Kat sat down by her things and unstrapped her wristguards.

"Hey, Kat! Thanks for reffing tonight." Kara plopped onto the floor across the way, her own belongings strewn about the area.

"Yeah, of course."

Kara started untying her skates. "Are you gonna come again on Thursday?"

"I'm thinking about it." Kat pulled her helmet off and shook out her sweaty hair.

"You totally should! We loved having you last time!"

"Thanks! I'll try. I have a lot going on this week."

It was a fantastic feeling, knowing her presence was wanted. It always seemed too easy for a divide to form between skaters and refs, which sometimes made it difficult for Kat to really feel like a *member* of the league. But Thursday night had done a lot to change that.

Kat finished gearing down and packing up. As she rose from her seat, a voice called to her.

"Kat! I wanna catch ya before ya leave!" Vee came running over. "Y're reffin' at MAD again this year, are ya not?"

MAD, short for Mid-Atlantic Derbycon, was a major annual event hosted by the Liberty City Rollers. Teams traveled from around the world to play, watch, and celebrate derby for one action-packed weekend in June. As it took place only an hour from Crosscannon, CRD skaters and officials attended every year.

"Yeah, my application got accepted months ago. Why?"

"We're just accounting for all the league members who're participating this year." Vee raised her brow inquisitively. "Would ya mind if we posted a photo of ya on social media along with some of the skaters goin'?"

"Um . . . no, that would be fine."

"Grand! You'll do us proud! I mean, we give ya shite sometimes, I know, but if we're bein' honest, y're the best there is."

"I . . ." Kat was speechless. That last comment—those weren't words she'd heard from a skater before. Well, from Lynn and Jet, maybe, but they were her friends. Vee was the captain of the Heavy Metal. Given her casual delivery, it seemed clear she had no idea how gratifying and affirming this was. "Thanks!" was all Kat could manage.

"Aye, sure. Alright, take care and have a good night. Thanks for everything."

"Uh . . . you too, Vee."

Kat watched her walk away. She was still a little stunned.

"Haha! You're, like, glowing!" Kara had been quietly watching the exchange. "She's right, ya know. You rock at what you do. We're lucky to have you."

"Jeez." Kat felt her cheeks flushing. "What is this? Boost Kat's Ego Day?"

"D'aww, you're turning pink." Kara giggled.

She had a contagious sort of laughter. Kat couldn't help but join her.

* * *

Kat was on cloud nine as she pushed open the rink doors and stepped out into the darkened parking lot. She walked to her car at a leisurely pace, singing under her breath. Damn, it felt good to be appreciated.

She popped the trunk and lowered her skate bag into it. She checked that the pins on the outside of the bag were securely fastened, especially the catnip pin. Satisfied, she closed the trunk with a *thud*.

"Kat."

That familiar, husky voice. Kat turned to look . . . and there was Dot, standing several yards away, on the edge of the lamplight, her van some distance behind her.

"Hey! You're still here!" Kat's eagerness rang in her words despite her efforts to rein it in.

"Hey. Yeah." Dot sounded a little raspier than usual. She started to take a step closer but hesitated. "Can I talk to you?"

Once again, Kat was stunned. Yes . . . yes, of course Dot could talk to her! Her heart was suddenly racing, but there was no way she'd pass up this opportunity.

"Y-yeah! Come on over. I can barely see you in the dark." Kat leaned back against the trunk and motioned for Dot to join her.

As Dot approached, Kat could see that her eyes were red. And a few salty remnants of tears remained on her cheeks. She was still limping slightly.

"What's up?" Kat's forehead creased. "Is everything okay?"

"Yeah. Yeah, fine." Declining the offer to lean on the car, Dot stood with her feet apart and her arms folded. She looked Kat in the eye and cleared her throat. "So . . . I want to ask you something."

"Of course, ask away."

Dot shifted in place. "Out here on Thursday night . . . I told you I liked your photography."

"Yeah."

"And you said that meant a lot coming from me. What did you mean by that?"

Kat grinned. "*That's* what you came over here for?"

Dot was silent for a moment. Then she looked away. "Sorry, never m—"

"No!" Kat's face went serious. She leaned forward and touched Dot's arm. "I just—I'm sorry, I thought it was obvious. It meant a lot because it came from a fellow artist. And your work is—well, it's beautiful."

Dot's brow furrowed. She studied Kat's face. "You're being serious."

"Of course I'm being serious! You're an amazing sculptor."

Dot's doubtful expression began to crack into a smirk. "A sculptor? Jeez. Hardly."

Kat folded her arms too. "You make sculptures, do you not?"

"I guess, technically." Dot put a hand behind her head and relaxed her stance. "I just never thought of myself as a *sculptor*. I couldn't sculpt in clay or wood to save my life."

"Well, maybe so, but I love your . . . um . . . your junk sculptures?"

"My trash art?" Dot chuckled. "*Junk sculptures* works."

Kat beamed. She loved Dot's laugh. She loved seeing Dot *smile*. It was as though clouds had just parted.

"So—but," Dot went on, "I think the only place I posted pictures publicly was on L&M."

"Yeah, that's where I saw them. I like that you provide photos from all different angles. There's so much detail to appreciate on each piece."

"I . . . well, I tried. I'm not the photographer you are." A pink hue was overtaking Dot's cheeks.

"So yeah." Kat's voice grew softer. "That's what I meant. Anyway, what did you think I meant?"

At that question, Dot's face went a bit deer-in-headlights. "Uh—I don't know." She lowered her eyes. "I didn't really think anyone paid attention to my art. I guess I was afraid—well, not *afraid*, but I mean . . ."

She was speaking quickly. The color drained from her face. Was Dot nervous? Kat had never seen her like this, like she'd been cornered.

"Never mind. It's not imp—"

"Oh god." Realization hit Kat. "You didn't think I was being sarcastic, did you?"

Dot didn't answer. Her eyes said it all.

"No, I would never . . ." Kat stood up straight and took a step toward Dot.

"Sorry. Ya know how . . . when you don't know . . ." Dot paused and exhaled. "You jump to the worst conclusion."

Kat was horrified to know Dot had been uncertain about her intent—and living with that for days. "Now I understand why you asked. I'm really glad you did."

A little smile returned to Dot's face. She met Kat's eyes again.

"And seriously," Kat went on, "don't sell yourself short with regards to your art."

"Yeah, well . . . truthfully, I've yet to sell one piece."

"Maybe you're just marketing to the wrong crowd. People going to L&M probably aren't looking to buy sculptures—for the most part." *Kat* would buy Dot's art in a heartbeat, if she had the extra cash to spend.

"Could be." Dot looked lost in thought. She stared at Kat just a little too long, as if transfixed. Then she seemed to snap out of it. "Sorry, I'm, uh . . . keeping you."

"Not at all! I really like talking to you!" Kat surprised herself with her directness. She was feeling bolder than usual tonight.

The pinkness in Dot's cheeks was renewed. "Yeah. This was good."

Kat's instinct was to hug Dot goodbye, but she wasn't sure. She just ended up hesitating.

"Okay. I'm gonna . . ." Dot pointed a thumb toward the van.

"Right." Kat flashed her a smile.

She watched as Dot walked away. Wow. They'd just had a full conversation! A short one, but a productive one, to be sure. Comfortable, even, all things considered.

Kat got in her car. They were the last two in the lot now, so she waited to see that Dot's van started. Then Kat pulled out of her spot and headed for the diner.

Lynn and Jet were going to flip when she told them about tonight. Well, the highlights, anyway. She figured some of the details ought to stay between Dot and her.

CHAPTER 4

Hawed

Dot went to the studio early the next morning. She'd woken up feeling inspired. Hopeful. She walked in with a protein bar clenched in her teeth, a set of keys in one hand, and her purse in the other. She took a bite and surveyed the room while she chewed.

Everything remained where she'd left it the day before. The Burger Life screens lay on the steel counter, clean and awaiting their inaugural run. Tee shirts, tank tops, and hoodies were on one of the tables, folded and piled by size and color. Tubs of ink sat ready next to the screen printing press, in the colors that best matched Lynn's original design.

Dot had been hoping to launch into that job today. As such, she'd left herself little to do in terms of prep work. So her eyes moved instead to the table that held her dragon sculpture. She was close to finishing it.

She came around the table and inspected the figure. The creature's arms, or front legs—whatever dragons called them—lay at its base, waiting to be attached properly. Each one was covered in tiny clamps, which had held them together while the adhesive cured. The clamps would be ready to come off by now. As she chewed the last bite of her protein bar, she threw the wrapper in the trash, then sat down in front of her project.

Careful to avoid the claws, which were actually quite sharp, she removed the clamps one by one and lightly tested the strength of each connection. She ran her fingers over the scale pattern on the back of the arm. The texture had turned out great—very lizard-like, and consistent with the rest of the sculpture—so she was pleased with that.

Satisfied that it was ready to be attached to the creature itself, Dot lifted the arm up and held it against the dragon's existing stump. She would need to apply the adhesive and then put the part in place freehand. Not only that, but she'd need to hold it still while applying clamps. There would be room only for tiny adjustments once the adhesive had been applied.

Dot could see in her mind's eye how she wanted the piece positioned—where it would connect to the larger structure. But she couldn't quite get it in place. It wasn't that the size was off or the arm was shaped wrong. It was just that her hand kept quivering. Strange. Dot normally had very steady hands.

She put the arm down, held her hand up and observed it. Not even the slightest tremor. Steady as can be. She picked up the part and tried again. But as soon as she got it mostly in position, there was that quiver again. *Dammit.*

What was the deal here? Was she nervous about getting this right? It's not like there was anything riding on it. Could it be the time of day? Any time before noon *was* early for her, after all. Maybe if she just walked away and came back to it later . . .

In the meantime, she'd just try to relax and center herself. She went to the mini fridge and perused the beer selection. Some IPAs, a stout, a lager . . . ah, Upstarts' Brazen Tart witbier. That was a morning sort of brew, right? If she drank it in the AM, then sure it was.

Dot pulled the bottle off the door. There was an opener on top of the fridge. She popped the cap, shut the door with her foot, then took a swig while she walked over to the computer desk. She put the beer down next to the keyboard and sat in the cushioned chair. Time to get lost on the web for a while.

First stop was to check orders on Lizard & Mouse. Hmm. Only one more since Lynn's report the night before. Okay, then on to the CRD member discussion forum. Nothing especially exciting there. Debate over a change in the rules. Signups to promote CRD at Pridefest. Dot had already signed up, so no need to worry about that. Nothing else of interest.

Next was Facebook. Eight notifications. Some likes on a link she had shared. New posts from Jet. And one friend request—from Katrina Brooks.

Dot stared at the notification. They had seventy-three mutual friends? Jeez, that included most of the league, plus a lot of Dot's derby connections outside of CRD. Now that she thought about it, maybe it did look a bit weird that she and Kat weren't at least Facebook friends.

The previous night's talk must have prompted Kat to send the request. This wasn't at all out of line with the way she'd been acting lately, but Dot still wasn't sure what to make of that whole situation. Regardless, accepting the request was the only real option, wasn't it? Dot would look like an asshole if she declined.

The sound of keys in the door. The knob turned. No time to think. Dot clicked "confirm." The notification was still showing! She closed the browser.

"Hey, lady!" Lynn cast her a smile. "I saw you made a new friend!"

"Wait . . . what?" Dot swiveled the chair to face her. "How . . . ?"

"Oh please. We saw you in the parking lot last night." Lynn hung her tote bag on a coat hook. "It's not like it was a very clandestine meeting."

"Ah." Of course. Duh.

"I mean, you looked pretty engrossed, so I don't blame you for being oblivious. But we *were* all leaving the rink at about the same time."

"Uh. Yeah." Dot could feel her cheeks flushing.

"I'm just glad you finally took my advice and talked to her!"

Dot cringed. "Well, it wasn't what you think."

"No?" Lynn narrowed her eyes at Dot. "So, what did you two talk about, then?"

"Art."

"Art!" Lynn slapped Dot's shoulder. "That's great!"

Dot gave her a puzzled look. "I thought you wanted me to talk to her about penal—"

"I'll take what I can get!"

"O . . . kay . . ." Dot was lost.

Lynn looked her in the eye and folded her arms.

"Okay, listen." Lynn's tone became much more solemn. "Frankly . . . you looked like shit when you left the rink yesterday."

Dot sighed and turned away.

"We both know you were in a bad place. I'm not judging you for that." Lynn paused, watching Dot's face. "But something had to give. Am I right?"

Dot met Lynn's eyes again, though her expression was stony.

"I don't care what you talked to Kat *about*," Lynn said. "I'm just glad—hell, I'm *impressed* that your stubborn ass talked to her at all."

Dot snorted, breaking into a smile. She covered her mouth with her hand.

Lynn laughed. "You know you're stubborn, do you not?"

"I guess a little," Dot said with reluctance.

"A little," Lynn repeated, her tone heavy with sarcasm. She made her way around Dot and sat down at her drawing table. "Alright. Well, I'm not gonna pry all the details from you, but I will say you look much better this morning. So whatever she said to you, it must have been good."

Dot was silent. She tried to will herself not to blush. It was a losing battle. Lynn seemed to take notice and raised an eyebrow.

"Is that what has you in the studio this early?" Lynn's eyes went to the beer. "Day drinking?"

"Maybe." Dot reopened the web browser and typed in the address for Lizard & Mouse again. "I did sleep better last night."

"Oh?" Lynn opened her sketchbook to a fresh page.

"I woke up feeling pretty good, so I wanted to come over and get something done." Dot sipped her beer.

Lynn looked around the room. "Doesn't look like you got very far."

"Yeah, well. The beast wasn't cooperating."

Dot clicked to view one of her sculptures on the L&M site—a large mask, just over two feet tall. The actual piece was mounted on the wall above the desk where Dot was sitting. All-green, with details resembling vines or branches, it looked like a nature goddess from several feet away. But upon closer inspection, one would see that the entire structure was built out of little plastic army men, which Dot had melted together.

She looked from the screen to the actual mask and back again.

"Hey, do ya think . . . ?" Dot stopped, not sure how to phrase her question.

"Think what?"

She took a moment to consider her wording. "Should I try putting my junk sculptures out there more? Like, would people be into them?"

"Junk sculptures? I've never heard you call them that before." Lynn was inspecting the tips of her colored pencils. "Yeah, dude, people would love them. I've been telling you that for years. What has you thinking about it now?"

"Um . . ." Dot felt her cheeks getting hot again. What was *with* this? She picked up her beer and took a long gulp before continuing. "As it turns out . . . Kat really likes them . . . believe it or not."

Lynn almost fumbled her pencils, catching the box upright just in time. She let out a sigh of relief, then looked at Dot. "Oh, I believe it." She put the pencils down on the drawing table. "Yeah, you should get, like, gallery space or something."

"Gallery space? For my trash art?" Dot cocked an eye at Lynn. "Are you nuts? Besides, that's expensive. I'd have to actually sell some pieces to recoup the cost."

Lynn's face was incredulous. "You don't think they'd sell? *I* think they'd sell."

"I . . . Call me doubtful. No one's ever shown interest in buying them before. Except my dad."

"Hardly anyone's seen them yet!" Lynn looked around at Dot's sculptures, scattered about the edges of the room, on top of cabinets, on the walls. "Alright, so, what if you just start small? You have decent pics of them on L&M. Put those on Facebook and stuff. I'll share them, and I'll get Jet to. I bet they'd get a crap ton of likes."

Dot clicked through the various photos of her art. "I just—I worry that it's not good enough. Or that the whole medium is a cop-out."

Lynn shifted in her chair. She looked pensive. "Okay, first of all, the medium may be non-traditional, but it is in no way a cop-out. Few people could transform these materials the way you do. But if you feel that way, why even put the stuff up for sale on L&M?"

"I don't know." Dot tensed up. "I thought maybe that would make it legit? Otherwise I'm just playing with junk in my dad's garage. L&M seemed like a safe enough place—where, eh . . . probably no one would actually see it." She chuckled at her own expense.

"Uh-huh." Lynn smirked. "And then Kat saw it, and you found out you have an actual fan. And that got you thinking."

Dot took another swig from her beer. "Mmhm."

"You are way too hard on yourself, my dear. I think you're too close to your own work to see how good it is. And believe me, I get that."

Dot leaned back in her chair and stared at the mask on the wall.

Lynn went on, "Trust your fans, Dot. Kat, of all people, likes your crazy trash art. That's gotta say something, right?"

"I suppose it does." Dot smiled. "Maybe it says she has terrible taste."

Lynn shook her head. "Jesus, you're hopeless."

* * *

Thursday evening. Kat turned the key and stepped in the front door of the house. The aroma hit her immediately—onion, garlic, chili, tomato . . . That had to be Lonnie cooking.

"I'm guessing enchiladas!" Kat yelled as she shut the door behind her.

"Damn, sis!" Lonnie called back. "You're getting good at this! Where you been?"

Kat rounded the corner into the kitchen. "I picked up a shift at the camera shop. Jake called me this afternoon."

Lonnie glanced at her between adding ingredients to his saucepan. "I thought you'd be at the rink, skating with your new girlfriend."

"She's not my . . ." Kat turned red, but she was grinning. "Shut up."

"You better make your move, girl. Strike while the iron's hot."

"You're such a dude. It's not always that simple." Kat cleared her throat and collected herself. "Anyway, I couldn't pass up this shift."

"You need the money?"

"Well, I mean I always need the money." Kat took a seat at the table. "But I also want to stay in good with Jake. He lets me do prints there, basically at-cost."

"I can see how that would be important." Lonnie spoke without looking at her, his eyes focused on food prep.

"Yeah, especially with Pride coming up. I'm gonna be printing like crazy next week. Which reminds me—you're sure your brother's okay with me borrowing his tent?"

"Yeah, it's totally cool. I'll get it from him this weekend."

"Awesome." Kat leaned back in her chair. "You're a life saver."

Lonnie shrugged. "I know."

There was a momentary lull. Kat spied an open bag of tortilla chips on the table and reached out to take one. "So, anything new with you? How'd that interview at the bar go?" She popped the chip in her mouth.

"Eh, it was okay." Lonnie shook his head. "I don't think they're gonna hire me."

"No?"

"Just the vibe I got." He opened the cabinet and pulled out a casserole dish. "But in other news, I have a date tomorrow night."

"Oh, good for you!" Kat swallowed and grabbed another chip. "Where'd you find this one?"

"Tinder." He glanced back at her. "And don't spoil your appetite. There's plenty here for you too, if you want some."

"Mm!" Kat nodded enthusiastically, her mouth full again.

"Honestly, I'm not super pumped about meeting this chick. But it's something to do on a Friday night."

"Hey, you never know. She could defy your expectations."

"Yeah, we'll see." Lonnie peeked inside the oven briefly. The smell of roasting corn filled the kitchen. "How about you? Where *are* you with this girl now?"

Kat chewed for a second while she considered her answer. "Well, I told you we talked."

There was a pause.

With his free hand, Lonnie motioned for her to continue. "Yeah, I remember. And?"

"Annnd now we're friends on Facebook?"

"Ooh, big step! You sure you're ready for that?"

Kat threw her head back and groaned.

"Alright, alright." Lonnie turned around, licking his finger, and leaned back against the counter. "I know. It's complicated. Good on you for making progress, sis. Really."

"Thank you."

"Do I get to see what this Mouse looks like at least?"

"Oh!" Kat's eyes lit up. "Yeah! One sec."

She pulled her phone out of her purse and opened the Facebook app. It was already showing Dot's page. Kat touched the profile pic to make it full-screen. It was a waist-up shot of Dot holding up a beer and shouting at someone off camera.

"Here." She turned the phone around and held it out to Lonnie. He stepped closer and took it from her.

"Aw, she's way cute!" He smirked. "Yeah, you gotta lock that down!"

Kat rolled her eyes.

"Dorothy, huh? I like her hair." Lonnie tapped the screen and checked out Dot's other photos. "Damn, and she's built. I mean, not like super cut, but she looks like she could kick serious ass."

"She *does*." Kat grinned.

Lonnie flicked through a few more pictures. Then he tapped a couple times. "Alright, here, hold on." He started typing something.

"Hey! Hey!" Kat nearly leapt out of her chair, reaching for the phone. "What're you *doing*?"

Lonnie evaded her grasp. "Relax! I'm not gonna send it, I promise." He finished typing and handed the phone back to Kat. Then he turned to the stove and gave the sauce a stir. "Just a suggestion, sis."

Kat looked at the screen. True to his word, Lonnie had left the message unsent.

hey grl. come w me 2 3rd sat mkt this wknd? bst frnd bailed on me. also i rly supr like yr face n wanna touch yr butt

"No. Way." Kat burst out laughing. "That is not me *at all*."

"Okay. Then how would you word it?"

Kat pursed her lips. She didn't respond, just stared at the screen.

Lonnie peeked over his shoulder. "You're thinking about it, aren't you?"

"No." She was definitely thinking about it. "Maybe."

She deleted Lonnie's message. How *would* she word it? *I know we've only talked for like 5 minutes total, but do you want to spend the day with me?* Ugh. It was too soon. Why was she thinking about this? She was torturing herself.

She leaned her elbow on the table and propped her head on her hand. "Why do you do this to me, Lon?"

"Because"—he turned to look at her—"in all seriousness, you should ask her."

"It's just . . . it would be all day. That seems like a lot, for a first . . . ya know . . ."

"A first date?" Lonnie chuckled. "Don't think of it as a date, Kit Kat." He casually waved his spatula. "It's just a trip to the market."

"Right . . ." Kat stared into the middle distance, thinking. "And I guess it would be a productive trip for her too. She could find some great materials to sculpt with. You remember the guy that was there last time selling boxes of old circuit boards?"

"Yeah, and we were like, 'Who would buy that?'"

"A junk artist, that's who—if it's cheap enough. Regardless, I'm sure she'd find *something* useful at TSM."

"Well, there's your angle." Lonnie turned his attention back to the stove.

As Kat sat in contemplation, she started to notice her bra was itching and her feet were sore. She checked the time on her phone. 9:12. "How long do you think 'til that's ready?"

"When this is done I gotta fill the tortillas and bake 'em. A little over half an hour?"

"Okay." Kat leaned forward and lifted herself out of the chair. "I'm gonna run upstairs and get changed. I'll be back by then."

"Cool."

* * *

Once in her room, Kat put her purse on the desk and threw her phone onto the bed. She pulled her collared shirt off over her head. Arching her back, she reached up and unhooked her bra, then let the straps slip down her arms. Ahhh, the feeling of air against her skin. Relief.

She threw the clothes into the laundry basket that served as her hamper. Then she sat down on the edge of the bed, untied her boots, and pulled each one off, letting it fall to the floor.

She blew out a breath and fell backwards onto the bed, eyes closed. She'd been on her feet for hours. She spent a minute just lying there, reveling in the comfort of being home.

Her tranquility was soon interrupted by a buzz from her phone. She picked it up and checked it. Nothing important—someone in her photography circle had posted new shots. But there were other notifications as well, among them a reminder that she had events coming up this weekend, including Third Saturday Market.

She really did want to go. She *needed* to go. She needed frames—a lot of frames—to display her prints at Pridefest, and it was a safe bet she'd find them for cheap at TSM. But she really, really didn't want to go alone. Tough-skinned as she was, it was easy to feel intimidated, and even a little unsafe, among the throngs of people there. The buddy system was key.

Could she ask Dot? It didn't seem like such an outlandish idea when she looked at it in practical terms. And the two of them had just recently connected over art stuff. If she wasn't so *into* Dot, this would have been a no-brainer from the start. So yeah . . . it wouldn't be a stretch.

But if she was gonna do this, she'd better do it soon. The market was less than two days away. That meant messaging Dot tonight.

Alright, Kat, don't overthink it. She rolled over onto her belly and opened the Messenger app.

* * *

Dot pulled her van in next to Jet's white Camaro. Jet and Lynn had already gone inside and grabbed their favorite booth.

Dot opened the visor mirror. Her helmet had left her hair matted down. She took a moment to play with it—pinned it back on the sides, tried to fluff up the top a bit by pulling it forward and messing it about. She brushed it away from her eyes and took a look. Definitely an improvement. She grabbed her purse and hopped down out of the van.

When Dot walked into the diner, Jet cried out, "There she is! The queen of the rink!"

Some of the diner staff applauded. Dot smirked and shook her head.

Tonight's practice had ended with a drill called Queen of the Rink—a free-for-all, last-skater-standing game which involved trying to knock each other down or off the track. It was one of Dot's favorites. Coming out on top always felt pretty badass.

When she reached the booth, she threw her purse onto the seat and slid in across from Lynn and Jet.

"You guys are dorks," she said. "Did you order yet?"

"Of course not," a voice answered from behind before Lynn or Jet could get a word in. "You know I wouldn't let them order without you." Maggie, their waitress, came around and stood at the end of the table. "Hey, stud."

Dot gave her a bright smile. "Hey, hot stuff!"

Maggie was a curvy redhead with big, green eyes. She and Dot had a long-standing tradition of tongue-in-cheek flirtation.

Maggie leaned down to hug Dot.

Dot inhaled deeply. "You smell divine! Is that a new fragrance?"

"You noticed!" Maggie beamed. "Ricky didn't have a clue."

Dot cringed at the mention of Ricky. "How *is* the boy toy?"

Maggie curled her lip. "Besides being oblivious? Messy. Stinky. Nothing like *you*."

"Me? Not stinky?" Dot laughed. "Please. I smell like death right now, I'm sure." She sniffed the crux of her elbow. As expected, she reeked.

"Aw, nonsense. You've just been working hard." Maggie lowered her voice to a purr. "You have that natural feminine musk about you."

"Oh yeah?" Dot laid her arm across the back of the seat, opening her body toward Maggie. "Is it calling to your inner animal?"

"Jesus, you two." Lynn wrinkled her nose. "Gross."

Dot and Maggie giggled.

Jet added, "Yeah, I would barf, but I haven't even eaten yet."

"Alright, alright." Maggie stifled her laughter and collected herself. "What can I get you ladies?"

She readied her pen and pad. Jet looked at Lynn.

"Oh, me?" Realization shone on Lynn's face. "Okay, I'll do the burger combo. Jack cheese, black-and-white shake. Please."

"Okay. Ms. Rocket?"

"Grilled cheese, chocolate shake," Jet said. "And fries."

Maggie turned to Dot. "And the usual for my muskrat?"

"You remember?" Dot raised an eyebrow.

Maggie threw her a knowing glance while writing. "Of course I remember! It hasn't been *that* long."

"Yes, thank you!"

"Okay, I'll put this in." Maggie tore off the slip.

"Thanks, Mags!" Jet said.

Maggie smiled, and winked at Dot, then she was off.

Jet turned to Dot. "So how about *you* killing it tonight!"

"Not just Queen of the Rink, either," Lynn said. "You were on fire the whole time."

"Yeah." Dot grinned. "It felt pretty good, like I was just *on*. I can't believe Coach used me as an example for the Dynamo."

The Dynamo, so named by Fiend, was one of the new offensive moves they'd been working on.

Lynn snickered. "I like how you just started calling it the 'Mo."

"Well it takes too long to say 'Dynamo.' It has to be an immediate reaction."

"And that's why Coach wanted *you* to demonstrate." Jet pointed at Dot. "It's all about timing, and you had it down. You made me a hole every time with the 'Mo."

Lynn snorted. "Oh my god, I hope this catches on."

"Anyway, yes, you rocked tonight." Jet was emphatic. "I'm glad it felt good. You needed a good night."

Just then, Maggie came by with three glasses and straws. "Water for my thirsty girls."

"Aw, you're the best." Lynn took a glass eagerly.

"Shakes'll be out in a few." And Maggie was off again.

Dot began unwrapping her straw. "Are either of you working Pride?"

Jet was taking a long sip of water.

"Nah." Lynn plunged her straw through the ice. "Well, Jet's

volunteering with the LGBT center, but I assume you mean working the CRD tent."

"Yeah."

Jet swallowed. "We worked First Friday, so we don't need the event credit. Are you?"

Dot nodded. "I'm on the noon shift. Any idea who else is working?"

"Let's see." Jet's brow creased. "I don't know who's on what shift, but I think Siren, Peaches, Jocelyn, Domme—"

"Domme's back?" Dot's face lit up.

Jet shook her head. "She's not skating yet, but she's doing better. And I don't know if Vee is *working* Pride, but there's a good chance she'll be hanging out if Domme's there."

"I hope she's on my shift. I haven't seen her in ages." Dot leaned closer to Jet. "What's the deal with those two, anyway? Are they dating?"

"Who? Domme and Vee?"

"Mmhm."

Jet laughed. "No! They're not dating, they're derby wives."

"Ah, okay." Dot waved a hand dismissively. "I never got the whole derby wife thing."

"I used to have one," Lynn said. "She moved to California."

Bzzz-bzzz.

Lynn continued, "That was way back, though. When I was still skating with LCR."

Dot dug in her purse and found her phone. She pulled it out just far enough to unlock it and check the screen. She started to put it back, but she did a double take and checked it again.

"What's up?" Lynn eyed the purse, then Dot.

Dot brought the phone up above the table as she silently read the message.

Hi! Question: Would you be interested in coming to 3rd Sat Market this weekend? I know we've only talked briefly, but my buddy can't go and I think you might dig it. Huge flea mkt w/lots of crafty stuff. Sry for asking last minute.

"It's . . . a message from Kat."

"Oh yeah? What about?" Lynn extended her hand to take the phone. Dot gave it to her.

"She's asking if I wanna go to a flea market."

Jet leaned in to read over Lynn's shoulder. Her eyes went wide, and she gave Lynn several little punches in the arm.

"Ow. Stahp." Lynn elbow-nudged her in protest.

"What?" Dot looked at Jet.

Jet bit her lip.

Lynn answered, "It's Third Saturday Market! You know what that is, right?"

Dot squinted at her. "I mean, I know it's a flea market."

"That's kind of an understatement. TSM is enormous. I haven't been there in years, but I remember needing a map to get around. It's like a little city with its own different neighborhoods, all sprawled out on this field." Lynn paused to sip her water. "There's a section that's all artists and crafters that I loved. There's even a little sort of punk rock flea market area. Like a market-within-a-market."

"Oh wow." Dot tilted her head pensively, her curiosity piqued.

"But that's just a fraction of it. You could find just about anything at TSM, if you know where to look."

"Hmm." Dot folded her arms and slouched back against the seat.

"Are you gonna go?"

"It sounds interesting." Dot weighed the idea. "But going with Kat . . . I . . ."

Lynn and Jet were both silent, staring at Dot expectantly.

Dot sighed. "What if you guys came with?"

Jet shook her head. "No can do. We have dinner at Lynn's parents' on Saturday."

"Come on, Dot," Lynn said. "You afraid to spend the day alone with your biggest fan?"

Jet raised an eyebrow. "Yeah, I think at this point we can pretty much confirm she doesn't hate you."

Dot tapped her foot against the leg of the table. "I guess she was cool on Tuesday."

Cool? She'd been Dot's *lifeline* on Tuesday! Dot could see those gentle blue eyes practically lifting her off the floor. She heard the words echoing in her head again—*give credit where it's due.* But she so hated being wrong. *Cool* was her compromise.

Dot was spaced out, lost in thought. Lynn's voice brought her back to the present.

"You should go." Her tone was more serious now. "I know you're reluctant 'cause she's confusing or whatever. But that's all the more reason, isn't it? Get to know her and see what makes her tick." She handed the phone back to Dot. "Plus I know you have no other plans Saturday."

Dot read the message again. "Where is this place, anyway?"

"Like half an hour away. You could even meet her there. Then if you decide you wanna leave, make up some excuse and bounce."

"Yeah." Dot liked that idea. Reluctant as she was, the prospect of flat-out saying no just . . . well, it felt like a dick move. And if there was one thing she hated more than being wrong, it was feeling like a dick.

She started typing.

Sure! Just tell me

No. She wasn't that eager. Delete.

Yeah, that could be cool. Where and when do you wanna

Delete. Too conversational. Keep it short and direct.

I'm game. Details?

Yeah. That would do.

Send.

"What are you typing?" Jet asked impatiently.

Dot held the phone out and showed them the screen.

Jet's mouth formed a silent "O." She high-fived Lynn.

Dot looked at them blankly. "Wow, you two are really invested in this."

Lynn and Jet froze for a second. They looked at each other, then back at Dot.

"Uh. Well, you know . . ." Lynn shrugged. "This is an adventure. It's exciting."

"We're living vicariously," Jet added.

"Yeah, that's it."

"Shakes!" Maggie showed up with her hands full, bearing three thick, frozen beverages in oversized glass mugs—a black-n-white and two chocolates, one of which had swirls of extra chocolate sauce.

"Perfect timing, Mags!" Lynn flashed her an eager grin.

"Awwwesome." Dot's mouth watered as she took the double-chocolate mug. "Mags, it has been too long since I last tasted your milkshake."

Maggie put her hands on the table and leaned forward, pressing her ample bosom in Dot's direction. "I knew you'd be back for it, baby."

CHAPTER 5

Instinct

———————

Orders started coming in on Friday morning, giving Dot plenty of print work to do. She stayed in contact with Kat over Messenger, though the conversation remained largely impersonal. They exchanged phone numbers and worked out the practical details of the Market trip. Otherwise, Dot kept herself busy, and the hours flew by.

Only in bed that night did Dot find herself dwelling on the next day's plans. She was looking forward to Saturday, though she wasn't entirely sure of the reason. Was she anxious to get it over with? Or eager to get some answers? A little of both? Or—if she was honest with herself—was she just looking forward to seeing Kat?

That last one was a real possibility. After all, it was nice to have a fan. Surely that was why she felt so drawn to talk to Kat again, right? Right. Satisfied with her rationalization, Dot began drifting off to sleep.

* * *

The alarm went off far too early for Dot's liking. 6:00 AM was an absurd time for anyone to be awake, as far as she was concerned. But she was supposed to meet Kat at seven, when the Market opened, to try to beat the crowds or some nonsense. Dot was liking this whole idea a lot less right now. Still, an image flashed in her mind—of Kat leaning against the trunk of her Corolla, waiting—and seemed to kickstart her wakefulness.

Dot was in and out of the shower. She'd always been quick about that. Back in her room, she dug hastily through a basket of clean laundry, throwing articles of clothing on the bed as she found them—a fitted Heavy Metal t-shirt with the neck cut out, green cargo shorts, bra, socks, undies. Once dressed, she pulled her old high-top Chucks out from under the bed and put them on. Kat had suggested comfortable shoes that Dot didn't mind getting dirty.

Makeup-wise, Dot applied just a light layer of foundation to even out her skin tone. She generally went for a pretty minimalist look.

She put a bit of mousse in her still-damp hair and blew it out to give it its signature wild style. Then she pinned it back on the sides and swept the top toward the back.

Lastly, Dot grabbed her purse and a backpack, as suggested by Kat, and threw a pair of shades on her head. She was out of the house by 6:35.

She arrived only a few minutes late at the address Kat had given her, which turned out to be a massive field with what looked like a tent city in the middle of it. Market employees directed her as far as where to park. Kat had said to meet at the "nearest entrance," rather than specifying one, and this was why.

Dot ended up parking closest to the "orange" entrance. It looked like one could enter anywhere along the perimeter, but the major gateways were color-coded. As she trekked across the grass, she pulled her phone out and texted Kat to say she was arriving.

Dot had her shades down at this point. The sun was low on the horizon and downright blinding whenever she looked east. It cast long shadows across the field and reflected brightly off the tops of the tents.

As she approached the entrance, she spotted Kat waving to her. Kat was a little taller than Dot and wore a heather-grey tank top under an open white shirt. She had on mid-thigh, cut-off denim shorts and Doc Martens laced halfway up. And shades. She'd been right—the shades were a must-have. In addition to wearing a backpack, she was pulling some kind of folded-up contraption on wheels.

"Hey! You made it!" Kat was grinning ear to ear.

"Hey!" Dot's eyes went from Kat to the wheeled device. "What's that thing?"

Kat looked down at it. "It's a collapsible wagon. Lonnie and I invested in it after we'd been coming here a while. Really cuts down on trips back to the car."

"Lonnie?"

"Yeah, he's the one who couldn't make it today. We usually come every month together."

Dot tilted her head. "And he's your . . . ?"

"Oh! Housemate! And friend. Yeah, people always think we're a couple." Kat flashed a disapproving sneer.

For some reason, Dot felt a sense of relief at that answer. She didn't dwell on it. "Cool." She put her hands on her hips. "So . . . what's the plan? What's first?"

"First, let me give you a map." Kat pulled a square of paper from her back pocket and unfolded it. It was just a yellow sheet with a simple map on one side and a long list of vendors on the other. She sidled up next to Dot. "Okay, here's where we are right now. This section is Clothing and Personal. Personal refers to, like, makeup and stuff."

Dot nodded.

"Over here is Art and Handmade. And then across from us is Antiques and Used Goods." Kat pointed to the map as she explained. "Those are the main areas. Then on the borders between them, you have these smaller, sort-of hybrid sections."

"Yeah, Lizzy mentioned something about a punk rock market here that was like that."

"Oh, yes. That's there, between Antiques and Handmade. You can actually see it from here." Kat turned to the east, peering over top of the nearby vendors. "See that big black tent in the distance? It's under that."

"Wow." Dot shielded her eyes from the sun as she followed Kat's gaze. There was indeed a massive black tent that covered a decent-sized area.

"I always visit there," Kat said. "But I generally hit the entire Antiques section anyway, and most of Handmade. Hell, I'll browse the whole market if there's time. You never know what you'll find. They try to group it into these sections, but it's far from perfect."

"Like this guy selling clothes and lamps over here?"

"Exactly. It's a flea market—it's full of surprises." Kat returned her gaze to Dot, un-squinting as she looked away from the sun. "Oh jeez, have you eaten yet? Or need coffee?"

That piqued Dot's attention. "No, yeah, I could definitely go for something."

"Me too. Let's head for the food court while we talk."

They started toward the center of the Market. Dot glanced around at the vendors as they passed. It was certainly an eclectic mix—tie-dye everything, Islamic headscarves, teen girl fashion, band tees . . .

"Of course," Kat said, "I won't make you do the whole market with me. I mainly need to hit Antiques and Used."

"What do you need there?"

"Frames, mostly. I got a tent at Pride to show my photography, and now I'm scrambling to prep for it."

"No way! That's great!" The first smile of the day crossed Dot's lips. And before any caffeine!

"It's gonna be a challenge." There was concern in Kat's tone.

Dot glanced at her. "I'm sure you'll do fine."

Kat smiled back. "What about you? Any particular areas you'd like to check out?"

Dot thought for a moment. "Well, you mentioned over Messenger that I might find some junk in the Used section. Although I have to say, I'm not used to actually paying for the stuff I build with."

"No?" Kat raised an eyebrow. "How do you get all that stuff? People just getting rid of it?"

"Well, some of it. And some I just already had laying around. But mostly . . . ehh . . ." Dot fidgeted, adjusting her backpack.

"Mostly?"

"Mostly I—" Dot cleared her throat "—pick it out of the trash."

"Iew, like dumpster diving?" Kat wrinkled her nose.

"No! I don't actually climb into dumpsters and stuff! Except for that one time. Well, two times."

Kat laughed. "You're nasty!"

"Hey, art is dirty work sometimes!"

"I'll say!" She looked sideways at Dot. "Just tell me you showered this morning."

"Awhaw! Come on, it's not like I'm crawling around in garbage all the time. But yes, I showered before entering your presence, princess." Dot turned to Kat and half-curtsied.

Color filled Kat's cheeks. "Oh stop." She smirked. "Sorry, I didn't mean for it to come off that way."

"S'okay. Next you'll be calling me a scruffy-looking nerf-herder."

Kat feigned insult. "I would never!"

Dot chuckled and shot her a smile. Kat's hand reached for Dot's. Dot took it instinctively, only realizing it once they were linked. Why did this feel so easy? This was the longest conversation they'd ever had, yet it felt like they already knew each other well.

"Here we are." Kat brought them to a stop.

They'd entered what looked like an old warehouse building in the center of the Market. The food court. Folding tables and chairs were set up throughout the central space, and vendor booths lined the walls. Only a few of the vendors were present yet, selling mostly breakfast items.

Kat looked to Dot. "Coffee?"

"Uh, sure. I'm not a big coffee drinker, but I could use the boost. Mostly I need to eat something."

"Why don't you look around while I grab the coffee, then? What do you drink?"

Dot squinted an eye. "Um, something not too coffee-y? I like mochas."

"Iced?"

"That works."

* * *

When they reconvened, Dot had a sizeable breakfast burrito in her hand. "These things are huge!"

"Ah, you went to Benny's! Yeah, they rock." Kat had a drink carrier with two iced coffees in one hand. The other hand was holding a bag and pulling the fold-up wagon. She put the stuff down on a nearby table. "Here, let's sit a minute."

Kat handed Dot her mocha, then reached into the bag. She pulled out a poppy seed bagel with cream cheese already spread between the two halves.

"I'm gonna regret this when the seeds are all stuck in my teeth." She paused, eyeing the coffee and the wagon. "Do you mind if we sit here while I eat this? I don't have enough hands."

Dot answered with her mouth full. "Fine wiff me." She swallowed. "I'm just along for the ride."

They sat in surprisingly comfortable silence for a few minutes, each of them preoccupied chewing. Halfway through her burrito, Dot realized she'd been practically inhaling the thing. She slowed down and took a sip of her mocha.

"This is really good." She raised the cup. "Thanks. I owe you one."

Kat shook her head. She finished her mouthful of bagel before speaking. "My treat. For coming with me today."

Dot took another, smaller bite and thought while she chewed. "So for these frames . . . do you have a vendor in mind already?"

"Mm." Kat nodded. "There are a couple that I think are good bets. I want to hit them first."

Kat described their locations. She talked about those and some of the neighboring vendors while the two of them finished eating. Then with their coffees in hand, they ventured out of the old warehouse and into the Antiques & Used Goods section.

They passed by numerous vendors selling furniture of all kinds. There were also toys and games, small appliances, home decor, china and flatware. Some vendors had seemingly random assortments of goods.

As they walked, Kat described what she was looking for and how her tent would be set up at Pride. Dot kept an eye out for frames and anything else Kat could use.

"Hey, there's the doll vendor." Kat pointed. "We'll have to swing back this way so I can show you what she has."

"Doll vendor," Dot repeated. "That alone sounds creepy as fuck."

Finally they came to a vendor with lots of home decor items, including boxes upon boxes of frames.

"This is one of them." Kat stepped out of the foot traffic lane, pulling Dot with her. "Looks promising, but I'll have to dig through the selection to find what I need."

Dot approached one of the boxes and flipped through a few of the frames. They were all mixed up. Some old, some new-ish. Metal, wood, and plastic. Some with glass, some without. Kat unfolded her wagon. It was made of dark blue canvas, with a metal frame, and looked big enough to fit two of these boxes.

Dot nodded at the little cart. "Will that be able to carry enough for your purposes?"

"Hopefully." Kat eyed the frames. "This could take me a while. If you want to go look around while I do this, that's—"

"Nah, I'll help you look." Dot didn't really want to walk around by herself. She was here to hang out with Kat, after all. "This is the main reason we came, right?"

Kat nodded.

Dot's inner team-player kicked in. She was all business now. "You gave me a good description of what you're looking for. Let's do what we came to do."

"Okay."

Kat smiled, but creases lined her face. Dot couldn't tell if she was happy or . . . disappointed? But that didn't make sense. Anyway, there was work to do.

"So how about I start at that end"—Dot gestured to the furthest bin—"and we can work towards each other?"

Kat perked up a bit. "Yeah, sounds good."

They spent the better part of an hour going through frames. The vendor, an older gentleman, came by and offered a couple of empty boxes. Slowly but surely, Kat and Dot filled them to capacity with simply-styled wooden frames and matching-size glass.

"How many is that now?" Kat asked as Dot added another frame to the collection.

"That makes fifteen of the big ones and twenty of the smaller ones."

"That should be enough."

The vendor had taken to wrapping the glass in paper and packing it such that it wouldn't rattle in the wagon. He was finishing the last one as Kat approached him to pay.

Dot watched the interaction. She heard Kat say, "Thank you so much for doing that."

The guy was harder to understand from where Dot stood—he was quieter—but she did catch him saying, "My pleasure. You and your girlfriend have a wonderful day." At that, a pink hue definitely overtook Kat's face and arms. Was she blushing? It was adorable.

"And thank *you*." Kat made a beeline for Dot. "Thank you so much. You were a huge help."

"Hey, no prob—"

And pulled her into a tight hug.

"—lem."

Dot reciprocated the gesture. Kat smelled really good. The natural sweetness of her sweat mingled with the faint florals of her deodorant, filling Dot's senses. It was . . . a bit of a rush, actually. When Kat ended the embrace, Dot felt the loss.

"Okay, well . . ." Kat looked down at the wagon. "I guess that takes care of that." She sounded almost despondent, the corners of her lips hinting at a frown.

Dot gave her a questioning eye. "Shall we haul this back to your car?"

"Yeah."

"Then we can come back and have some fun."

Kat opened her mouth, then paused. She lifted her shades. "You want to?"

"Of course I want to."

A relieved smile crept across Kat's face. "I was afraid you weren't really into it."

Dot put her hands on her hips. "You got me up at the ass crack of dawn. You'd better show me around this place."

Kat beamed. She pulled her shades back down with authority. "Alright, then! To the car!"

They took turns pulling the wagon. Kat led them on a shortcut through the Handmade section that greatly reduced their walk. On the way to the car and back, She related the story of how she and Lonnie had first started coming to TSM, and she talked about some of the items she'd found here in the past.

"So the syringes in your photos are from here?" Dot asked.

"Yup. Not the needles though. Those were just blunt craft needles I put on them to complete the look. Anyway, that was a very rare find, those syringes."

"What else have you found here?"

"Let's see." Kat pondered. "One of my lenses. You know, for my camera."

Dot nodded.

"Maybe half the furniture and stuff in my room. Of course, we needed Lonnie's truck for that."

The conversation never lulling, they entered through the Clothing section again. This time, they moved at a leisurely pace, stopping here and there along the way. Kat tried on a faux-leather motorcycle jacket. Dot thought she wore it well, but Kat said it wasn't quite *her*.

The crowds had started building, so Kat suggested they hit the punk rock market before it became a mob scene. She took Dot's hand and they cut through the Handmade section again, this time making their way directly to the black tent.

When they stepped under the tent, Dot's breath caught in her throat. It was so high, and it seemed to stretch on and on. The underside of the canopy was decorated with banners displaying the logos of iconic musicians. A path ran around the perimeter of the tent, lined with vendors on either side. More vendors filled the oval space in the center.

"They come from all over," Kat said. "It gets bigger every year."

Dot and Kat started along the outer path. There were jewelry vendors, vinyl records, lots of handmade items, old and obscure toys. And the clothes—latex, leather, ripped up tees and denim, you name it.

Kat found another motorcycle jacket. This one, she said, spoke to her—right fit, right price, and as she told a stunned Dot, "When I caught you drooling, I knew I had a winner."

Not far from there, Dot picked up a new pair of eight-gauge, rainbow-anodized steel earrings. Kat chose them for her, after holding up several styles to see how they looked with her blue hair.

By eleven, the crowds really were packing the place. Dot hadn't seen the entire punk rock market yet, but they were both itching to escape to a more open area.

So they headed out the other side of the black tent, into the Antiques & Used section proper. Kat took Dot to the doll vendor, who had not only tons of dolls, but boxes of broken dolls and doll *parts*. While interesting—and creepy—the vendor was asking far more than Dot was willing to pay. The parts were clearly intended for actual doll enthusiasts, not junk artists looking for cheap materials.

On the upside, they discovered the circuit board guy was still there and still trying to sell those boards. Dot looked through his selection and found a board from an old TR-808—a classic drum machine used in EDM, and lots of other music for that matter. It was clearly destroyed, unsalvageable with regards to its original purpose. That was a crime. But Dot could definitely use it for *something*. A few dollars later, she felt a hell of a lot richer.

Dot and Kat looked around a bit more, but before long both of their stomachs were rumbling. They'd been roaming the Market for nearly five hours. At Kat's suggestion, they headed back to the food court for lunch.

* * *

"Holy crap." Dot stood with her mouth agape.

Stepping into the old warehouse was a far different experience this time than it had been that morning. The pungent aromas of countless dishes from all different cultures permeated the air. The building was a hive of activity.

"Wow. It is *really* crowded," Kat moaned.

Dot's brow creased in sympathy. "We don't have to eat here. The entire Market's getting jam packed. We could call it a day and get outta this zoo."

"Yeah, thinking the same. I'm super hungry though. Maybe I'll get something here and eat it in the car."

"Or we could sit on the floor of the van and eat together."

Kat answered with an eager grin. "I think that's an awesome idea."

"Alright, cool. Now then . . ." Dot surveyed the food selection. The sheer number of choices was overwhelming. "What do you recommend?"

"Hmm." Kat considered the options. "Can you do spicy?"

"Sure."

"Are you vegan or veggie?"

"Nope."

"Okay." Kat scanned the far end of the massive room. "I'm kinda feeling Cajun today, if you're up for that. There's a place near the corner over there. I've had their jambalaya, and I definitely recommend it."

Dot began salivating. "Oh man, I haven't had jambalaya in ages."

"It's decided then!"

Kat took Dot's hand and guided her through the crowd, between tables and chairs, to the back of the line for Ameline's Kitchen.

The line wasn't too long, and it was moving quickly. The smells coming from the little stand were glorious. Dot checked out the chalk board menu—po' boy sandwiches, chicken jambalaya, shrimp étouffée, and hush puppies. Six kinds of hot sauce were lined up next to the napkins. Dot could do spicy, but she wasn't one to pour hot sauce on everything.

"You two ordering together?"

"Oh, no, separate." Kat let go of Dot's hand. "You go first."

Had they been holding hands that entire time?

"Uh, the um, jambalaya please," Dot managed. "And an order of hush puppies."

How did she keep doing that without even realizing it? It was just *natural*. This whole day had felt natural.

Dot moved aside and paid, lost in thought. Kat started putting in her order.

"Mouse, what are you drinking?"

"Hm?"

"You didn't order a drink. Your water bottle's empty."

"I didn't? Uh, Coke, I guess." Coke had become Dot's go-to beverage while she was stocking up on cans for the dragon.

Kat turned to the woman behind the counter. "And a Coke and a water."

"Thanks," Dot said.

"Yeah, no worries. I'm gonna eat some of your hush puppies, though."

Food in hand, they made the trek back toward the orange entrance.

It was too noisy now to really hold a conversation, and too crowded to walk side by side anyway.

Once outside the market, Kat dropped back to walk beside Dot. It was much quieter out here. Peaceful. The two of them exchanged glances and smiles, but neither one said anything until they'd reached Dot's van.

"Lemme open the windows." Dot pulled her keys out of her purse. "It's probably hotter than hell in there."

She climbed into the driver's seat and put the key in the ignition, just to roll down the front windows. Then she went into the back, cracked all of those windows as far as they would go, and opened the sliding door from the inside. Kat was there waiting.

"Welcome aboard!" Dot sat down on the edge of the floor. Kat joined her.

"Welcome aboard," Kat repeated, snickering. "You're corny."

Dot smirked. "Sorry."

"No, don't apologize." Kat flashed her a grin. "It's cute."

Dot felt her cheeks flush. She hoped Kat didn't notice.

Kat opened her container. The scent of shrimp wafted from it.

Dot glanced over. "You got the étouffée?"

"Yeah, I've never had it before. You're welcome to try it." Kat passed a fork to her.

Dot opened her own container. "Oh man, this looks awesome." She opened the bag of hush puppies and set it between them.

Dot shoveled the first forkful into her mouth, and she had to close her eyes. Kat hadn't been messing around when she'd picked this place. This was damn good jambalaya.

"So . . ." Kat shifted and got comfortable. "Tell me about screen printing. I've always been fascinated by it."

At that, Dot seemed to glow with enthusiasm. "Sure! What do you wanna know?"

"Well, I understand the basics, transferring ink through the screen and all that. But how do you make the screen itself?"

"Okay, so"—Dot sat up straight and prepared to explain her craft—"the process is similar to developing a photograph, only kinda simplified. You have this stuff called photo emulsion ..."

Dot could get pretty passionate explaining what she did. She ended up illustrating with her hands a lot—or in this case, her fork. She spent the next five minutes largely neglecting her food while talking Kat's ear off.

"So is that what you went to school for?" Kat asked.

"Yup. Got my bachelor of fine arts in printmaking." Dot scooped up a forkful of chicken and rice. "What about you?"

Kat broke her gaze, looking down to her food. "I was an English major, actually."

"Oh, so the photography ... ?"

"Self-taught."

"Holy shit." Dot was stunned. "That's fucking impressive."

Kat couldn't seem to help a little smug smile. "Thank you. I'm proud of it. Still trying to figure out how to make a living doing art though."

"Ah, well if you find the answer, let me know."

"What? Please." Kat's expression was incredulous. "You and Lizzy must be doing pretty okay to afford your own studio."

"Eh heh ..." Dot cringed. "Well, we don't exactly *afford* it, per se."

"What do you mean?"

Dot sipped her soda before answering. "It's kinda ... my dad's garage."

"Oh! Sorry, I assumed—"

"I mean, don't get me wrong, it's a real studio! We put a lot of work into it, my dad and I. Totally renovated the space. It's, like, seriously professional looking. And functional. We just ... don't have to pay rent."

"Oh, well that's awesome, then!" Kat looked relieved.

"Yeah, it's pretty good. And Lynn and I make enough to help out with utilities. I just, uh ..." Dot turned her eyes away. "It'd be nice to be able to move out of my dad's *house*."

"Hey." Kat caught Dot's eyes with her own. "At least you *have* your dad. And he sounds like a good guy."

"True. He's pretty dope."

Kat chuckled. "Pretty dope?"

Dot laughed at herself. "Eh, yeah. Heh. I picked that up from Jet. Polly. Somehow she's able to say it and not sound like a total dork."

Dot pulled a hush puppy out of the bag.

Kat watched her bite into it. "I almost forgot about those."

"Help yourself." Dot eyed Kat's étouffée. "Can I snag a shrimp?"

"Of course!"

Dot pierced one with her fork. "So where do you do *your* work?" She popped it into her mouth.

"In my room, mostly. I do my printing at Jake's Cameras. But editing, matting, framing—I do it all at home."

Dot frowned. "On the third floor?"

"Yup."

"Well that's gonna be a pain in the ass getting ready for Pride, prepping all those frames you bought today."

Kat nodded. "Tell me about it. Not looking forward to hauling them up the stairs."

Dot considered this. "Why don't you do it at our studio? We have plenty of space."

"I . . ." Kat blinked. "I could do that?"

"Yeah, why not?" Dot stole another shrimp. "Bring your materials over tomorrow, and you can set up wherever. I just finished a thing I was working on, so there's a whole table open."

Kat was speechless for a moment. "That's . . . really generous. I'd *love* to see your studio." She caught Dot sneaking into her étouffée again. "Do you just wanna trade? I could totally get into that jambalaya."

"Oh! Yeah, definitely! Sorry, I keep stealing your food."

"Ha! It's okay, I'm glad you like it."

They swapped meals. And forks, as it happened.

Dot narrowed her eyes at Kat. "What got you into photography? After majoring in English."

Kat's answer came readily. "I've always loved being behind the lens. When I was a kid, I'd compose pictures with my toys, or take shots of random objects that caught my attention. Got my first camera when I was six." She scooped a bite into her mouth.

"Oh, so photography really came first, then."

Kat took a moment to chew. "Yeah, I don't know what I was thinking in college." Her eyes fell. "I was in a really weird place then. Not a good place."

Dot didn't say anything, but her sense of concern must have been showing.

Kat glanced at her and went on, "It's history now. Don't worry about it."

Curious but not wanting to pry, Dot opted to fill her mouth with food instead.

They kept the conversation relatively light after that—Burger Life designs, Lonnie's vegan cooking, finding treasures in the trash.

It felt like the sun ought to be setting, but it was only midday. They'd just packed a lot into the hours they'd spent together. The exhaustion was real, though.

Dot yawned. "God, I could go for a nap."

"That's what I'm doing when I get home. That's my afternoon every third Saturday." Kat started to clean up the trash.

"Just leave that stuff here. I'll chuck it when I get home."

"Okay, that works." Kat got to her feet and stretched, then leaned one hand against the van. "Thank you so much for coming today. Seriously."

"You kidding? Thanks for the invitation! Here, wait." Dot stood up and dug in her pocket. She pulled out two matching woven bracelets—rainbow with black lace trim. "I picked these up in the punk rock tent. Just thought they looked cool." She held one out to Kat. "For luck with your stuff at Pride."

Kat's eyes teared up. "Oh my god." She covered her mouth. "You are *so* corny."

Dot snorted, laughing.

Kat took the bracelet and tied it around her wrist. "I'll wear it with . . . well, pride!"

She hugged Dot again. Wow, did Kat smell good.

"See you tomorrow?" Dot felt a swell of hopeful anticipation as the question left her lips.

"Definitely." Kat broke the embrace and looked at her. "Afternoon? You have practice in the morning, right?"

"Yeah, I'll text you when I'm in the studio."

"Sounds good."

With a wave, Kat walked off toward her car.

Dot closed the side door of the van and climbed into the driver's seat once again. She started the engine and took hold of the gearshift, but she stopped. There were some things she needed to process.

First of all, she was going to have to eat crow in front of Lynn and Jet. She wasn't looking forward to that, but there was no denying it now—she'd been dead wrong about Kat. Kat was cool. No. More than cool. She was . . . impressive. Interesting. Fun to talk to. Easy to be around. Frankly, Dot liked her a lot.

Which brought Dot to her next question—had today been . . . a date? She didn't think it was supposed to have been. But it had certainly felt like one at times. And not at all in a bad way.

* * *

Kat slung her camera bag onto her back and locked the car. She followed the path through the breezeway and around to the back.

So this is where Dot lived, huh? A white split-level house with a detached garage. The garage was much bigger than Kat had expected.

She stepped inside and shut the door behind her. Immediately to her right was a tiny powder room, and on her left a row of coat hooks. Then, with two steps down, the space opened into the studio itself.

Dot, wearing an old, ink-spattered tank top, was placing the last of Kat's things on a long, wooden worktable. All together, there were two boxes of frames, a stack of mat boards, and a backpack containing tools and supplies for mat cutting and hinging.

Kat stepped down into the room and put her camera bag on the table. Then she backed up and took in the scene.

The walls were *covered* in art. Lynn's drawings were everywhere, but Kat's eyes were drawn to the sculptures that stood out between them.

To her left, over the computer desk—the green mask. The "dryad," as Kat thought of it. A beautiful tree spirit. She'd seen it a thousand times in photos, from all different angles. But now, here in the room with it, those empty eyes seemed to be watching her.

Further over, a frozen waterfall burst forth out of the wall, cascading down into a sconce, where it ended in a splash and a cloud of mist. Light flickered, sparkled, and refracted through the entire structure. Kat recalled that the "water" was made of clear plastic cutlery. How Dot had produced the mist effect remained a mystery.

On a shelf in the corner to Kat's right stood a rearing pegasus. But the wings were those of a sci-fi spaceship. Where they connected to the body of the horse, wiring and realistic scarring made it look as though the wings had been surgically attached. The effect was jarring. Painful. Even more so in person than it had been in photos.

On a table in the far corner was a piece Kat hadn't seen before—a red dragon, with some flecks of silver and white, taking flight. It was powerful. Majestic. Alive. How did Dot do that?

Kat returned her gaze to Dot, who stood watching her with a satisfied grin.

Kat put her hands on her hips. "Well don't you look proud of yourself?"

"Eh heh." Dot's cheeks turned red. "I've just never ... ya know ... seen anyone look at my work that way."

"What way?"

"Well ... like you're awestruck."

"I *am* awestruck!" Kat stepped closer. "This . . . these"—she gestured around the room—"are unbelievable!"

Dot's grin widened, if that was possible.

"What's the dragon made of?" Kat admired the creature again.

"Coke cans."

"Coke . . ." Kat's brow furrowed. "That's not Coke cans." She looked at Dot. "That's Coke cans?"

"That's Coke cans."

"It has *muscles!* You made muscles out of *soda cans?*"

Dot nodded.

"You're insane!"

She snickered. "It's got scales too."

Kat shook her head. "And you don't show these to anybody. We've gotta change that."

"I'm starting to think you might be right." Dot looked down at the tabletop now littered with Kat's things. "So anyway, I thought you might want to use this table. Or feel free to use the floor if you want, too. There's plenty of floor space."

There was indeed a large, open swath of laminate wood floor between the tables and the far wall. Windows on that wall allowed natural light to flood the room.

"So make yourself at home." Dot kicked the edge of a canvas drop cloth that lay out across part of the floor. "We can move this if you need."

Kat was overwhelmed. "Thank you. This is incredible. Working in here is gonna be . . . well, a dream come true, honestly. An actual studio."

She slid her things to either end of the table, clearing the center. She pulled a few frames from the boxes and laid them out in front of her.

"I wish I could get started right now, but I don't have the prints yet." She stared at the various frames, envisioning which of her images she might like to mount in each one.

"Ah, nuts." Dot's face fell. "I thought it'd be cool if we were, like, working side by side today." She eyed a contraption on the next table over, closest to the sink.

The device was bolted to the corner of the table. It had four short arms extending from the center, each one holding an aluminum frame in the air. Each frame had a screen stretched across it.

Kat could just make out the design imprinted on one of the screens. "Oh, those are the silkscreens!"

"Yeah, I have a big batch of Burger Life shirts to do today."

"You do?" Kat's eyebrows rose. "So, does that mean I get to see screen printing in action?"

"Well . . ." Dot frowned in consideration, then shrugged. "I mean, sure, if you want to. But once I ink the screens and all, I want to run the whole batch. That'll take a while. It could get pretty boring."

Kat smirked. "I wouldn't worry about boredom. This room's like a little art museum." Her eyes wandered to a row of smaller sculptures on a shelf above the sink. "I'll keep myself entertained."

"Alright, then come around here and I'll show you how I set this up."

Kat started to round the table, but she stopped halfway. "One thing." She put a hand on her camera bag. "Would you mind if I took pictures?"

Dot shrugged again. "I don't mind. If you think it's that interesting."

"Awesome!" Kat beamed. She quickly opened her bag and pulled out her Nikon D750. She also selected a short telephoto lens that she could easily swap on and off, depending on the shot.

Meanwhile, Dot had started laying and centering light grey tank tops on a series of pallets that rotated under the screens.

"Okay." Dot pulled the lid off a tub of amber ink. "First I have to stir these really well." She picked up a metal paint spatula and thrust it into the ink. "This is plastisol ink, which is really goopy. Stirring will make it easier to work with."

Three other tubs awaited their turn at being stirred. While Dot wrestled the ink into a more manageable consistency, Kat studied the way the lighting in the room was affecting the scene.

"Would you mind if I played with the lights?"

Dot shook her head. "As long as I can see what I'm doing, knock yourself out."

Kat found the switches near the door. She turned off all the studio lights except for those directly over the screen printing area. Daylight was still streaming in through the windows, but the overall ambient light around Dot was now reduced. Kat returned to Dot's side and studied the results.

Yes, good. The shadows were now more pronounced. They revealed the muscle definition in Dot's arms, the curves and valleys of her shoulders and clavicle. The metal frames of the screens shone brightly where the light hit them, with starkly shaded surfaces underneath.

Kat took a few test shots of Dot stirring a tub of ink, her arms flexing with the effort. Studying the pictures on the small camera screen, Kat noticed the color of the ink stood out particularly well. She liked that, especially since Dot had splotches of it as far up as her elbows—though this in itself was baffling.

"How are you already covered in that stuff?"

Dot laughed. "I don't know. I have a knack for making a mess of myself. As long as the shirts stay clean—that's the important thing."

With the tub in her right hand, Dot rotated the screens, stopping at one of them and pulling it down over the shirt. "Okay, come 'ere."

Kat stepped closer, practically looking over Dot's shoulder.

Dot scooped a dollop of red ink onto the screen. "See the stencil on this screen? This is gonna be just the red parts of the design—the helmet, part of the skates, the fry box, that's the ketchup there, and also parts of the words." She reached behind her to the steel counter and picked up an object—a long, wooden handle with a rubber blade running the length of it. "And this thing is called a squeegee."

"And you spread the ink with that?"

"In a minute I will, yeah."

Dot rested the squeegee on the screen, where it met the arm of the machine. She raised that screen and rotated the next one into position.

While Dot repeated the process for the other three screens and ink colors, Kat snapped photos of her working. Close shots of her hands manipulating the ink. Shots of Dot reaching for the next frame with an ink-speckled arm.

Dot shot her a glance. "Now that I've got these set up, I can start actually printing."

"Ooh!" Kat lowered the camera and watched.

Dot gripped the squeegee and pulled the ink across the screen. In its wake, it left a thick smear of red. "I've flooded the screen, and now this is a print." She pushed the ink back, piling the goopy substance at the far end, away from the stencil. Then she lifted the screen and turned to Kat. The stencil pattern had been transferred flawlessly onto the grey tank top.

"That's so *cool*."

"Isn't it?" Dot smiled. "I've been doing this for years, and I still think it's the coolest thing." She reached away from Kat and flipped a switch on another machine. "Now, this thing is a flash dryer. I'm gonna pass each shirt under it while I print the next one, but I can't leave them too long. Which means I need to develop a rhythm and keep everything moving."

"Okay, so this is the part where you slave away for hours while I creep on you and take pictures."

"Hours?" Dot chuckled. "Maybe *an* hour."

"Oh, that's not bad!" Kat narrowed her eyes at Dot. "You thought I'd get bored in an hour? Clearly you underestimate my attention span."

"Clearly!"

Kat hefted her camera. "I wasn't distracting you with this, was I?"

Dot squinted. "Eh . . . a little."

"Oh no." Kat scrunched up her face. "Sorry, then I won't—"

"I don't . . . mind."

Kat blinked.

Dot went on, "It's more just the sound. The clicking of the camera. Makes it hard to find my rhythm."

"Well, do you wanna . . . ?" Kat gave a moment's contemplation, then snapped her fingers. "What if we put on some music?"

Dot pointed at her. "Exactly what I was thinking!"

Kat's eyes lit up. "Okay, what do you want on?"

"Actually, there should already be a playlist up on the computer, if you just wanna hit 'play.'"

Kat wandered over to the desk. She leaned down to grab the mouse. Sure enough, a playlist was already loaded and paused. She unpaused it. Electronic music emanated from speakers in the corners of the room.

She looked at Dot. "How's the volume?"

"Turn it up." Dot jutted her thumb upwards. "I'll take it as loud as you can stand it."

As loud as Kat could stand it, huh? The words of someone who'd never been on a road trip with her, windows down, The Distillers at full blast.

Kat opened the volume control on the computer. Oh, it was already at a hundred percent. Must be a knob on the speaker, then. Yup. She cranked it up and turned around to look at Dot.

"How's that?" she yelled.

Dot shrugged. "If that's the loudest you can go!"

Hmm. Alright, maybe Dot *could* handle it. Kat turned it up until she could barely hear herself think. The EDM beats flooded her reality, drowning out every other sound. She looked at Dot again. Thumbs up! Wow, okay then!

One thing Kat noticed was that the bass seemed low in the mix. Dot probably had it set that way so it wouldn't shake the art off the walls.

Kat crossed the room again and picked up her camera. Dot had already found her rhythm and was working away. She moved so quickly. One shirt after another. Her motions flowed like liquid. Reach, pull, push, lift. She was captivating to watch. Entrancing, even.

Click!

Kat flinched. She'd startled herself by hitting the shutter release. Anyway, that's what she should be doing—taking pictures, not staring.

Kat approached Dot and contemplated the scene, the angles, the framing. She started with the printing process itself, getting a few shots of the open ink tubs in front of the spider-like printing press.

She inched closer, getting a somewhat higher angle. She snapped shots of Dot's hands pulling the squeegee across the screen. Then pushing it back. Forearm muscles shifting. Powerful fingers grasping.

Kat moved up and framed a shot of Dot's head and upper torso. Illuminated from above, Dot's features cast shadows under her brow, nose, lips, and cheeks. The contrast made her face appear statuesque. Kat caught shots of her mid-stroke, as her shoulders and upper arms flexed, shimmering beneath the light.

This gave Kat another idea. She stepped in as she had earlier and watched over Dot's shoulder. Looking down her arm like that, Kat could not only see what Dot was seeing, she could feel the strength of her. It was visceral. If Kat could manage to capture that . . . She brought the camera up and played with the focus. It was tricky, but she took a number shots from that vantage. Hopefully one of them would turn out.

From where Kat was standing now, she could smell Dot, sweating from the exertion. The scent of her was sharp, but warm. Animal. Magnetic. There was a strong urge in Kat to reach out and touch Dot's shoulder. Her neck. Run fingers up into her hair. She envisioned Dot turning around and . . . Was it getting hot in here?

Kat stepped back. Her head was swimming. She needed to cool off. She backed into the steel counter and leaned against it a moment, her free hand gripping the cool metal. She closed her eyes and exhaled.

Turning around, Kat noticed for the first time the assortment of items on the counter. There were a few squeegees and paint spatulas, and a stack of frames. Everything looked well-worn—scratched, pitted, dented, stained. The tools of an artist.

Kat raised her camera and photographed the scene as it stood. Then she inspected the frames, lifting the top one, then the next. They all had screens stretched across them—some blank, some with stencils still present. Old Burger Life designs, mostly.

She took a couple of stenciled frames and leaned them against the stack, facing her. Another cool shot. Then she put them back as she'd found them.

Now that she had her wits about her again, Kat returned to the screen press. With her short telephoto lens affixed, she went around to the other side of the table, opposite Dot, and lined up a shot from the front. Dot noticed her and mugged for the camera.

Kat flashed a smile back, but she wanted something real. Natural. She framed Dot's face and waited for her to look again. The next time Dot looked, she didn't mug. A little smirk crept across her face. Her cheeks flushed. That's when Kat snapped the photo. Perfect.

Kat continued snapping away, thinking of new angles, different ways to capture Dot at work. When, at last, she ran out of ideas, she instead took a stroll around the studio.

She studied the dragon up close. It really was made of soda cans. Unbelievable. There were other sculptures, too, that she'd never seen before—older sculptures, it looked like. Simpler. How long ago had they been made, she wondered. How long had Dot been honing this ability?

Kat studied piece after piece. It was a thrill to finally see them up close. To see the tiny details. To break the illusion, only to then step back and have it restored.

She was tempted to photograph Dot's work, but she felt it would be bad form to do so without explicit consent. And anyway, she'd rather do it right. Really compose the shot. Set up a backdrop, figure out individualized lighting for each piece. God, if she could, though.

The volume of the music dropped significantly. Kat turned around to find Dot bent over the computer.

"Hey," Kat started. "Are you done?"

"Just about." Dot stood up and gestured toward the screen press. "But before I clean up, do you wanna try your hand at it?"

"At . . . screen printing?" Kat's eyes went wide. "Oh my god, can I?"

"Yeah, I'll walk you through it."

Kat put her camera down. Moments later, she was standing at the screen press with Dot next to her. The screen with the amber ink hovered in front of her. Dot had made this look so easy, but Kat felt entirely out of her element.

"Don't worry." Dot touched the back of her arm. "We're gonna go one step at a time. I'll tell you what to do, and you just be my hands."

Kat swallowed. "Be your hands. Got it."

"First, lower the screen over the shirt."

Kat pulled it down gently.

"Good. Okay, take hold of the squeegee."

Kat gripped the wood handle the way she had seen Dot do it.

"Angle it a little higher. Now, apply a little downward pressure, and pull the ink back towards you. Nice. Now you're gonna pick up the squeegee and get it behind the ink. Good. Lower your angle a little. And push. Excellent."

Excellent, she said! As if.

"Now lift the screen and see how you did. Just make sure you lift it all the way. One of these arms is wonky and doesn't like to stay up."

Kat lifted the screen slowly. When she saw the shirt, her mouth formed an "O."

"I did it!"

"You're a natural!" Dot grinned.

"You're a good teacher."

"Just three more colors to go. Slide that baby under the dryer for a few seconds."

Kat did as instructed. On the next two colors, she didn't need as much prompting. She worked her way through the steps methodically. Lower the screen. Angle up. Pull. Angle down. Push. Lift.

"Fast learner." Dot leaned against the table with her arms folded. "I bet you can handle the last one without me."

"Oh yeah?"

"Easy. You got this." Dot pushed off the table and straightened up. "You want a beer?"

"Uh, sure! Yeah!"

"IPA? Lager? Stout?"

Kat nodded. "A stout would be delightful. Please."

"You got it."

Kat eyed the last screen—the red one. Here goes. She took hold of it and pulled down. It hitched a little at first, but it came. She lowered it onto the shirt.

Angle up. Pull. Over. Down. Push. The screen looked clear. That should do it. She lifted it off the shirt just as Dot was setting the beers on the table.

"Ooh, look!" Kat stepped to the side and turned, beaming at Dot. She pushed the screen up and let go of it. "It's beautif—"

She saw it in her peripheral vision. The screen was falling. The wonky arm, she'd forgotten!

"No!" Kat turned to catch it.

Too late. When it reached the bottom of its arc, the impact shook the screen. Red ink splattered into the air. Kat raised her arms to cover her face. She stepped back reflexively, but her foot caught the corner of the drop cloth and slid out from under her.

Dot rushed forward, but she didn't have a chance of catching Kat. Kat's left foot twisted underneath her as she landed butt-first.

"Ow." She winced, awkwardly stuck in a half-sitting position.

"Jesus. Are you okay?" Dot knelt next to her, put one hand on her back, and took Kat's hand with the other.

Using Dot for support, Kat lifted herself off of her foot and slid it out from under her. Then she put her butt down on the floor and breathed a sigh of relief.

"Hoo. I think so."

Kat moved to shift herself to a kneeling position, facing Dot. Then, holding onto both of Dot's hands, she managed to stand up—first on the right foot, then tentatively adding weight to the left. It was painful, but not cripplingly so.

Kat blinked. She could feel ink on her face. She raised her eyes. She could *see* ink on Dot's face, just inches away.

"You're a mess." Kat's voice was a near-whisper.

Dot chuckled a little. "You should see yourself."

"Sorry."

"Hey." Dot gave her a warm smile. "It's okay. That's why I dress like this in here."

Kat could smell Dot's sweet breath, feel its delicate warmth on her face. It was intoxicating. Dot's eyes were locked on Kat's. Her mouth was so close. Kat felt a pull that was nearly irresistible. Dot's smile slowly faded, her lips relaxing. Her hands gripped Kat's. Could she be feeling it too?

The door shut with a thud, just audible over the music.

Kat let go of Dot's hands. Or did Dot let go of hers? She wasn't sure. They turned to face the door.

Lynn hopped down the two steps and looked up. "Oh shoot. Am I interrupting?"

"Uh—!" Dot motioned to the screen press. "We were . . . just . . . printing, and . . ."

"I made a mess and fell on my ass," Kat finished.

"Uh-huh." Lynn eyed the table full of framing materials.

"She has a tent at Pride!" The explanation burst forth from Dot. "She's gonna prep here. I offered."

Lynn beamed. She looked at Kat. "Cool! So we'll see more of you this week?"

Kat nodded.

"Right on! I'll try to stay out of the way. Of your work, I mean." Lynn made her way to the drawing table and put her bag on the chair. "You two know you've got red speckles, right?"

"Oh. Yeah." Dot turned to Kat. "We should get cleaned up."

* * *

"So lemme guess what happened next." Lonnie sat across from Kat. It was Monday happy hour at Upstarts. "You took your inky clothes off and showered together."

Kat cackled. "Oh my god! You are such a dude!" She took a sip from her pint glass, then wiped the foam from her upper lip. "But you're half right."

"I knew it!" Lonnie put his hand in the air.

Kat shook her head and grudgingly indulged him with a high five. "It wasn't like that, though."

"What do you mean? What was it like?"

Kat put her elbow on the table and leaned her cheek against her knuckles. "We just took our tops off."

Lonnie's eyebrows went up.

Kat smirked. "Not the bras, just the shirts."

Lonnie's brows retreated.

"And then we wiped eachother down."

"Hot!"

"With cleaning fluid and old rags, Lon."

"Still hot."

Kat bit her lip and looked down at her beer. "It was a little hot."

"I knew it! My girl!" He folded his arms and leaned on the table. "So what happened after that?"

"Well, I helped her clean up. Or rather, I folded the shirts she'd printed while she cleaned up."

"Did you guys get any more alone time? A goodbye kiss?"

Kat blushed. "Just on the cheek, when we hugged."

"Aw man." Lonnie leaned back in his seat. "If only Lizzy hadn't shown up, right?"

The pink in Kat's cheeks turned to red. "I know. I keep thinking about that." She looked at Lonnie. "What do you think? In a moment like that . . . do I go for it? On the chance that she feels the same?"

Lonnie regarded her frankly. "Honestly, she's crazy if she *doesn't* feel the same. I don't know what to tell ya, though. That's one of those things, you just gotta feel it out. Or ask her, 'Can I kiss you?'"

"Really?" Kat turned a skeptical eye at him.

"Yeah, seriously. Doesn't hurt to ask. Just imagine if *she* asked *you* that."

"Eh heh." Kat smiled sheepishly. "Good point."

"Anyway, look at you! Thinking boldly!"

"Yeah, well . . . the whole weekend was an adventure." Kat paused to sip her beer. "It *makes* you bold, getting out of your comfort zone, ya know?"

Lonnie was in the midst of drinking. "Mm." He swallowed. "Oh, I know. Friday night was decidedly not in my comfort zone."

"Really? What happened? Bad date?"

"Mmm, not exactly. The date was fun. We got along great. She invited me back to her place."

"Uh huh?" Kat listened attentively.

"But there was a catch."

"Uh oh."

Lonnie took another sip, then looked down at his beer as he continued. "Yeah. See, she already had a boyfriend."

"Oh dear."

"Annnd they were looking for a third."

"Oho! Kinky!" Kat grinned in anticipation. "Did you do it? Tell me you did it."

"I had conditions."

Kat's eyes went wide. "You *did it?*"

Lonnie snorted.

"You're fucking with me." Kat's expression hardened.

"I just wanted to see your reaction."

"You . . . I'm gunna . . ." Kat reached across the table and slapped his arm.

"Aw, that stings!" Lonnie was still laughing.

"Yeah, well, you mess with the bull . . ."

"Haha! The bull, huh? I think that Mouse chick is rubbing off on you."

Kat smirked. "Maybe so."

Lonnie downed the last of his beer and planted his empty glass on the table. "I'm gonna hit the bathroom and stop at the bar on the way back. You want anything?"

"Nah, thanks. Still working on this."

Lonnie got up and ambled away, leaving Kat with her thoughts.

She'd been putting on a cool facade for him, so he wouldn't worry. And for herself as well, trying to convince herself she wasn't nervous. She was, though—nervous about tomorrow's scrimmage. About seeing Dot in that context. It would be their first time back at the rink together since . . . well, since they'd become friends. Or whatever they were. Now, on the verge of returning to the weekly routine, Kat feared the old tension would pick up again where it had left off.

She fiddled with the bracelet on her wrist—her little piece of concrete reassurance. She knew she'd feel better once she got to the rink and looked into Dot's eyes—and saw them look back the way they had in the studio. She took a deep breath and exhaled slowly. Tomorrow night couldn't get here fast enough.

CHAPTER 6

Revelations

Kat pulled the door open and walked gingerly into the rink, still moving with a slight limp. Around her neck she wore lanyards carrying her whistle and stopwatch, but her skate bag was conspicuously absent.

She rounded the corner of the entryway to find several skaters standing around talking. The early birds. The seats usually claimed by Dot, Lynn, and Jet were as yet vacant.

That afternoon, Kat had made up her mind that she was going to be bold. She and Dot had laid down the roots of something good, and she wasn't going to leave room for old tensions to grow back like weeds. To that end, she sat down in Dot's usual seat to await her arrival.

This action prompted looks from a few of the assembled skaters, ranging from confusion to concern. Kat folded her arms and crossed her legs, mentally doubling down on her occupation of the seat.

Leah came around the corner, pulling her skate bag behind her. She had bright green hair down to her shoulders and wide, innocent eyes. Freckles adorned her ivory cheeks, lending warmth to her sharp features. She stopped in her tracks when she spotted Kat.

"Hey, Kat." Leah glanced around at the other faces nearby. "Are you sure you want to sit there?"

Kat eyed her defiantly. "This *is* Mouse's spot, isn't it?"

"Yeah." Leah arched an eyebrow. "Okay, I clearly missed something. Do I want to be here when she shows up?"

Kat chuckled. "Don't worry. She and I are on good terms."

"Really! I thought you two were mortal enemies." Leah took a seat on the island bench opposite Kat. "Shows what I know."

Wow. Had things really looked that bad to everyone else? Kat thought back on previous scrimmages, Dot's eyes aflame as she vehemently—and loudly—disagreed with one of Kat's calls. But her bark was worse than her bite. Didn't they realize that?

Come to think of it, Dot didn't really bark at anyone else as much as she barked at Kat. Maybe that said something. *What*, exactly, Kat didn't know. And anyway, that was a hell of a way to say whatever it was. But she suddenly felt as though she'd known Dot for a long time in a way no one else really did.

Sure, Kat had never enjoyed being yelled at by Dot. But she'd also never felt intimidated. In general, she liked Dot's passion. Her only concern had been the underlying tension and what that meant for her chances of ever getting close to Dot.

Kat checked the time on her phone. Dot wouldn't normally arrive for another ten minutes or so. It was probably wishful thinking, hoping to catch her early.

Kat looked across at Leah, who was pulling her knee gaskets on. "I haven't talked to you in a while, Siren. Are you still seeing that girl you brought around a couple months ago?"

"Kristin?" Leah curled her lip and shook her head. "No, we didn't last long after that."

"What happened?"

"Ehh . . ." Leah sighed.

Kat waved dismissively. "It's okay, you don't have to tell me."

"No, I don't mind." Leah stood up and started her pre-practice stretches. "I think she was having trouble with the whole trans thing, really."

Kat wrinkled her nose. "Oh, I'm sorry."

"Aw, don't be. Rather than talk to me about it—or, ya know, break up with me like an adult—I found out she was fucking somebody else."

"Shit."

"Yeah." Leah shrugged. "I ended it. She offered some weak apology, but I told her to fuck off."

"Good for you. You deserve better."

Leah slowly rolled her head around, stretching her neck. "I'm thinking maybe I'll hold off on dating for a while. It's just . . . a lot. Life is a lot right now."

Kat nodded. She hated to see Leah discouraged, but she understood.

"What about you?" Leah asked. "You seeing anyone?"

Hmm. Kat wasn't sure how to answer that. Vaguely, maybe.

"Uh, not . . . really." *Not really?* Way to go, Kat. That won't prompt more questions at all.

"Not really? So, sort of?"

Kat cringed internally. She tried to sound casual, but her answer came out a little rushed. "Well, I mean, there might be someone, but I don't know yet."

Leah smirked. "Ahh, right. Yeah, I know what that's like. Anyone I know?"

"It's me, isn't it?" Lynn crossed between Kat and Leah, taking her seat beside Kat. "Sorry, chica. I'm spoken for."

Kat let out a relieved laugh, grateful for the well-timed rescue. "Aw, Liz! A girl can dream, can't she?"

Lynn pulled her shades off her head and put them in her purse. "I know, it's frustrating to want what you can't have. Dream all you like, darlin'." She looked up and glanced at the door, then winked at Kat and whispered, "Turn around."

Kat turned to the door. There was Dot, striding toward her in tight, mid-thigh athletic shorts and a fitted black tee with the sleeves cut off. She grinned broadly when her eyes met Kat's.

Kat felt warmth rush through her body, into her face and arms. There was the look she'd been waiting to see. As Dot reached her, Kat stood and opened her arms. Dot received her eagerly, gently squeezing her torso in a firm embrace.

Leah watched them. "Wow." She looked at Lynn, who flashed her a knowing smile. Leah's face perked with realization. "Oh!"

Kat was vaguely aware that some kind of interaction was happening behind her, but it seemed so far away in that moment. She inhaled Dot, forgetting that she'd even been nervous about seeing her. Kat was enveloped in Dot's powerful arms. She could feel Dot's left hand gripping her side, the right resting against her ribs. This was perfect.

She had no idea how long the hug lasted. At some point, they pulled away from each other and locked eyes, both of them grinning.

"Hi," Kat managed.

"Hey."

Kat didn't know what else to say. She'd learned what she'd been waiting to find out. She hadn't thought much beyond that. A twinge of self-consciousness came back to her at last.

"Uh, sorry, I've been in your seat." Kat gestured to the chair, stepping aside to make way for Dot.

"That's okay, sit. I'll sit here." Dot took the next seat over, so that she and Lynn were on either side of Kat. "No skates? Are they over by the refs?"

"No, my ankle's still hurting."

Dot's expression went grim. "Shit, I'm sorry."

"It's okay." Kat touched her arm. "It's not your fault. And it's not that bad, anyway. I'm just gonna stay off skates for a few days. I think it'll be fine."

Dot's smile recovered. "Alright, good."

"Hopefully they can use me as an NSO tonight."

"Probably," Leah said. "We never have enough."

Jet came around the corner. She lit up when she saw Dot and Kat together. Kat waved to her, prompting Dot to turn and do the same.

"Hey, guys!" Jet headed for her seat on the other side of Lynn. She almost sat down, but she stopped, her gaze fixed on Dot's and Kat's wrists. "Oh. My. God. You guys. Are adorable."

"Hm?" Lynn followed Jet's line of sight. "Ah."

"Matching rainbow friendship bracelets? And what is that? Black lace?" Jet's eyes were wide. "That is so cute I can't stand it!"

As she went on, Dot and Kat turned ever-deepening shades of pink.

Jet slapped Lynn on the shoulder. "How come we don't have something like that?"

Lynn craned back to look at her. "Uh, because we're so much more than friends?"

"Uh-huh." Jet gave her a playfully skeptical eye. "I'm getting us a pair. I love that."

Kat held hers up. "Mouse got them at the Market on Saturday."

"See, that's so thoughtful! Well done, Mouse." Jet gave Dot a sly smile. Dot's cheeks flushed red.

When Kat turned back in Dot's direction, she noticed several of the officials had arrived and were gathering in the ref area.

"Oh hey, Smith and Scrunch are here." She looked to Dot with reluctance, not wanting to leave her side. "I should go see what they want me to do."

Number Scruncher—"Scrunch" for short—was the head non-skating official, or NSO. She was in charge of jobs such as scorekeeping, jam timing, and the like.

"Of course!" Dot gave Kat an encouraging smile. "Do your thing! I'll see you later!"

Kat beamed at that simple sentiment. "Right! See you later!" She jumped up and walked briskly off toward the ref area, glancing back briefly to flash a smile at the skaters.

Just then, Vee's voice boomed, "Everyone start yer off-skates warmups! Let's go! The sooner we start, the sooner we play!"

* * *

TWEEET!

Down a blocker, Dot, Lynn, and Fiend set up in a tripod defense against a black-clad Vee. Vee made a move for the outside lane, and Dot slid over to cut her off. But while that was happening, Princess Peaches plowed into Fiend from the left, leaving the inside lane wide open. Vee juked to the inside. Dot tried to mirror her movement and block off the opening, but Peaches moved to intercept Dot, delaying her for a split second. That was all the time Vee needed to slip through and take lead jammer status.

TWEET-TWEET!

Without hesitation, Jet pulled the star off her helmet and passed it over the heads of the black blockers to Lynn, who was quickly on Vee's tail.

In the brief confusion of the star pass, Jet sneaked past the black blockers to join Dot and Fiend in the front. With the pack already moving at a fair speed now, Dot directed the white team to keep up the pace.

Vee came around the track on her first scoring pass, approaching the pack as it went into turn three. With Lynn nipping at her heels, Vee drifted out on the straightaway and cut in on the turn. At the inside track boundary, her feet left the ground. In a majestic leap, she soared over the edge of the infield.

It was a beautiful apex jump—and a move Dot had seen coming a mile away. She was waiting as Vee made her descent. Instead of Vee's feet hitting the ground, her ribs met Dot's shoulder. She twisted in the air and hit the floor on her side, her knee and elbow pads clattering against the wood. Immediately, she rolled onto her back and touched her hips to call off the jam.

TWEET-TWEET-TWEET-TWEET!

Dot stood over Vee and offered a hand.

"Nice hit, Mouse." Vee accepted Dot's help and got to her knees with a grunt, then popped up onto her feet. "Well timed."

"Thanks." Dot gave her a heartfelt grin. It *had* been a solid hit, and Dot was feeling pretty damned proud of herself for knocking the mighty Geneva Convulsion out of the sky. It was early in the second half, and so far it had been a good night. Dot was sitting at only two penalties, and she hadn't even been holding back.

She rolled off the track with her shoulders back and her head held high. Her eyes went automatically to the spot on the sidelines where Kat stood recording the score. Kat looked up from her clipboard and met Dot's gaze with a victorious smile and a little fist pump.

Dot felt a surge of warmth at that sight. There was a deep sense of satisfaction in knowing Kat was cheering for her. Somehow it felt even better than landing that hit on Vee.

"Dude! You dropped her like a rock!" Jet rolled up beside Dot. "Hm?"

Jet smirked. "You didn't even hear me, did you?"

"Sorry, I was, uh—"

"I know, I know. Don't sweat it. How's that going, by the way?"

"How's what going?"

Jet snorted. "That!" She nodded in Kat's direction.

Dot looked at Kat, then back at Jet. "Oh. Uh. It's good. Things are good."

"Things are good, huh? I certainly hope so. You've been making eyes at her all night."

"I—we—" Dot's voice hitched, and she cleared her throat. That surge of warmth was getting uncomfortably hot all of a sudden. "Is it that obvious?"

Jet snickered. "Why? Are you embarrassed?"

"Nnhh. I don't know if that's the word."

"Self-conscious, then?" As they rolled to a stop in the bench area, Jet folded her arms and turned her body to face Dot. "I wouldn't worry about other people noticing. It's obvious to me 'cause I'm watching. Lynn told me you two had an interesting weekend."

"She did?" Dot folded her arms too. She looked down at the bracelet resting just above her wristguard. "Yeah. It was ... better than I expected." She paused, weighing her next words, and finally muttered under her breath, "You and Lynn were right."

Jet inhaled sharply, her mouth agape.

Dot rolled her eyes. "Don't rub it in."

"I wouldn't dream of it!" Jet grinned and slapped her on the arm. "I'm glad you had fun."

Dot's gaze wandered back to Kat, who was focused on her task. "Do you think it's obvious to her, though?"

"What?" Jet took a moment to realize. "Oh! The way you look at her?"

Dot nodded.

"I don't know. Do you want it to be?"

Dot sighed. "I don't know. I don't know what I want. I'm still trying to wrap my head around who she is. I mean, I thought—well, you know what I thought."

"You thought she was a bitch who had it in for you."

"Yeah, that." Dot picked up her water bottle and took a swig from it. "God, that sounds so harsh now. I feel like an ass for ever thinking that."

"In fairness, you *are* kind of an ass."

Dot gave Jet a dull glare. "Thanks."

"Any time!" Jet spun in place on her skates, obviously pleased with herself. "So, you gonna ask her out or what?"

"Jeez, you don't beat around the bush, do you?"

"Ha! No, I dive right in," Jet said matter-of-factly. "Lynn'll tell ya. Speaking of which—she said she interrupted the two of you getting messy together in the studio. Did you guys ... ya know ... ?"

"No." Dot answered quickly, but she was distant, deep in thought. "That is, I think we *almost* ... did something." The memory came to the forefront of her mind. She remembered distinctly the feel of Kat's hands and the rush of inhaling her breath. Goosebumps rose on Dot's skin. A tingling heat pulsed beneath the fabric of her shorts, prompting her to self-consciously tense up.

"Oh man, you've got it bad, don't you?"

"I do n—mmh." Dot shifted in place, not sure how to say what she felt. Flat out denying Jet's observation seemed futile. "It's just . . . it feels kinda surreal, ya know? That *that's* Kat. The weekend felt like it was some kind of dream. But then I get here tonight, and the dream's still going."

"Oh yeah. You've got it real bad. Now it makes sense why you invited her to move in."

"Move *in?*" Dot laughed. "Oh god, don't call the U-Haul yet! She just brought some stuff over to the studio."

"That's what I meant! Move into the studio!" Jet shrugged and raised her hands in mock innocence. "Although, I like how you said *yet.* Don't call the U-Haul *yet.*"

Dot let out an exasperated sigh. "Oi, Jet. Gimme a break for one second."

"Okay, okay! I'm just teasing! Trying to lighten the mood. You seem a little keyed up."

TWEET-TWEET-TWEET-TWEET!

Jet grabbed a star helmet cover off the rink wall. "Here." She thrust it at Dot.

"Aw, no." Dot winced. "Why do you do this to me?"

"Come on, it's scrimmage. Everybody jams at least once. Just pretend you're blocking and smash your way through."

Dot groaned. "Fine." She took the cover from Jet.

Jamming was the worst. The *worst!* It always made Dot feel inadequate. She didn't have the instinct for it or the raw agility of someone like Vee or Jet. She knew well the defensive tactics that would be used against her, yet she could never seem to outmaneuver them. Jamming, for Dot, was an exercise in frustration.

She rolled up to the jammer line with an air of insecure reluctance.

This was going to be a chore. She pulled the star cover over her helmet and glanced to her left. Kara was there, wearing the star for black, looking her cheerful self. She offered Dot a grin. Dot reciprocated half-heartedly.

Scrunch called out, "Five seconds!"

Dot turned to her right, her eyes going straight to Kat. Kat bit her lower lip, watching Dot with visible anticipation. Dot smiled, this time genuinely. She couldn't help it. Kat beamed in response, her eyes shining. She was radiant. Somehow, in that moment, a weight was lifted. It was only practice. Just relax and play. Dot blew out a breath and looked ahead at the wall of black blockers. Yeah, maybe she could do this. For those eyes, she felt like she could do anything.

TWEEET!

* * *

"Your girlfriend says she'll be here in five." Lynn was at the computer, with Dot's phone next to her. She'd been watching for texts from Kat.

"She's not my . . ." Dot began automatically. She knelt in the middle of the drop cloth, attention focused on the sculpture in front of her. "I don't know what she is, okay?"

Next to Dot, a small collection of enamel hobby paints sat on top of a scrap wood panel. She had one of the little glass bottles in her right hand and a fine-tip brush in her left, with which she was applying detail to the dragon's left eye.

"You like her, though," Lynn said.

Dot heaved a sigh. "I swear to god, between you and Jet—yes, fine, I like Kat." She put the bottle down and straightened her back, stretching while she inspected her work. "Since you're so interested anyway, do you think she . . ." Shit. Dot had started the question without thinking. Now that it was halfway out, she felt a little immature asking it. "I mean . . . did you see anything yesterday that, like . . ."

"Are you trying to ask if I think she likes you too?"

"I guess, yeah." Dot twisted around to look at Lynn. "Just, ya know, from what you've seen."

Lynn chuckled. "Dot. Are you blind? The two of you are like smitten teenagers together. Of course she's into you."

"Really?"

The tables were obstructing Lynn and Dot's view of one another. Lynn swiveled the chair around and rolled a few feet to the side, where Dot could see her. "Girl, what happened to your game? You never stress like this. I've seen you hit on women within seconds of meeting them. Remember the first time we met Maggie?"

Dot half-smiled. "Heh. I was on fire that night, wasn't I? My smoothest strike-out ever."

"Yeah, well, you made an impression, and things turned out fine. You and Mags are buds now."

Dot shifted around to sit facing Lynn. "But nothing was at stake there, going in. I didn't know Mags from a hole in the ground."

Lynn raised an eyebrow. "From a hole in the—?"

"I know, wrong . . . whatever. You get it."

"So, there's more at stake with Kat? After, what, three days of hanging out?"

Dot gave a side nod. "It's also derby. Ya know, dating within the league? You remember how anxious you were about getting with Jet."

"True."

Dot put her hands on top of her head, interlacing her fingers. A slight blush filled her cheeks. "But yeah. Even besides that. I don't wanna fuck it up."

"Alright, well, she's gonna be around a lot regardless, until Pride. You don't have to rush anything." Lynn leaned back in her chair and smirked. "Jet wasn't kidding. You do have it bad."

Dot took a long, deep breath. Lynn was right. No rush. There was still a week and a half to feel things out before Pride, starting tonight.

Kat had been working at the camera shop since eight o'clock that morning. It was getting close to six now.

A car door shut just outside. Dot perked up. She couldn't see from where she sat. While she got to her feet, Lynn peered out the window.

"There's your girl. Got a couple'a bags with her."

Dot spotted the figure coming up the driveway and disappearing around the side of the studio. She hurried to Kat's table and began clearing space.

The door creaked open, voices just audible on the other side.

"You go ahead, I've got the door." That was Dot's dad.

"Thanks . . . um . . . Mr. Mauser?" Kat stepped in, carrying a large, flat portfolio case, a loaded plastic shopping bag, and her purse.

"Nah, call me Ben." Ben sidled in behind Kat. He had a light beard and chin-length, shaggy, salt-n-pepper hair. He wore glasses, jeans, and an open button-down shirt over a tee. Overall, he had a casual kind of grunge-grown-up style about him.

Dot rushed forward to take the plastic bag from Kat. "Here, I made some room."

Lynn waved from across the studio. "Hey, Mr. M!"

"Hey, Lizard!" Ben waved back, then turned to Dot. "Hey, kiddo, you gonna introduce me to your friend?"

"Oh! Yes!" Dot put the bag on the table, then gestured to her guest. "Dad, this is Kat. Kat, this is my dad."

Kat extended her hand. "Nice to meet you."

Ben took it with a smile and a slight bow. "A pleasure!" He looked past her to the table full of materials. "Another artist, I take it?"

Kat nodded. "Photographer."

"Fine art," Dot added. "She's brilliant. I'll have to show you her galleries."

Ben's smile broadened. "Great! Well, welcome to the Mouse Hole!"

"Aw, Dad!" Dot cringed. "Don't call it that."

Ben winked at Kat. "I only do it 'cause it bugs her."

Kat snickered. "Naturally."

"Okay, so anyway"—Ben looked to Lynn, Dot, and Kat in

succession—"I have pizza on the way from Tracy's, if you girls are hungry. I didn't realize there'd be four of us—"

"No no." Lynn stood up. "I have to take off, but thank you." She was already in the process of gathering her things.

"Aw. Okay, Lynn." Ben turned to Kat. "How about you?"

"I'm . . ." Kat shot a quick glance at Dot before continuing, "I'm starving, actually. I had an early lunch."

"I got a sausage-and-pepper and a white-with-spinach. That okay?"

Kat grinned. "Sounds perfect!"

Dot smiled, but her stomach was doing flips. She hadn't exactly been planning on dinner with the parent just yet. Her dad was a pretty easygoing guy, so it could be worse. She'd just been hoping to have a better idea of where she stood with Kat before introducing him.

"Great!" Ben took a small step backwards, toward the door. "I'm gonna head back and wait for the guy. Just come on in the house when you're ready to eat."

"Cool," Dot said. "Thanks, Dad."

"Yes, thanks!" Kat added.

With a serene smile and a little nod, Ben pivoted and headed out of the studio.

Kat watched the door close behind him. "Wow, your dad seems pretty chill."

"Yeah, he never really made it out of the nineties. He's got that whole Gen X slacker vibe going on. You'd never guess he works his ass off."

"What's he do?"

"Computer systems field support or something." Dot leaned her butt on the table. "He travels a lot to deploy new software and stuff. Actually, I didn't even know he was home."

"Oh." Kat's mouth hung open briefly as her expression turned to mild concern. "I hope you don't mind that I took him up on the pizza. I don't want to in—"

"No! Yeah! Of course!" Dot took hold of Kat's hand in an effort to reassure her.

Relieved joy washed over Kat's face. "Okay." She smiled and gripped Dot's fingers gently.

Dot's stomach stopped flip-flopping, but butterflies still fluttered. She nodded toward the table. "This stuff can wait. Let's head over. I'll show you the house."

* * *

"CBGB, huh?" Ben eyed Kat's tee shirt as he folded his pizza slice.

"Hm?" Kat looked down. She swallowed her bite. "Oh yeah, I forgot I wore this."

"You a punk fan?"

"Yes!" Her eyes sparkled as she raised them again. "Classic stuff mostly. Patti Smith, Ramones, The Clash, Dead Kennedys . . ."

"Mm! Good taste!" Ben lifted a finger while he chewed for a moment. "I got to see the Ramones in Philly, back in—what was it, eighty-seven?" He squinted across the table at his daughter.

Dot chuckled. "Don't look at me! I wasn't born yet!"

"Don't you catalog all my concert stories in that young brain of yours? That's the main reason I had a kid." His delivery was impeccably dry.

Dot smiled and shook her head.

"I got to see Patti in twenty-twelve," Kat said. "That was an almost spiritual experience." She sipped her iced tea. "Man, I'd love to go back in time and see those bands coming up in New York, though."

Ben arched an eyebrow. "I did go to a show at CBGB once, in the eighties."

"No way!"

"Don't get too excited." He looked down and picked up a pepper that had fallen off his pizza. "It was some no-name band on a Monday night. A couple of bands, probably. It all kinda runs together, thinking back. Anyway, the place was a dive—at least when I was there."

"Heh, yeah, I've heard that." Kat took a small bite, then cheeked it as she continued, "One article I read said it had the worst bathroom in rock-n-roll."

"Ha! You do your research, eh?"

"Oh man, I love that history. Everything today was influenced by that scene."

Ben beamed. "Dottie, where'd you find this girl? Can we keep her?"

Keep her? Dot knew he was kidding, but her heart leapt with eagerness. She felt a burp rising and eased it out silently, putting her fist against her mouth. It bought her a few seconds to collect herself. What was that first question again?

"Uh, she's in derby with me, Dad. You've seen her before."

Ben's brow creased as he studied Kat. "I *thought* you looked familiar, but—are you on Heavy Metal too?"

Kat subtly cocked her head. "I'm a ref, actually."

"Ah!" Realization shone in Ben's eyes. "Okay, now I can picture you in your gear. It's the stripes that were missing." He took a long sip of his beer. There was silence for a moment. He put the bottle down slowly. "Wait a minute. Aren't you the ref Dottie's always shouting at?"

Fgnt! Dot coughed with a mouth full of Coke. "Aww." She closed her eyes and sniffed, setting her glass back on the table. "Soda in my sinuses."

Kat snickered as she passed a handful of napkins to Dot. "You okay?"

Dot nodded. "Yeah. Yeah, just gimme a minute. Oh, it burns."

Trying to suppress her smile, Kat turned back to Ben. "Yeah, we butt heads sometimes, I guess."

Ben got that serene look again. "And yet here you are! I'm glad she hasn't scared you off."

Dot rolled her eyes.

"Ya know, she sounds like her mother when she's angry."

"Dad."

Kat looked from Ben to Dot. "Your mom—is she . . . ?"

"We're divorced," Ben said.

"Oh. Sorry, I—"

"Don't worry." Ben waved away her concern. "It was ages ago. We got married way too soon. Had Dottie early on. After several years of tormenting each other, we uh . . . well, we decided to call it quits while we were still capable of being friends. For Dottie's sake, especially."

Kat's expression relaxed. "Ah, so you're still in contact?"

"Yup." Dot nibbled at her crust. "She's in New York now."

"She's with a law firm in Manhattan," Ben added.

Dot went on, "Sometimes I'll head up there and crash with her for a few days. She's okay. Her boyfriend's a tool though."

Ben cackled. "He is, isn't he? Probably drives him nuts when you drop in and become the center of Mom's attention."

Kat grinned. "Sounds like you three have a good arrangement. Does she ever come here? Has she seen the studio?"

"We usually do holidays here," Ben said.

"Oh yes, she was duly impressed the first time she saw the studio." Dot straightened up in her chair. "Speechless. Couldn't believe dad and I did all that."

Kat's eyes widened. "You did it all yourselves?"

"Most of it." Ben squinted in thought. "We got an electrician. And a plumber. I didn't want to mess with that stuff."

"We did the rest," Dot said. "Dad was the mastermind."

"Well, I had done a lot of renovating in the house, so I'd picked things up along the way. I had never done a project that big, though."

"How'd you do the ceiling?" Kat asked, her face scrunched inquisitively. "It's pretty high."

"Oh, that was a pain in the ass." Ben started gesturing as he described the process. "We insulated up there, and covered it with drywall. We needed a lift for that part. Dottie wasn't such a beefcake yet back then."

Dot snorted at that. She reached across the table and pulled another slice out of the box.

As she listened to her dad telling Kat about the studio, Dot realized her butterflies were all but gone. Kat fit right in here. And it seemed her dad was steering clear of asking about the relationship between the two of them.

Dot relaxed into her chair. She put her elbows on the table and started into the fresh slice.

* * *

Half an hour later, back in the studio, Kat was laying out the contents of the plastic bag onto the table—spray-on wood stain, plain black spraypaint, wood touch-up markers, glass cleaner, and paper towels.

"For the frames?" Dot picked up the wood stain and investigated the small print on the can.

"Yeah, some of them are a little beat-up. Some just don't have color yet."

Kat's portfolio bag sat on the floor, leaning against the leg of the table. She crouched down and unzipped it. Reaching in, she produced a folder about half the size of the bag, which she laid on the table and opened. In it were numerous photo prints in various sizes, stacked smallest to largest.

"Oh! You got them!" The prints stole Dot's attention away from the can. She slid over next to Kat, who gently spread a few of them out.

"I thought maybe you could help me pick which ones to frame and display."

"Me?" Dot's brow wrinkled, but she didn't take her eyes off the photos.

"Yeah, you're a visual artist." Kat glanced at Dot briefly, then joined her in studying the prints. Each one took on a different feel under the bright studio lights than it had on the digital screen, but they were all so familiar—extensions of herself, expressed on paper. "And I'm so close to these, I'm not sure I'm being objective. I trust your opinion."

Dot was silent for a moment, watching Kat flip through the pile. "Okay. I can do that."

Kat grinned. She felt a sense of security, having Dot's hands in this project. It was comforting not to be figuring this out on her own.

"Anything else I can do to help?" Dot looked over the tabletop, now cluttered with materials.

"Well . . ." Kat faced her and leaned a hip against the table. "I don't want to pull you away from your own projects."

"Nah, don't worry about that." Dot's eyes went to the dragon on the floor. "I'm just fucking around with it at this point. You have a deadline here."

"Okay . . . then, if you want, you can help me start staining the frames tonight. They'll need time to dry."

At that, Dot seemed to glow with purpose. "Yeah, sure! Lemme move the dragon and we can set up on the drop cloth."

Dot was quick to clean up her project from earlier in the night. The sculpture went back on the corner table. The wooden plank got tossed on the floor underneath it. The hobby paints went back in their box on the steel counter, with the brushes on top.

Soon, frames were stacked on one corner of the drop cloth, with the spray cans next to them. Dot opened the nearest window for ventilation, and the two of them settled on the floor with several frames scattered between them.

Kat picked up the wood stain and looked at Dot. "Something tells me you have more experience with spraypaint than I do."

"Heh, yeah, I'd say that's likely." Dot took the can from her.

"Would you be willing to do that while I use the markers to clean up the scratches on some of these?"

"You want me to use this one?" The stain in Dot's hand was a dark mahogany color.

"I hadn't really decided." Kat picked up the black spraypaint and handed it to Dot as well. "I'd say use your best judgement. I don't know much about wood stain, but for this I figure the darker the better. Ideally, all the frames would be black. Makes it simpler and more uniform, ya know?"

"Oh, I can do black." Dot shook the black spray can. "This stuff should take to the wood just fine. We got all unfinished frames, right? No varnish or anything?"

"Right."

"Yeah. I don't know how long this one can will last, though."

"Oh . . ." Kat's face fell.

"It's okay, I have some more black in the closet."

Kat lifted her eyes to meet Dot's. "You don't mind using it?"

"For you? Of course not!"

The words came so readily. Dot's willingness was really touching. Kat smiled. "Thanks."

"Sure."

Dot turned a little pink. Kat didn't say anything—she felt flushed herself.

"Right. So." Kat started sorting the frames. "You can start with the unstained frames. I'll take the ones that already have color and even out the scratches before I hand them off to you."

"Sounds good!"

Before long, Kat was diligently touching up one frame while Dot sprayed the first coat of paint on another. Silence reigned for a few minutes, apart from the *pssst* of the aerosol and the occasional clatter of wood. Finally, it started to get to Kat. It wasn't uncomfortable, but she longed for some interaction with Dot.

"So . . . 'Dottie,' huh?"

Dot's face went stark. "Oh no. Don't you start too. Do you know how long it took to get Jet to stop calling me that after she met my dad?"

Kat giggled. "Aww. Well, I usually call you Mouse, anyway. Maybe I'll call you Mousy."

"Don't even."

"I'm kidding! I'm kidding!" Kat glanced at Dot. She was so cute when she got riled. Kat couldn't resist, but she also couldn't bring herself to drag it on too long.

"I would never do that that to you. My family used to call me Kitty. Drove me nuts."

Kat's heart jumped. She swallowed. She'd surprised herself, bringing up her family.

"Aw, Kitty. Heh. How'd you get them to stop?" Dot continued working while she talked, seemingly unaware of Kat's sudden discomfort.

"I didn't, really. Um. Sorry, I don't—"

"No, I'm sorry!" Dot squinted, peering at a spot she had just sprayed. "We talked about *my* parents all through dinner. I didn't even ask about yours."

Kat felt she had a decision to make here. She could downplay this whole topic and bring up something else, if she wanted to. Or she could let Dot in. "Yeah, I kinda... changed the subject on purpose." She opted for the latter.

Dot looked up from the frame. "You did? Why? What's—"

"I haven't talked to my family since college." There. It was out.

Silence fell again for a long moment.

"Shit." Dot put the spray can down. "How... how long?"

"Ten years."

A hesitant pause. "I'm sorry."

Kat looked down at the frame in front of her. She picked it up and resumed searching its surface for blemishes.

"Yeah, don't be. They're the ones who should be sorry." Kat's voice was low. Controlled. She was determined not to let it waver.

"Can I ask? I mean I understand if you don't want—"

"Junior year, they found out I was dating a girl. That I'd *been* dating girls." Kat's jaw felt tight as she spoke.

Dot's mouth hung open. "They didn't..."

"They cut me off. Refused to pay for school unless I broke up with my girlfriend and swore off women."

Dot turned her body to fully face Kat. "They stopped talking to you?"

"Not exactly. They wanted me to move home. *Get help.*" Kat took a deep breath and exhaled through her nose. "I never went home."

Dot frowned. "Where'd you go?"

"My girlfriend's, at first. 'Til we broke up. Some friends' couches after that." Kat fixed Dot with an assertive stare. "Look, nobody knows this. Lonnie knows a little, but . . . this is . . ."

"I get it. Doesn't go beyond me."

Kat half-smiled. "Thanks." She focused on the frame again. "I . . . ya know, I thought they'd come around. I kept the same number and everything. My—" she cleared her throat "—my mom called a few times early on. Tried to get me to . . . I dunno . . . compromise. Once it was pretty clear I didn't want to change, I stopped hearing from them."

Dot didn't say anything at first. She picked up a frame and turned it in her hands, staring at it. Finally, she looked at Kat again.

"So that pin . . ."

Kat nodded. "He'll be eighteen soon, Eli."

Dot's eyes widened. "He made that when he was eight?"

"Seven, actually. With help, at school. But he designed it himself."

Dot nodded. "You have a sibling too, then."

"An older brother, yeah." Kat shook her head. "He always drank the Kool-Aid."

She put the frame down. It had been a long time since she'd talked about this stuff. There was a lot to tell, and she had never really told all of it to anyone. It was a bit too much to think about right now, especially with so much to do.

Her eyes wandered across the drop cloth and then up to Dot's. "Hey. If we could just . . . be done talking about this for now . . ."

"Yeah. Yes. Of course." Dot looked around as if just woken from a daze, her hand grasping for the spraypaint. "Let's get this stuff done, right?"

Kat brightened up. "Right." She waited a moment, watching Dot turn back to her frame and get settled again. "I'm glad I got to meet your dad. You were right, he is pretty dope."

Dot laughed. "I'm never gonna live that down now, am I?"

"I don't know. It's starting to grow on me."

CHAPTER 7

Repercussions

———————

Dot pulled her van in next to Jet's Camaro. Her phone had buzzed during the short drive here. She retrieved it from her purse. A reply from Kat.

Omw now! See you soon!

It was Thursday night. Kat hadn't made it to practice because of her ankle, so Dot had invited her to meet up at the diner afterward.

Dot fixed her hair in the mirror. She took a little more time, put a little more care into it than she ever had for Maggie. No rush, she reminded herself.

When she stepped into the diner, Dot headed straight for the restroom. She spent a few minutes scrubbing the stink off her wrists and elbows, lather running the length of her arms as though she were prepping for surgery.

She emerged feeling a little cleaner. Through the window, she spotted a red Corolla that looked like Kat's. Sure enough, when Dot came around the counter she saw three familiar heads occupying the usual booth.

Jet beamed at Dot as she approached. "You didn't tell us you texted Kat!"

Dot smirked. "What? You're my keeper now? I tell you everything?" She slid in next to Kat, who took Dot's purse and tucked it into the corner of the seat with her own.

Kat twisted to face Dot and greeted her with a hug. "Hey, you don't smell terrible!"

"Haha! Thanks, I did my best." Dot sniffed her arm. It smelled . . . not terrible.

"The gang's all here at last!" Maggie rounded the corner of the booth. "Hey, stud! You made it!"

Dot folded her arms and sat back. "Hey, sexypants!"

"Oh come now, muskrat." Maggie stepped closer and leaned her hip against the table. "You know I don't wear any pants under this uniform."

Kat gave her a skeptical eye. "Like, *any* pants?"

Maggie lowered her voice in mock secrecy. "Shhh, hush darlin'. I'm just tryin' to rev Blue's engine. You'll thank me later." She winked at Kat.

Feeling pressed between Kat and Maggie, Dot was starting to sweat. She eyed Lynn, sending a silent distress signal across the table. Lynn just smiled and shrugged.

This could be a good thing, though, right? Maggie's apparent assumption that Dot and Kat were an item. She'd skipped over asking, which was a relief.

"Anyway!" Maggie took a step back, easing off the flirtatious air. "I can't believe I finally got all four of you together! I feel like I caught all the Pokémon!"

Dot froze, confused. "All four?"

She glanced at Kat, who was biting her lip but otherwise unreadable.

Lynn had been snickering at the Pokémon comment, but she was quiet now. Jet was giving Maggie big eyes that seemed to say "stop talking."

"Oh." Maggie cringed.

Okay, Dot *had* only been confused, but now she was getting suspicious. "What?" She looked from Maggie to Jet.

Jet's big eyes focused on Dot. "Mags, would you—?"

"Give you a minute. Yup." Maggie motored off to the kitchen.

Dot turned to Kat. "Have you—do you know Maggie already?"

Jet spoke before Kat could answer. "There's something we should probably tell you, Mouse."

Now Dot was worried. "This isn't some kind of intervention, is it?"

Lynn snorted. The tension eased slightly.

Jet went on, "We kinda . . . well, we already . . ."

"We've been hanging out with Kat," Lynn finished.

"For a while," Jet added.

Dot looked at Kat again, who was still biting her lip. Kat nodded.

"Whaddya mean?" Dot narrowed her eyes at Lynn. "Like how long?"

"I dunno . . ." Lynn shot a questioning glance at Jet. "Weeks? Months?"

"Three months."

"THREE MONTHS?" Dot's shout drew looks from the other patrons. She lowered her voice. "Three months? You assholes! What the *fuck?* You've known her all this time?"

Dot was livid. The implications of this knowledge were streaming into her mind faster than she could process them. All that time, all those conversations about Kat. How? Why? Lynn and Jet offered her apologetic stares, which didn't help. Dot wanted to tear into them. This was *not cool.* It was manipulative. A betrayal of trust! How many other secrets were they keeping? How many other people knew about this?

She turned again to Kat, who gave her a pleading look and took hold of her hand on the seat between them. That's what gave her pause. Time slowed down. Those beautiful blue eyes threatened sorrow, and it was more than Dot could bear. In that moment, she could see herself spiraling. She stopped and breathed. Focused on the touch of Kat's fingers. The sounds of distant conversations. The ever-present scent of coffee. But most of all it was those eyes that grounded her, helped her find control.

Dot clenched her teeth to keep her jaw from shaking. She looked at the faces across the table. Talked herself through the haze of anger. These were her friends. Her teammates. They wouldn't just stab her in the back. There had to be an explanation.

She closed her eyes and released a long, controlled sigh. When she finally did speak, she managed softer, measured tones. "What the actual fuck, guys? Why didn't you just tell me she was so cool?"

Lynn lifted her furrowed brow. "We tried. Sorta."

Jet folded her arms. "Come on, Dot. Would you have taken us directly at our word?"

"You were . . . pretty adamant," Lynn said.

Dot fell back in her seat. "Seriously? You don't think I woulda listened?"

Kat squeezed her hand. "You *are* a little bullheaded."

Dot rounded on her with a piercing glare.

Kat responded with a calm smile and muttered quietly, "Not everybody can handle it head on."

After a beat, Dot's expression relaxed. There'd been no accusation in Kat's statement—just observation. And even acceptance, which was a comfort. Dot lingered for a moment in their silent connection, considering Kat's words. Maybe she had a point.

"Look," Lynn said. "We knew if we could get you to talk to her, you'd see for yourself."

Jet added, "We did try, did we not?"

It was true. How many times had they urged Dot to open a dialogue? More than she could remember.

"Yeah . . . I guess you did." Dot's eyes fell. "Constantly. God, you guys drove me nuts."

"That said . . ." Lynn cringed and seemed to shrink in her seat. "Sorry

I flat out lied a couple times. About knowing Kat. I feel kinda shitty about that."

Dot hadn't even considered that part yet. The thought of it stung fresh. She acknowledged Lynn with a nod but couldn't meet her gaze.

"We were gonna tell you this stuff," Jet said. "Mags kinda took it out of our hands there."

Dot exhaled. She stared at the table, collecting her thoughts. Her heart was still pounding in her chest. Well-meaning or not, her friends had just put her through the ringer, and she couldn't help but feel she owed them a little payback. She considered her next words carefully.

"I won't lie. This hurts. I... I don't know if we can be friends anymore, after this. I mean, how can I trust you two?"

Jet's and Lynn's expressions went stark. A pall fell over the table. Lynn swallowed audibly.

"I might have to quit derby. Then there's L&M..." Dot's voice broke. She pursed her lips, trying to hold back a self-satisfied smile.

"She's fucking with us," Lynn said.

Jet started breathing again. "You shit." She kicked Dot under the table.

"Ow! I had to! I never get opportunities like that." Dot brandished a smug grin which quickly found itself bordering on a sneer. "Anyway, you had it coming."

Kat smiled and shook her head.

Dot was more than annoyed with her friends. She was simmering beneath the surface, just barely holding tears at bay. But she wouldn't let them see that. Anyway, they *had* tried, in their way. Dot did believe that, and she was frustrated with herself for not having listened to them sooner. At least it was all out in the open now.

"Assholes," she muttered, severity returning to her voice. "No more secrets, please."

Lynn nodded. "Agreed."

"Fair enough," Jet said.

A few seconds passed in silence. Dot blinked slowly and rubbed at her temple, her hand trembling. "I could use a beer."

"Well . . ." Kat looked around the table. "I don't have to be up in the morning. Why don't we go somewhere for drinks after this?"

Lynn perked up. "Ooh, good idea."

Jet leaned forward on her elbows. "I'm down."

"Yeah, okay," Dot said with an appreciative glance at Kat. "Nothing crazy, though. Just one round."

"Sure thing." Kat stroked her thumb over Dot's rough knuckles. "Whatever you need."

A moment later, Maggie approached, practically tip-toeing as she eyed the four of them. "Is it safe to come back?"

"Oh, yes! Please!" Lynn waved her over. "I'm starving here."

Maggie grinned and readied her pen and pad. "Awesome! What can I get for my favorite crew tonight?"

* * *

The weekend came and went quickly. Kat picked up a shift on Saturday. Dot had practice Sunday morning. Otherwise, they spent most of their time toiling away in the studio. Kat began to feel like she only ever went home to sleep.

She made a mental note to do something nice for Dot after Pride, to thank her. Having the studio in which to work was making this project infinitely easier. And Dot was being extremely generous not only with her space, but with her time and energy. Honestly, Kat was skeptical now that she would have been able to pull this off alone.

By the time Tuesday rolled around again, they'd made significant progress. The frames were painted, the matting cut to size, the prints chosen. Most of the mats and prints were even mounted to the backboards already. They were coming down to the final stages now.

It felt like weeks had passed since the previous scrimmage, they'd packed in so much activity. Kat's ankle was feeling normal, and she was back on skates. Reffing would be a nice mental respite. The black-

and-white world of the rules. When the time came, it felt good to don
her stripes again—figuratively, anyway. In actuality, Kat was wearing a
Velvet Underground tee that she'd cut into a tank top.

TWEEET!

The start of a jam. It was the fifth one of the night, and Kat was
finding her groove again. That never took her long.

The action on the track unfolded like music in her mind. Each skater
moved in harmony with the others, acting and reacting, working in
tandem, colliding and avoiding. A breach of the rules stood out like a
dissonant note.

TWEEET!

"White two-three, multiplayer!"

Kat maintained objectivity. There was no room for bias. She saw
jersey colors and numbers, while the faces of the skaters became blurs in
the periphery of her consciousness. That made it easy to keep personal
feelings out of the equation.

TWEEET!

"White five, blocking out of play!"

Except when Dot looked directly at her, the way she was now. Dot's
eyes met Kat's with a disapproving squint. But Dot didn't shout. She
didn't say anything. She turned and left the track.

Dot's first penalty of the night. Kat hoped there wouldn't be many
more. She couldn't stand to see Dot looking defeated the way she had
two weeks prior.

Kat was jam-reffing tonight, following the black jammer—number
nine-seven at the moment. Nine-seven was not lead in this jam, but
Smith had called a penalty on the white jammer, which meant this
would go the full two minutes.

Nine-seven came around on her first scoring pass, Kat analyzing her
every move. Nine-seven took the inside. Got knocked out of bounds
by a legal hit. Skated back. Re-entered behind all relevant skaters. No
cut. Slipped between two white blockers. Forearm contact, no impact.
Points earned for opponents in the box. A juke, then a turn around

a third white blocker. Nine-seven exited the pack and left the engagement zone. Five points.

Kat held five fingers in the air. She glanced at her scorekeeper. He was holding up five as well, confirming receipt.

Kat continued tracking black nine-seven. Nine-seven's movements were calculated. Rapid. Clean. It was poetry. By the time the jam ended, she had racked up thirteen points.

TWEET-TWEET-TWEET-TWEET!

Between jams, Kat grabbed her water bottle and took a sip. She scanned the sidelines for Dot and found her deep in conversation with Lynn. No time to wait for her to look this way.

"Five seconds!"

Kat lined up to track the new black jammer—number four-five-one.

The period continued on in this manner. After each jam, Kat would look for Dot briefly. Every so often, she would catch Dot looking back and get a smile out of her. The rest of the time, they were each in their own little world—ref and skater.

TWEEeeeEET!

By the end of the first half, Kat had called one more penalty on white five—a failure-to-reform—and had unfortunately gotten to see Dot's scowl again. Polly Dactyl, one of the other refs, had also called a penalty on her.

Three penalties at this point didn't bode well. Maybe if Kat could talk to her during halftime, she could boost Dot's spirits. But that would have to wait, as Coach Rex had just called the Heavy Metal skaters together for a team discussion.

Kat took the opportunity to refill her water bottle. She rolled off the rink floor toward the drinking fountain.

"Hey, Kat!" Kara called to her as she and Peaches approached.

Kat was leaning over the fountain, but she turned her head to greet them. "Hey, what's up?"

"We have a question about that last jam," Peaches said.

"Sure. Go ahead, I'm listening."

"Alright, so, I was here," Kara began, "and Jocelyn came up like this." She gestured to indicate the positions of other skaters as she laid out the scenario.

Kat screwed the lid back onto her bottle, then patiently responded to their inquiries. They discussed what had actually happened, then went into some hypothetical situations. It was a nice distraction while Kat waited for her chance to catch Dot.

Time seemed to fly when Kat was talking rules—apparently not enough time, though. While Kara and Peaches' curiosity had been sated, the Heavy Metal meeting was still going on.

Kat checked the scoreboard clock—about five minutes left of intermission. She didn't want to get involved in another conversation and possibly miss Dot, so she opted to keep herself occupied by checking her phone.

Kat's things were in the ref area. Smith had wanted to discuss a rules update at the beginning of practice. Otherwise, Kat would have preferred to gear up with Dot. Her purse sat where she'd left it, under the seat. She picked it up and dug out her phone.

A missed call? Probably from Lonnie. Not many people would be calling her. But no, it wasn't Lonnie. Just some random number. Never mind. She hit the "back" button. Wait, though—what had that area code been? She looked again. Three-one-five. That was upstate New York. Her parents' area code.

Kat's heart both sank and sped up. She didn't recognize the rest of the number. What were the chances that . . . ?

Oh! There was a voicemail! Shit . . . If that *was* her family, did she want to hear it right now? Maybe wait until after scrim? Was it better to know? Either way, it would weigh on her. Then again, it *could* turn out just to be a stupid robocall, or even a wrong number. In either of those cases, she would be able to relax. That decided it. She hit "play."

A few seconds of silence . . . then some rustling . . . more silence . . . or was there a voice in the background? . . . then it ended.

Kat stood with her eyes closed and the phone to her ear. Her pulse resounded in her head. She'd been holding her breath. She exhaled. Swallowed. The sounds of the rink came rushing back into her consciousness.

Well, that had offered no answers. Maybe she could look up the number. She opened the web browser. Wait—did she have time for this? She turned around and checked the clock again. No. Thirty-four seconds. Dammit, and she'd missed Dot!

Kat stuffed the phone back into her purse and shoved it under the seat. She breathed deep as she rolled back onto the rink floor. She scanned the sidelines for Dot and found her looking down, adjusting her helmet. No comfort there.

TWEEeeeEET!

Start of the second half. Focus, Kat.

Smith rolled up beside her. "You wanna keep tracking black?"

"Hm?" It took a second for Kat to register what she was being asked. "Oh. Sure, doesn't matter."

Skaters lined up on the track.

"Five seconds!"

TWEEEET!

The familiar sounds. The familiar rhythm of the game. It calmed Kat. She fell back into her groove with relative ease, and that phone call became a distant speck in the back of her mind—something for another Kat to deal with at another time.

TWEET-TWEET!

Kat's jammer burst out of the pack and took lead. Number six-seven made long, powerful strides as she came around the track. She hit the back of the pack at speed, swerving into white nine's hip and knocking her off-balance.

Six-seven drove forward, but much of her momentum had been lost. She was met by white five, who caught six-seven with her chest and stopped her dead. Six-seven tried to spin to the side, but white five's teammates had reformed around her and restricted six-seven's options.

Relying on pure brute force, six-seven pressed forward into white five, who slid some distance before hunkering down and bringing six-seven to a halt. White five became immovable, a vision of strength, with her quads and calves flexed and her core tight. She was Herculean. But she needed to give ground. The rules required her to maintain some movement in the direction of play while blocking. Maybe white five didn't realize how long she'd been holding six-seven at a dead stop. But that was irrelevant. Kat had to act on what she saw, and it had been too long.

TWEEET!

"White five, stop block!" Kat signaled the penalty and directed white five to leave the track.

Dot grudgingly yielded to Lynn. Immediately, all the intensity with which she'd been blocking Lynn transformed into ire directed at Kat.

"Ghaa! What the—Kat!"

Dot had never actually shouted Kat's name on the track before. It was startling, but Kat let it roll off. She was confident in her call. All of Dot's fury couldn't change the facts.

Black six-seven—Lynn—touched her hips to call off the jam.

TWEET-TWEET-TWEET-TWEET!

Kat signaled four points to the scorekeeper before peering over her shoulder. Good, Dot was on her way to the box. Kat would have been heartbroken if she'd had to call an insubordination on Dot, especially in the first jam of the second half.

Dot turned around and sat down. She didn't look back at Kat.

Following that episode, the second period was . . . rough. During jams, Kat was on point. The rhythm of the game kept her focused. But between jams and during time-outs, she would look for Dot, try to catch her eyes, get some reassurance that she was okay—that *they* were okay—and she never got it.

In the sixth jam, Kat had to call another penalty on white five. And again in the tenth. Dot was getting reckless. She didn't yell, though. She didn't even give Kat the evil eye—or look at her at all.

TWEEeeeEET!

Dot ended the scrimmage with a total of six penalties—five called by Kat, and that one from Dac. She raced back to her seat with Lynn close behind her, the two of them clearly arguing. No doubt, she was in a pretty bad place.

Kat hurried to her own seat. She quickly pulled off her helmet and untied her skates.

"Kat, good job tonight, as always!" Smith seemed in good spirits.

Dac rolled up from behind him. "Yeah! Thanks, Kat. Thanks, Smithy."

"Thanks, guys." Kat didn't look at them. She unstrapped her wristguards and dropped them on top of her bag while keeping an eye on Dot.

* * *

Dot finished cramming her gear into her bag and started wrestling the zipper up.

Lynn leaned in, speaking quietly enough that nearby skaters wouldn't hear. "Dot, seriously, don't let this fuck things up."

"I won't, okay?" Dot was less mindful of her volume. "I just need to cool off. It'll be fine."

"If you walk outta here without . . ." Lynn gestured urgently in Kat's direction, but Dot was ignoring her. "Dude, you haven't so much as looked at her since like halftime!"

"I *can't* look at her right now."

"Dammit, Dot, would you get your head outta your ass for like two seconds here?"

"Outta my . . . ? You know what—fuck you, Lynn, okay?" Dot got the zipper shut. "I'm trying! Just, fucking . . . *let* me." Jaw clenched, she stood up and extended the handle on her bag. She gave Lynn a cold glance, then turned and marched away, certain not to make eye contact with anyone else on her way to the exit.

Dot was the first one out of the rink. She made a beeline for the van, walking around to the far side of it, to the sliding door. She pulled it open and practically threw her skate bag inside. She put her hands on the door frame and leaned forward, hanging her head, fighting the urge to hit something. She needed time.

Not even a minute had passed when she heard footsteps approaching.

Kat rounded the back of the van and stood with a hand on it. "Hey."

Dot exhaled in frustration. She didn't want to do this. Not while she couldn't think straight. Not *ever*, preferably, but especially not now.

"Dot . . ." Kat inched toward her.

Fine, whatever. Screw it. Dot raised her head and turned to face Kat. "Okay. What gives?" she asked sternly, biting back her inclination to shout.

"Excuse me?" Kat looked taken aback. Confused. What the hell did *she* have to be confused about?

"Why am I such a target?"

Kat's brow furrowed. "What are you talking about?"

"The penalties. Every little thing I do." Dot raised a dramatic hand in front of her. "The slightest fucking—"

"Wait." Kat took a step forward. "Are you seriously putting this on *me* right now?"

"Well if it's not you, then explain to me how *I* get called on *everything* while other people get away with so much." Dot's tone bordered on belligerent. "Where were the forearm calls and the low blocks? God, the low blocks tonight!"

Kat bowed her head and glared at Dot. "Listen to me. I call what I see. That's all I can do. I can't be everywhere."

"So why do you have to be all over *me?*"

"'Cause you happened to be in my perception, that's why."

"This has been an ongoing thing though!" Without thinking about it, Dot had just doubled down on her argument. If this confrontation was happening, it was happening all the way. No backing down. No half-measures.

"Ongoing?" Kat put her hands on her hips and stood up straight.

Dot straightened up in response. "Every week, I'm the one with the most penalties. How do you think that looks to Coach? To Vee?"

"Well maybe if you'd stop breaking the rules, you wouldn't get so many." Kat's tone remained even, but fire flickered in her eyes.

Faced with Kat's unwillingness to yield, Dot started seeing red. She lashed out. "Maybe if you had eyes in your head—!"

"If *I* had eyes?" Now Kat's voice was raised. "What kind of penalties do you get? Huh? Direction, out of play, destruction, failure to reform." Kat counted them off on her fingers. "Maybe if *you* had eyes, you'd have better track awareness." She took another step closer.

"God dammit!" Dot looked away, balling her hands into fists. "This is such bullshit!" As Kat came nearer, conflicting emotions were playing havoc. Dot didn't know whether she wanted to shout or cry.

Kat folded her arms and planted her feet on the pavement. She tilted her head to the side. "What is this about, Dot? Do you seriously have a problem with my reffing?"

"YES!" Dot's answer was immediate. For better or worse, it was raw honesty, but saying it left her feeling like she'd been punched in the gut. She staggered, pressing her hands to her head. She'd managed to avoid this moment for so long, and now that it was here, it was complicated by other factors. She closed her eyes and inhaled. The next words came forcefully. "And I don't fucking know how to feel about it, 'cause I really like you!"

Dot opened her eyes. Kat was staring silently, her face stony, her jaw set. She bored a hole in Dot with her gaze. Dot had never really seen her angry until tonight, and frankly it was intimidating.

"I . . . *pride* myself," Kat started, emoting with her fist over her chest. For the first time, her voice began to shake. "Do you have any. Fucking. Idea . . ." She cut herself off and stood silent, apart from the occasional stilted breath.

Dot's heart pounded. For these few seconds, she felt paralyzed.

Finally, Kat closed her eyes and sighed. "Fuck it." She opened them again and stepped into Dot's space.

"What?"

In one movement, she cupped Dot's face in her hands and pressed her lips to Dot's.

Dot hadn't seen this coming. Her mind reeled. The world turned upside down. Kat's lips were like flower petals. The tears Dot had been holding back spilled silently down her cheeks. Though she was still trembling, still unable to think through the hurricane of emotions, the reasons seemed to be slipping from her grasp.

She inhaled deeply through her nose. "Nng!"

Kat pulled away. "What is it?"

"Your wrists . . . stink."

"Do you want to do this or not?"

Dot nodded.

"Then shut up." Kat closed the gap again. She didn't move her hands.

Dot allowed her head to tilt back as the slightly taller Kat eased closer to her. Kat's breasts just barely grazed Dot's. Hesitantly, Dot placed her hands on Kat's sides, just below her ribs. She slid them around to Kat's back and pulled her in, bringing their hips together.

Goosebumps rose on Dot's arms and neck. A warmth rushed through her. Instinct told her to breathe more heavily, but Kat's hands remained where they were. So Dot took torturously shallow, controlled breaths. Her lips parted and shifted against Kat's, meeting them again eagerly. Kat's nose brushed against Dot's cheek, tickling as Kat exhaled.

At last, Kat showed mercy and slid her hands down. She gripped Dot's shoulders, stepped and turned, forcing Dot to turn with her. She pushed into Dot, driving her back against the van door. She pressed her hips forward, her thigh sliding up between Dot's legs.

Kat slid her fingers down Dot's arms to her wrists, which she took hold of firmly. She pulled Dot's hands off of her and forced them up against the door. Dot dared not resist.

Kat brought her mouth to Dot's once more. She parted her lips as she interlaced her fingers with Dot's.

Dot felt Kat's tongue searching and opened to receive it, meeting it with her own. Now she breathed deep. Kat ground slowly on her crotch, awakening a tingling heat. Dot wanted to move against Kat's leg, but she had no leverage. Kat had all the control.

The hot sweetness of Kat's mouth, the caress of her tongue—Dot craned upward, hungrily seeking to take in more of her. But Kat bowed her head to meet Dot's brow and, with a gentle nuzzling motion, pushed Dot's head back against the van.

Dot was pinned. Her body ached for more—more touch, more friction, anything. Kat fed her slow, deep kisses, probing her mouth and then pulling back, keeping her begging.

Kat undulated her hips, grinding herself tantalizingly against Dot. She stoked the fire between Dot's legs but wouldn't give her the satisfaction of letting it escalate. She kept it smoldering. Kept it aching.

Now it was Dot whose breaths grew stilted. Tasting, touching, but helpless, hoping Kat would give her more. She no longer cared about coming out on top. She just didn't want this to end.

Then, voices. In the parking lot. Dot and Kat were hidden from view for the moment, but that likely wouldn't last.

Kat removed her thigh and ended the kiss, pulling away from Dot. Dot tried to move with her, but Kat put a hand on her chest and held her against the van. Wordlessly, with a commanding gaze, Kat looked from Dot to the open doorway of the van and back again.

Dot's heart began to race. Hope swelled in her. She obeyed without protest, sidling over to the opening and sitting on the floor of the van, her eyes on Kat the whole time.

Kat approached slowly. With a nod and a glance, she directed Dot to move further in. Dot did so, turning and scooting into the back of the vehicle. Kat stepped in gracefully on one knee, then the other. She reached behind her and pulled the door shut. The sounds of the outside world fell away.

Dot propped herself up on her elbows. Kat knelt in stark silhouette against the interior light shining from the ceiling. She dropped to her hands and knees and crawled over Dot, straddling her left leg. Dot lay back on the floor beneath her.

The light went out. Dim illumination streamed in through the windows, allowing Dot to see the shadowy figure hovering above her, engulfing her field of vision.

"Look at me." Kat's husky whisper was more than enough to pierce the deafening silence.

Dot searched the shadow looming in front of her. Her eyes began to adjust, and the shape of Kat's cheeks and jaw emerged from the darkness. Then the curvature of her lips and her nose. Her hair hung down, damp with sweat, haloing her face but for the side she had shaved. And her eyes shimmered, heavily lidded and locked on Dot's.

"Good." Never removing her gaze, Kat inched her knees back and lowered her hips, settling her crotch against Dot's thigh. She pulled herself forward, sliding in tight against Dot.

The heat of her, the pressure. Dot could feel her own wetness absorbing into the fabric of her form-fitting shorts. She pulsed against Kat's leg. Dot raised her right knee to create more contact. She ran her fingers around Kat's bare waist, exposed where her shirt had ridden up. Dot began to push the shirt up further as if to remove it.

"Uh-uh." Kat shook her head ever so subtly. "Just fuck me."

She pulled her hips in, rubbing right against Dot's sensitized clit. At the same time, she dropped to her elbows, descending to capture Dot's mouth with her own.

"Mmhh." Dot moaned with satisfaction at the renewed contact. She thrust up against Kat, who continued to roll her hips—no longer teasing, now fully indulging.

Kat delved into Dot's mouth, her tongue dancing against Dot's. Dot couldn't get enough. She wanted to drink in as much of Kat as possible. She slid her hands up Kat's back, under her shirt, wrapping her arms around Kat's middle. The sound of their heavy breathing filled the small space.

"Huhh." Kat throbbed against Dot's thigh. Her heat was building, her juices soaking through her own leggings and Dot's. Kat moved her head to the side, putting the two of them cheek to cheek. Her breath excited the tiny hairs on the side of Dot's neck, at once cooling and igniting.

Dot's arousal climbed higher. Every thrust of Kat's hips sent a shockwave through her. Every sensation was heightened. Her mind was swimming, filled only with the immediacy of Kat's presence—the weight of Kat's body as it pressed against her, the slickness of the sweat where their cheeks met, the heady scent of Kat's exertion mixed with the fruity aroma of her shampoo and the biting odor of derby gear.

"Hhhah," Dot vocalized as Kat rubbed against her again. "Ahh . . . faster."

"Don't . . . huh . . . tell me what to do," Kat breathed. She pressed her hip hard into Dot.

Pain. Dot's eyes went wide, and she inhaled sharply. Pain, but pleasure too, as Kat rolled up against her clit. Only once did Kat press so hard. A tear left the corner of Dot's eye.

Kat raised her head and looked at Dot. "Don't talk." Their breath mingled for a moment before Kat's lips met Dot's again. She lightly bit Dot's lower lip, then licked and soon devoured her, seeking Dot's tongue.

The taste of Kat's mouth drove Dot closer to the edge. Kat did speed up the motion of her hips, grinding herself against Dot with abandon. Her thrusts came harder and faster.

"Hmmh." Kat broke the kiss. "Are you close?"

Dot nodded, remaining obediently silent.

With that, Kat forcefully recaptured Dot's mouth and closed her forearms around Dot's head. She moved in rapid circles against Dot, their roaring fires merging into a single, raging inferno. Instead of single thrusts, single shockwaves inching her closer, now the continuous, driving force of Kat's movement carried Dot toward the precipice.

"Mmhmmm!" Dot tried to communicate without breaking away. Her breathing intensified. Kat seemed to understand. She didn't let up, but stroked herself with rapid purpose on Dot's now-drenched thigh.

"Ah . . . ahah." Kat kept her open mouth close to Dot's, their lips still touching as she nuzzled Dot's face. "Oh god," she whispered. Dot felt the words being spoken. Breathed them in. She opened herself to Kat, pushing upward to meet each little circular stroke. Kat shivered in her arms.

Kat's legs flexed and squeezed Dot's thigh, and Dot hurtled over the edge herself. Her breaths grew quick and shallow. Her clit throbbed wildly against Kat. Internal pressures found release, flowing through her in euphoric waves, tensing her muscles and wiping her mind blank.

Arms trembling, Dot tightened her embrace and pulled their bodies together as one. Kat took small, erratic tastes of Dot's mouth, tangling her fingers in Dot's hair. The flame which had begun below roared through them both, burning away all other thoughts in exquisite, pulsing heat.

How Dot had longed for this connection. Her desire for Kat had come only recently, but swiftly. And powerfully. Now, in this moment of ecstatic vulnerability, there was *only* Kat. Dot felt as though the two of them were inextricably intertwined. Nothing could come between them.

The intensity began, gradually, to ebb. Kat continued to move her hips in gentle circles, massaging and drawing out the blissful sensation. She kissed Dot again, this time in slow, patient exploration. As the flames slipped away, Dot dissolved into the welcoming embrace of Kat's mouth. She savored every stroke of Kat's tongue against hers.

The waves of pleasure slowed and abated, transitioning into mere echoes. Finally, feeling oversensitized, Dot was grateful when Kat slowed her gyrations to a stop.

With one last, long taste, Kat pulled her lips away. She lifted herself up, from elbows to hands, and stared down at Dot. Sweat dripped onto Dot's chin.

Dot smiled, gazing up at Kat. But Kat's face was serious—troubled, as much as Dot could tell in the dark. Kat rolled off of Dot and lay on the floor.

Dot turned to her, still panting. "That was . . . intense."

Kat stared at the ceiling and said nothing.

"Hey." Dot reached for Kat's hand, but Kat pulled it away.

"Don't ruin it." Kat sat up. Her voice was unsteady. "I really don't want to talk to you right now." She got to her feet, crouching under the ceiling, and went to the door. She reached for the handle.

"Wait." Dot pushed herself off the floor.

Kat paused for a second. Two seconds. Then she pulled the door open. She glanced back at Dot. Beneath pained eyes, Kat's cheeks glistened in the moonlight. Sweat or tears? Or both? She turned away and jumped out of the van.

Dot got to her feet just as the door slammed shut. By the time she opened it again, Kat was halfway to her car, running. Dot stepped down onto the pavement.

"Kat!"

But Kat didn't respond. Dot watched as she got in her car and pulled out of the spot, drove to the parking lot exit, turned onto the main road, and disappeared out of sight.

Dot staggered back and sat down in the van doorway. She slumped forward and pressed her brow into the heels of her hands.

"Fuck."

Chapter 8

Reconstruction

———————

Dot stumbled up the stairs, into the kitchen, wrapped in a bath robe. Her hair was matted and disheveled. Her head and arms, as yet unwashed, itched with the memory of derby gear. She could smell it on herself. And she could smell Kat as well, and feel the salty residue of their shared sweat. She could taste Kat on her lips.

Her head hurt. Probably dehydration. Lack of food. Lack of sleep. She'd come in late and downed two beers prior to taking all her clothes off and falling into bed. And now she was up early, after a few hours of restlessness.

Cereal. She should eat. She pulled the Frosted Flakes box off the top of the fridge. Moved a bowl and spoon from the drying rack to the table. Opened the fridge. Grabbed the milk. Poured the things in the bowl.

She put the milk back and grabbed a beer. Pulled the bottle opener magnet off the fridge and popped the cap. Took a swig before sitting down at the table.

Images and moments from the night before kept replaying in her head. She couldn't think about anything else. She felt sick, but she shoveled cereal into her mouth anyway. She needed to eat.

The stairs creaked as her dad came down from the second floor wearing a tee shirt and lounge pants.

"I thought I heard you up." He squinted as he stepped into the kitchen, where sunlight streamed through the window above the sink. "Beer for breakfast. Coffee stout?"

Dot's mouth was stuffed. She shook her bleary-eyed head.

"I know, you hate coffee." He ambled over and took a closer look. "Red ale, huh?"

Dot turned the bottle to look at the label. She hadn't totally been paying attention to what she was picking up. Or tasting.

"Hair of the dog? You go out with the girls last night?" Ben walked across the kitchen and opened a cabinet, pulling out a stack of coffee filters. "Or just you and Kat, maybe?"

He separated one filter and put it on the counter, then put the rest back in the cabinet before glancing at Dot. She was looking at him with tears streaming down her face. She swallowed her cereal.

"Oh, baby, what's wrong?" Ben dropped what he was doing and strode toward her.

She stood up, pushing the chair back with her leg. Her father enveloped her in a gentle embrace. She threw her arms around his middle and sobbed into his shoulder.

"Dad . . . I fucked up."

* * *

Ten minutes later, they were sitting at the table together. Ben sat listening with an open beer of his own. Dot had filled him in on the events of the night before—the details of the conversation, the basic gist of what had followed.

"I called and texted, but she wouldn't answer." Dot wiped the drying tears from her cheek. "So I left her alone after that."

"Probably a good idea." Ben squeezed her hand.

"I don't know what to do, Dad." Dot stared vacantly across the room.

"Hey." Ben tilted his head and drew her eyes back to his. "God, I haven't seen you like this in years. Not since Rachel in high school."

Dot pressed her lips together and sniffled in response.

"You really care about this woman, don't you?"

She nodded, blinking back more tears.

Ben sighed sympathetically. "Look, it's not over. You had a fight. That's all."

"Yeah, but—" Dot choked back a sob "—I don't know how we resolve this."

Her father's brow creased with concern. He looked at their clasped hands on the table, then back at Dot. "What do you mean by resolve it, kiddo?"

"I . . . um . . ." Dot searched for the words. "Like I said, she's not gonna back down."

"And neither are you?"

"Right." Dot bit her lip, fighting hard not to let herself start bawling again in frustration. "And it's not like there's much of a middle ground here."

Ben picked up his bottle and took a swig before responding. "Well, you know I'm the master of relationships, obviously."

Dot snickered. Ben's face brightened at the sound of her laughter.

"Okay, so look. Maybe you can't resolve it. You won't always be able to find an answer. That's what makes this relationship shit hard, but that doesn't mean you can't make it work."

"So what are you saying?" Dot eyed him skeptically. "We agree to disagree? On derby?"

Ben bobbed his head side to side in deference. "Maybe I'm wrong. I don't know the rules or the game the way you two do."

The way you two do. Dot liked the sound of that. If only she and Kat knew derby the same way.

"But bear with me here." Ben took a moment to compose his thoughts. "Let's say you're right. For the sake of argument. Say we can prove that she has some kind of bias against you, even if it's totally subconscious. You have proof of it in your hand. All you have to do is present it to her, and she'll know she's been wrong. Could you do it?"

Dot's eyes fell. Arguing with Kat was one thing, but she hadn't truly considered what winning that argument would look like. If she had *proof*... Kat had so much pride. Something like that would devastate her. "I mean..." Dot considered the implications. "I think she would want to know. For that reason alone, I would have to show it to her, but..." The idea of Kat looking so defeated put knots in her stomach. "But as far as..." She looked her dad in the eye. "For the sake of proving I'm right? Honestly, I think I'd rather be wrong."

"So, her feelings are more important than your pride on this issue."

"Yeah." A sob crawled up Dot's throat. She swallowed it back down. "Definitely."

Ben smiled. "Then I think you're answering your own question here."

Dot gave him a pleading look. "So you really think we can make that work? Agreeing to disagree?"

He shrugged. "Hell if I know. You got anything better?"

Dot laughed. There was relief in this idea, at least. Her dad had helped her see what her priorities were. Things looked a little clearer now.

"But how do I...?" Dot sighed. "What if she doesn't answer my messages?"

"She will." Ben squeezed her hand again. "Give her time."

* * *

"So I asked her, flat out, right, 'Do you serous—ser-i-ous-ly have a problem with my reffing?'"

Kat was halfway through her fourth pint of Kickback coffee stout. She had passed "buzzed" about an hour prior. Upstarts' brews tended to have a relatively high alcohol-by-volume, and Kickback was no exception.

She sat across from Lynn in one of the big wooden booths in the dimly-lit brewpub. Lynn had barely started her second Rancor IPA and was nursing it.

Kat leaned on the table. "And almost before I can finish asking the question, she blurts out, 'Yes!'"

Lynn exhaled pensively. "How did you respond?"

"I was pissed!" Kat hit the heavy wooden table with an open hand.

"I would be too." Lynn's eyes were sympathetic. Her tone was calm. Soothing.

"I felt disrespected, Liz!" Kat began to raise her voice. "You know how long I've been doing this? How hard I've worked? I'm a good ref, dammit!"

"You're a *great* ref."

"I love this game." Kat eased her shoulders back a bit.

"I know you do."

"I was kind of in disbelief that she'd actually said that, ya know? So I didn't say anything right away." Kat sat back and leaned to one side, keeping an elbow on the table. "And then she says . . . she says she doesn't know how to feel about it 'cause she really likes me!"

"She said that?" Lynn raised an eyebrow. "Wow, okay, so—"

"And here I am thinking maybe when she said yes she didn't really mean it, right? Like, I'm trying to give her the benefit of the doubt here." Kat lifted her hands in exasperation. "And then she says *that*. And it's like, fuck, she's really thought about this!"

"Shit. I wasn't even looking at it that way." Lynn rubbed her eyebrows, muttering more to herself than to Kat. "Oh Dot, what did you do?"

"So I said I'm done, right? I'm so done with this bullshit. Where the fuck does she get off, huh? God, I wanted to—" Kat clenched her jaw. "I wanted to—I dunno—I wanted to scream. I almost tried to *explain*, like she would listen."

"Almost?"

"I was so mad, I was shaking." Now Kat's voice was quivering. Tears welled in her eyes. "And just . . . fucking heartbroken."

Lynn reached across the table and took her hand. "Kat, I . . ."

"I didn't know what else to do, so I kissed her."

Lynn's eyes went wide.

"I wanted to stop fighting with her."

"Well that's *one* way to go about it."

Kat balled her hand into a fist under Lynn's. "I was so mad at her."

"How did she react?"

"She said my wrists were smelly!"

Lynn scrunched her nose. "She what?"

"Well, my hands were like right here." Kat leaned over the table and demonstrated on Lynn's face.

"Oh. Yeah, I guess that would—"

"I told her, 'Deal with it.'"

Lynn snorted. "Nice!"

"I hadn't even meant to do that, but it served her right anyway. And still . . . she still wanted to . . ." Kat closed her eyes. After a beat, she shook her head and smiled. "We finally kissed."

"So it was good?"

"It was so good. Her mouth tastes like . . . I dunno, the best . . . sweet . . ." Kat licked her teeth, lost in her reverie.

"Ah, so there was tongue." Lynn smirked.

"Not at first. But once I had her up against the van, yeah."

"Up against the . . ." Lynn's smirk disappeared, replaced with an impressed frown. "This turned into a heck of a makeout session." She picked up her beer and started taking a long sip.

"Well I mean, we fucked in the van, so . . ."

Pffft!

Lynn managed to catch most of her expelled beverage, though some ended up on the outside of the glass or in a puddle on the table.

"You guys—" Lynn cleared her throat "—you really cut to the chase there." She put the beer down and went about drying her face and hands on her cloth napkin.

Kat sighed and rested her head in her hand. "I'm not sure it was the right thing to do."

"Ehh, I will say it's not where I expected this story to go." Lynn lazily folded her napkin and put it on the table. "But yeah, this leaves you two in kind of a weird place, doesn't it?"

Kat took a sip of her beer as she stared into the middle distance. "Part of me thinks I should'a told her to fuck off."

"But you didn't."

"No." Kat's eyes came into focus and she looked at Lynn. "It was like, all I could see was . . . us . . . ya know, the idea of us . . . me and her . . . crumbling. And I couldn't let that happen, not yet. I needed to know."

Lynn put her elbows on the table and interlaced her fingers, staring intently at Kat. "Needed to know what, exactly?"

Kat shrugged. "If there was something there. If we had a connection, or, like, had I been chasing a ghost all this time?"

"And you found something."

Kat took a long, deep, uneasy breath before responding. "Yeah. I did. But now I—I . . ." Choking on the words, she closed her eyes and swallowed.

"Now you have to reconcile that with, uh . . . Dot being an asshole to you."

Kat nodded. Lynn laid an open hand on the table. Kat took it.

"She's crazy about you, ya know," Lynn said. "But she has issues."

Kat cocked an eye. "Ya think?"

Lynn stifled a snicker, biting her lip while she composed herself. "Seriously, though. I've known Dot a long time." The humor drained from her face. She looked almost somber. "She has . . . *difficulty* . . . accepting her own failures. Most of the time she avoids any situations where she would risk falling on her face."

Kat's brow furrowed. "What do you mean *avoids?* She charges right in, as far as I've seen."

"In the heat of the moment, yeah. Before she has time to second guess. But take a longer view, and you'll see." Lynn paused and sipped her beer, then set her glass down. "I mean, look. Why do you think she's never seriously tried to sell her art? Or even shown it to anyone?"

Kat's expression softened. "Shit."

"Yeah. She's afraid. And that's okay. I mean we all have our issues, right?" Lynn leaned closer. "The problem is, she projects her insecurities onto the rest of us. When she does fall on her face, it's always someone else's fault, and she's the victim. I don't think she even realizes she does it. It's just a coping mechanism or something."

Kat's mouth hung open as Lynn's words registered. "Jeez, that's some insight."

"Yeah, well. I took a few psych courses in college."

Kat chuckled a little.

A fleeting smile crossed Lynn's lips before she went on. "Really, mostly I just know Dot. I've seen her shit play out too many times."

A sorrowful realization weighed on Kat. "So this is about way more than just me."

"Kat . . ." Concern etched Lynn's face. "It's not even about you at all."

"Well now I kinda feel bad for her."

"Oh, don't start with that." Lynn straightened up. "We're all at the mercy of our own fucked up shit sometimes, but that doesn't mean we get to take it out on other people."

Kat stared down into her beer.

Lynn craned her neck down, trying to catch Kat's eyes. "Hey, you were mad at her, and you *should* be. Hell, I'm mad at her *for* you. It's emotional abuse, her trying to put her shit on you like that."

"But . . . why, though?" Kat looked up from her glass. "How'd she get that way? I mean, we all do our share of fucking up."

Lynn shook her head. "Now you're asking me questions I don't have the answers to. But listen . . ." She opened her mouth, paused a second to think, then went on, "Please don't get me wrong about Dot, okay? I love her. She's a good person, in spite of her issues."

Kat recalled the Dot who'd spent countless hours in the studio, helping her with her project. The loving, selfless Dot. "Yeah, she can be pretty great."

"And I do think she's capable of overcoming this. Of being better."

Kat raised hopeful eyes at Lynn.

"But in the meantime," Lynn went on, "you don't deserve to be treated like this."

Kat sighed. "I know."

"On the other hand"—Lynn met Kat's gaze and offered a small but reassuring smile—"you don't *take* her shit. I've never seen anyone go toe to toe with her the way you do."

Kat smirked. "Well, she's all bark."

"I don't know about that." Lynn's smile waned. "Sometimes her words can bite pretty deep."

Kat was silent. After the previous night's argument, she knew that was true. She sipped her beer, her eyes glassy as she considered all of this.

"Is it stupid of me to still want her?" she asked at last.

"Kat." Lynn leaned forward and took her hand again. "All I can say is . . . whatever you decide to do here, you'll have my support. Like I said, I love Dot, but I love you too." She squeezed Kat's fingers. "I wouldn't blame you if you decided to walk away."

The thought of it started a sob forming in Kat's throat. Her eyes welled up again, surprisingly quickly.

Lynn continued, "But I wouldn't think you were stupid if you wanted to stick it out. I'll have your back. Jet too."

Kat smiled through her tears, almost coughing as she spoke. "Thanks, Liz."

"Shit, come 'ere." Lynn got out of her seat and slid in next to Kat, pulling her into a tight hug.

Kat belched, mid-sob, right next to Lynn's ear.

Lynn started cracking up. "Oh my god, Kat. You're a mess!"

"Yeah, I think I might be a little drunk."

* * *

Kat lay on the floor with her headphones on, plush carpet under her fingers, pastel pink ceiling above. No music was playing.

Knock-knock-knock.

"Katrina Jacobs." Her father's voice. "Kitty, come outta there. We've been calling you. Aunt Devon is here."

Aunt Dev! Aunt Dev was here! Kat's heart leapt.

She sprang off the floor and looked in the mirror. Skinny jeans and a babydoll tee. Barefoot. Her light brown hair was so long and messy. She pulled it back into a ponytail, using an elastic hair tie from around her wrist.

Where was her makeup? On her bureau, she found her black eyeliner pencil. Returning to the mirror, she started applying it, but it appeared light blue on her skin. She checked the pencil's label—"Raven." Why wasn't it working? No, wait . . . of course . . . she wasn't allowed to wear black makeup.

There was no time to worry about this. Aunt Dev was waiting. Every second counted.

Urgency struck Kat. She burst out the door of her room and bounded down the stairs. The white paint on the old banister was smooth, like she remembered it.

Aunt Devon stood facing away from her in the doorway to the kitchen. Devon had short, pixie hair—platinum blonde, like Lynn's. She was about Kat's height. And thin. Even thinner than last time.

"Aunt Dev." Kat's voice was weak. She couldn't seem to catch her breath.

Devon turned to face Kat, her mouth broadening into a grin. "Hi, birthday girl!"

"Aunt Dev . . ." Kat struggled to speak. Her chest felt tight.

"For you." Devon held out an envelope. Kat took it. It was heavier than it looked.

She studied her aunt's face. Devon was pale, except that her eyes were dark. Sunken. Her cheekbones were pronounced. She looked gaunt. So much of her was already gone.

Kat looked at the envelope in her hand. She ran her finger under the edge and opened it carefully, trying not to create a jagged tear. Inside was a card, and with it a compact disc.

She peeked at the disc without removing it. It had a handwritten label—"KITTY BDAY MIX." Kat pulled the card out and read the front.

May you walk with the Lord on your special day.

In the card was a folded paper—a letter, also handwritten. She hastily unfolded it and began to read.

My sweet Kitty,

Now, on your 16th birthday
everyone's eyes will be on you. Be
very careful what you . . .

There was a lot to the letter, but Kat didn't read the whole thing. She knew where the real message was—the first letter of each line.

NEVERMINDTHEBOLLOCKS

Her mouth fell open with shocked delight. The CD was The Sex Pistols, disguised so her parents wouldn't know. She clutched the letter and envelope to her chest and met Devon's eyes.

"Aunt Dev . . ." Again, speaking proved difficult.

"Shhh." Devon put a hand on Kat's arm.

"Aunt Dev . . ." She pushed through it, forcing the words out in a near-whisper. Tears formed with the effort, blurring her vision. "Aunt Dev . . . I'm like you."

Devon nodded. Kat knew she understood.

"Oh, Kitty." Devon pulled her into a firm embrace. She was still stronger than she appeared. She spoke softly into Kat's ear. "Don't let them hear. Understand? If they ever find you out . . . you run."

Kat tightened her arms around Devon, holding on as though she might blow away.

"Promise me." Devon's voice faltered.

Kat nodded. "I promise."

"Run, my sweet baby."

"Aunt Dev . . ."

* * *

Kat woke with a start. She was soaked in sweat. And thirsty. So thirsty.

A bottle of water and two Aspirin were waiting for her on the nightstand. She swallowed the pills and chugged half the bottle. Light peeked in between the closed blinds. What time was it?

On the floor by the side of the bed, she found her purse. Her phone was inside, but it was dead. She plugged it into the charger on the nightstand. It would be a few minutes before it had enough power to start up.

Kat propped her pillow on the headboard and sat up against it. She was breathing heavily. When she closed her eyes, she could still see Aunt Devon.

The dreams tended to come when she was stressed. They were a little different every time. And she always knew things she wouldn't have known back then. She knew what was coming, though not always the how or the why. And she knew she couldn't stop it. Time was always running out.

Kat's head hurt. Her stomach felt hollow, and her muscles ached. She didn't want to dwell on the dream. She slid her feet off the bed and lowered them to the floor. She stood up slowly and stumbled across the room to her desk, where she fell into the chair.

She opened her laptop and squinted as her eyes adjusted to the light of the screen. The clock in the corner showed 1:32 PM. Thursday.

New Facebook notifications were showing. Kat looked through them, but there was nothing especially interesting. Curiosity demanded that she check Dot's profile. No activity there at all.

Email? Of course there was new email. There was always new email. Updated terms of service for her website, upcoming concerts in the area, some junk mail that had gotten past the spam filter, and one personal email from . . . Eli Jacobs.

Kat stopped breathing and stared at the name. She scanned across the line to the subject: "Aunt Kitty?"

She got up and walked away from the desk. Her head was not in a place to deal with this right now. She picked the bottle off the nightstand and downed what water remained. Without giving herself time to think, she opened the door, crossed the hallway, and descended the stairs.

She moved with purpose, focusing her attention on the immediate task—going to the kitchen and refilling the bottle. Trying not to let her mind wander. Or wonder.

Standing at the kitchen sink, she filled the bottle with cold water, drank some of it, and filled it to the top again. Then she turned around and surveyed the room. She should eat something, she knew. As far as she could remember, she hadn't had any dinner the night before. Just alcohol.

Bananas. In the produce basket on the table. Someone had gone shopping. Thank you, Lonnie. Kat pulled one from the bunch and started peeling it. She sat down at the table, broke off a piece, and popped it in her mouth.

She closed her eyes while she chewed, taking slow, deliberate breaths. With each piece she swallowed, she felt a little better. It made a world of difference, just getting those first few bites of food into her stomach.

The house was quiet. Everyone else was out. Kat sat alone in the stillness, the faint ticking of a clock audible in the next room. Much as she dreaded thinking about it, her mind kept going back to the email.

Eli had been eight years old when Kat cut ties with her family. Eight years. She'd been gone longer than that. For the past decade, in her mind, he had remained that child. Innocent. The one pure memory she'd held onto, and the one person she'd most regretted leaving behind.

If this email really was from Eli, then reading it would mean learning things Kat wouldn't be able to unlearn. It frightened her. There'd been a certain comfort in the past being the past, her old life an unchanging image in her memory, frozen the way she'd left it. She'd grown to depend on that as a constant.

She wished Lonnie were home. He and Dot were the only ones who had any knowledge of her old life. Neither of them knew much, but the fact that she'd told them anything spoke volumes.

As it was, Kat had only herself for company. She could either read the email now or continue to stew over the unknown. There was already no going back, no unseeing it in her inbox.

She got up and threw out the banana peel. One banana wasn't really enough nutrition. Kat wasn't especially hungry, or in the mood to cook, but she needed something else. She grabbed a protein bar out of the cabinet, then picked up her water and left the kitchen.

Back in her room, Kat closed the door. She sat down at the desk, placing the water and protein bar next to the laptop. She took a deep breath and moved the mouse to wake up the screen.

There it was. Don't think too much, Kat. Just do it.

Click.

Ms. Katrina Brooks,

My name is Eli Jacobs. I'm searching for my aunt, whom I haven't seen in some years. I have reason to believe you might be she. If I am wrong, I apologize for the confusion. In that case, please disregard the remainder of this message. Thank you. – Eli

Aunt Kitty?

It's E. I don't know where to start, so please bear with me. First, if you got a voicemail from a strange number the other night, that was me. I'm sorry I didn't say anything. I didn't really expect the number to work, and then I heard your voice. You sound the same as I remember. I guess I froze. Mom was around, so I had to be careful.

For years, they wouldn't tell me why you left. I don't think they ever told me the truth. If you want to be left alone, I'll respect that. But if you're willing to talk to me, I'd like to know you again. You can email me or reach me at that number. It's my personal cell. I've missed you, Aunt Kitty.

With love,
E

P.S. – I still have the Canon Sure Shot you gave me, and I graduated to a Minolta SRT202. I'm majoring in photography!

Kat exhaled. She reread the postscript several times, her eyes hovering over "Canon Sure Shot." She'd handed that camera down to Eli when he was six years old—the same age she'd been when it was given to her, brand new in the box.

She looked back over the rest of the message. It was polite and open. He didn't seem to be putting any expectations on her, which was very mature of him. Eli had always been a good kid. Respectful.

He didn't offer much information about himself. But that made sense, especially if he wasn't sure he had the right person. Majoring in photography, though—was that Kat's influence at work? Even after all these years?

That question and a thousand more flooded her brain, and she found herself itching for answers. And more than that, she found herself eager to answer Eli's questions. Her favorite nephew was looking for her, and here she was! She wanted to put his mind at ease, tell him his search was over!

But as she stared at the blank reply window, debating where to start, second thoughts began to creep in. Kat had still been envisioning the nephew she remembered. Little E with his camera. But this wasn't little

E anymore. This was a young man just coming out of high school. A young man with ideas and beliefs and motivations. A young man she really didn't know.

Sure, Eli had memories of Kat, but the fact was he'd lived a life without her in it. Without her influence. She'd left him alone among the wolves, and for all she knew he might have become one himself. What was his goal here? Was he *just* hoping to reconnect? Or would this turn into an effort to bring Kat back into the fold?

She wanted to be optimistic. She really did. But she needed to protect herself. If only she had a little more information to go on.

The easiest thing would be to look up Eli on social media. She'd very likely find him and get a better impression of the man he'd grown into. But if she found Eli, she'd almost certainly find the rest of her family connected to him—photos and news about her brother, sister-in-law, father, and mother. Probably extended family too.

She didn't want to go there. She couldn't. The thought of it put knots in her stomach. She'd buried all of them long ago, and they needed to stay that way.

Kat sat back in her chair and closed her eyes as she sipped from her water bottle. She breathed. Tried to clear her head. What other, safer options did she have?

What she *could* do was a bit of targeted searching on Google. Maybe Eli's name, number, or email address would bring up some informative links. That felt like a promising idea.

Kat tried those as search terms. The email got very few hits, none of them useful. The phone number appeared on countless websites listing basic cell information, but again none of the results really told her anything. So she focused on his name.

"Eli Jacobs" alone proved too broad a search. She tried it in combination with some other terms—their hometown, the local high school, his major... That did it. "Eli Jacobs photography." Among many irrelevant links to other Elis and Jacobses and photographers, there was one article about college scholarships.

Seventeen-year-old Eli Jacobs of St. Lawrence County, New York had been awarded an art scholarship based on the merit of his photographic work. He would be attending Maryland Institute College of Art, beginning in the 2018 Fall semester.

Right name, right age, right location, and right major. That had to be him. No photo, though, and no further information. But it was something.

Kat went back and continued searching. She tried including "scholarship" and "Maryland Institute." She searched his name in combination with different clubs, hobbies, church groups, blog sites—anything that would speak to his beliefs or politics, especially. She spent the better part of an hour brainstorming search terms, but no more leads were coming up. She seemed to be out of luck.

Finally, exhausted of ideas, she was back at square one. Once again, the cursor flashed on the screen, waiting for her to begin her reply to Eli.

She didn't like this. She felt like she was flying blind. Before sending any kind of response . . . she needed help. She didn't want to do this alone.

Kat closed the laptop, put her elbows on the desk, and interlaced her fingers under her nose. She stared at the wall. *Didn't want to do this alone.* When was the last time she'd said that? Kat had spent the past decade being careful not to lean on anyone. Looking out for herself. The people she considered close friends were few in number—Lonnie, Jet, Lynn, and now Dot. And even then, while she would confide in them to a degree, she didn't want to *depend* on them for anything.

But this situation was different. Eli had the potential to shake her foundations—to bring her old life back to haunt her. Kat would be taking a chance by reconnecting with him. For the first time in a long time, she was willing to admit she needed support. Someone to be her anchor, to root her in the present. Someone she trusted.

She trusted Lonnie, and she'd known him the longest. It would make the most sense to bring him in on this. She could talk to him as soon as he got off work. But as sensible as that would be, it wasn't Lonnie she wanted right now. At the forefront of Kat's mind, more than anything else, was the feeling of Dot's hand in hers, the way Dot had held on tight as they'd worked their way through the crowds that day at the market. That's what she wanted—*whom* she wanted.

Was that foolish? Tuesday night had shown how turbulent their relationship could be. God, they'd been so angry at each other. And for what? Pride? Over roller derby?

Proverbs 16:18. "Pride goes before destruction." Kat could still hear her father quoting that verse. The hypocrite. Well, maybe that was the solution then. Unlike him, she would show that she could actually swallow her pride.

She stood up and crossed the room to her bedside table, picked up her phone, and turned it on. It took a minute to power up, buzzing repeatedly as notifications appeared. Kat ignored most of these—app updates and the like. But there was one new text message as well. From Dot.

I miss you. Can we talk?

It had been almost two days. *Only* two days, but it might as well have been a week. Kat didn't even hesitate.

Yes. Please.

CHAPTER 9

Agreement

Music thumped at high volume. Kat didn't know EDM well enough to recognize the artist, but she didn't find it disagreeable. It was mellow, and thick with layered beats and instrumental harmonies.

She stood at the top of the entryway and surveyed the studio. It looked like Dot had stepped out, as no one was present. The room appeared amazingly clean—or at least uncluttered. When Kat had left it last, there'd still been frames scattered across the drop cloth and on the counter. Scraps of mat board had littered the tabletop. Tools and paint and adhesive had been left out.

Now all was tidy. Everything had been put away in boxes, it seemed, except for a few frames laid out neatly on the table. Kat stepped down into the room and took a closer look at those frames.

The prints in them—she didn't remember mounting those. No, she hadn't gotten to them yet, had she? They looked great. Finished and ready for display.

Kat walked around the table. Four of the boxes were office-style cardboard—the type with lids and handholds—but they'd been painted black, and the lids were nowhere to be seen. Two boxes sat atop the table, and two on the floor, each filled with horizontally-stacked, matted prints. Each print was wrapped neatly in its own transparent plastic sleeve. Kat hadn't supplied those sleeves. Or the boxes. This was all new.

Also on the floor were three larger boxes—these unpainted. They had flaps to close over the tops but remained open at the moment. These boxes held the rest of the framed prints, also stacked sideways. Thin bubble wrap had been woven over and under each frame, padding it against the next. Again, the packing materials were new.

There'd still been at least a day's work left to do, as Kat had left things. Now, as far as she could tell, the project was done and ready for transport to Pridefest.

The door opened, and Dot stepped in, soundless in Kat's music-saturated perception. There was a gentleness in Dot's eyes as they met Kat's. Dot's mouth hung open slightly, as though she meant to speak. She quickly shifted her attention and strode toward the computer. She reached for the mouse and stopped the music. Silence fell abruptly over the room.

Dot turned to face Kat, who had her hand on the edge of one of the tabletop boxes.

Kat looked from the box to Dot. "You finished it."

Dot took a tentative step toward her. "Yeah. Sorry, I had to. Pride is only two days away, and I didn't know if . . . um . . ." Her eyes fell from Kat to the table.

"Don't apologize." Kat felt herself wanting to smile, to reassure Dot, but it wouldn't quite come. There were too many things yet to be said.

Dot came closer, gesturing to the boxes. "I, uh . . . I got these for the prints that aren't framed. They work okay as displays, I think—you know, so people can flip through them." She glanced briefly, almost timidly, at Kat, then moved to the frames on the table. "And I matted and mounted the rest of the prints. I hope they're okay. I did my best."

She stepped back from the table and interlaced her fingers on top of her head, watching Kat expectantly.

Kat followed her around the table, eyeing the framed prints. "Perfect." She spoke softly and raised her eyes to meet Dot's. "They're perfect. You did great. Thank you."

Dot blushed. A smile flashed on her face, but it was gone as quickly as it had appeared. There was a long silence as she seemed about to say something. Kat waited patiently.

When she spoke, Dot's tone was almost pleading. "I . . . don't want to fight."

Kat was ready with her reply. "Neither do I."

Again, Dot stood in nervous silence. Kat reached out and cupped the side of her face, brushing Dot's cheek with her thumb.

Kat went on, in a broken whisper, "I missed you too."

Dot put her fingers over Kat's and lowered their joined hands. Her gaze focused on Kat again, this time without reluctance, though concern wrinkled her brow.

"I had an idea." She searched Kat's expression. "But you might not like it. I'm not sure if I like it."

"Try me." Kat's response was immediate. Eager.

"Okay, but . . . listen, before I tell you the idea"—Dot held her hand tightly—"I want you to know, whatever this is that we have . . . I want this."

Kat's heart swelled. Her cheeks flushed.

Dot continued, "I want to be with you. If you want to be with me."

Kat nodded, a grin at last pushing its way out.

Dot beamed for a moment, but worry quickly lined her face again. "So, here's the thing." She looked down. "What if there was a way we could . . . agree to disagree? When it comes to derby."

Kat could already feel the ire rising. The defensiveness. *Agree to disagree?* Is that all this was to Dot? A disagreement? It was Kat's very competency at her job in question here! Her years of work and experience! Her pride as a ref!

Her *pride*.

Kat closed her eyes and took a deep breath. She'd known this wasn't going to be easy. It wasn't fair. It wasn't right. But it was . . . only derby. It was only one facet of her life. And there were more important things to worry about right now. She could swallow her derby pride, at least long enough to hear out Dot's idea.

Kat exhaled. "Agree to disagree. How do we do that?" She opened her eyes.

Dot seemed to untense a little. "Well . . . uh . . . by keeping derby separate."

Kat's face contorted with skepticism. "What do you mean keep it separate?"

"I mean . . ." Dot took a breath and collected herself. "I mean, in the context of derby—when we're at the rink, or a bout, or whatever"—she met Kat's eyes—"we're different people. I'm a skater. You're a ref. That's it. We don't, uh . . ." She swallowed and looked away again. "We don't talk to each other. We don't know each other."

Kat was stunned, her eyes wide. This sounded crazy. She might have settled for a promise of mutual respect, or a "no talking derby while angry" clause. Something less overkill. "That's . . . severe."

"I know."

Well, this idea put things in perspective a bit. Lynn's insight was coming back to Kat now. This wasn't even really about her. This was about Dot avoiding confrontation. She was afraid to be wrong—afraid enough to consider this ridiculous plan. Kat's anger became tempered with sympathy. If she could understand what it must be like inside Dot's head . . .

She looked at Dot. Looked into her eyes. Felt the grip of her fingers. This is what Kat had come for. She needed Dot. And if this is what Dot needed from her right now, then so be it. Maybe, in time, Dot would come around. At least until then they wouldn't be at each other's throats—assuming this worked.

Kat tilted her head, holding Dot's gaze. "Could you really do that?"

"I'd be willing to try. I..." Dot hesitated. Kat could feel her trembling. "I don't want to repeat—"

"Then okay." Kat squeezed her hand.

Dot froze, surprised. "Okay? Really?"

Kat pressed her lips together and slowly shook her head. "I don't know, but I'm willing to try too."

A little smile crept across Dot's face. "Okay."

They stood looking at each other. Dot wasn't trembling anymore. A slight sense of relief had taken the edge off, but something still felt unfinished. Neither of them said anything for several seconds. Kat wasn't sure what should come next—although she knew what she *wanted* to come next. She broke the silence.

"Would you kiss me alrea—"

Dot's lips were on hers before she could finish. She inhaled Dot's scent and pulled her in close. *This* was relief. The sweet taste of Dot, the feel of her body against Kat's. Pride be damned. This was where Kat belonged. This was home.

She couldn't help but laugh as the remaining tension melted away. Just a little, joyful laugh, as her tongue met Dot's. They were gonna be okay. She could feel it. And that was all that mattered.

When the kiss found its natural end, they stood holding each other. Kat rested her forehead against Dot's and gently nuzzled her brow. They breathed one another's breath. Kat simply reveled in finally being here, safe in Dot's arms.

Eventually, Kat pulled her head back and looked at Dot. There was still so much more to say, so much Dot didn't know. Kat wanted to let her in.

"Dot." Kat studied her face. "There's something I want to tell you about. Something that happened today."

Worry pulled at the corners of Dot's eyes again. "What is it? Are you okay?"

"Yeah. Yeah, I'm okay." And that was the truth. Here, now, with Dot, Kat was more than okay. "It's about my family."

"Oh." Dot's expression softened.

"Yeah. It could be a long story. I'll have to fill you in on some things that . . . I've never told anyone." God, that was true. There was so much about Kat's past that she'd never spoken of. Now, on the verge of breaking that silence, it felt as though she'd been holding back a flood.

"Well, let's get comfortable somewhere, and you can tell me everything." Dot rubbed Kat's back reassuringly. "Are you hungry?"

Kat hadn't realized it until now, but her appetite had returned in full force. "I'm starving, actually."

"Why don't we go in the house? I'll make us something to eat while I listen."

Kat lit up. "That would be amazing!"

Dot smirked. She leaned in and kissed Kat softly. Then she released her embrace and pulled away, finding Kat's hand and taking hold of it.

"You called me Dot." Smiling, Dot walked backwards toward the stairs, bringing Kat with her. "Instead of Mouse."

"Yeah." Kat's cheeks turned pink. "I feel closer to you if I use your real name. Is that okay?"

"Yes! Please, keep doing it."

Kat grinned. "Okay, Dot."

* * *

"Are instant scalloped potatoes okay?" Dot's head was hidden behind the cabinet door. "I'm pretty good at doctoring them up."

"Honestly, whatever you make is fine. I can barely boil water, so as far as I'm concerned you're about to do magic over there."

Kat sat at the kitchen table with a tall glass of iced tea. Dot had the makings of a meal laid out on the counter next to the stove—fresh pork chops she'd found in the fridge, frozen green beans, several different herbs and spices—and now she was pulling out milk and butter for those potatoes. Kat just watched in amazement.

"Okay, olive oil, salt, pepper—that looks like everything." Dot started measuring, pouring, heating. It was like watching Lonnie work, except entirely different. Dot had her own rhythm, her own flow. Lonnie always seemed smooth and controlled in the kitchen, ahead of the game. Dot's method was a little more chaotic, like she was constantly playing catch-up.

"So." Dot drizzled olive oil in a pan as she glanced over at Kat. "Where do you wanna start? I'm listening whenever you're ready."

"Uh . . ." Kat sat up. In the last several minutes, she'd begun to dread this moment. Dot's prompting helped. "I guess I'll start with today and . . . fill in as I go. You remember Eli, right?"

"The nephew who made the pin." Dot opened the bag of green beans and dumped them into a large bowl.

"Yeah. He emailed me today."

"He *what*? How did he . . . ?"

"I don't know." Kat ran her fingernail along a groove in the design on her glass. "He didn't say. He wasn't sure he had the right Katrina Brooks, so I guess that's why he didn't go into much detail. But, um . . . there's some background to that, too, that I should tell you."

"Background to what?" Dot licked butter off her finger.

"My last name. It isn't really Brooks." Kat watched Dot's reaction carefully. "It's Jacobs."

Dot raised her eyebrows. "Wow. So he must have done some digging to find you."

"Yeah, maybe." Kat relaxed. The name revelation didn't appear to have fazed Dot. "He has my phone number too, though. Now, see, I haven't changed my number since college. So my family still has it. But little Eli didn't. Which begs the question—did he find it on his own, or did they give it to him?"

"You think they wanted him to contact you?"

"I don't know." Kat sipped her iced tea, then set the glass down. "I was excited when I first read the email. He basically just says he misses me and wants to reconnect. And he still has the camera I gave him when he was six."

"Aw, that's adorable!" Dot poured the contents of a pouch into a pot and started stirring it with a fork.

"He's majoring in photography. I did a little digging myself and found out he's going to MICA."

"No shit! That's a great school."

"On a scholarship." Kat couldn't help but feel like she was boasting on behalf of little E.

Dot looked at her and smiled. "You sound proud."

"I know." Kat's eyes fell. "It's a problem. I keep thinking of him as my little eight year old Eli. But he's not. I don't know who he is now."

"Um, so, what is it that you're afraid of, exactly?" Dot rapped the fork on the edge of the pot, then placed it on the counter.

"A few things, I guess." Kat rested her elbows on the table and ran her fingers through her hair. "I'm afraid my family got to him. That he grew up to be like my dad and my brother. That the kid I knew is gone."

"Well, one way or another, he grew up. He was always going to."

"Yeah, but if I'd been in the picture . . ."

"Ah. I see." Dot laid a pork chop in the pan. It started sizzling immediately. "But you had good reason to leave, right?"

Kat was distant. "Yeah . . ."

Dot glanced over to find Kat red-eyed, staring at the window. "Hey. Kat."

"Hm?"

"Could you help me with this?" Dot picked up the fork and poked around in the pot. "Just keep stirring these so they don't burn?"

"Uh. Sure." Kat got up and walked to the stove, stepping to the right of Dot. She took the fork. "You trust me with this job?"

"About as far as I can throw you, but you looked like you were gazing into the abyss over there."

"The abyss!" Kat chuckled. It cleared her head. Brought her back to the here and now. "Yeah, I guess I was. Thanks."

"Of course." Dot put her right arm around Kat while she turned the pork chops with her left. "If you wanna wait to talk about this stuff, it's okay."

Kat considered it for a moment before responding. "I kinda want to get this out."

"Okay. Whatever you need." Dot squeezed her close.

"So, I'm also worried that he'll try to get me to reconnect with the rest of my family. Or even just tell me about them. And I don't want that. I don't want to know anything."

"They were that bad?"

"It was . . . complicated. I had to leave for my own survival, but that didn't mean it was easy." Kat sighed. "God, that sounds so dramatic."

Dot's brow creased as she flipped the chops over. "What do you mean *for your survival?* Did they hurt you?"

Kat sniffed. There was a lump in her throat. She tried to focus on stirring the potatoes. "No, they would never hurt me. Not on purpose. They thought they were helping. They were doing their best, but they didn't understand. I mean, how could they?"

"Kat. Helping how?"

Kat swallowed. "Have . . . have you ever heard of reparative therapy?"

The tongs slipped out of Dot's hand. They clattered against the stove and fell on the floor. She ignored them and turned to fully face Kat, gripping Kat's upper arm. "No fucking way. Like conversion therapy?"

There was rage in Dot's voice. Maybe this had been a bad idea.

"They didn't know the damage, Dot."

Dot put her other hand on Kat's cheek and looked her in the eye. "They did that shit to you?"

"Not to me." Kat's voice was little more than a whisper. "My aunt, Devon. But they weren't trying to hurt her. They thought her soul was on the line. It's not that they . . ." Dammit. Why was she defending them? "Anyway, it's not something they do *to* you."

"Isn't it, like, *Clockwork Orange* shit? Aversion conditioning?"

Kat shook her head. "Not anymore. I—I don't think. At least, not that Aunt Devon told me."

Dot released her death grip on Kat's arm and bent down to pick up the tongs. "Then, what did they do?" She took them over to the sink, on the other side of Kat.

"Mostly just talked. I think these might be done."

Dot peered over at the potatoes. "Nah, they can go a bit longer. Would you lower the heat on them though? To like three?"

Kat adjusted the dial and gave them another stir. She turned around and leaned back against the counter.

Having rinsed the tongs, Dot returned to the pork chops and checked their undersides. "So it's just talking?"

"As far as I know." Kat watched as Dot prodded the meat. "But you can really fuck someone up with words."

The scent of the food, and the herbs Dot had rubbed into the chops—rosemary, sage—Kat didn't know what else, but her mouth was watering.

"This smells amazing, by the way."

Dot grinned smugly. "Thank you! Last thing, would you throw that bowl of beans in the microwave over there? For four minutes?"

A glimmer of a smile crossed Kat's lips. "Happy to." She was grateful for these little distractions.

"So, yeah." Dot pulled two plates out of the cabinet and set them on the counter. "I know words can be powerful." She picked forks and knives out of the silverware drawer. "But they couldn't make you do it, could they? You're not a minor. You weren't when you left."

Kat started the microwave, then turned to face Dot. "No, technically they couldn't make me."

Dot checked the chops again, giving them gentle nudges with the tongs.

Kat went on, "But you don't understand. Living in an evangelical household, in a life where everyone you know is a member of the church . . . you can't escape it."

Kat's voice was starting to falter. Dot stopped what she was doing. She turned to Kat and just listened.

"Refusing the therapy . . . I'd never hear the end of it. The guilt of turning my back on my family, walking away from Christ. The shame of it. Of not even *wanting* to get better. Of being that selfish." Kat put a hand to her mouth, trying to smother a sob as it escaped.

Dot quickly turned off the stove, crossed the kitchen, and wrapped her arms around Kat. She whispered in Kat's ear. "You're right. You're right. I don't understand what that's like. I'm sorry, baby."

Kat held onto her, resting her cheek against Dot's. "Aunt Devon tried. I don't know what they say in therapy, but it screwed her up for good. I came out to her when I was sixteen, and she said if they ever found out, I should run."

"Sounds like she loved you."

Tears streamed down Kat's face. She was barely audible. "Yeah."

Dot's eyes weren't entirely dry now either. "Is it okay if I ask? Is she still . . . ?"

Kat gripped the fabric of Dot's shirt. "The last time I saw her was Christmas, when I was seventeen. She overdosed on January third."

"I'm sorry." Dot gently rocked Kat from side to side. "I'm so sorry. I'm glad you told me."

Kat exhaled, her breath shaking. "Me too." She closed her eyes and relaxed into Dot's embrace. "I think maybe I do need a break from talking about this."

"Okay, no problem." Dot slowly rubbed Kat's back, soothing her.

Kat's breathing calmed. The smell of herbs called to her stomach, reminding her she was safe in the present. With a beautiful girlfriend who cooked for her and held her while she cried. And just two days to go until Pride. It was Thursday night. She opened her eyes as a startling thought occurred to her.

"You missed practice!"

Dot barely reacted, except to give Kat a gentle squeeze. "Of course I did. This was more important."

Kat beamed, even as tears still glistened on her cheeks. She ran fingers into Dot's hair and wrapped her arm around Dot's head, pressing her face close.

Dot spoke softly. "Would you want to stay over tonight?"

Tonight or any night, Kat was certain there was nowhere she'd rather be. "I'd like that."

CHAPTER 10

Connections

———————

Scent was the first thing to hit Dot as she woke—faintly floral and fruity on top, and as she inhaled she was wrapped in stronger, pungent currents. Slight, pleasant sour notes hovered over a deep sea of musky warmth that begged her to sink into it.

It was the sleepy, sweaty, animal aroma of her favorite human. Dot instinctively strove to be closer to the source. She nestled her nose just behind Kat's ear and gently tightened her left arm around Kat's torso.

Under the covers, Kat's bare skin pressed against Dot's naked breasts, belly, pelvis, and thighs. Dot shifted a little, the subtle movement of skin on skin a palpable confirmation of their physical connection. Kat's fingers closed over Dot's hand in response. Dot lazily opened her eyes.

In the darkened room, Kat's phone was the only source of light. She lay holding it with her free hand, scrolling slowly through a screen of text. Dot's eyes took a moment to adjust to the brightness, but they were soon able to focus and landed on the words "Aunt Kitty."

Dot planted a simple, patient kiss on the back of Kat's neck while peering over her shoulder.

Kat turned her head slightly. "I'm sorry, I didn't mean to wake you."

"You didn't," Dot whispered. "How long have you been up?"

Kat checked the clock on her phone. "Maybe half an hour."

"You stayed still here all that time?"

Kat interlaced her fingers with Dot's. "I didn't want to move."

A wave of joyous warmth flooded Dot's being. She grinned and inhaled deeply through her nose, savoring Kat's presence, before focusing again on the screen.

"Is that the email?"

Kat cleared her throat softly. "Yeah. I've been thinking about how to respond."

Dot could see the entire screen clearly from where she lay. "Is it alright if I read it?"

"You want to?"

"Of course."

Kat lifted Dot's arm and turned over to face her. The light of the phone lit their faces from below, reflecting in Kat's eyes. Kat leaned forward and kissed Dot hesitantly. Dot pressed into it, seeking more. With that, Kat parted her lips and welcomed Dot's advance. Dot could feel her smiling. Their connection became playful, tongues chasing and retreating before meeting.

Finally, Kat committed fully and lifted herself over Dot, planting a hand on the other side of the bed. Dot went with it, resting back against her pillow while Kat explored her mouth. She ran her fingers up the back of Kat's neck.

It was a long, slow kiss. Gentle and deep. Kat tasted like the grogginess of morning, her sweet saliva tainted with thick, hot bitterness. But Dot didn't care. She was just as gross, she knew, and it obviously wasn't fazing Kat one bit. There was something beautiful about that, she thought—about being hungry for one another even at their ickiest. It felt raw and pure. Frankly, it was turning her on.

Kat pulled away and gazed down at Dot with half-lidded eyes and a satisfied grin. She placed her phone on Dot's chest.

"I'll leave this with you while I go to the bathroom." She caressed Dot's cheek and ran her thumb over Dot's lips. "If the screen locks, the code is seven-two-eight-eight-four."

Dot's eyebrows rose. That was a big show of trust. She nodded at Kat. "Seven-two-eight-eight-four."

Kat slid her fingers down Dot's belly as she lifted herself away. Then she tore her eyes from Dot's and rolled off the bed.

She reached for the floor lamp in the corner. "Okay if I hit the light?"

"Sure."

Dot squinted as the room was illuminated. The soft light of the sixty-watt bulb shimmered on Kat's ivory skin, accenting the curves of her perky, wide-set breasts. Kat bent down and picked a purple tank top off the floor—Dot's Thorn City Rollers shirt. She pulled it on and headed for the door on the opposite side of the room, casting a wink at Dot.

Once Kat had shut the door behind her, Dot sat herself up against the headboard with a pillow, then turned her attention to the phone. Seven-two-eight-eight-four. The email was the first thing to appear on the screen.

Ms. Katrina Brooks...

Dot took her time reading through the message. She tried to keep in mind everything Kat had told her the night before, to put Eli's words in context. But even then, there just wasn't much to read into.

Kat re-entered the room while Dot was nearing the end of her second read-through.

Dot looked up from the phone. "You're right, he doesn't say a whole lot."

Kat crawled into bed and got under the covers, nestling her head against Dot's side. Dot brought her knees up and rested the phone on her thigh.

"So tell me..." She stroked Kat's head, running fingers through her hair. "What can I do to help with this?"

Kat peered up at her. "I guess just be there? While I respond to him. And especially when I read his response back."

Dot nodded. "I can do that. I was also thinking—when he does write back, would you want me to read it first? Sort of screen it?"

"*Could* you?" Kat's enthusiasm was clear.

"I'd be happy to."

"That would make me feel so much better about this." Kat wrapped a hand around Dot's thigh and smiled up at her with adoration.

"Do you know what you want to say to him yet?"

"I've been thinking." Kat's eyes went to the phone. "I have so many questions, but I want to keep the first message simple. Like, one, 'Yes it's me.' Two, 'Don't tell me about our family.' And three, 'What are your intentions?'"

"Not, 'How did you find me?'"

"Mm, not in the first correspondence. I want to know that so badly, but not until we have an understanding of what's okay to talk about."

"Well . . ." Dot hit the reply button and handed the phone to Kat. "Why not get the first one over with, then? You know what you want to say. And I'm right here."

Kat took the phone carefully. She looked up at Dot, then back at the screen.

"Here, sit up next to me." Dot propped a pillow against the headboard for Kat.

Kat sat up and scooted back beside Dot so that their shoulders and hips were touching. "Okay." She took a deep breath and exhaled slowly. "Getting it over with. Where do I start?"

Dot put a hand on her leg and gave a reassuring squeeze. "Maybe start with what's familiar. How would you have greeted *little* Eli? That's who he was the last time he saw you, so that's what'll be familiar to him too."

"Right." Kat bit her thumbnail as she thought.

"Would it help if I don't look while you write?"

Kat shook her head. She started typing.

Hi E,

She paused. After a moment's consideration, she changed it.

Hi Buddy,

Yes, you found me! I've missed you too! I'm sorry I didn't get to say goodbye. I'll tell you everything they wouldn't about why I had to leave. But before we go any further, I need to lay out some ground rules. They might seem harsh, but they're important to me.

One, please don't tell me any news about our family. My parents, your parents, anyone. I don't want to know what they've been up to. When you find out why I left, hopefully you'll understand. Until then, please just respect that request.

And two, I have no intention of reconnecting with anyone other than you. I'm never going back home to Culson or returning to the church. I'm home already. Not that I assumed you would try to bring me back, but I had to make that clear just in case.

If you're okay with these rules, then I would love to get to know you again. It breaks my heart that I wasn't there to see you through your teens. You may come to regret reaching out once you learn the truth about me, but I hope not. Write back soon and let me know if you still want to talk, okay?

Love always,
Aunt Kitty

P.S. – I still have the catnip pin you made for me. I display it proudly all the time.

Kat worded the letter carefully, making numerous changes and adjustments on the way to this final version. When she typed "I'm home already," Dot felt a touch of elation, but she refrained from reacting so as not to break Kat's concentration.

Kat scrolled through it one last time, making no further changes. "What do you think?"

Dot rubbed her leg. "I think it's perfect."

"It's not too, like . . . harsh?"

Dot looked at Kat, who remained fixed on the screen. "Babe. It's not harsh. It's assertive, and that's exactly what you need it to be."

"I'm a little afraid I'll scare him off."

"Hey, look at me." Dot put a hand on Kat's cheek and locked eyes with her. "He'll understand. You've been gone for ten years. He must know you had some heavy reasons for leaving." She watched Kat's expression. Kat didn't seem entirely assured. Dot went on, "If I'm wrong? If this is enough to scare him off? Then he isn't ready. We knew that might be a possibility, right?"

"Yeah."

"This letter is excellent, Kat. If he's the Eli you want to hear from, he'll get it completely."

That got a little smile from Kat. She turned back to the screen and hovered her finger over "send."

Dot kissed her on the cheek. "You got this."

Kat touched the button and the email went off into the ether. She sighed in relief, then slid down and laid her head on Dot's shoulder. "Now we wait."

Dot rested her cheek against Kat's head and took her hand. "Proud of you." She gave the moment time to sink in. After a small stretch of silence, she asked, "Do you have anywhere to be today?"

"At some point, I have to get the tent from Lonnie. Other than that I'm free." Kat put the phone down on the bed. "You?"

"No, I was kinda hoping to spend the day with you."

"Oh really?" Kat sat up and turned to Dot with a sly look. "What *ever* would we do with a whole day to ourselves?"

Dot smirked. "I could think of a whole list of things."

"Hmm." Kat licked her teeth seductively "Well, as long as that list starts with coffee, I'm probably game for the rest."

"Ha! Coffee first, huh? Alright." Dot rolled up to her hands and knees such that she was straddling Kat, then turned and stepped off the bed. "Then let's get brewing!" She extended a hand. Kat took it firmly and rose to join her.

* * *

"Strangers at derby? How the fuck is *that* gonna work?" Reggie wasn't one to mince words.

Also known as "Domme"—short for Dominomatrix—Regina Leone was part of the Heavy Metal's jammer rotation. Or she *would* have been, if she wasn't currently on medical leave for a torn ACL.

Reggie and Dot were staffing the CRD tent together at Pridefest. Though the consummate goth, for this occasion Reggie had added rainbow colors to her usual black lipstick and eye makeup.

Behind the two of them hung a banner displaying the Crosscannon Roller Derby logo. In front of them stood a table covered with flyers, bout schedules, and a small assortment of CRD merch items—tee shirts, hats, and bandanas.

Reggie sat forward in her folding chair. "Seriously, you know this is a monumentally stupid idea, right?" She took a corn chip from the bag in her hand and popped it into her mouth.

Dot folded her arms defiantly. "If it's so stupid, then what's your alternative?"

"I don't know. Talk it out?"

Dot sighed. "Trust me, it's an argument that leads nowhere."

Reggie raised an eyebrow. "*I* heard it leads into the back of your van."

Dot sat bolt upright. "My—how did you . . . ?" She glanced around. "Did Lynn . . . ?"

Reggie snorted. "It's hardly a secret. A bunch of people were in the parking lot that night. And you know what they say—if the van's a-rockin' . . ."

Dot turned bright red.

Reggie leaned back, grinning. "Relax! Nobody cares. Anyway, good on you. Angry sex is the best."

That coaxed an embarrassed chuckle out of Dot. She dropped her elbows onto to her knees and covered her face with her hands, groaning. "Yeah, well, I'm partial to the non-angry variety, myself."

"You have no taste for the finer things, my friend." Reggie thrust her hand back into the chip bag. "Speaking of your van, what time did you and Kat have to get here this morning?"

Dot pulled her fingers down and raised her head. "Uh, about nine-thirty. We loaded everything up last night, so basically we just rolled out of bed and came here."

Reggie frowned in consideration. "Damn, that's early for you. And she stayed over two nights in a row? You two are, like, really coupling."

"Mmhm." Though blushing only mildly now, Dot beamed to the point of glowing.

"Oh, Mouse." Reggie smirked and shook her head. "I didn't know it was like this. I guess it *would* have to be pretty special, though, to be worth all the, uh . . . complications."

"Dude, you don't even know." Dot's reply was swift and certain. "She's amazing. Have you ever talked to her?"

Reggie shrugged. "Sort of. Just in passing." She crunched another chip.

"I'll introduce you later. And you can see her work, too. She's a killer photographer!"

"So I've heard. Yeah, I'd like that."

Dot was glassy-eyed, daydreaming as she looked forward to seeing Kat again. After a long moment, she realized the conversation had lulled and that they'd basically been talking about *her* the entire time.

"So what about you?" She squinted at Reggie curiously. "Are you coming back to skate soon?"

"Mm!" Reggie swallowed a mouthful of food. "Next week!"

"No way!" Dot blinked in surprise. "Will you be able to skate at MAD?"

"That's the hope. We'll see how things feel."

"Man, that'll be a relief, if you're able to play." Dot folded her arms again, this time conversationally. "I mean, we're favored over Second Bridge anyway, but we need to beat them pretty handily to improve our ranking enough for playoffs."

Reggie's brow wrinkled. "Like, by how much?"

"Pixie did the math. I think she said we need about one and a half times their score. So if Second Bridge has a hundred points, we need a hundred and fifty."

"Doable."

Dot nodded. "With our full jammer rotation? Definitely!"

"Is this about MAD?" Vee approached from behind the tent and put her hands on Reggie's shoulders.

"Yeah." Dot tilted her head up at Vee. "Is that the right point differential? One and a half times their score?"

"Aye, a wee bit less than that, actually. We need t' score fifty-nine percent of the total points in the bout."

Reggie craned her neck back to look at Vee. "Baby, if your hands are gonna be there, they'd better be massaging."

"Oy! Yes mistress!" Vee cast a look of mock distress at Dot but started rubbing Reggie's shoulders anyway.

"That's better." Reggie closed her eyes and grinned.

"Anyway, Reg my love, I came over here to ask an important question."

"Mhm?"

"D'ya fancy a shift in front of the cannon? Siren's takin' pictures."

Dot contorted her face. "Fancy a *what?*"

Reggie opened her eyes a slit. "A make-out session."

Vee winked at Dot.

"Uh-huh." Dot eyed Reggie, then Vee. "I don't get this arrangement. Like, why aren't you two dating already? You're so obviously into each other."

Reggie cackled. "Dating within the league? Are you crazy? Oh, that's right, you *are!*"

Dot glared at her, unamused. "Ha ha."

"See, I know you have this good thing with Kat, and I wish you the best, I really do. But in my opinion, that's just playing with fire." Reggie looked up at Vee. "Right, baby?"

Vee just laughed, then leaned down and kissed her.

Dot rolled her eyes. "Right. 'Cause you two aren't playing with fire *at all.*" She laid the sarcasm on extra thick. "Are all derby wife couples like this?"

Reggie opened her eyes fully and narrowed them at Dot. "I dunno, *you* tell *me*. Do you and Lizzy make out?"

"Me and Lynn? We're not der—"

"Bull-*shit* you're not derby wives." Reggie snickered smugly. "You two are the *quintessential* derby wives. Best friends? Can count on each other no matter what? That's your derby wife."

"Oh! That's all it . . . ?" Dot was genuinely astonished she'd never realized that.

Vee gave her an assuring nod.

"Uh, well, no—I most definitely do not make out with Lynn."

"So no," Vee said through a chuckle, "not all derby wives make out. Reg and I just, em . . ."

"Have a special bond," Reggie finished with a smirk.

"Oh lord." Dot shook her head. "At least I learned something here." She picked up her phone and checked the time. "Anyway, we have about an hour left in our, uh . . . shift. Then you guys can go shift or snog or whatever at the cannon."

"I'd rather shift in front of the protesters, frankly." Reggie motioned toward the west end of the park, where a small anti-LGBTQ group was gathered with signs. She looked up at Vee. "Whaddya say, baby?"

Dot peered off in that direction. A couple of guys were having it out with the group. "Yeah, if you wanna end up in a shouting match."

Vee didn't even look. "Aye, let's not go instigatin' confrontation. That's what they want."

Reggie groaned. "It's infuriating, though. We don't go protesting at their churches and lobbying against straight marriage."

"That's 'cause we're bein' the bigger women here, love. Mouse is right. If we go over there, we'll just end up in a shoutin' match. We should be enjoyin' our day an' leave the protesters bored out of their feckin' minds."

"Pffft. Fine," Reggie grudgingly ceded. She cocked an eye at Dot. "Since when are you the voice of reason? You're usually the one doing the shouting."

"Ha!" Dot sat back and crossed her legs. "I'm multifaceted! Who knew?"

"Yeah, yeah." Reggie's expression softened. "Really though, I think this thing with Kat has chilled you out some. Overall, I mean. You seem happier."

Dot's eyes fell and a grin crept across her face.

"I like it," Reggie said. "It looks good on you."

* * *

"Thank you so much! I'm really glad you like it!" Kat pocketed a crisp twenty-dollar bill as a smiling patron walked away with one of her unframed Lady Godiva prints. That made nine sales so far today—a hundred and fifty dollars all together.

Kat turned around and scanned the tent again, as had become habit at this point. Hours into the event, it still felt daunting to have her art physically displayed for sale. To be peddling it in person. She kept checking to make sure everything looked neat and professional.

The vendor tent was dark green, with canvas "walls"—heavy curtains, really—on three sides, leaving only the front open. The framed prints were hung directly on the canvas. Ideally, Kat would have had sturdier, actual walls or some other display device, but she was making do on a tight budget. As it was, a strong breeze would occasionally rattle the frames and leave some of them crooked, so Kat was constantly adjusting them.

The boxes of unframed prints were set up on a long table under the wall on the right. A single folding chair sat vacant in the back. Kat hadn't done much sitting since arriving on site that morning.

She made the rounds again, anxiously straightening each frame, starting with the left wall. Every so often, she would stop to wipe a fingerprint from glass, or simply to scrutinize the quality of a photo, judging herself in hindsight for things she might have done differently.

Near the end of the right side, above the table, hung one such photo—an eleven-by-fourteen-inch print in a sixteen-by-twenty frame. It was a shot from the shadowy interior of a decrepit old house. The browns and greys of dust and rotting wood dominated the foreground. Off-center to the left was a large window, through which could be seen a landscape of lush, colorful vegetation under a bright sun, stretching off to the horizon.

When she'd taken the photo, Kat had loved the contrast between the indoor and outdoor scenes. She remembered being so proud of her find. But looking at it now, she questioned its worthiness in taking up a framed spot on the wall. It was an older photo, after all. Her technique had improved since those days. Examining it now, she sensed glaring errors in exposure, light balance, positioning . . . God, she really hadn't made the most of that shot. The print had been one of Dot's picks. One of her favorites, actually. But people coming into the tent hadn't been paying it much mind, and Kat wondered if it just didn't measure up next to her other pieces. Maybe she ought to switch it out, put a different print in the frame.

Kat unhooked the frame from the canvas wall and laid it at the end of the table. She sidled over to the nearest box and began flipping through prints, seeking a suitable replacement. Another abandoned building scene? Maybe one of her most recent pieces, something more expertly shot?

"May I ask what you're doing with this one?"

"Hm?" Kat looked up to find a woman delicately lifting the frame off the table.

"Has it sold already?"

She was a striking figure—taller than Kat, with an air of cool authority. Her voice was deep, full and decisive, with just the faintest creak. She wore an outfit of loose, flowing linen. The orange fabric, with flecks of copper and gold, complimented her warm, caramel brown complexion. Select pieces of silver jewelry served to tie in the silver of her short-cropped, curly hair. Her discerning eyes were focused sharply on the image in her hands.

"No." Kat's immediate reaction was to reach for the frame, but she stopped herself. "I'm switching that print out for something else."

The woman frowned. "Now why would you do that?"

Kat cleared her throat. "Well, it doesn't seem to be, uh . . . holding anyone's attention for long. Until now, I guess." She felt nervous all of a sudden, as though her art was being graded while she watched.

"Mmm. Have a little faith in your work, my dear." The words were at once admonishing and assuring.

"Faith?"

The woman was silent for a moment as she continued to examine the photograph. "Give it time to speak to the right person." She looked up at Kat. Her gaze still carried scrutiny, though of a gentler sort than she'd been giving the photo. "Tell me, why did you choose to frame this print in the first place?"

"I . . . didn't, actually. My girlfriend did."

"Hm!" The woman grinned, her eyes softening. "Well, she has good taste. It's my favorite of the lot."

"You've seen the rest?" Kat glanced around the tent.

"Oh yes. While you were busy criticizing yourself over here, I toured the collection."

"Ah." Kat winced. "Sorry, I didn't mean to ignore you."

The woman chuckled. "It's quite alright. I understand."

Kat raised a skeptical eyebrow. "So that's really your favorite?"

"If I'm being honest, it's hard to decide. But I do truly adore this one. How much are you asking?"

Kat had spent hours the day before mulling over prices. With nine sales under her belt now, she'd learned to quote them with some confidence. "Thirty with the frame."

The woman cringed. Cringed!

Kat panicked. "I can go lower!"

The woman shook her head. She put the frame down and stepped closer to Kat. "Darling, listen." She reached into her purse and pulled out her wallet. "I've appraised a lot of art in my time. Bought many, many pieces. I have an eye for it." She placed a hand on Kat's arm and looked her in the eye. "Now, I'm going to pay you what I think it's worth, and I don't want to hear any arguments."

That last comment snapped the remaining nervousness out of Kat. Who did this woman think she was? Kat would go as low as twenty-five for the print and the frame, but lower than that and she would *have* to argue. She had to hold to some standard if she ever hoped to make a living at this.

Before Kat could muster a response, the woman pressed a single folded bill into her hand. Kat gripped it with her thumb, furrowed her brow, and looked down.

A hundred dollars.

Kat's heart started to race.

One. Hundred. Dollars.

She looked at the woman. This couldn't be right. "H-how much do you want back?"

"Oh, honey." The woman spoke frankly, without missing a beat. "That's all yours. You are a rare talent." She picked up the frame and admired the print again. "I know just where I'm going to hang this."

Kat was speechless.

The woman turned to her again. "What's your name, my girl?"

Kat swallowed. "Katrina. Brooks."

"Verona." She extended a hand. Kat took it. "You're the highlight of my day, I'm telling you. Do you have a card with your information? A website?"

"I . . . I don't have a card, but I'll write it down." No business cards? Stupid! Kat would have to remedy that soon. She reached under the table for her purse, which she'd hidden in one of the empty boxes. She found a pen, but paper was not forthcoming.

Verona spoke with patience and ease. "Just write it on the bag, dear. I'm not fussy."

Of course, a bag! She hadn't even offered one. Get it together, Kat!

Paper bags were tucked sideways between two of the boxes on the table. Kat pulled one from the stack and quickly jotted her name, website, and email in the upper corner. Then she held it open while Verona deftly slipped the frame into it.

"Wonderful." Verona smiled warmly. "I can't wait to see where your art takes you. Well done, Ms. Brooks."

"Thank you." Kat was near-breathless, a mix of excitement and disbelief still gripping her. "Thank you so much."

"My pleasure. Good luck to you."

When Verona had left the tent, Kat finally sat down in the chair, still gripping the hundred-dollar bill. She was already rethinking her prices. Were her pieces really worth that much? And even if they were, was it reasonable to expect that much at a street fair like this? Regardless, maybe she should ask a little more than she had been. She grabbed a paper bag, folded it in quarters, and started listing the different print sizes.

* * *

"A hundred bucks for one piece?" Dot's jaw dropped, and her eyes went wide. She swept Kat up in her arms and lifted her off the ground. "I knew it! I told you your stuff is worth more!"

Kat grinned ear to ear as her feet touched down again. "Okay, yes, you were right!" She rested her hands on Dot's shoulders. "I re-priced after that. Take a look and tell me what you think." She nodded toward the table, where she'd left her price notes.

Dot picked up the folded paper bag and read down the list. "I don't see any hundred-dollar listing here."

"Well, see, I figured even if Verona was right about the value, I don't think the average person would pay that much. So I compromised." Kat looked over Dot's shoulder at the notes. "They're still over twice what they were, which is big."

"No kidding! Have you sold any at the new prices?"

"No, but it's only been like twenty minutes." Kat drifted away from Dot, toward the front of the tent, and peeked out along the path. "I need to get business cards, too. She asked for one, and I ended up writing my info on the bag."

Dot spied the pen on the table. "That's not a bad idea, ya know. For today, in lieu of cards." She put the notes down and slid the stack of bags out from between the boxes. "I can start on that now."

Kat whirled around. "You don't have to do that. *I* should be—"

"You should be ready to greet customers. I got this." Dot sat down with the bags and grabbed the pen.

"Okay. Then . . . thanks." Kat wandered back into the tent and went about adjusting the frames again.

Dot soon had a rhythm going, writing name, email, and website on one bag after another. "So this woman. She wanted your info. Do you think she'll buy more prints?"

"Maybe. She sounded like an avid collector, and she did say something about seeing where I go with my art."

"That sounds promising!" Dot finished her tenth bag, flipped the corner down, and started on the eleventh.

"Yeah, it got me thinking, actually. About what I want to do next." A hint of concern entered Kat's tone. "I haven't added anything new to my portfolio in months, 'cause I haven't come across, ya know, inspiration—the right subject."

Dot looked up from her task. "I'm sure you'll find something. When you least expect it, probably."

"Well, I was about to say, there *was* one thing recently. Or technically a bunch of things." Kat slowly pivoted to face Dot, biting her lip. "And I want to ask you if it's okay."

Dot tilted her head, oblivious as to where Kat was going with this. "If what's okay?"

"Your sculptures."

Dot blinked. The words took a moment to sink in, then her eyes went wide. "Oh! You wanna take pictures of . . . of my . . . ?"

"Yeah. If it's okay with you." Kat had that pleading look in her eyes.

Dot sat up straight. "Of course! You're more than welcome to!"

The concern was wiped from Kat's face. Excitement began creeping in to replace it.

Dot continued, "Yeah, you don't even need to ask. I'm just surprised. I mean, *that's* your one thing? My junk art?"

"Yes! Without a doubt." Kat beamed as though she was barely containing herself. "Sometimes you find a subject that just calls to you, ya know? It demands to be photographed. And the moment I stepped into your studio, I heard that call from all directions."

Dot chuckled self-consciously. She looked down, her eyes scanning the web address she'd just written. "Okay, if you heard the call, then go with it."

Kat walked over, kneeled next to Dot, and kissed her on the cheek. "Thank you."

Dot turned and gave her a peck on the lips. Then she frowned in thought. "Wait, so—you took all those pictures of *me* that day. Didn't you take any of the sculptures?"

Kat shook her head. "No, I was too nervous to ask you back then. Taking pictures of *you* is one thing, but shooting your art—using *your* art to make *my* art—I don't know, that felt like a whole other level."

Dot gave her a knowing smile. "I'm happy to have you make art out of my art. Anyway, you'll probably make it look better than it does in real life."

"Hey, friends! Happy Pride!" Jet rounded the corner of the tent, wearing a purple tee shirt that identified her as a Pridefest volunteer. "How's business?"

"Jet!" Dot put an arm around Kat and pointed to her. "She sold a piece for a hundred bucks! To some big-time collector!"

"No way!" Jet bounded into the tent, her slender frame radiating enthusiasm.

Kat blushed. "It wasn't like . . . I don't know . . ."

Dot side-eyed her and smirked. "You're gonna act like it wasn't a big deal?"

"Eh heh." Kat grinned. "Okay, it was kind of a big deal."

Jet opened her arms toward them both. "It's totally a big deal! You two should celebrate! I was actually just coming by to see if you've had a chance to walk around Pridefest and see everything."

Kat shook her head. "I haven't been away from this tent since setup this morning."

"Yeah, I was here with her before my CRD shift," Dot said. "I haven't seen much else."

"Well, you should!" Jet's eyebrows rose. "What if I watch the tent for a while? You guys can get lunch and enjoy the festivities. Vee's band is going on in like ten minutes at the pavilion."

Kat turned to Dot, then back to Jet. "You'd do that?"

"Of course! Go have some fun together!"

Dot was already a step ahead. She held up the stack of bags and showed Jet the writing. "Just make sure if anybody buys anything, use the bags with Kat's info on them. And here's the price list." She grabbed Kat's notes off the table and thrust them at Jet.

Jet laughed. "Okay! I got it!"

"Sorry, it's kind of an amateur setup." Kat dug in her pocket. "I'll leave some cash with you for change, and my phone for credit cards."

"Oh, right." Jet's tone sobered up. "That would be pretty important."

A few minutes later, Jet was all set to watch the shop. With a promise to return in an hour, Dot and Kat left the tent. They walked hand in hand, matching bracelets side by side.

As they hit the path leading toward the pavilion, Kat gave Dot's fingers a squeeze. "Thank you for everything you did getting ready for today. I couldn't have pulled this off without you."

Dot just looked at her and smiled. When their eyes met, she could feel her cheeks flushing. This moment felt so much like that first day they'd spent together. The same rush of connection, the same natural feeling. Only, now she wasn't questioning it. She just felt extremely lucky.

When Dot looked forward again, she spotted the old cannon up ahead on their right. "Fancy a shift in front of the cannon?"

"A what now?"

Dot snickered. "It's something Vee said to Domme. *Shift* means *make out*."

"Ah! Well then I do fancy a shift! Also, what's the deal with those two? Are they dating?"

Chapter 11

Game On

_____

Aunt Kitty,

It's really you! I've been looking for you off and on for so long, I can't believe I found you. Now I really don't know where to begin. I feel like there's so much to say.

I guess I'll start by saying yes, I totally agree to your terms. I am 100% not trying to get you to come back, I promise. And I'll do my best not to mention anything that's happened with the Jacobses since you left.

Frankly, I can't wait to get out of here in August and get away from them. I don't know where your faith stands these days, but I've been gravitating toward a much more progressive interpretation of the Bible, and of course that's not something I can talk about at home. But I've connected with some people online who think like me. Once I get to school, I want to check out a UCC congregation.

On a different note, I've been to your website. Your work is beyond words, Aunt Kitty. It's inspiring. All these years later, I still find myself hoping to be like you when I grow up. What else have you been doing? What's life in Crosscannon like? I'm excited to catch up. And you can ask me anything—I'm an open book!

With love,
E

Dot looked up from the phone. She leaned back against the screen printing table and took in the scene around her. The studio was certainly a different sight than it had been only two hours prior.

She and Kat had placed the big, old, heavy table under the center window, long edge against the wall. They'd covered it with a huge swath of black velour, and behind it they'd draped a curtain of the same fabric, such that it both blocked the light from outside and served as a photo backdrop. On the floor next to the table stood a pair of telescoping light stands with diffusion umbrellas attached.

A smaller table near the computer desk had become home to a box of light filters as well as Kat's camera bag, in which Kat was currently digging. She had lenses and accessories strewn about the tabletop.

Next to Dot, taking up the last bit of open surface on the screen printing table, there sat a stack of assorted fabrics—alternate backdrop materials, Kat had said. She'd collected them over the years for cheap, mostly at TSM. They included a bleach white cotton fabric, a natural beige muslin, and other materials in green, brown, and grey.

Kat looked up from the camera bag and surveyed the room. "Shit. I kinda took the place over, didn't I?"

"Hm?"

"Sorry. Once I'm all set up, I'll move the things I'm not using into a corner."

"Oh!" Realization hit Dot. "No, I'm just marveling at how quickly you jumped into this project. I thought you'd want a break after Pride."

Kat chuckled. "Are you kidding? This *is* my break. This is what I'm most excited about doing." She resumed searching the bag's pouches. "I won't have a chance to work on it again for like a week, so I want to get started while I can."

Dot's brow furrowed. "A week?"

"Yeah, you know I have that gig at the restaurant on Wednesday." Kat would be doing photos for the new vegan place opening in Crosscannon.

"I know, but you're staying over Thursday and Friday, right?"

"I am, but I won't have time to do *this*." Kat gestured vaguely around the studio. "I'll be busy editing photos from Wednesday. And then I'm reffing Skyline Valley's double header on Saturday, and a hangover bout the next morning. I won't get home until late Sunday."

Dot cringed. "Damn, you have a long week ahead of you."

"Yep. No rest for the wicked, as they say."

Dot looked up and glared at the familiar green face hanging above the computer desk. "You're sure you want to waste your free time on these . . . things?"

Kat followed Dot's gaze. She didn't answer right away, instead taking a moment to admire the piece. "You really are hard on yourself as an artist." She turned back to Dot with sympathetic eyes. "You can't see how, just, utterly beautiful your creations are?"

A reluctant smirk emerged on Dot's face. She folded her arms. "I mean, they're *okay*. But the way *you* look at them, you'd think they were masterpieces."

Kat tilted her head. "If they're only okay, then what's motivated you to keep at it all these years?"

"I don't know. I feel like I have to." Dot lowered her eyes and stared at the desk while she contemplated how best to explain. "I find materials . . . and I see the potential of what they could be. And yes, if I could accomplish what I see in my head, it would be beautiful. But I always fall short."

Listening intently, Kat stepped around the small table and moved toward Dot.

Dot went on, "I guess with each new piece, I think maybe this is the one where I get it right."

Kat frowned. "You don't think you've ever gotten it right?"

"Hm!" Dot shook her head. "Not even close. If I could show you what that mask was *supposed* to look like . . ."

"Supposed to, huh?" Facing away from the mask now, Kat took a long look at the dragon in the opposite corner. And the pegasus. "I think maybe you're unduly punishing yourself, hon. Nothing ever turns out exactly like the original vision." She stepped into Dot's line of sight and met her eyes. "How about this? I'm gonna make it my mission to show you what *I* see. To show you your art through my eyes."

Dot raised her eyebrows, at once curious and doubtful. Much as she would love to see whatever the hell Kat was seeing, a photograph wouldn't show it. It was all in Kat's head. But Dot didn't have the heart to voice her cynicism directly.

"That . . . would be something," was all she could manage.

Kat smiled. Now standing just inches away, she reached out and spoke softly while straightening Dot's bra strap. "So yes, I'm sure I want to spend my free time on these *things*. There's nothing else I'd rather be doing."

At those words, Dot's eyes took on a playful glint. Her focus drifted down to Kat's lips. Kat's proximity was igniting some alternative ideas.

"Nothing else? Really?" Dot unfolded her arms and placed the phone on the table beside her. "Not even that thing you did with your tongue last night?"

"Oho!" Kat's jaw dropped into an open-mouth grin. "We're going *there*, are we? Well, it is fun watching the way you wiggle when I do that, I have to say."

"Wiggle?" Dot laughed. "That sounds real sexy. I'm sure you made me do more than wiggle."

Eyes half-lidded now, Kat put her hands against the table on either side of Dot. Barely making any bodily contact, she purred in Dot's ear. "And writhe. And shake."

Dot had actually thought, for a moment there, that she might be the one to play seductress this time. But suddenly Kat was giving her a lesson on how it's done. Somehow Kat seemed able to flip a switch and make Dot's knees go weak.

"Hold still." Kat brought her face in front of Dot's again. "Is this what you mean?" Tilting her head sideways, she extended her tongue and ran it across Dot's parted lips. In slow motion, she mimicked the strokes she'd performed *elsewhere* on Dot the night before.

Dot remained obediently unmoving while Kat's slick tongue glided back and forth, tracing her upper lip, then her lower. Dot's clit throbbed with the memory of that sensation, sending a wave of heat surging throughout her body. Her breath was stilted as she uttered her response.

"Uh . . . uh-huh."

Kat withdrew her tongue to speak. "But we have all night for this, baby." She gave Dot's lips one last, slow lick. "I'll tell you what—you help me get the mask off the wall and hung in front of the backdrop, and tonight I'll make your legs shake 'til you forget how to skate."

Dot nodded, searching for words in the pink haze that had overtaken her mind. "Just, uh . . . give me a second here to remember how to *walk*."

Kat laughed and kissed Dot earnestly, shaking off the sultry act. She took Dot by the hand and stepped back, pulling her away from the table.

"Alright, alright." Dot scanned the room for the mini stepladder they'd been using. She found it under the window on the left and moved it next to the computer desk.

Kat stood beside her, examining the mask. "So, here's my idea. I'd like to suspend it from the ceiling if I can. I have some invisible wire that's rated for fifty pounds." She turned to look at the ceiling above the backdrop. "The track lighting rail looks pretty sturdy, and we could hook it to the curtain rods for stability. Do you think that would support it?"

Dot gave a cursory glance at the track lighting. "Yeah, that should work fine. It's really not that heavy." She ascended the ladder, with one hand against the wall for support. She reached her other hand through the eye of the mask, easily lifted it off its hook, and passed it down to Kat, who took it gingerly with both hands.

"Wow, it's lighter than I would have guessed!" Kat carried it across the room and laid it gently on the velour-covered table.

"One of us might need to stand on that table, actually," Dot said. "To reach the ceiling."

Kat looked up. "Ah, good point."

"Just lay it on the floor. It'll be okay." Dot finished descending the ladder, then picked it up to move it under the track lights.

After some searching for a suitable location, Kat set the mask down on the drop cloth.

As Dot eyed the long, steel rail that held the lights above her, she couldn't help but feel she'd gotten sidetracked from something—some good news she'd meant to share with Kat. "*Oh!*"

"What?" Kat turned with a start.

"Before we get into this, you should read Eli's email."

Kat gasped, her face aglow with anticipation. "So it's good?"

"From what I can tell. Sounds like he accepts your terms with enthusiasm."

"Oh my god, that's great!" Kat practically leapt to the screen printing table and scooped up her phone.

"Ah!" Dot raised a hand. "Speaking of god, there was one thing in there I didn't know. What does UCC stand for?"

"UCC." Kat paused with her finger over the phone's screen. "United Church of Christ?"

Dot shrugged. "He's thinking about joining it. Is that good?"

Kat's eyes widened. "Good? That's awesome! Holy shit, his parents would kill him."

"For joining a different church?" Dot squinted in confusion.

"Well, for joining a liberal church, specifically. UCC is really open and accepting. Cool with queer and trans folks, very social-justice-oriented. Our family would say it's been corrupted by Satan's influence and that it's a mockery of Christianity."

"Oh, so two thumbs up, then!"

Kat laughed. "Exactly!" She returned her attention to the phone and tapped the screen. "Okay, lemme read this."

Dot nodded. She turned her own attention back to the task at hand, locating the spool of wire next to the camera bag. There were no wire cutters to be seen, but she knew the toolbox in the storage closet contained a pair.

They spent the next couple of hours on this rainy Monday afternoon working out the kinks in their makeshift wire rig. It took countless adjustments to get the mask positioned *just right*. But thanks partly to Eli's message, the mood remained positive in the face of little frustrations. When they were done, the visage of the green goddess hovered center-stage in a sea of black velour. Even Dot had to admit there was a magical quality to it.

* * *

TWEEET!

"White five, blocking out of play!"

Dot didn't look at the ref. She left the track without a word. But as much as she tried to pretend otherwise, she knew it was Kat who'd made the call. Dot could avoid looking, but she couldn't avoid hearing.

She sat down in the penalty box, closed her eyes, and exhaled. Their first scrimmage with the agreement in place, and she could already tell how difficult this was going to be. Not looking at Kat, not reacting to her—it took tremendous force of will. It was exhausting. Not to mention it meant Dot wasn't letting off any steam. She just kept swallowing her anger. Bottling it up.

TWEET-TWEET-TWEET-TWEET!

The jam ended with Dot in the box. Jaw clenched, she leaned back in her chair and rolled her eyes up to look at Pixie.

Pixie checked her now-paused stopwatch. "Twelve seconds."

"Thanks." Dot turned back to the track to find the white team had fielded a full four blockers. Unbelievable. Was no one paying attention?

"YO, WHITE! AM I *INVISIBLE* OVER HERE?" Her ire rang out through the venue. Startled eyes looked at her from all directions. She threw her hands up. "What! I can't yell at my own teammates now?"

Kara exited the track, leaving three white blockers. That had been the whole point, but Dot could still feel eyes judging her. She folded her arms defiantly.

TWEEET!

Start of a new jam.

"White five, stand."

Ten seconds later, Dot was released back into the fray. She managed to get through the last five minutes of the first period with no further penalties. That put her at three, going into halftime.

She retrieved her water bottle from the rink wall with the intention of refilling it at the fountain. But she thought better of that idea when she spotted Kat heading in the same direction. Whatever. Water could wait.

"HEAVY METAL!" Coach Rex's voice boomed. She had a way of shouting with a cool, commanding tone, quite unlike Dot's abrasive outburst. "Take a minute to do whatever you need to do, then meet me in the corner!"

Good, another strategy discussion. That would keep Dot's mind occupied—and keep her from accidentally making eye contact with Kat.

"Mouse, do you have a minute?"

Dot turned to find Coach's authoritative gaze fixed on her. "Uh. Yeah, what for?"

"What for?" Coach quirked an eyebrow. "Come on, Mouse. It's pretty obvious you aren't quite yourself tonight."

"Ehh. Yeah. See, Kat and I—"

"Yeah yeah, I know about the thing with Kat. The deal you two made where you're not acknowledging each other."

Dot swallowed. "You do?"

"Of course I do. I'm your coach." She put a hand on Dot's shoulder.

"Look, how you guys decide to navigate that whole thing is none of my business. But its effect on your play *is* my business."

Dot cringed. "Shit. Am I doing that bad out there?"

"Well ... not exactly. You're not playing poorly, as an individual. It's just that you're playing like you're out there by yourself." Coach glanced at the bench area. "It's like you're not just ignoring Kat, you're ignoring everybody. You haven't even been talking to your teammates on the sidelines tonight."

Dot closed her eyes and sighed. "Yeah. I know. I'm sorry, Coach."

"Hey, look at me." Coach waited for Dot to open her eyes again. "It's okay. I don't need you to be sorry. I just need you to focus. You know these plays and strategies better than anyone, and your teammates need you to lead them on the track."

"I ..." Dot was taken off guard. A compliment like that from Coach Rex was a rare thing. She seemed to reserve them for moments when her skaters most needed to hear them. Dot's heart swelled with pride, but she found herself speechless.

"Forget how many penalties you have. Leave the refs to me. Just talk to your teammates and focus on the game. Can you do that?"

Dot nodded.

Coach smiled. "Good. Now let's get everyone else on board. We have a bout to win in less than three weeks."

* * *

Gameplay wasn't the hard part for Kat. She just went into ref mode and did what she did best. It was ignoring Dot the rest of the time—while gearing up at the beginning of practice, and between jams. She'd had to part ways with Dot at the studio so the two of them could drive to scrimmage separately and begin this whole charade. That had felt awful.

Come halftime, Kat actually found herself missing the old tension. She'd have preferred getting barked at to this total non-interaction. Treating Dot like a stranger, constantly avoiding eye-contact—it just felt wrong. At least she didn't really need to think about it while Dot was busy with the team meeting.

For her part, Kat spent the break talking to Smith about carpool arrangements to Virginia, for the Skyline Valley bouts. On her budget, there was no way Kat could afford gas and hotel costs alone. But packing four officials into one car made a big difference, and they'd be crashing at a friend's place for free—one of SVRD's skaters, whom Smith knew from way back, had offered couches and guest beds.

TWEEeeeEET!

End of halftime. Good. Back to work for one more period, and then Kat could gear down and get the hell out of here. She returned to her position on the infield as inside pack ref.

Dot rolled onto the track and set herself in formation with her teammates. As usual, she took the brace position.

"Five seconds!"

TWEEET!

From the first moment of the first jam, Kat could tell something was different. The white defense was stronger, more solid. White five was more controlled. Whatever Coach had said to her, it must have had an impact. But Kat couldn't ponder that thought right now. She filed it away and focused on the present.

White five moved with precision, providing support to her teammates. She directed them so as to counter the black team's attempts at offense. Black nine-seven rolled to the outside lane, and white five was there like a mirror twin to block her. Black's offensive assist plowed a hole through the center. The white defense let her through and reformed immediately behind her, staying focused on the jammer.

Move for move, white five was playing the game like a chess match, always one step ahead of her opponents—rotating her team to fill gaps before they even appeared, catching the black jammer in tricky traps on the inside and outside lines. All maneuvers that required the white blockers to work in tandem.

When the black jammer finally did break through, white five stayed with her teammates and quickly switched to offense. She read the black defense like a book, called out the play, and the white skaters swiftly opened a lane for their own jammer.

This trend continued, jam after jam. On rare occasion, white five would go rogue, go for the big hit, and almost get herself into trouble, but a quick "Mouse!" from Coach Rex was enough to rein her back in.

With about eight minutes left in the second period, Coach called an extended time-out to give everyone a rest. It also gave Kat a chance to reflect. She'd always known Dot to be a formidable skater, but this was something else. She was proving to be quite a mastermind of the game as well. Not only that, but she was playing cleaner than ever, only picking up one more penalty since halftime.

Following the timeout, Kat resumed her duties for a handful of jams, but before she knew it the clock had run down and the final whistle was blown. Mercifully, the second period seemed to have flown by.

Kat was in awe. She wanted so much to skate over to Dot and congratulate her on a scrim well-played, but she knew that was off-limits. Much as Kat hated this agreement, she wanted to respect it. And anyway, what if it had something to do with this turnaround in Dot's play? God, if Dot could stay focused and perform like this at MAD, Heavy Metal would make it into playoffs for sure. Kat definitely didn't want to mess that up. Maybe it would be best to avoid talking about scrim at all, then, even outside the rink.

In any case, she was still itching to get out of here and drop this pretense. She picked up her water bottle and hurried to the changing area. Within seconds of her butt hitting the seat, her skates were untied and off her feet. She tore her helmet off, removed her gear with purposeful haste, and was packed up before some of the skaters had even left the rink floor.

"So we're on for Saturday?" Smith came rolling leisurely in Kat's direction.

Kat stood up and extended the handle on her skate bag. "Yeah, you'll message me when you know the time for sure?"

"You got it." Smith moved closer and lowered his voice. "And good job tonight. I know it couldn't have been easy, given the thing with Mouse. You're a—"

"You know about that?" Kat narrowed her eyes at Smith.

Smith shrugged. "Hey, it's derby. There are no secrets."

Kat groaned. If Smith knew, then everyone knew.

"Don't sweat it." He patted her on the arm. "I'm rooting for you two."

"Yeah. Thanks."

Kat strapped her purse across her body and offered Smith a little farewell wave. As she turned toward the exit, she glanced in Dot's direction. Old habit. Luckily Dot wasn't looking, but Jet caught Kat's eye and grinned. Kat smiled back before marching out the door.

Almost there. She crossed the parking lot, unlocked her car, and threw her bag in the trunk. Once in the driver's seat, she dug her phone out of her purse. Then she sat back and watched the rink doors through the rear view mirror.

She didn't have to wait long. Dot burst out into the parking lot with Lynn close behind. They split up and headed for their respective vehicles. Kat looked down at her phone and started a new text—to Dot, Lynn, and Jet.

Diner?

As soon as Dot climbed into her van and closed the door, Kat hit "send." Now it was up to Dot. If she needed time alone, Kat would just have to be pat—

Buzzzz.

See you there, baby <3

Chapter 12

Bliss

Hi E!

I know, I always called you buddy, but you were a little kid then. I'm thinking maybe I'll let it go. What are your thoughts? What should I call you now that you're grown?

Thank you for agreeing to my requests. That's a huge relief, and it really means a lot to me. Honestly, it's also a relief to hear that you've found a more progressive understanding of your faith. I know it's hard for you at home right now, but it'll get easier once you get to school. I think you'll really like the UCC. As for me, I still have a kind of faith. I take a very liberal view these days. I'd love to pick your brain about this stuff if you want to get into some scholarly religion talk.

Life in Crosscannon is good! Busy, for me. I try to make a living as an event photographer, but I still dream of supporting myself with my art. I sold some prints at a local festival on Saturday. That was a first! My other passion is roller derby. I'm a referee for the league here in Crosscannon, but I travel a lot to help other leagues too (going to Virginia this weekend). That's a subject I could go on about for days.

So, my main question for you, before anything else: How on Earth did you find me? How did you know to look for Katrina Brooks? That has me very curious.

Love always,
Aunt Kitty

* * *

"This week has been dragging, Lynn." Sunday afternoon, Dot was once again seated cross-legged on the drop cloth, with the hobby paints to her right and the dragon in front of her. She was staring into one of the beast's cat-like eyes. "I'm telling you, I don't know what I did with my time before she came along."

Lynn set her sketchbook down on the drawing table and put her backpack on the chair. "What do you mean? She's been around this week, hasn't she? She just left yesterday morning." She started pulling art supplies out of the backpack—fresh erasers and pencil sharpeners, a new bottle of turpenoid solvent, and a pack of colorless blending pencils.

"Well yeah, but she's been so busy this week." Dot screwed the lid back onto a tiny bottle of purple paint. She squinted at the dragon. "God dammit. Why do these eyes look so cartoony?"

"I thought she was here, though. Didn't she bring her laptop over?" Lynn set her bag on the floor, then walked leisurely toward Dot. "And you've been at that damn dragon's eyeballs for days. It's not like you've been twiddling your thumbs."

"I know." Dot sighed. "It's different, though. We're in our own little worlds. I miss working *with* her like we did on the Pride project."

Lynn grinned. "Aw, sounds like the honeymoon's over. Back to the grind for both of you." She crouched behind Dot, looking over her shoulder, and examined the dragon's face. "Those eyes look great! I don't know what you're complaining about."

"No, they look stupid," Dot muttered. "I'm going for realistic here. They just don't look . . . I don't know. *Believable*."

"Hmh." Lynn shook her head. "Dude, it's a dragon made of soda cans. It's not gonna look realistic up close like this. Stand back and look at it. It really does come to life then. That's how all your stuff works."

Dot groaned. "That's fine and all, but what if she takes close-up shots?"

"Oh! Ha! Now I see what's going on here." Lynn stood up and backed away. She turned and headed for the fridge.

Dot twisted around to face her. "What?"

"You. Obsessing over that one little detail all week." Lynn bent down and pulled an IPA off the door of the fridge. "I knew it seemed unusual." She popped the cap, turned around and leaned against the corner of the wall near the entryway. "You want it to look perfect for picture day, don't you?"

Dot put down the paint and brush. She got to her feet and ambled in Lynn's direction, eyeing the fridge herself. "Anything good left in there?"

"Just IPAs. You want one?"

"Yeah, I guess that'll work."

Lynn opened another bottle while Dot shook the blood back into her legs.

"Thanks." Dot accepted the beer and took a swig before continuing. "So, maybe I do want it to look perfect. Wouldn't you? No one's ever photographed my shit like this. The whole world's gonna see it now."

She leaned back against the screen printing table. The space between the two of them, where the big table would normally be, remained conspicuously open.

Dot's eyes went to the mask hovering in relative darkness, unmoved since Monday. "I'm thinking of revisiting my old pieces too. Refining some of the details. What do you think?"

Lynn shot her a cautioning glare. "Don't you dare start down that road, Dot. You'll never be happy, no matter how much you do to them."

"But—"

"Leave them be."

Dot froze, biting her tongue.

Lynn went on, "Trust me. From one artist to another. That way lies madness."

Dot exhaled. She scanned the room, giving each of her pieces a critical look.

Lynn sipped her beer, watching Dot thoughtfully. "*Trust*, Dot. You know Kat's work. You know she has incredible instincts, right?"

Dot nodded.

"She wants to photograph your work just the way it is. Even if you don't understand that, you gotta trust her. Show her that you believe in her."

Believe. Lynn certainly had a way of giving perspective, setting Dot's faith in herself, which was admittedly lacking in this arena, against her faith in Kat.

"I do believe in her," Dot said. "It's just . . . it's occurring to me that this is gonna be the first big exposure I get. This isn't just her project, ya know? I'm entrusting my fate to her instincts, here. It's not easy."

Lynn chuckled. "First big exposure, huh? You make it sound like a magazine spread or something." She pushed off the wall and approached Dot with arms folded and an understanding smile. "It's never easy. But if it helps, I think you're making this a bigger deal than it actually is. It's just Kat's Instagram and her website. The only way it's gonna go beyond that is if people really like it, and if that's the case then you have nothing to worry about anyway."

"Heh." Dot's cheeks turned rosy. She glanced at Lynn, then looked down. "Alright. Point taken." She blew out a breath. "Maybe I am getting ahead of myself."

"It's okay." Lynn walked past Dot and headed for the drawing table. "I know what it's like. I've had my work in publications before, and it's on all the Burger Life stuff. It's always nerve-wracking. You just learn not to show it." She sat down facing Dot. "Try to relax. Kat'll be home soon, won't she?"

Dot straightened up. "Not for a few hours yet." She carried her beer over to the computer desk, taking a seat beside Lynn. "But I haven't checked email in a while. She's been waiting for a message from someone, and she was gonna forward it to me if it came this weekend."

"Good. As long as it gets your mind off that dragon." Lynn started unwrapping her new supplies and putting things away.

Dot opened the web browser and navigated to her inbox. She had a few messages waiting. There was a confirmation of her weekend pass to MAD. There was an email from her mom, asking if she'd like to visit in July. And yes, there was one from Kat, but the subject wasn't what Dot had been expecting—"Fwd: Lovely meeting you at Pridefest."

> Baby! We're just hitting the road now. I couldn't wait until I got home to share this with you! I'm too excited! xoxo – K

> – – – – –

> Ms. Brooks,

> I hope the rest of your day at Pridefest was fruitful and enjoyable. Your print is prominently displayed in my office. I don't mind telling you it's gotten more than a few compliments over this past week, and deservedly so!

> The selection of work you brought to Pride was only the tip of the iceberg, I see. You continue to impress me as I peruse the galleries on your website. I won't waste time flattering you, though. After decades of doing what I do, I've found words are cheap unless one is prepared to back them up. So I shall cut to the backing.

> I would like to host an exhibition featuring a selection of your work, at no cost to you. We would go over the details together in person before setting any plans in stone. All I seek from you at this time is confirmation of your interest. Please contact me as soon as possible by phone or email.

Your true devotee,

Verona Fairchild
Owner/Director, Warfield Gallery

"Uhh. Lynn."
 "Yeah?"
 "Does an exhibition at the Warfield count as big exposure?"

* * *

That night, Kat's phone buzzed on the nightstand. She reached out carefully, so as not to wake Dot, and tilted it to look at the screen. Email notification: "Eli Jacobs – How I found you."

She picked up the phone, bringing it closer and resting it sideways against the mattress. Dot's arm was nestled snugly around her. She could feel Dot's warm breath against her neck. Kat knew this email had to contain things she was nervous about facing, but she couldn't ask for a safer or more comforting place in which to read it. She tapped the screen to open it.

Aunt Kitty,

You can still call me buddy! E is fine too, if you want to try it on for size, but I don't mind buddy. You were the only one who called me that, so it was always a special thing to me.

Sorry for the delay getting back to you. This is kind of a long story, and I wanted to find some time to sit down and type it all out. I have to warn you, it might bring up some memories that are difficult for you. I don't know for sure, because I don't have all the details. I'm actually hoping maybe you'll fill in the blanks. If you want to. No pressure. At this point it would only be to satisfy my own curiosity.

I never forgot about you after you left. Like I said, I searched for you off and on. Every few years I would get curious and go looking for answers. Your disappearance was always this great mystery I wanted to solve. No one else seemed interested in helping figure it out. I felt like the rebel detective who wouldn't give up on the case. There were lulls in the "investigation," of course. But the older I got, the better I understood how things worked, and I would get new ideas as far as where to look for clues. When I got access to the internet, I started searching for you there. I tried everything I could think of—Gran's maiden name, your middle name. I thought maybe you'd become a travelling missionary or something, which tells you how off-base some of my searches were, lol. I was still pretty deep in the family faith back then. Turned out they'd done a good job of hiding anything relevant that would have helped me find you.

Last year, I was up in Gran and Pop's attic. I'd never been allowed up there as a kid, and naturally that only made me more curious. Nobody stopped me this time. Either they didn't know, or they forgot what was up there. Or they thought I'd stopped looking, I don't know. Anyway, this is where things finally got interesting. I found an unlabeled shoebox full of old photos and notes and clippings. It was like stumbling on a lost treasure. Everything in there was about either you or this person named Devon Brooks, who turned out to be my great aunt. I don't remember ever hearing about her, so I knew right then that the mystery was deeper than I'd thought. In that box, I found a sticky note with a phone number—your phone number, though I wasn't sure of that until I tried calling it just recently. I also found some clues about this Devon Brooks that I could follow. I knew there had to be a reason you and she were put together in that box. There were invoices from a therapist and a rehab facility. I looked them up and found out what kind of services they provided. I also found her obituary. It said she was survived by a husband, George Brooks. He still lives nearby, so I went to see him in person.

When I found George, I think he gave me the first honest answers about any of this stuff. He tried to get me to leave at first, when he heard my last name was Jacobs. It took some perseverance to convince him I didn't know anything and I was genuinely looking for answers about you. George said he remembered you. What follows in this story, you probably already know, but it was new to me. He told me about his wife, Devon, and that it was really his sister Elizabeth who was in love with her. George married Devon for show, so she and Liz could live together without our family getting suspicious. I won't lie, I teared up a little when he told me that. I blamed teenage hormones, but really it was the sweetest thing I'd ever heard. To take a leap like that in his early 20s, for the sake of his sister's happiness . . . Talk about selfless, right?

Aunt Kitty, I know you already know the rest, so I won't mind if you don't read on. You can already see how I put together that I should look for Katrina Brooks. The rest of the story is just to let you know what I know, but I understand if it's hard to read.

So, George told me Devon was never really well. He said the marriage and everything happened in the years following her "therapy." She was still so troubled by what she'd been through, it poisoned her relationship with Liz. George didn't know all the details about that, but after a couple years Devon and Liz separated. Devon was so heartbroken, on top of the issues she already had, and she turned to drugs to cope. And of course the Jacobses blamed the drugs on her being gay, giving up on therapy, and "welcoming Satan into her life." And they blamed the Brookses for "enabling" her, which explained why George was so reluctant to talk to me.

George said he and Liz saw less and less of Devon. But he said she always had a special connection with you. That's when it really hit me that you might be using her last name. After that, it didn't take me long to find you on Facebook, which links to your website, which has your email.

That's also when I put something else together. In that shoebox—those therapy invoices. There were a bunch with Devon's name on them, but there was also one with *your* name on it—a phone consultation, dated right around the time you left. Aunt Kitty, I know what that therapy is for. I want you to know, if that's why you left, I understand. Especially after what they did to Devon, I can't blame you for disappearing.

Our family is so backwards. Didn't Jesus tell us to love each other and warn us against judging one another? I don't think they'll ever get it. I wish I'd had the chance to know Devon. And I'm not taking for granted how lucky I am to have you in my life again.

Well, that's how I found you, and then some. If you want to talk about any of this, I'll listen. If you'd rather talk about something lighter, I'd love to hear more about roller derby! Either way, I love you, and I hope you've been having a great week.

Your buddy,
E

"Is everything alright?" Dot whispered softly.

Kat put the phone back on the nightstand, then turned over to face her with watery eyes and a wide grin. "Everything's fine. I'll tell you all about it in the morning."

"Okay, good."

Dot gathered Kat into her arms and intertwined their legs. She was out cold again in seconds.

With her head nestled under Dot's chin, Kat listened to her lover's rhythmic breathing and drifted off to sleep herself.

* * *

Birds were singing outside as Kat unlocked the door to the studio, using the extra key Dot had given her. It was early—much too early for Dot to be up—but Kat couldn't wait to get back to work on her project.

It was dark inside. The windows faced west, so the sun wouldn't actually shine into the room until later in the day. Kat hit the switches in succession, and artificial light cascaded across the space.

Directly across the room, the face of the dryad hung in the air, watching her. Finally, today she would get to play with it. Kat stepped down the entryway stairs and found her camera where she'd left it, on the small table. Beside the camera was her laptop, which she opened and started up.

Kat brought up on screen the test images she'd snapped a week prior. She pulled from her camera bag a small notebook and flipped to the most recent page, where she'd written down the camera settings from those shots. She laid the notebook open on the table and went to close the shades and curtains over the two exposed windows.

Next, she turned on the diffused lights, which remained just the way she'd positioned them previously. Then she stood back and observed the subject.

She turned off the light on the left, leaving the mask illuminated from above and to the right. Hmm. No, she needed the ambient light to be dimmer. She went to the entryway and, with eyes on the mask, began turning off ceiling lights.

With some experimentation, between those and the diffused lights, she managed to find an agreeable balance. With just the right amount of shadow, the surface of the mask revealed its texture vividly—the countless tiny army men entangled together. Up close, a green sea of horror. From a distance, a face of singular beauty. Kat knew, if she could find just the right angle and lighting, and zero in the focus and exposure, she could showcase both aspects in a single shot.

Without any further fussing, she went to work. Only by testing the current setup would she know for sure what needed adjusting. With steady hands, Kat snapped a series of photos from various angles. When she was satisfied that she'd captured what she wanted, she transferred the images to the laptop for a closer look in Lightroom.

This was both the beauty and the agony of having unlimited time and control over the scene. She knew that she could sit down right now, start editing and touching up this series of photos, and she would very likely end up with some images she'd be happy with. But she also knew she could do better if she made some adjustments to the scene and tried again.

And try again she would. Over the course of the next couple hours, Kat shot and reviewed several more series of photos, making tiny changes after each pass. Fortunately, she really did enjoy this process, tedious as it could be. It was a labor of love, shaping a scene to perfectly capture a subject—and doubly so, given the source of the subject in this case.

The click of the camera. Kat's footsteps on the laminate floor. The chirping of birds outside. These were the only sounds in the otherwise silent studio—until the door creaked open and another set of footsteps entered.

"I had a feeling I'd find you in here." Dot stood in the entryway, grinning at Kat.

"I told you where I was going, silly. You must have been answering me in your sleep."

"Eh, yeah, I do that. Sorry." Dot jumped down the steps and opened the fridge, retrieving a bottle of water. "Did you eat?"

"Yeah, your dad made eggs."

"Aw, I missed eggs? I had cereal."

Kat shook her head, smiling. "If you want what's cooking, you gotta be up with the chef."

Dot raised an eyebrow. "Never heard that one before."

"Something Lonnie says." Kat looked up from the laptop. "Speaking of Lonnie, he wants to know if we're doing Third Saturday Market this weekend. I'd love for you to meet him."

Dot sat down at the computer, spinning the chair around to face Kat. "Yeah, count me in! That was . . . like . . ." Dot's cheeks flushed. "I really had fun with you that day."

Kat gazed dotingly at her. "You. Are. Adorable. Look at you blushing." She bent down and planted a short, tender kiss on Dot's lips. "I had a really good time that day too. Can't believe it'll be a month already."

Dot sipped her water and screwed the lid back on. "Have you been working in silence all this time?"

Kat had her eyes fixed on the little screen of her camera. "Yeah, I hadn't really thought about it. You wanna put on our mix?"

"Yes!" Dot swiveled around and opened the most recent playlist—a combined collection of their favorites. "What's that one of yours that I really liked?"

"'Lust for Life.' Iggy Pop."

"Yeah, sweet! I'm starting with that!"

As the opening drums came in, Dot lowered the volume so they could still speak comfortably.

She turned back around to face Kat again. "So what was going on last night? I vaguely remember waking up and thinking you were crying, but you said you were okay. Or did I dream that?"

"Oh! No, you didn't dream it!" With a gleam in her eye, Kat put the camera down and grabbed her phone. "Sorry I woke you."

"That's okay."

"I got a response from Eli." Kat opened the email and handed the phone to Dot. "You don't have to read it all this minute. It's pretty long. The abridged version is that he found me by learning about Aunt Devon."

Dot's brow creased with concern. "Oh. So is that what—?"

"Yeah, I got a little choked up reading about her. It's okay. Anyway, her married name was Brooks. That's where I got it."

"Married name? But I didn't think . . ." Dot's concerned look turned to confusion. "I'm lost."

"Sorry, I'm jumping ahead." Kat was speaking quickly now, enthusiasm getting the better of her. "Eli explains it pretty well. It's all in there."

"Okay, okay. Maybe I should just read it. It doesn't look *that* long."

"Right. Yeah, that's probably the simplest. I'll give you a few minutes."

Kat picked up her camera. She took a deep breath and tried to relax. She wasn't usually this excitable, but there seemed to be so much going on, and all of it positive—Eli, Verona's offer, Dot meeting Lonnie, Dot *killing* it at derby. Not to mention just being home, being free to work on this project, being with Dot. Kat had never expected her life would lead to a place like this. She'd never expected to be happy. It was almost more than she could stand. She smiled to herself. *Almost.*

Kat got back to what she'd been doing, transferring the latest batch of photos to the laptop. She looked them over, comparing them to previous shots, while Dot read.

"So he had already figured out . . ." Dot started. "No, scratch that. He sort of . . . found you *by* figuring out that you're queer."

Kat laughed. "Oh my god, I guess he did! I hadn't even thought of it that way!"

"That's pretty fucking cool. I mean, it sounds like he's totally fine with it."

"I know." Kat beamed. "I can't believe he came from my family. Do you know what a relief this is?"

Dot squinted a curious eye at her. "Well, we already knew he was all liberal and queer-friendly, didn't we?"

"Heh. In *theory*, yeah. It's one thing to be okay with it in theory. It's a whole different story when it's a family member you look up to."

"I guess." Dot pursed her lips in thought. "I guess I'm pretty lucky to have my family. It's always been a non-issue."

Kat snapped a photo of Dot looking contemplative. And another when she gave the camera a smirk.

"I love watching you go with that thing." Dot rested her elbow on the arm of the chair, her chin on her knuckles. "You said you responded to Verona already, right?"

"Yup! First thing, as soon as I got her email." Kat lined up a shot looking up at the mask from the lower left. *Click.*

"Are you gonna use the same photos from Pride?"

"I don't know. I'm not sure how it's all gonna work yet—if I'm gonna be picking them, or if Verona will, or what." From the upper left. *Click.* "If I'm picking them, I want you to help me."

Dot's eyes went wide. "Me? I . . . That's a big responsibility."

"I know it is. You have good taste." Center left. *Click.* Kat pivoted to face Dot with a knowing smile. "I told you it was one of your favorites that Verona bought. The one *I* was second-guessing."

"True. I mean, I'm willing to help."

"Good." Kat pivoted back and lined up the next shot.

Dot put the phone down and opened her water bottle. "What about today? Is there anything I can do to help with this?" She took a sip.

Lower right. *Click.* "Well . . . I did have an idea."

"Yeah?"

"How would you feel about taking this outside?"

Dot sat up. "The whole setup?"

Kat chuckled and turned to her. "No, just the mask. I'd like to try tying it to the big oak tree in the yard. If the light hits it right, it'll look really cool."

"Oh, yeah." Dot relaxed. "Yeah, we can do that for sure."

"Awesome! Thank you!"

"Of course! When do you wanna do it?"

"Mm." Kat eyed the dryad, as if to ask what she thought. "Maybe in like an hour? I think I've almost got this nailed down here."

"Sounds good to me." Dot swiveled to face the computer. "I'll check on L&M, then." She opened the browser and settled into her usual online routine.

The Sex Pistols' "Pretty Vacant" ended. The next song opened with ominous chanting—one of Dot's EDM tracks.

Kat recognized it. "I like this one. What's it called?"

Dot peeked back at her. "This is 'Dreams,' by Nero. You're into this?"

"Yeah, it's cool. Wanna turn it up?"

"Totally!"

Dot cranked the volume just in time for the beat to drop. Kat continued snapping away in a world now saturated with sound.

Following a couple more rounds of photos inside, they took down the mask and carried it out to the oak tree in the backyard. After much careful positioning, they tied it to the west side of the trunk.

Dot and Kat spent the better part of the evening side by side in lawn chairs, watching the mask as the light changed. The setting sun shone between the house and the studio, striking the tree with an orange glow that gave eerie life to the eyeless face. It seemed to become part of the tree, the two entities blending as one in the wash of color. This was exactly what Kat had been hoping for.

She captured the scene from different angles and in various hues as the sun dipped in the sky. At times, she looked back at Dot and found her transfixed. In those moments, she knew Dot must be catching a glimpse, however fleeting, of the wonder she herself had wrought.

CHAPTER 13

Dream

At the 2018 Tri-State Beer Brawl, Upstarts' Triticum Get Some hefeweizen took home a gold medal for Best Wheat Beer. This prompted Upstarts to change the name of that particular batch to Triticum Laude. A glistening twenty-two ounce glass of this cloudy golden brew awaited Dot as she returned from the pub's restroom.

She sat down across from her dad in the dimly-lit wooden booth. In front of him was a pale amber-colored beer of some kind—probably a Rancor IPA, knowing his taste. Between them on the table sat one of Upstarts' ever-popular hot pretzel appetizers—a favorite of Dot's.

It was check-in night for the Mausers. Check-in night was more than just going out for dinner with Dad. More than just catching up. Check-in night was a dedicated block of time set aside for heart-to-heart conversation. It was understood that serious matters would be shared and discussed, and that difficult questions might be asked. Check-in night meant really checking in on one another's mental and emotional well-being.

Nights like this happened on a semi-regular basis—every two or three months, generally. But Ben always made a special point of having a check-in night during periods when there was a lot going on. Right now, for instance.

He raised his glass. "What shall we toast to?"

Dot gave the question a moment's thought. "To Pride?"

Ben smiled. "To Pride. Happy Pride month, kiddo."

Dot lifted her glass and clinked it against his. There was a brief silence as they took their first sips.

She swallowed and licked the foam from her lip. "So, Mom emailed me on Sunday. Wants me to visit in July."

"Oh yeah? When in July?"

"She said any weekend is good, but she'll have some extra time towards the end of the month. The twenty-sixth and twenty-seventh? Whatever that Thursday and Friday are." Dot took another small sip and set her glass down.

"Do you have anything going on then?"

"No, I'll probably go." Dot sneered a little. "I'm kinda dreading it though. Every time I go up there, she ends up riding me about still living at home."

"Mm." Ben pressed his lips together. "She has her opinions. I don't care what she thinks. There's no shame in living at home." He met Dot's eyes. "Anyway, I love having you around. You know that, right?"

She stared blankly, studying his frank expression. After a beat, she nodded.

Ben went on, "She used to get on my case too, ya know."

Dot squinted. "What'd she get on *your* case for?"

"Oh, I leaned on my parents a lot in my twenties." He took a short sip. "I didn't live at home then, but they rescued us financially a few times. Especially after you were born. Your mother didn't think I had a real direction and doubted I'd ever make anything of myself." He looked down as he set his glass on the table. "One of the many things we fought about."

Dot reached for the pretzel with both hands, tearing off a small chunk. "But you did make something of yourself. Look at your career." She dipped it in the accompanying cheese sauce.

"My point. It took me a while to get off the ground, but I got there."

"Yeah, but I'm older now than you were then. I'm twenty-eight already." She popped the piece into her mouth.

Ben's brow creased in sympathy. "But you're also following a different path, sweetheart. And it's a different time. You're getting there. Look at L&M!"

Dot frowned and tucked the pretzel bite into her cheek. "L&M wouldn't be able to support itself if we didn't have a rent-free studio."

Ben conceded a side nod. "Maybe not. But you have a serious customer base. You have fans out there waiting to see what the next design is gonna be."

"Yeah, fans of Lynn's art." Dot swallowed her food.

Ben bowed his head slightly, catching her with an assertive stare. "But the business belongs to *both* of you. She couldn't do it on her own. You're the printmaking expert." He reached for the pretzel.

"I guess."

"And look at all you do besides that. With your sculptures, with derby." He dipped a piece in the sauce. "Maybe they're not income sources, but baby, life is not measured by income."

Dot smirked. "Says the guy with the six figure salary."

Ben chuckled. "True enough. Okay, maybe in a certain context, yes. If we're talking about poverty and quality of life and that kinda stuff, income is a very big deal." Cheese dripped from his pretzel bite as he held it over the plate, using it to point at Dot. "But even then, it doesn't define your worth as a human being." He popped it into his mouth.

"So what defines *you*, dad?"

Ben smiled and shook his head. "Dottie . . ." He took a moment to finish his mouthful of food before continuing. "Okay. Did I ever tell you, once upon a time, I wanted to be a musician?"

Dot raised an eyebrow. Where was he going with this? "I remember you used to play guitar sometimes."

"Mmhm." Ben picked up his glass. "I was in a band in college. We used to play shows at the student rec center all the time. We thought we were pretty hot shit."

"What happened?"

He shrugged. "Well, we could *play*, for sure. We had fun and all, but something was missing. My heart wasn't in it. I didn't have a passion for my art the way that you and Lynn and Kat do." He sipped his beer, savoring it for a moment before swallowing. "So, at some point, I met your mother and kinda got sidetracked. And for a little while there, ya know, your mom was right. I didn't know what I wanted. I felt like I was drifting, going through the motions." He gazed at Dot with gentle eyes. "Things didn't really come into focus for me until you came along. Everything changed then. You became my world."

Dot looked down at her beer.

Ben went on, "You want to know what gets me out of bed in the morning? Why I don't mind traveling so much for work?"

Probably because it got him away from his crazy daughter. Dot tilted her glass slightly, watching the liquid move. "Why?"

Ben leaned forward and softened his voice. "'Cause it means *you* don't have to worry about the money. So you can define your life by following your dreams, not by worrying about a paycheck."

Dot raised her eyes to meet his. "But what about *your* dreams, Dad?"

Ben let out a patient sigh. He reached across the table and put his hand on Dot's. "That's what I'm getting at, kiddo. This *is* my dream. I'm living it right now."

Dot looked down again, but a slight smile graced her lips. "Yeah, okay."

Ben let go of her hand. He folded his arms, elbows on the table. "That said, I understand your desire to support yourself. To help with utilities, to buy your own groceries. I get it. And that's fine. But you know I'll always have your back, financially or otherwise. That's what I live for."

Dot nodded, the slight smile fading.

Ben sat back, studying his daughter's face as he took in a mouthful of ale. She didn't look up. He waited, gave her a few seconds, before breaking the silence.

"Change of subject?"

She nodded.

"Okay, you got it." He tore off another pretzel piece. "How're things with Kat?"

That brightened her up. Color rushed into Dot's cheeks, and a grin spread across her face. She looked sheepishly at her dad. "Things're . . . good."

Ben licked salt from his thumb. "How's the agree-to-disagree working out?"

"Okay, I think." Dot bit her lip for a moment. "It was pretty rough at first, but now Coach has me so preoccupied that I don't have time to think about it."

Ben's brow furrowed. "Preoccupied how?"

"Well, I know the strategies better than anyone else on the team, so she specifically wants *me* to take command on the track."

"Oh wow!" Ben beamed with pride. "That sounds like quite a compliment coming from Coach!"

Dot's face fell, twisted in discomfort. "I don't know." She glanced up. "I mean, it is! It's a huge compliment. But I don't know how I feel about it. I don't like leading. I don't want everyone looking to me, depending on me like that. It's too much."

"Stress?"

"Yeah. They're trusting me to make decisions for them, and if I fuck up, we all fuck up." The color drained from Dot's cheeks.

"Hmm." Ben squinted and interlaced his fingers under his chin. "Well, how's it going so far?"

"Um . . . so far it's . . . working? I guess?" Dot flashed a brief, uncertain smile. "But I feel like I'm constantly behind the eight ball. Like I can barely keep up. And this is at scrim, against skaters I'm familiar with. I'm not gonna be able to read Second Bridge's skaters as easily."

Ben's expression began to tense with concern. "If this situation makes you that uncomfortable, have you talked to Coach about it?"

"No, but what's the alternative anyway? If I don't step up and do this, no one else can." Dot shrugged. "Well, someone would have to try, obviously, but . . ."

"But no one could do it as well as you can."

"Yeah. So if I don't step up, I'm letting the team down. And if I *fuck* up, I'm letting the team down. I'm stuck." The statements had tumbled out of Dot without her stopping to think. She wished she could snatch them out of the air before they reached her dad's ears.

Ben was silent. The concern in his eyes turned to outright worry.

Dot exhaled. "I know. I know what this is sounding like."

"Tell me. I want to know what it sounds like to you."

Dot swallowed. "A . . . a little extreme."

Ben pushed the pretzel plate aside and laid both hands on the table, palms up. Dot instinctively put her hands in his. He gently clasped her fingers. Her knuckles carried faint scars from the years of abuse she'd put them through—from the oak tree so many years ago to the van door just recently. Most people didn't notice, but Dot knew her dad could see them at a glance.

He raised his eyes to meet hers. "I know how important derby is to you. This is a big game coming up. I just want to know you're gonna be okay if it doesn't go perfectly."

"Yeah. Dad . . . I'll manage. I can do it."

Ben held her gaze. "When was the last time you talked to Dr. Frye?"

Dot closed her eyes momentarily while she thought back. "Um . . . we had a phone session in November. I talk to her once a year now. Just for a status update." Outside of these annual sessions, it had been more than five years since she'd last needed to see her psychiatrist, who doubled as her therapist.

"Would it help to see her before the bout?"

"No. I'm okay, Dad." Dot answered quickly. Insistently. "Really. I'm a little anxious, but I have it under control."

"Okay, okay." Ben lowered his eyes and nodded. "Sorry. I worry." He squeezed her fingers. "You're my baby."

Dot squeezed back. She took a long, slow breath. "I know. It's okay."

Ben set his jaw as if he was about to say something else, but he hesitated. With his thumb, he caressed the knuckles of Dot's left hand. Finally, he spoke. "Have you told Kat yet?"

Dot's heart jumped. Her pulse quickened. She shifted rapidly through a deer-in-headlights feeling and into full-on defensive mode. No, she hadn't told Kat yet! And so what? It was *her* love life, not his! Who was he to—?

She started to pull her hands away but stopped herself. She froze. Breathed. Actively reminded herself that her dad wasn't *accusing* her. He was just asking, and only because he cared. She was lucky he cared so much. She knew this logically.

Dot did her best to let the intense feeling run its course and pass through her. In the meantime, she tried to answer authentically without biting her father's head off.

The words came out through a restrained, nervous laugh. "What? That I'm a nutjob?"

Ben remained serious, his tone full of compassion. "That you're in *recovery*, sweetheart."

"No. God. Talk about scaring her off." Dot seemed to shrink in her seat. She couldn't look at him.

Ben half-smiled. "Dottie, she's already felt the brunt of it, and she's still around. That says a lot."

"The brunt of it." Dot's eyes were glassy. "She hasn't seen the brunt of it."

Ben tilted his head. "Hasn't seen . . ." He gave her a puzzled look. "You mean the worst it's ever been?"

"The worst *I've* ever been."

His expression softened. "Baby, you were a teenager. It's been a very long time since then. You've worked so hard, and it shows."

Dot didn't respond, but glanced at him briefly.

He continued, "You're the strongest person I know. I'm extremely proud of you, and Kat is lucky to have you."

Slowly, the corner of Dot's mouth pulled up into a reluctant smirk. "I'm lucky to have *her*."

Ben grinned at that sight. "I think that's true too. I like her. She seems like a good egg. And I'm happy for you."

Dot extracted her left hand from her dad's and reached for her beer. She took a long, slow, contemplative gulp. As she put it down again, she looked at Ben. "When I'm ready."

Ben nodded. "Okay. When you're ready."

* * *

Kat placed a tea light on the wide metal base of Dot's dragon sculpture. She pulled the wick up and snipped it short with scissors. Then, a few inches away, she placed another. As the sun finished setting and the sky overhead grew dark, Kat worked her way around a small, circular table, laying many such candles in a rough ring surrounding the metal creature.

Ben stood several feet off to the side. With Dot away at practice tonight, Kat had requested his assistance on this portion of the project. He'd helped her move the table and sculpture out here to the patio at the far end of the backyard, and now he was sticking around to watch the creative process unfold.

The night sky went black and the stars twinkled brightly. Kat produced from her bag a long-nosed butane lighter and began igniting the tiny wicks. Softly flickering light illuminated the dragon from below, reflecting off the undersides of its wings, causing its scaled skin to glisten and come alive. With each new flame born, the effect intensified.

Kat spent several minutes adjusting the positions of the candles, using the lighter to nudge them—this one just an inch closer, that one a hair to the right—making sure the eyes pierced and the fangs shimmered just so. She crouched beside the table and peered up at her handiwork. The resultant scene, as viewed from this vantage, gave the impression that the dragon was looking down over a burning village—or perhaps a torch-bearing mob, come to slay it—while silhouetted against the clear, starry sky. She couldn't have been more pleased with the outcome.

She slung her camera around from behind her, deftly catching it and popping off the lens cap in one fluid motion. She wasted no time bringing the viewfinder to her eye and snapping a few test shots. Referencing the results on the camera's small screen, she made adjustments to aperture setting, shutter speed, and ISO. She played with the depth of field while searching for the perfect lighting balance.

Before long, a clear rhythm was established. Like a hummingbird at the mouth of a flower, Kat flitted this way and that, capturing the scene from multiple angles. After a number of shots, she would stop to examine the photos before altering her settings and starting again.

Ben stuck around while she worked. As he gazed upon the dragon, he wore the same transfixed look Kat had seen on Dot. She glanced at him now and then, tempted to snap a candid photo of him to show side by side with his daughter, but she wasn't sure how he'd feel about it. And anyway, she doubted there was enough light to get a decent shot.

Regardless, capturing the dragon was her mission tonight. She'd been planning this shoot for the last week and a half, hoping for a clear, windless evening. And without Dot here to witness the process, Kat could keep it a secret and make the final product a surprise. To that end, Kat was determined to get as many varied takes as she could before Dot came home, to be certain the collection would contain some workable images.

The surreal nature of the candlelit presentation kept drawing Kat in, such that time seemed to stand still. But the seconds ticked by nonetheless, turning into minutes, and soon surpassing an hour. She was looking down, checking the latest batch of photos, when a light appeared in her peripheral vision. She turned to see Ben checking his phone.

"I think we'd better wrap this up if you want to keep it a surprise," he said. "Dottie'll be leaving practice soon."

Kat's eyebrows rose. "It's that late already?"

Ben gave her a consoling glance. "Yup. Time flies, kiddo. Er—Kat, I mean."

Kat laughed and shot him a smile. "I don't mind 'kiddo.'" She replaced the lens cap and stood up, slinging the camera around to her back again. "It's kinda nice."

She took one last long look at the beast surrounded by the horde of little flames. Then she leaned down and started carefully blowing out the candles. Ben stepped closer and helped her. When the final light was snuffed out, they found themselves standing in relative darkness, staring at countless little cups of molten wax.

Ben turned to Kat. "Any idea how long these'll take to cool?"

"Oh yes, I planned this all out. I figure about ten minutes and they should be just cool enough to touch."

"Alright. I'll set us a timer." Ben's phone lit up again, illuminating his face. He tapped the screen a few times. "Ten minutes and counting." He looked up. "Have you eaten yet? I was thinking of making burgers when Dottie gets in."

Kat had been so preoccupied she'd forgotten about dinner. "Um, no, I . . . Is that an invitation?"

"Of course it is! You're always welcome at our table." Ben's face was hidden in shadow again, but his tone was warm and sincere.

Kat hesitated, but she answered eagerly. "Yes! Thank you, I'd love to. And, uh"—she gestured to the dragon—"thank you for helping me with this."

"Oh, it's my pleasure. Anything for you, kiddo. You make my little girl happy, and that's . . . ya know . . . the most important . . ."

He trailed off. There was a brief moment of heavy silence, but for the sound of crickets. The weight of his words hit Kat, and she was suddenly grateful for the darkness, as she could feel heat flushing her entire face and neck.

Ben cleared his throat. "Sorry, I'm probably embarrassing you."

Kat tripped over her tongue as she answered. "N-no, n-not at all!" Ugh. So much for hiding it. "A-a little, maybe."

Ben chuckled. "Alright, well, I'll just say you're welcome, then. How's that?"

Kat's eyes were adjusting to the dark now, and she could just make out Ben's sympathetic grin. Her self-consciousness began to dissipate. "That's okay," she said timidly. "I liked your first response."

Ben had such a comforting smile. Without uttering a word, he could convey a feeling that everything was gonna be okay. So unlike Kat's own father. The more time she spent at the Mausers', the more she came to believe this is what "home" was *supposed* to feel like.

Ben turned his gaze to the house, then glanced back at Kat. "You want anything from inside? I'm gonna grab a drink."

The question broke Kat's train of thought. "Hm?"

"We've got Kickback in the fridge."

Kickback coffee stout. Her favorite. He'd remembered.

"Oh! Sure, I'd love one."

"You got it." Ben started down the yard's slight incline. He crossed the deck, opened the door, and disappeared into the house.

Kat listened to the crickets. She watched fireflies dance near the oak tree. Here she stood, in a backyard in a quiet suburban neighborhood, with a loving father figure nearby, waiting for her girlfriend to come home.

But "home" was seductive. Dangerous. What was she doing? She'd been letting her guard down. Kat's legs tensed. She felt an impulse to run. She could get in the car and take off right now, leave this all behind before it had a chance to break her heart—before she could allow herself to grow dependent.

But the impulse passed as quickly as it had come. It was irrational, she knew. Of course she wouldn't run. She just . . . This was . . . Things were going so *well*. She was happy, mostly. She felt safe and accepted and loved. How had this become her life?

And when was the other shoe going to drop?

* * *

Hey Buddy,

Your detective skills are pretty stellar! You're dead on about everything that happened. Thank you for sharing all that. I did read the whole thing, btw. You were right, some of it was hard, and I don't think I'm ready to go into further detail. But I'm glad you know.

Your suspicion about my sexuality is right too. Thank you for understanding. Thank you *so much*, Eli. You're the first blood relative since Aunt Devon to accept me for who I am. I promise I will tell you about her someday. You would have loved her.

I used to be ashamed. When I was your age, I was afraid to be this way. I'm very lucky now to have a community that embraces me. That's my derby league, Crosscannon Roller Derby. The sport is what brings us together, but the league is so much more than that. CRD is my safe space, and I guess some of the members are sort of my family now. I take a lot of pride in being a good ref, because I love this sport, and I love the people, and it takes all of us to make it happen. We actually have a big event next weekend—sort of a tournament, but not really. It's complicated. Anyway, teams from leagues all over the world come to this thing to play against each other, and I'll be working with officials from all over as well. It's a lot of work, but also a lot of fun. It's a bit of an escape from everyday life, like a derby vacation. A derbycation!

Well I've got to run. I'm expecting company soon. Have a great weekend!

Love always,
Aunt Kitty

* * *

"Yo! Kat, you didn't tell me you had all these toys!" Dot lifted a purple vibrator out of the nightstand.

Kat turned with a start. "Oh, get out of that drawer! Lonnie's gonna walk in here any second. I don't want him seeing that stuff."

"Aww." Dot put the device back and slid the drawer shut.

Kat had been kneeling over the foot locker, looking for a lost memory card. Now she settled back, sitting on her feet, and followed Dot's gaze to the music posters adorning the walls—Iggy Pop, Patti Smith, The Clash, Siouxsie and the Banshees, Tegan and Sara, and L7.

"How long have you had these posters?" Dot asked. "They look like they've seen better days."

"Since college, so at least a decade. They lived in the trunk of my car for a while. Anyway, a lot of the stuff in here is from college." Kat's eyes wandered to the lamp on the nightstand, the alarm clock on the dresser, the wastebasket next to the desk—just a few of the items that had journeyed with her since her days in the dorm.

She hadn't spent much time in this room lately. Or in this house. She'd been stopping by now and then to check the mail, do laundry, or pick up photographic equipment for her current project, but apart from last night, she'd only slept here once in the past two weeks. She was looking forward to spending some time with Lonnie.

Things weren't looking good for today's market trip, however. Torrential rain continued to batter the window, as it had been doing all morning. Even so, Dot sat ready on the edge of the bed, with her old Chucks on her feet and shades on her head. It was really touching to see her so eager for this.

"Hey, sis, I got bad news!" Lonnie's voice echoed up from the floor below. Seconds later, his footsteps could be heard ascending the creaky wooden stairs. "These thunderstorms are supposed to go on all day." He reached the top, crossed the hall, and swung around the door frame into Kat's room. "Looks like the market's a bust."

Kat looked at him and then glanced toward Dot. "Lon, this is—"

"Ah! You must be the Mouse!"

Kat's response was automatic. "It's just Mou—"

"That's the *Dread*mouse to you, mister!" Dot stood up from the bed and sauntered toward Lonnie.

Lonnie quirked an eyebrow. "Oho! Like the Dread Pirate Roberts!"

"Indeed." Dot didn't miss a beat. She stopped in her tracks and narrowed her eyes as though sizing him up.

Lonnie stepped further into the room, away from the door, and approached Dot cautiously. He extended his right hand. Dot did the same.

Lonnie took hold of Dot's hand, his eyes locked with hers. "You seem a decent fellow," he started in his best Inigo Montoya accent. "I hate to kill you."

"Oh no." Kat closed her eyes.

Dot snickered at Kat's reaction, but she managed to restrain her laughter enough to come back with, "*You* seem a decent fellow. I hate to die."

Kat glared at Dot, incredulous. "God help me, not you too."

Lonnie's smirk extended into a broad, toothy grin. There was a twinkle of mischief in his gaze as he held it on Dot.

Taking it as a cue, she asked, "Why are you smiling?"

"Because I know something you don't know." Lonnie paused for effect. "I am not right-handed."

Kat sighed. "Lonnie, that's not even the line."

"Well," Dot said, "there's something I ought to tell *you*."

Kat shook her head. "Okay, I've created a monster."

"I'm not right—"

"Neither of you is right-handed!" Kat covered her face with her hands.

Dot and Lonnie started cracking up and finally broke the handshake.

"Aw, Kit Kat, this is great!" Lonnie patted Kat on the shoulder. "Your girl's the shit!" He turned back to Dot. "Very nice to finally meet you, by the way."

"Likewise!" Dot nodded at him.

Kat smiled in resignation. "Okay, but, just *please* don't spend the whole day quoting *The Princess Bride*."

At that, an impish gleam shimmered in Dot's eyes. She hesitated, lips pursed tightly, and then uttered a quiet, "Aaas yooouuu wiiiiish."

Lonnie lost it. Kat snorted, trying desperately not to laugh. She slapped Dot's arm. Seconds passed as the three struggled to compose themselves enough to hold a conversation.

"Alright, so what—" Dot tried, but she was still giggling and had to pause. She began again. "What's the plan if the market's a no-go?"

"Hmm." Kat looked at Lonnie. "If the rain wasn't so heavy, maybe thrifting. I'm not too keen on going out in this, though."

Lonnie shrugged. "Netflix and chill?"

"I could be up for that." Kat turned to Dot.

Dot's face was twisted in a hesitant mix of confusion and disgust. "The . . . the three of us?"

"Hm?" Now Kat was confused. Then realization hit her, and her eyes went wide. "*No!* No no." She started laughing again.

"Oh shit." Lonnie grinned and covered his mouth. "Sorry, my bad. *Platonic* Netflix and chill. Like, as in actually hanging out on the couch watching Netflix."

Relief visibly washed over Dot. She resumed breathing. "Jesus, dude. Why would you call it that, then?"

Kat raised her hand. "Eh. That's my fault. Back when I first moved in, I, uh . . . didn't realize it was a euphemism." Her cheeks turned pink. "And I might have suggested it to Lonnie."

Lonnie cocked an eye at Dot. "Imagine my confusion."

"Oh, Kat." Dot smiled and shook her head.

Kat ventured a meek glance at her. "After that, it just stuck."

Dot chuckled softly. "Alright, it's all good. You guys just had me nervous for a second." She put her hands on her hips. "So, rainy day inside, huh?" She looked from Kat to Lonnie. "Well shit, yeah, I'm down for some movies! Let's do it!"

* * *

"How have you two never seen *Heathers?*" Lonnie sat with his palms up, baffled.

He'd laid claim to the right side of the couch and currently held the remote. Kat had given the left side to Dot and planted herself in the middle.

"I don't know." Dot shrugged. "It was before our time."

"Okay, first of all, Winona Ryder and Christian Slater are timeless. And secondly, we're gonna fix this problem right now." Lonnie hit "play" and settled back into his seat. "Buckle up, ladies! We're goin' to the eighties!"

Dot and Kat settled in as well—Kat sitting cross-legged and hugging a throw pillow, while Dot leaned back and spread herself out.

Heathers completely defied Kat's expectations. She'd heard it described as a high school dark comedy, which it certainly was, but that hadn't prepared her for its surreal presentation and brazenly cynical social commentary. No wonder it was a cult classic. This was a movie she'd be thinking back on later, for sure.

What's more, Kat found the character JD oddly familiar right off the bat. Then, with more context, it finally it hit her. It was Christian Slater's delivery of the dialogue. She often heard that voice come through in Lonnie's conversation style, especially when he was being sarcastic or cheeky. She wondered how many *Heathers* references she must have been missing over the years.

When *Heathers* ended, the next movie choice fell to Dot. Looking for a change of pace, she picked *Stardust*, a favorite of hers which Kat had never seen. This was met with enthusiastic approval by Lonnie.

"It's the *Princess Bride* formula!" he said. "It's not as quotable, but you can't go wrong with a well-executed fantasy-adventure-comedy-romance."

Kat squinted at him. "Romantic comedy, you mean?"

"Ehh"—Dot wobbled her hand in a so-so motion—"maybe *technically?* But Julia Roberts and Hugh Grant this is not. You'll see. You'll love it, I promise."

"Well, in that case . . ." Kat smiled at her adoringly.

Dot grinned back. She had her arm up behind the couch and her torso open to Kat. Kat turned, scooched over, and tucked herself against Dot.

Stardust was a definite change of pace—full of wonder and action and suspense. Hilarious and utterly heartwarming. Kat grew ever more glad she'd snuggled up next to Dot for this one. She rested her head back against Dot's arm and sank into her.

Kat was also rather ecstatic that Dot and Lonnie were getting along so well. They continued quoting *The Princess Bride* to each other as the day went on. Now, see, Kat loved that movie as much as the next girl. It was just that when Lonnie got started quoting a movie, he would go on and on, and she could only take so much. But today she found she didn't mind listening to the two of them go back and forth. Maybe it was the fact that they had cast her as Buttercup to Dot's Westley. Or simply that this was their chosen medium over which to bond. Whatever the reason, Kat had never been so gratified at hearing that script recited.

Halfway through *Stardust*, hunger began to set in. Lunch would soon be an imperative, and Chef Lonnie leapt into action. Having already seen the movie several times, he wasn't missing anything by making a few trips to the kitchen. He'd been keeping a batch of homemade three-bean soup in the freezer, waiting for an occasion such as this. It seemed the perfect comfort food for a rainy Saturday morning.

When the movie ended, lunch was just about ready. The aroma of garlic, onions, and chilis had filled the first floor. Lonnie served up three big bowls of his hearty concoction while Dot handed control of the movie selection over to Kat.

Kat sat back on the couch, placing an old throw pillow on her lap and settling her bowl into it. She grabbed the remote off the cushion next to her and navigated directly to "search." She already knew what her pick was going to be.

"This is another one I haven't seen, that I've been meaning to." She started entering the title, and the movie soon popped up—*Blue is the Warmest Color*. She turned to Dot with questioning eyes. "I know Lonnie hasn't seen this. Have you?"

Dot smiled knowingly and shook her head, her blue mane flowing back and forth. Kat then looked to Lonnie.

He nodded. "Let's do it."

Kat hit "play." At the first spoken line, Lonnie made an offhand comment.

"French with subtitles. Fancy."

That was the last thing any of them would say for quite a while. The heavy atmosphere of the independent film soon drew them in, eyes glued to the screen so as not to miss any dialogue.

The story was moving. The cinematography raw and visceral. The performances intense and authentic. While *Stardust* had certainly been romantic in its storybook way, this was . . . *real* romance—frightening and exhilarating and tragically relatable. Kat's heart ached for these characters.

With their empty bowls on the coffee table, it didn't take Kat long to reposition and curl up next to Dot. At times, she found herself gripping Dot's leg or squeezing her hand—touching her for the simple comfort of knowing she was there.

By the end of the three-hour epic, Kat was wrapped snugly in Dot's arms, tears streaking her face. She turned to find that Dot's eyes weren't dry either. Even Lonnie had clearly been affected.

"That was intense." Dot was still staring at the screen.

"No kidding." Lonnie sat up and glanced toward Kat and Dot. "At the end—did that say 'chapter one of two'? Please tell me that's what it said. It can't end like that."

Dot turned to answer. "It said 'chapters one *and* two.' *Et* means *and*. That was all of it, bud."

"Ah, shit."

Kat giggled. "Lon, you got really invested, didn't you?"

"How could I not?" He groaned. "Man, let's watch something light next. My heart can't take another movie like that."

"Well it's your pick." Kat grabbed the remote and offered it to him.

While Lonnie scrolled through the movie options, Kat wiggled out of Dot's embrace. She scooted her butt to the right and then reclined, laying her head on Dot's lap.

Dot ran fingers through Kat's hair, sweeping it away from her face. She lightly caressed Kat's cheek and neck. It was pure bliss, that simple touch. Knuckles brushed against wispy little hairs, nearly tickling but not quite—just enough to say "I'm here." Dot draped her right arm over Kat, finding the back of Kat's hand and interlacing their fingers. Kat clutched Dot's fingertips to her chest, squeezing gently.

She couldn't get enough of these little palpable reassurances, especially with the story they'd just seen weighing on her mind. It seemed Dot could sense that, or was at least feeling the same. Kat wondered if Lonnie could tell—if he had a clue how reflective and appreciative she and Dot were feeling in this moment.

Kat closed her eyes and listened as Lonnie and Dot talked. They went back and forth between discussing *Blue* and debating the next film choice. But more than their words, Kat listened to the sounds of their voices—the way they communicated with such familiarity already. Like Kat at the Mausers', Dot was a natural fit here.

Rain continued its endless rapping on the windows, a constant blanket of white noise in the background. With an ear against Dot's thigh, Kat tuned into the rhythm of her heartbeat. She drifted in the sensation of Dot's presence, in the contentment of family, of "home." As she dozed off, reality and dream became indistinguishable. She began to feel that maybe she *could* believe. Maybe there was no other shoe after all. Just maybe.

CHAPTER 14

Wake

———————

In the week leading up to MAD, the Heavy Metal spent most of their practice time refining strategies and perfecting communication skills on the track. Bout schedules for the weekend were released, revealing that CRD would play SBRD at noon on Saturday.

Officiating schedules were sent out privately to participating refs and NSOs. Agent Smithereens was assigned to work the CRD bout, along with officials from various other visiting leagues. Kat, unbelievably, was not assigned to ref on any of the three tracks during that time block. This, of course, meant that she would be free to watch Dot play—to cheer for her in the most important bout of her derby career to date. Kat was so thrilled at this she could scream, but she opted to save it for game day.

Given this news, and the nature of MAD overall, Dot and Kat made an amendment to their agreement. They would be spending three days immersed in the derby world, and neither of them had any intention of treating the other as a stranger the entire time. To that end, they determined the agreement would only hold if Kat was reffing and Dot was playing in the same bout. And yes, this situation remained a possibility at MAD, as Dot would be playing in several just-for-fun "challenge" bouts in addition to Saturday's sanctioned bout. In such an event, the agreement would remain in effect until both parties changed out of uniform afterward.

Once it had been determined they'd be spending MAD *together*, Kat and Dot began really looking forward to their weekend derby getaway. They would be mingling with skaters and officials from around the world, relaxing in the pool, dancing it up at the afterparty each night, not to mention seeing some of the top teams face off against each other—Empire, Garden City, and Violet Crown were all due to be at MAD this year.

Kat channeled her excitement by throwing herself into her project. Apart from shooting more of Dot's art, she put countless hours into reviewing and editing the photos she'd already taken. After MAD—after Heavy Metal secured their place in playoffs—Dot would have a little bit of a break from all the derby pressure. Kat figured that might be a great time to unveil some of her finished work. Perhaps it would inspire a little confidence in Dot regarding her sculptures.

Dot and Lynn spent the better part of the week prepping Burger Life merchandise to sell at MAD. L&M was going to have its own vendor table there, and the duo needed plenty of tee shirts, tank tops, and patches ready to go. That meant lots of screen printing work for Dot. She printed tons of the new "WILL SKATE FOR BURGERS" design, as well as smaller batches of some old favorites, including "Drive-thrUnicorn" and "#LivingMyBestBurgerLife."

On Thursday evening, Dot closed the lids on several plastic tubs full of merch. She loaded them into her van while Kat put the finishing touches on one last photo of the dragon. Just as the sun was disappearing beneath the horizon, they locked the door to the studio and headed into the house. Not long after dinner, Dot and Kat bid goodnight to Ben and disappeared downstairs, early to bed in anticipation of the three long, exciting, and *exhausting* days ahead.

* * *

Dot rolled up to the jammer line with a carefree smile, wearing a red tank top. She shot a quick glance directly at Kat, who was sitting trackside on the floor by turn one.

Kat cupped her hands around her mouth. "Let's go, baby!" After reffing the previous bout, she had hurried to the locker room and changed out of her stripes. Now she wore Dot's spare black jersey, proudly displaying the name "Dreadmau5" on her back for all to see.

"You can do it, Mouse!" Jet's voice came from behind Kat. Jet was tending the L&M table, which was set up back by the wall, next to the other vendors.

TWEEET!

"RRRAAHH!!" Dot roared as she plunged herself into the wall of purple blockers.

From Kat's point of view, Dot had disappeared among her opponents, seemingly caught up. But seconds later, the entire purple defensive formation began to pick up speed. Suddenly, Dot emerged, chest to chest with the foremost blocker.

TWEET-TWEET!

The other jammer burst out of the pack, taking lead status and speeding off around turn two.

With a quick pull-back, Dot crouched low and drove her shoulder into her opponent's sternum. The purple blocker nearly fell backwards, catching herself on one knee instead. But that was all Dot needed. She stepped around the downed skater and chased after the purple jammer.

Dot shouted across the track, "Take the front!" Her red teammates quickly maneuvered around the purple blockers, who scrambled to catch them. The pack began to speed up. Dot eyed the other jammer with a predatory grin. She was closing the distance between them.

TWEET-TWEET-TWEET-TWEET!

The purple jammer called it. No points scored.

Kat punched the air in celebration. "Yeah, Mouse! Way to force the call!"

Dot flashed a smile as she rolled back to the red bench. That had been her second time jamming in this half-hour challenge bout, the theme of which was "Infrared versus Ultraviolet."

Most challenge bouts had themes. Some were purely fanciful—Ninjas versus Pirates, Pancakes versus Waffles, and so on. Some reflected styles or attributes of the skaters on each team—Gender Benders versus Femme Fatales, or Goths versus Pin-Ups, for example. They had little bearing on actual gameplay, beyond perhaps determining jersey colors. Themes were just an added layer of fun and creativity.

Dot was in rare form tonight. Skating alongside players from a variety of other leagues, she was socializing as much as she was competing. And on the track, she was all smiles, regardless of her role. In the past, Kat had heard Dot say she hated jamming. Yet here she was, volunteering for the job and having fun with it. Whether it was the celebratory atmosphere of MAD, or the low stakes of the challenge bout, or some combination of factors, Kat didn't know. Regardless, it was an absolute thrill to see Dot so thoroughly enjoying herself.

A plastic cup full of beer descended slowly in front of Kat's face. She took it hesitantly, with both hands, and craned her head back to find Leah standing over her.

"Hey, Siren!"

"Hey, Kat! Mind if I sit with you?"

"Of course not!" Kat grabbed her bag from the floor beside her and pulled it around in front of her, making room for Leah. "I thought you'd be watching the Empire-Liberty bout."

Leah settled herself cross-legged next to Kat, cradling a nearly-full beer of her own. "I was, but it's such a blowout. And then I heard you guys were over here." She took a sip, her eyes following the action on the track. "Are you sticking around after this or heading back to Crosscannon?"

"Oh, we'll be around! We're staying at the hotel, so no hour-long commute home. Thanks to Dot's dad."

"Nice!" Leah glanced at Kat. "I'm sharing a room with Kara, Fiend, and Julie."

"Julie's the new girl, right? The transfer—AWW!" Kat straightened up suddenly as Dot took a hard hit that knocked her to the floor. Dot slid several feet, but she used the momentum to roll over, up to her knees, and back onto her skates. "Yes! Go, baby!"

"Yup, she's still a freshie. This is her first MAD."

"Oh cool! She's gonna have a blast."

"Anyway," Leah said, "there's no official afterparty tonight, but word is a lot of people are hitting the hotel bar right after the last bout, if you and Mouse wanna come."

Kat raised an eyebrow. "That sounds fun. I'll see what Dot wants to do. I know she's not drinking until after the Heavy Metal bout tomorrow, but maybe we'll just make an appearance."

"Totally understandable. I'm only having this one beer, myself." The current jam ended. Leah took her eyes off the track and turned to Kat. "You gonna be there to cheer us on tomorrow?"

"Most definitely!" Kat beamed. "Si, you have no idea how excited I am to be able to cheer for her. Even just tonight. But especially tomorrow, when it counts."

Leah smiled. "I can see it in your eyes. I don't think I've ever seen you this happy."

"Eh heh." Kat blushed. "I, uh . . . don't think I've ever *been* this happy, honestly."

"It suits you." Leah's smile dropped. "But you're not gonna stop reffing now, are you? Now that you two are a thing?"

"Stop reffing?" The very idea struck Kat with momentary panic. "Who said anything about stopping reffing?"

"Nobody!" Leah answered quickly. "Nobody, I just—well, you don't usually get to do this because of reffing, so I thought . . ."

Kat relaxed and chuckled. "No, no. I'll still ref. Any time I get to cheer for Dot, I'm gonna enjoy it to the fullest, but never at the expense of reffing."

Leah exhaled, relieved. "Good, we need you out there."

"Aw, thank you." Kat smiled graciously. "It feels good to hear that. I've put a lot of years into it. A lot of work. It's the best way I know to support this sport. And to support Dot, for that matter."

A new jam started. Kat scanned the track, but she didn't find Dot until her eyes got to the bench. Dot was standing in front of the row of chairs, holding her water bottle. When she turned and saw Kat, a wide grin exposed her turquoise mouthguard.

Dot made it into three more jams before the short bout came to an end. Infrared beat Ultraviolet 87-to-65, but to look at the faces of the skaters you'd never know the winners from the losers. Both teams offered grateful smiles as they circled the track, high-fiving the gathered audience members.

Dot grabbed her bottle and towel from the bench, then made a beeline for Kat, landing in her waiting arms. On her skates, Dot stood quite a bit taller than Kat.

Kat laid her head against Dot's chest. "My warrior on wheels," she muttered, just loud enough for Dot to hear.

Dot threw her arms around Kat. "Thank you for cheering, baby."

"Oh, of course! You kicked so much ass." Kat pulled back, her hair now matted with Dot's sweat. "Feeling warmed up for tomorrow?"

"You know it!"

"Siren was saying there's an unofficial afterparty at the hotel tonight, if you wanna stop in before bed."

Dot pursed her lips in thought. "Maybe for a minute. I need to get a good night's sleep, though."

Kat brushed a drop of sweat from Dot's brow and gave her a reassuring nod. "That's what I figured. Just thought I'd let you know."

"I mean, I don't mind if you wanna stay up and party for a bit, catch up with people. Anyway, let me go get outta this gear, and I'll see you in a few."

"Sounds good!"

Friday night—day one of three—and MAD 2018 was shaping up to be the best yet. Kat had been to Mid-Atlantic Derbycon each of the five previous years. She'd always tried to enjoy herself, but as an official these events could often start to feel like working weekends. At least, for Kat they could.

Truth be told, Kat wasn't very close with many people in derby. She hadn't developed personal bonds over the years, just "professional" connections. She had cordial relationships with everyone, but when her fellow refs would let loose together after a hard day, she'd always feel a little out of place.

This year marked Kat's first trip to MAD with real friends—not only friends, but a very special someone as well—and the experience was proving wholly different from anything that had come before. There wouldn't be anyone else she'd care to "catch up with" at this afterparty, but she would gladly go just to spend more time with the people she loved.

* * *

"How's the water?" Dot's voice echoed in the hotel bathroom.

"It's good! Great pressure. Nice and warm now." Kat stood under the shower head with her eyes closed. The soothing stream soaked into her hair and cascaded down her back.

She felt a momentary gust of somewhat cooler air, then heard the *thud thud* of feet stepping onto the fiberglass floor.

She opened her eyes and grinned at what she saw. "Hey, baby."

Dot stood at the far end, eyes half-lidded and a lazy smirk on her face. "I didn't really wanna wait for you to get out of the shower."

"No?"

"No." Dot stepped closer and took hold of Kat's hands.

Kat closed her eyes and tilted her head back, just far enough for the water to hit her hairline. "And why is that?"

"'Cause then you wouldn't be in here *with* me."

Kat felt the first contact, as Dot's breasts teasingly brushed against hers. Then their thighs touched. It was enough to make Kat's skin bristle and tingle all over. She smiled in anticipation.

Under the edge of Kat's upturned jaw, Dot placed a kiss. Gentle. Fleeting. Then another, next to it. And another. She slowly worked her way down the left side of Kat's neck.

"Oh, god," Kat breathed.

Dot traced a trail with her lips, winding toward the front and down to the hollow of Kat's throat. When she got that far, she pressed her body close to Kat's and nuzzled her nose and brow against Kat's neck.

Kat slowly lowered her head, searching for Dot's mouth. Dot looked up and found her, bringing their lips together.

"Mmmh," Kat moaned in satisfaction at the connection. They kissed lightly. Patiently. Sucking briefly, and then just grazing their lips against one another. Stretching out the moment.

"I'm so glad you're here with me." Dot spoke in a near-whisper. "At MAD." Kat could feel the words against her lips. "At all."

"Me too." Kat ran her fingers up Dot's muscular arms and over her shoulders. She got as far as Dot's neck, intending to cradle her face, when she stopped herself.

"Is something wrong?"

Kat laughed. "Um . . . I think my wrists probably stink. One sec."

She reached for the shelf in the corner and retrieved her lavender rose body wash. She squirted a dollop in her palm and replaced the bottle, then rubbed her hands together, spreading the lather up her arms.

"There." Kat placed her hands back on Dot's shoulders. She then drew her fingers up the sides of Dot's neck and under her ears, cupping the corners of Dot's jaw.

Dot brought her own hands around to Kat's back and pulled her out from under the water. Kat closed the gap between their mouths. She kissed Dot long and slow, their tongues moving against each other in a languid dance. They savored the taste of one another. Kat's slippery fingers glided around to the nape of Dot's neck.

Dot pulled the body wash down from the shelf again. Behind Kat, she squirted a generous amount into her hand, then put the bottle back. Resuming the kiss, she rested the edge of her hand against Kat's back and pulled upward, depositing the creamy soap along Kat's spine. Dot began lathering up Kat's milky skin with long, slow strokes.

Finally, Dot extracted her tongue from Kat's mouth and backed off, leaving a narrow space between their bodies. She moved her hands to Kat's sides, tracing the curve of her torso down to her hips, then gliding back up along her ribs, around her breasts, to her armpits.

Kat raised her arms as Dot reached this point, revealing tufts of short hair—a couple of weeks' worth of growth. Dot worked her soapy fingers into it without hesitation. Kat reveled in this. She loved the way Dot celebrated her body. In these kinds of moments, with her eyes locked on Dot's, Kat truly felt beautiful. Desired in her entirety.

Dot laid another drop of body wash on Kat's chest and proceeded to spread it with her fingers, up to Kat's shoulders and then down over the tops of her breasts. She stopped as she reached Kat's nipples. She gently closed her palms over them. Kat's breath hitched. Dot began a rhythmic massaging motion.

Kat's breathing grew heavy. She ran her fingers up the sides of Dot's head, into her hair. She could feel heat building between her legs.

"*God* I want you to fuck me," she moaned.

Dot grinned—almost the same predatory grin she had brandished on the track, except that the look in her eyes now was more a promise than a threat. She brought her hands lower, tracing the undersides of Kat's breasts before spreading the slippery soapiness down across Kat's belly.

Kat licked her teeth as she dropped her hands onto Dot's shoulders and pulled her in close again. Their bodies met. Kat thrust her left thigh, slick with lather, against Dot's crotch. She wrapped fingers around the back of Dot's head and whispered in her ear.

"Let's get you wet."

Dot snickered softly. "I already am."

Kat smirked. She pivoted, prompting Dot to turn so that they traded places. Then she gently pushed Dot back until the rush of water from the shower head began to soak into her blue hair.

Kat pulled her hands down around Dot's neck and watched the water stream over her chest and between her round, ample breasts. Stray droplets gathered and fell from Dot's large, brown nipples. Kat raised her eyes to meet Dot's and sank into those deep, dark irises.

Dot's sharp grin softened. She took the bottle of body wash and placed a few drops on her own chest. Then she cupped her hands over Kat's, begging them to descend. Kat bit her lip and ran her fingertips down over Dot's clavicle, pressing her palms into the soapy deposits.

Beginning with small circular motions, Kat spread the lather across Dot's upper chest, then down around the outsides of her breasts. She cupped them from underneath and brought her thumbs up to tease the edges of Dot's areolae. Dot inhaled sharply. Kat added her index fingers and gently pinched Dot's nipples, allowing them to slip from her grasp before repeating the motion. Again. And again.

Dot's eyes rolled up, her eyelids fluttering. She tilted her head back. "Jesus, Kat."

Kat let out a low, satisfied chuckle as she watched Dot become lost in the blissful sensations. Finally, she slid her hands around Dot's sides and enveloped her torso, pressing their bodies together. Dot brought her head forward again and rested her brow against Kat's, wrapping her up in powerful arms.

"This is an awfully inefficient way to get washed," Dot said. They shared a conspiratorial laugh. After a beat, she went on, with a wary tone, "At this rate we'll miss the party downstairs."

Kat answered with a smile of utter contentment. "I don't care. This is the afterparty I want tonight. Just you. This is perfect." She pulled her head back to look at Dot. "Is that okay?"

Dot nodded, almost imperceptibly. She found Kat's lips again and parted her own, their tongues meeting readily. Dot slid her thigh between Kat's. Kat could feel Dot throbbing against her leg. Her heat. Her longing. The message was clear. This was most definitely okay.

* * *

Aunt Kitty,

I'm glad you know who you are and that you're proud to be yourself. It makes me proud to call myself your nephew! Are you seeing anyone special? I had a girlfriend last summer and into the fall, but we broke up around Thanksgiving. That was hard. I really liked her as a person. We were just growing apart, looking for different things. It didn't feel right anymore, ya know? And now with me leaving for school soon, I've just kinda been content to stay single for the time being.

Speaking of school, there's something I want to run by you. You sort of live along my route to Baltimore. Not exactly, but close enough that I could make a detour to visit you on my way down. Classes start on August 27th, so maybe a couple days before? I'm taking a bus, so if I were to do that I might need you to pick me up at a station. It's just an idea! If you're busy then or you're not ready for that, I understand.

Anyway, I loved hearing about derby. Sounds like it's really an important part of your life. I'd like to see a game sometime, especially if I get to see you ref. I guess you're at that tournament thing as I'm sending this. Hope it's going well and you're having a ton of fun!

With love,
Your buddy E
xoxo

* * *

The next morning, Kat walked hand in hand with Dot as they once again entered the MAD venue—a massive warehouse-style building, the inside of which had been customized for rollersports. Three roller-hockey rinks with sport court floors took up the majority of the space, with bleachers extending from the walls nearest each rink. Dot's challenge bout the night before had been on Rink One, or Track One. The Heavy Metal bout today would take place on Rink Two.

Lanyards dangled from Kat's and Dot's necks, reading "Official" and "Skater" respectively and displaying the MAD 2018 logo. Kat nodded to the event staff watching the door, then began to scan the room for familiar faces. She didn't get very far before she spotted Ace Vantage, the tournament head ref, skating directly toward her.

"Katbot!" He came to a stop in front of her. "We have an issue. Lots of scheduling adjustments. You're gonna wanna check your bouts on the main schedule."

Kat's brow furrowed. "Adjustments? Why? What happened?"

"Well, I'm sorry to say, Agent Smithereens had a bit of a collision with a skater this morning. Fractured his fibula."

"Oh shit!" Kat's eyes went wide. "Is he—did they—?"

Ace motioned reassuringly with open hands. "Everything's okay. He's already at the hospital."

"Okay . . ."

"We just need to cover his shifts."

Kat sighed. "Right." She turned to Dot, who seemed to be listening intently. "Sorry, baby, I gotta run and—"

"I know." Dot was already nodding. "It's okay, I'll be around."

"I'll come find you." Kat planted a tender kiss on Dot's lips, then pulled back and gave her a smile before turning to follow Ace.

Skate bag in tow, Kat jogged around Rink Two to the officials' locker room in the far corner. She waved to the gathered refs, who were in the process of gearing up for the ten o'clock bout, then turned her attention to the massive master schedule that was taped up to the wall.

Kat ran her finger down the list of names. There she was, "Katbot." She followed the line across to—holy crap! She needed to be geared up and ready at Track Three in ten minutes! And it was basically non-stop after that until 6:00 PM! Shit, what about . . . ? Oh no. She was assigned to take Smith's place as outside pack ref for the CRD bout.

Her heart sank. There had to be a way to get out of that. Kat turned around to find Ace standing nearby.

"Ace."

He turned, eyebrows raised.

"There's gotta be someone who can switch with me, right? Take my place for the CRD bout?"

Ace squinted, wrinkling his face up doubtfully. "Staffing's tight, Kat. I mean, you could probably switch for a different bout in that same time slot, but that's it. We're already working with the bare minimum on Track One."

A different bout at the same time? No, no, that wouldn't work at all. Then she wouldn't even be *present* for Dot's bout. She had to be there.

Kat turned back to the schedule and scanned the noon column. It was true—all the refs were booked. That was it, then. The only way she would get to see Dot's bout would be by reffing it.

Ace rolled up beside her. "You wanna switch? I could put Ray or Zebes in for you and move you to Track Three."

"No, never mind." Kat's tone was flat. She couldn't hide her disappointment. "I'll do it."

* * *

Ten minutes into the second half, Vee was in the box, wearing the star. Second Bridge had a power start. Dot glanced up at the scoreboard as she rolled onto the track. Heavy Metal was up, 162-to-105—just barely beating the spread.

CRD lined up in the front, wearing black. Dot took the brace position. Lynn wore the stripe, alongside Jocelyn and Siren. They had to hold this jammer. Dot eyed the opposing blockers in their green jerseys as she tried to predict their offensive strategy.

"Five seconds!"

Dot muttered to her teammates, "Step out, set strong. Watch the lines."

TWEEET!

"Now!" Dot rolled backwards, her team moving forward to stay with her. They advanced several feet, then halted and hunkered down. Dot called out the green jammer's position using shorthand code. "Jammer one!"

Siren blocked off the inside line. Dot was in front of her, providing support.

"Out!" Dot mirrored the jammer's movement to the outside. "Three!"

Lynn and Jocelyn brought their hips together, blocking the jammer just as she moved to strike a path between them. Instead, she suddenly juked back toward the inside. The Heavy Metal blockers adjusted again. But while they did so, SBRD's blockers got the better of Lynn, driving her away from the outside line.

Dot reacted instantly. "Step out now! Rotate!"

The green jammer spun to the outside, toward the gap her teammates had opened. Just then, the green blocker on Lynn switched focus and plowed into Dot, keeping her from moving to intercept.

"Liz! Four!"

Lynn recovered, but not quickly enough to catch the jammer, who danced by on her toestops. Shit. Time for a last ditch effort. Dot spun around the green blocker and took a big stride toward the outside line. She turned and whipped her butt around, just barely clipping the green jammer.

That did it! Knocked her right out of bounds! Dot hit her toestops, flailing as she nearly fell backwards, but finding her balance. The SBRD jammer looked her dead in the eye, then stepped back in bounds and took off around turn one. Ha! An obvious track cut!

Dot expected a whistle any second. She looked to the outside pack ref. It was Kat. Kat signaled by moving one index finger around the other in a half-circle, indicating "no pass, no penalty."

No pass, no penalty? Where the hell was the track cut call? Kat had to have seen what happened! How could she have fucked that up? Dot stared at her, dumbstruck.

"Mouse! Jammer!"

Dot turned at the sound of Lynn's voice. The green jammer was coming around on her first scoring pass. She shouldn't even be on the fucking track! Whatever. Dot rolled back to her teammates and took her place in front of them.

"Out!" Dot started to move to the outside. Green jammer juked in. "In! Two! One!" The green blockers were swarming. Dot was focused on the jammer, who juked out again. "Liz! Four!" A green blocker slipped between Jocelyn and Siren and nailed Dot. Another knocked Siren out of bounds on the inside. The jammer slipped through.

Everything descended into chaos. There was too much going on. Dot couldn't react quickly enough. The SBRD skaters were all over her teammates. The CRD defense was still in shambles by the time the green jammer came around again. The jammer zipped around the pack untouched along the outside line.

"No!" Dot took off after her, swooped low, and caught her with a solid hit, knocking her clean off her feet. "Ha!"

TWEEET!

"Black five, blocking out of play!"

No no no no! Shit! Dot opened her mouth to shout.

"MOUSE!" Coach Rex's commanding voice rang over all the noise. Dot's gaze snapped in her direction.

Coach's stern expression was sobering. Dot couldn't disobey. She left the track and raced toward the penalty box.

She sat down, breathing heavily, her heart racing. It had all been going so well until now. She couldn't *think*. Think, Dot! Focus!

She watched the action on the track. Vee was back out there, going point for point with SBRD's jammer. But that wasn't enough. This bout was a matter of percentages, and Second Bridge was closing the spread. Heavy Metal needed to stop the hemorrhaging now! Dot needed to do her job!

"Black five, stand!"

Dot stood up with renewed purpose. Nothing was going to stop her.

She was a goddamn juggernaut, and her team was counting on her. There was no option but to succeed!

"Black five, done!"

She charged back onto the track, behind the pack. Vee had just finished a pass, picking up four points. Green jammer was approaching, about halfway around the track now. Dot needed to get up front with her team. Damned if she was going to be goated behind this green wall. Fuck this wall!

She hurtled forward, crashing between two green blockers. "RRRAAHHH!" They struggled to stay tight and hold her back, but Dot would not be stopped. She drove herself against them in a blind rage, forcing them to turn and separate. As they lost their footing, the wall parted, and Dot burst through.

TWEEET!

"Black five, back block!" The call came from an inside pack ref.

"Back block?" Dot retaliated. "That's fucking *bullshit!*"

TWEEET!

"Black five, insubordination!"

No! *No!* Shit shit shit!

Dot's heart was pounding out of her chest. She grabbed the sides of her helmet. The ref watched her expectantly. This couldn't happen. How had this *happened?* Everything was falling apart!

Dot was frozen. What was she supposed to do? She looked to her right. Kat was there, looking stricken.

"Black five," the ref repeated, "insubordination!"

Dot glanced at him, then turned and left the track. She didn't look at Coach. She sat down in the box. Shaking. Staring at the floor. Her knee bounced rapidly, her back wheels tapping. The jam ended. Another one began. Whistles blared. Voices echoed. Things shifted as if in a dream. None of it seemed real.

"Black five, stand!"

The penalty timer sounded like she was calling from a distant shore. Dot stood in slow motion.

"Black five, done!"

Dot rolled back onto the track. She got with her teammates easily, as the green blockers were occupied with Reggie. Beyond that, Dot couldn't remember what to do. She couldn't process. Everything was moving too fast. Her teammates were shouting, but it didn't make any sense.

At some point, the jam ended. Only on her way back to the bench did Dot realize she was sobbing. Tears poured down her cheeks and dripped from her chin. She sat down at the far end of the bench. Lynn sat next to her.

"Dot." Lynn spoke softly. "Dot, look at me."

Dot raised her eyes to meet Lynn's.

Lynn put a hand on her arm. "It's alright. Breathe."

"I can't . . . do it." Dot was hyperventilating, spurting words between quick, shallow breaths. "Can't . . . think."

"Shh." Lynn wrapped her arms around Dot. She said something else in her comforting tone, but it didn't register.

Dot was despondent. Her eyes burned. Her chest hurt. She was lost somewhere deep inside, gasping for air. Everything else seemed so far away and muffled.

Coach Rex approached the two of them. There was an exchange between Lynn and Coach. Soon after that, Lynn got up and skated onto the track, leaving Dot alone. Dot watched the skaters line up. That was her line out there—Lynn, Jocelyn, Siren, and now Fiend as the fourth. Lynn took the brace position.

TWEEET!

Following that whistle, it was all a blur. Dot sat on the end of the bench and watched the clock tick down. Both scores climbed consistently, strangling her, deepening the hole in the pit of her stomach as the point spread slipped away. The last fifteen minutes of the bout stretched on for an eternity.

Then, somehow, it was over. Coach hadn't put her in any more jams. Not that it mattered—she was useless anyway. Final score: 235-to-213.

Heavy Metal had won the bout, but they would not be going to playoffs. Nausea overtook Dot. While everyone stood in anticipation of CRD's victory lap, she slipped out the back door of the rink.

* * *

It was almost seven o'clock by the time Kat finished gearing down and packing up her things. The bouts had been running a little behind schedule. She'd been on skates since 10:00 AM, and her feet were killing her. Now back in her pink-and-black sneakers, she was looking forward to sitting down with a cold drink.

But priority number one was finding Dot. Everything else could wait. The last time she'd seen Dot was at the Heavy Metal bout, and Kat had been worried ever since. She'd seen Dot upset before, but never like that. That vacant stare. She'd looked so lost. Kat had searched for her briefly between shifts, but the venue was so huge, Dot could have been anywhere. And she wasn't answering her phone, but that didn't mean much—reception was terrible in this building.

Kat pulled her phone from her purse. No signal here in the locker room, but it would be worth a shot to step outside and try calling again. She rose, extended the handle on her bag, and headed for the door, turning to offer a wave to the other refs.

"Thanks, guys. See you tomorrow."

Ace looked up. "Thanks for everything, Kat. Good job today."

Kat nodded. Then she left the room and strode briskly toward the main doors of the venue.

Once outside, she began scanning the crowds—lines at the food trucks, circles of people gathered in conversation, streams of folks coming and going from the pool. Bright blue hair caught her attention a couple of times, but neither instance turned out to be Dot. Kat looked down at her phone. One bar. She walked further from the building, stepping off the sidewalk, onto the blacktop. Three bars. Four. That should do. She opened her recent contacts.

"Kat!"

She looked up to find Dot standing several yards away in the middle of the parking lot. Kat grinned, her heart leaping at the sight. "Baby! There you are!" She started toward Dot.

"That was fucking *playoffs!*"

The ire in Dot's voice stopped Kat cold.

Kat squinted, confused. "What?"

"Where the fuck was the track cut call? No pass no penalty my ass!"

Kat laughed hesitantly, still holding onto her smile. "You're . . ." She resumed walking toward Dot. "You're fucking with me, right? Come 'ere! I missed you!"

"That's the end of my season, Kat! That's it!"

Kat stopped again. Daggers were starting to pierce her heart. She silently begged for this to be some kind of bad joke. Her grin faded. She could see now the expression on Dot's face. Intense eyes. Jaw set. Kat's gaze wandered lower, and that's when she realized—Dot was still wearing her jersey.

Kat raised her eyes again to meet Dot's. "You're serious."

"You're damn right I'm serious!" Dot's response was immediate. "God dammit, Kat! Please tell me you're just fucking blind and you don't do this shit on pur—"

"No." Kat stood her skate bag up and let go of the handle.

Dot strode toward her. "You fucking—"

"NO!"

Dot halted her advance. Heads turned in the crowds around them.

"We're not doing this, Dot!" Kat let her arms drift to her sides, muscles tense. "I'm not taking this shit again!"

Dot's lip snarled. "We wouldn't have to go through this shit again if—"

"If what, Dot? *If what?* If I wasn't such a terrible ref? If I had eyes in my head? If I wasn't out to fucking get you? It's always my fault, isn't it? It's never you!" Kat could feel the eyes on her from all directions. "Well, guess what! Maybe it *is* you! Because I'm a fucking excellent ref, and I know it! I made the right call, and I don't need to explain myself to you!"

She took a tentative step closer. As she settled on her next words, she committed to the move, shifting her weight onto her front foot. "And it doesn't even matter, Dot." Her tone grew more controlled, even as her hands trembled. "I deserve respect regardless. I work *hard* at this. I've been reffing non-stop all day, so skaters like you could play this game. Because I *love* this game. I love what I do here."

Dot was silent. Kat glanced around at the faces of the onlookers. How much of this did she really want them to hear? After some consideration, she made a decision, marched across the distance, and stood face to face with Dot.

Dot stood defiant, hands balled into fists. "Kat—"

"Listen to me." Kat lowered her voice so only Dot could hear. "I love you." She swallowed. She hadn't been expecting to say that, but there it was. It was the truth. "I *love* you, Dot . . . but I can't do this anymore. This keeping derby separate thing. This is a big part of who I am, and I'm proud of it, and I'm good at it."

Dot's cheek twitched under her right eye, but her indignant expression was otherwise unmoved.

Kat matched her with a stern glare. "I don't know why you can't see that. I don't know why you're so insecure about this shit, or what the real issue is, but you need to figure it out." Despite her best efforts, Kat's voice started to falter. "And if you're not willing to talk about it or apologize to me, then . . . I . . ." She pushed through the lump in her throat. "I think we're done."

Dot's knuckles turned white. Her mouth twisted into a frown. But her gaze held fast. She didn't respond.

"Do you understand me, Dot?" Tears started to blur Kat's vision. She thought for sure she'd have gotten her point across. "Say something." The silence drove the daggers in. "Please."

Kat clenched her teeth to keep them still. Her heart pounded in her head. She stood trembling. Waiting. Praying.

Nothing.

Her eyes fell. "Okay." Kat's voice was little more than a whisper. She turned around and walked back to her skate bag, looking at the ground. She grabbed the handle and kept going, pulling it behind her.

"Kat!" Finally.

Kat stopped, holding her breath, and turned to look at Dot.

Dot's face was red, streaked with tears. Her firm demeanor had collapsed. "Everything's fucked now! Just tell me why!"

Tell her *why?* She was still blaming Kat. Still holding to that. Maybe she really believed it. Kat wasn't sure if that would hurt less or more. But she'd said everything she had to say, and now she was barely holding it together. She turned away and kept walking.

"Don't go! Kat!" Dot's tone was desperate. "What am I supposed to do now?"

Kat shut her eyes tight and put one foot in front of the other, biting back the sobs that racked her chest. She barely recognized the voice calling to her. It wasn't the Dot she knew.

"WHAT AM I SUPPOSED TO *DO?*"

CHAPTER 15

Fracture

Kat stayed with Leah that night. She would return to the venue in the morning to work her assigned bouts, regardless of Dot's presence. People were counting on her, and the ref crew couldn't afford to lose another from its ranks.

But Dot wouldn't be there. Lynn retrieved Dot's things from the hotel room and drove her home to Crosscannon.

* * *

Once inside the house, Dot watched through the window as the van pulled away. She and Lynn hadn't spoken much on the ride home.

Dot dropped her lanyard on the floor of the living room. She left her bags by the door and wandered into the kitchen, then down the stairs toward her bedroom, unsure where she wanted to be. Beer? Sleep? It didn't matter. Whatever she did, there would be no satisfaction in it. Nothing seemed of any great consequence.

She followed the hallway to the side door and went outside again, crossing the breezeway to the studio. The studio door was locked. Of course it was. Idiot. And her keys were all the way back in the living room.

Anyway, there was a spare key. Dot walked over to the back corner of the house and pried away a loose stone in the wall. The hole behind it was empty.

Oh. Right. That was the key she'd given to Kat.

Fucking Kat. Kat had ruined everything. She was *still* ruining everything. Dot strode back to the studio door, gripping the stone in her left hand. The idea of going back in the house to get her key . . . The thought of it was frustrating. Tedious. Embarrassing. Why couldn't this be simple? It was Dot's studio—just let her in! She tried the knob again, more forcefully this time. She rattled the entire door. Kicked it. Just fucking open! She hefted the stone, taking aim at the glass.

She stopped. Gritted her teeth and threw the stone at the ground instead. A piece chipped off of it and skittered across the pavement.

Dot took quick, shallow breaths. After a moment staring at the door, she turned and marched back into the house. Up the stairs. She snatched her purse off the floor, pulled her keys from it and dropped it again.

Leaving the house, she slammed the door behind her and returned to the studio. Unlocked the door. Thrust it open such that it hit the wall inside the entry hall. She hit the lights and stopped at the top of the steps. Why had she been so determined to get in here? She didn't even know.

She paused and looked around for answers. Reminders, maybe. But what was in here for her? Everything in this room reminded her of Kat. All her shitty trash art that Kat loved for some reason. The screen press she'd taught Kat to use that first day, when they'd almost kissed. The countless hours they'd spent together prepping for Pride. Doing photo shoots. Dot couldn't breathe. This room wasn't her happy place anymore.

And above it all, watching her, was that stupid green face—mocking her with its empty eyes. But she didn't have to take it. She jumped down the stairs and strode toward the desk, reached up and took the mask by the chin. A plastic bit snapped off of its back as she tore it down from the wall.

She dragged it along the floor, up the steps, out the door, and across the lawn to the oak tree. She pinned it up against the trunk with her right hand, holding it by the bridge of the nose.

Here's your goddamn dryad.

"RRRAAAHHH!"

She drove her left fist into its cheek with all of her strength. The plastic gave way and cracked, the face shattering into three large chunks and some smaller pieces. She let go and watched them clatter to the ground.

She lifted her foot, intending to stomp on the biggest piece. But a stinging sensation needled its way into her consciousness. The sharp plastic had dug into the skin of her fingers, drawing blood in places. The pain brought clarity—fleeting, but enough to tell her she would regret having done this. She put her foot back on the ground.

Still, the rage had to go somewhere. Anywhere. It was too much. She hated that fucking mask. She hated Kat. She hated herself. Just make it stop!

"AAAAAHHH!" She balled her right hand into a fist, reared back, and punched the trunk of the old tree, dead center.

Chk.

Something popped. In her hand. "Hhhuhhh." The pain was immediate. Intense. The clouds parted. She could breathe again. She could think. It hurt so much. She dropped to her knees and leaned against the tree, cradling her hand, which already seemed to be swelling.

Even this wouldn't last, she knew. This relief. The flood of emotions would return, especially the anger. It was too much. Too much. She needed help.

Dot stood up. On uneasy legs, she staggered back to the side door of the house. Through the hallway. Down to her bathroom. She rested her right hand on the sink. God, it was throbbing. Probably broken. And her knuckles were bloody.

She didn't care about that. She opened the medicine cabinet and reached for a prescription bottle on the top shelf. Olanzapine five-milligram tablets. Tucking the bottle against her body with her right arm, she managed to get the cap loose. Some pills spilled onto the floor, bouncing and scattering under the sink, behind the toilet, into the corners of the room. Fuck. Whatever, she only needed one. After setting the bottle on the counter, she carefully extracted a tablet.

Without giving herself time to second guess, she put the little white circle on her tongue, threw her head back, and swallowed it.

* * *

Aunt Kitty,

Run.

Your buddy,
E

Kat closed the laptop and turned around. Maxine lay naked on the bed, fast asleep. It was hot in the dorm room. Kat could never sleep in the heat.

She got up and tried the air conditioner again. No use. And maintenance staff was sparse during spring break. It might not get fixed until next week.

Kat's phone rang. She lunged across the room to pick it up before it could wake Max.

"Hello?"

A brief pause. "Kitty."

"Mom?"

"Kitty, please come home." She sounded forlorn, but firm.

"I . . . I can't, Mom. I have a project."

A sigh. "I know that's a lie."

"I . . . I . . ." Kat's heart started thumping in her chest. If it were possible to sweat more, she would.

"I spoke to the woman you've been seeing."

Kat's voice wavered. "Mom, I haven't been—"

"Don't lie to me. I know you and Dorothy have been sleeping together."

"Dot . . ." Knots started twisting up in Kat's stomach.

"You probably even think you love her, don't you? Do you call her your girlfriend?"

"Mom . . . she's not my—"

"You know that's impossible. You know that's the devil getting into you."

"It's not—uhhnng!" The knots turned to stabbing pain. Kat doubled over and fell to her knees.

"See? You can feel it, can't you?" Her mother's voice softened to a plea. "You know it's wrong. You've always known, because we raised you to know right from wrong."

Kat fought to speak through the pain. "It's . . . not . . . wrong."

"Just come home, Kitty. We can make this right, together. You still have a choice."

"No."

"You're my brave girl. I know you can—"

"NO!"

"Kitty . . ."

Then there was silence, but for the sound of her mother's distressed breathing. Was she crying?

Kat turned to see that her girlfriend was awake. No longer Max, now it was Dot who rose from the bed. She crossed the room and knelt with Kat. Embraced her from behind. Kat could feel Dot's cheek by her left ear, Dot's hands on her torso, arms wrapped tightly. Kat was safe. She was home.

Finally, her mother spoke again. "You're throwing everything away, Kitty. Just tell me why."

Kat found herself suddenly unable to catch her breath. She couldn't answer.

Her mother was sobbing now. "Just tell me why!"

"Be ... cause ..." Kat was out of air. Dot was squeezing too hard.

Run.

"Be ..." She felt lightheaded.

"JUST TELL ME WHY!" This time it came twofold, two voices, her mother's and Dot's.

Kat pulled the phone away with a trembling hand and looked at the screen. It was cracked.

Then there was just Dot, reduced to a whisper. "Don't go. Kat ..."

"Dot ..." Kat turned her head to rest her brow against Dot's temple.

"Don't go. What am I supposed to do?"

Run, my sweet baby.

Kat hung up.

She was alone.

* * *

Beats. Fast electronic beats. Deep drum tracks. A soaring instrumental melody with layers of harmonies dancing around it. The music had followed Dot into her dreams. Not that she could remember them now.

She woke gradually to the feeling of an off-beat rhythm. Painfully off-beat. Why could she feel it and not hear it? A heartbeat. A pulsing in her hand. That's what it was—her pulse. Shit. The memory came back. The pop. The pain. She dared not move it.

She opened her eyes. She was lying on her back. Her dad was sitting on the edge of the bed, to her left, inspecting the bottle of Olanzapine. She reached out and touched his hand on the mattress.

Ben turned to her immediately, concern weighing heavily on his brow, but a smile on his face nonetheless. He reached over and removed the headphones from Dot's ears. She'd grown so used to the high volume of the music, its sudden absence was jarring. A soft ringing lingered. The only other sound was that of Ben's movement—his denim shifting against the cotton sheets, the tap of plastic as he placed the headphones on the nightstand.

"Dad . . ." The word was an unintentional whisper. Dot cleared her throat.

"Hi, kiddo."

"I'm sorry."

"Shhh." Ben cupped Dot's face with his left hand and stroked her cheek with his thumb, brushing away the salt of dried tears. "I'm just glad you're okay. I'm sorry I wasn't there. My flight was delayed."

Dot swallowed. She didn't know how to begin to explain. In her groggy state, she felt disconnected from everything that had happened. From the anger and the reasons for it. She remembered it all, but almost as if it had happened to someone else. Right now, there was only the present—Dot and her dad, here in her bedroom.

Ben's smile shifted into a slight frown. "Your hands don't look so good, baby."

Dot managed a smirk and said flatly, "You should see the other guy." She tried to deliver the line with humor, but the effort required was more than she could muster.

Ben nodded. His eyes fell. "I saw." He laid a hand gently over Dot's left wrist, avoiding the scabby wounds on her fingers. "Dottie . . ." He looked her in the eye again. "I know you know I'm worried."

Dot's smirk disappeared. She nodded.

Ben went on, "You haven't . . . You've been preserving your art for such a long time. It's been, what, eight years? Nine now? Since . . . well—"

"Since I stopped destroying it."

Ben nodded again. He pressed his lips together in contemplation, took a deep breath, and exhaled slowly. He studied Dot's face. "How are you feeling now?"

Dot moved to lift herself onto her elbows, realizing quickly that the pressure on her arms made her hands throb. "Mmh."

"Here, kiddo." Ben stacked an extra pillow behind Dot's head. Then with his hands under her arms, he assisted as she scooted up to a half-sitting position. When she was comfortable, he settled back on the edge of the bed.

Dot looked at her right hand. It was more swollen than it had been hours prior. "My hand hurts, but . . . otherwise . . . pretty much numb."

"Okay." Ben brushed her hair away from her face. "First thing, I think I should take you to the ER to get that checked out. Agreed?"

"Yeah."

Ben paused. He seemed about to speak, but hesitated.

Dot looked at him expectantly. "Second thing?"

He took hold of Dot's fingertips, which she curled around his hand. "I hate to ask this again. I don't want to push you."

"You want me to see Dr. Frye."

Ben creased his brow questioningly. "Whaddya say?"

Dot sighed. "Yeah." She'd known this was coming. But her scrunch-faced look of discomfort didn't agree with her answer.

"What's wrong, baby?"

"I'm . . ." The thought embarrassed her. She didn't want to say it, lest it become real. "I'm just . . . afraid she'll put me back on the Zyprexa full-time."

Ben shook his head. "I don't think she will."

Dot eyed him warily.

"Dottie, this is a hiccup. We know you manage well without the meds. *She* knows that. She knows how hard you work. And she told us there would be hiccups along the way, didn't she?"

Dot nodded. "And she said she'd help me get back on track."

Ben offered her a smile. She could see the pride in his eyes when he looked at her, even now. It was enough to coax a little confidence into her.

"Okay."

"Okay." Ben gave her fingertips a gentle squeeze. "I'll give her a call later."

* * *

Ding-dong.

Standing in the front garden, Kat leaned her forearms against the house and bowed her head against her arms. It was so hot. She was dripping sweat, taking deep, heaving breaths. Her head throbbed mercilessly. Eyes open or closed? She couldn't figure out which was better. Either way, the world was spinning. Vomiting had brought little relief and threatened to strike again at any moment.

Lonnie opened the door in a tee shirt and running shorts. Leah stood on the concrete step, her slender frame clad in an athletic skirt and tank top. Her sweaty green hair was tucked behind her ears. Lonnie's eyes locked onto hers.

"H-hey, hi!" he blurted eagerly. He cleared his throat, quickly recovering his usual smooth demeanor, and extended a hand. "I'm Alonso. What can I do for you?"

"Heh." Leah smiled and shook his hand. "Lonnie for short, I take it?"

Lonnie gave her a nod. "That's me."

"Nice to meet you. I'm Leah." She eyed Kat, who was outside Lonnie's line of sight. "I brought your stray Kat home."

Lonnie stepped out the door and peered around the corner of the entryway. His face went stark. "Oh, sis, no . . . Let's get her inside."

Lonnie put an arm around Kat's torso and got her to lean on him. With Leah close behind, he half-carried Kat into the house and over the short distance to the kitchen. They eased her down into one of the chairs.

Kat's elbow was soon on the table, her head resting in her hand. "Thank you," she managed weakly. The cool air in the house was soothing.

Lonnie turned on the ceiling fan. "Don't worry, sis. We're gonna have you feeling a lot better soon." He looked to Leah. "How much did she drink last night?"

Leah cringed. "I don't know. A lot. We were at the afterparty. She was drunk before she even got there, and then she started doing shots."

"Oh boy." Lonnie opened the cabinet and grabbed a glass. "Alright, Kit Kat. Hold tight." He started pulling ingredients from cabinets and from the fridge.

Kat had to close her eyes. Lonnie's movements back and forth were nauseating to watch.

Leah dropped Kat's purse on the table. She went back outside and quickly returned with Kat's skate bag and backpack, which she left by the stairs. By the time she re-entered the kitchen, Lonnie was nearly finished his concoction.

She peaked over his shoulder. "What are you making?"

Lonnie glanced back at her. "This"—he stepped aside a bit—"is my hangover recovery system. OJ, electrolytes, B vitamins, ginger"—he added the final ingredient—top-shelf vodka—"and a little hair of the dog." He stirred the drink with a spoon, which he then removed and put in the sink.

Thunk. Lonnie set the glass down in front of Kat. She opened her eyes and was greeted by a fizzing, orange beverage. Her stomach twisted.

"Drink up, sis. You'll thank me later. And here." He placed two pills next to the glass. "Ibuprofen. For your headache."

Kat groaned. She took hold of the glass with her free hand. At least it was cold. She lifted it to her lips and took a sip. It . . . wasn't entirely disgusting. Actually, it was nice. Sweet. Spicy from the ginger, but not too.

Leah leaned on a chair and watched her. "Where'd you learn to make that?"

Lonnie was across the kitchen again, putting bread in the toaster oven. "I've picked up a few tricks over the years, tending bar."

Leah's eyes lit up. "You're a bartender? Where?"

"DJ's. You know, up Four-Twenty-Two?" Lonnie turned around and leaned back on the counter.

"I've heard of it." Leah sauntered over next to him and did the same. "That's cool! I've always wanted to learn to mix drinks."

Lonnie raised an eyebrow. "I could teach you."

"I'd like that." Leah smiled coyly.

Lonnie nodded, then returned his attention to Kat. She stared back at him with hazy, lidded eyes, then dropped her gaze to the table.

"So, sis . . . I've seen you drink, but a hangover like this is rare for you. What gives?"

Leah shot him a sharp glance. Kat just closed her eyes.

Lonnie turned to Leah. "What?"

"Do you mind if I tell him?"

Kat shook her head. "Doesn't matter."

"She, um . . ." Leah turned to face Lonnie, resting the side of her hip against the counter and folding her arms. "She and Mouse had a fight. They broke up."

"*I* broke up with *her*."

"Right. Anyway, I wasn't there, but apparently it was a pretty big public spectacle. Mouse blamed her for us not making playoffs."

Lonnie screwed up his face. "She *what?*"

"Exactly."

"Kat, I thought you weren't even reffing that game!"

Leah put a hand on his arm. "It's a long story." She glanced at the clock on the stove. "Unfortunately, I can't stick around to tell it. I have to get home."

"Oh, I didn't realize! Didn't mean to keep you."

Leah stood up straight and adjusted her purse strap. "No, not at all. It was nice talking."

"Yes, it was! And thanks for bringing her home." Lonnie accompanied Leah across the room. "And hey, listen, would you, uh . . . wanna go out sometime?"

"Catch a movie? Miniature golf?" Leah half-muttered the words as if reciting them. She laughed nervously. "Sorry, that's just me being silly. I'd love to—"

"Did you just quote *Heathers*?" Lonnie squinted curiously.

Surprise overtook Leah's face. "Yeah! You know it?"

Kat looked up as Leah reached the kitchen doorway. "Thanks, Si."

Leah offered her a sympathetic glance. "Oh, no problem, Kat. Feel better."

And then Leah and Lonnie were out of sight. Kat sipped her drink and listened as they exchanged phone numbers and said their farewells. The door shut, and Lonnie came back into the kitchen.

Ding!

He grabbed a plate from the drying rack and went to the toaster oven. Seconds later, he plopped the plate in front of Kat, presenting a single slice of heavily-charred toast. "I know you're not hungry, but nibble at this as much as you can. It'll help."

Kat lifted her head, expecting to feel sick at the movement, but the room had stopped spinning. "Actually, I feel a little better."

"That'll be the booze I put in there." Lonnie took a seat catty-corner from her. He leaned forward on the table. "I'm sorry to hear about Dot."

Kat took a bite of toast. "Yeah, well," she muttered between chews, "this is what I get."

Lonnie's brow creased. "For what?"

"For thinking I could have a fucking family." Kat swallowed. She took a gulp of her drink.

"Sis, you do—"

"Could you . . . not call me that?"

Lonnie frowned. "What? 'Sis'?"

"Yeah." Not meeting his eyes, Kat took another bite.

She chewed. Lonnie sighed. There was silence.

Finally, Kat swallowed. She downed the last of the hangover remedy, then stared at the empty glass. "Any chance I could get another one of these?"

"Not with the booze in it."

"Aw, Lon."

Lonnie shook his head. "You should get some sleep."

Sleep. She was exhausted. Her eyes burned. But the idea of going to bed, lying nestled in the covers, soft pillows cradling her head—it brought on the memory of her body intertwining with Dot's. Feeling secure in Dot's embrace. Feeling safe. Home.

She fought to keep the corners of her mouth from turning down. To blink back the tears. She took a deep breath and slowly exhaled, just managing to hold onto some fragile semblance of stoicism.

Lonnie laid a hand palm-up on the table, in invitation. "Hey. If you wanna talk, I'm here."

Kat shook her head. "No." She sniffed. "No, you're right, I should get some sleep." She pushed her chair back, stood, and grabbed her purse. She walked around Lonnie and out of the room, disappearing up the stairs.

* * *

Ben stood at the counter, chopping zucchini to the rhythm of David Bowie's "Let's Dance." His eighties playlist was in full swing.

A large pot simmered on the stove next to him. On this cool, rainy Tuesday night, he was making one of Dot's favorite comfort foods—giambotta, a southern Italian vegetable stew. This particular recipe had been passed down through her mother's family. The house smelled strongly of garlic, basil, and tomatoes.

Dot stared at her phone on the kitchen table. In the past twenty-four hours, she'd called, texted, messaged, and emailed Kat. And tried calling again. No answer and no reply.

Kat would be at scrimmage now. Dot had considered going, just to see her. She'd *strongly* considered it. Ached for it. But she knew better. If Kat wasn't talking to her, forcing it like that would be crossing a line. So she'd done the next best thing. She'd asked Lynn to talk to Kat for her. And Lynn had promised to report back as soon as possible.

So Dot sat staring at her phone, waiting.

"I should've told her."

Ben looked up from the cutting board. "Hm?"

Dot stood up and walked toward him, arms folded. "I should've told her, Dad."

Ben lowered the volume on Bowie. He replied soothingly, "You weren't ready, kiddo."

Dot stopped next to the stove and eyed the pot. "I don't know that I'm ever gonna be ready. It's news no one wants to hear." She raised her hands in mock celebration. "Surprise! Your girlfriend's borderline!"

"In *recovery*, baby." Ben put the knife down and turned to fully face Dot, one hand on his hip and the other on the counter.

"Yeah." Dot lowered her eyes. "It certainly didn't look that way on Saturday." She studied the blue splint covering her right hand and wrist.

"Well, you have your appointment with Dr. Frye tomorrow. You'll get it figured out. I know you will."

Dot replied forcefully, automatically. "It's not that *simple*, Dad. You don't just *figure it out*."

"I know, I'm sorry. I just mean—"

"I . . ." Dot closed her eyes. Her tone softened. "I know what you meant. I'm sorry I snapped."

"It's okay."

Dot opened her eyes. Ben opened his arms. After a beat, she stepped into his embrace, her own arms still folded under her breasts. She laid her head on his shoulder.

"It's okay," he said again.

Cyndi Lauper's "Time After Time" played quietly in the background. Ben swayed to the beat with Dot.

She sighed. "How do you put up with me, Dad?"

Ben chuckled softly. "Dottie . . . putting up with *you* is easy. It's the BPD that's hard. And I know as hard as that is for me, it's ten times harder for you. I'll never understand what that's like." He rested his cheek against her hairline. "I wish I could take that burden from you."

"Hmh. Be glad you can't. You're totally unequipped to handle the beast."

Ben rubbed Dot's back. "Like I said, you're the strongest person I know. I have faith in you."

Dot closed her eyes again, drifting to the music with her dad. A little smile crossed her lips. They stayed like that as minutes passed, enjoying the calm of the moment.

Buzzzz.

Ben lifted his head. "Is that Lizard?"

"Lemme see." Dot pulled away and walked to the table, eagerly picking up the phone.

Yes, a text from Lynn! Dot's heart jumped as she tapped the screen. But upon reading the message, a shadow of disappointment fell across her face.

"Kat isn't there tonight."

Buzzzz.

Dot continued reading. "Lynn says Coach is asking if I'm cleared to skate . . . so I can help ref." She looked up to find Ben listening intently. "I guess 'cause Smith is out. But me? Really?"

Buzzzz.

She checked the screen again. "Not just Smith, she says." Then she put her splinted hand over her mouth. She looked wide-eyed at Ben. "Kat's not coming back to derby." Panic started to rise in her. What if this was it? What if she never saw Kat again? She shook her head, unable to speak further as she waged a hopeless battle to hold back a rushing flood of tears.

Ben furrowed his brow questioningly. Dot held the phone out to him. He stepped forward, took it from her, and read the messages for himself.

"It says she's taking a *break*, kiddo. She just needs a little space. A little time."

But Dot was falling apart in front of him.

Ben's expression shifted, his gentle eyes becoming a safe haven amidst the storm. "Come'ere."

Dot lunged to him and threw her arms around his middle. He wrapped her up and held her tight.

"I know, baby. I know it hurts."

She sobbed into his shoulder, tears soaking into his shirt.

"Let it out. It's okay. I'm here."

Chapter 16

Salve

Hey Buddy,

No, I'm not seeing anyone. Good on you for recongizing that your relationship wasn't right and getting out. That's bery mature.

Actually I'm tking a break from derby now that MAD is done. Too much drama. Maybe sometimes I'll come down ans ref a bout in Baltimore.

I thibnk a visit would be fun! Why not come for a week! We can share tricks of the trade and I'll introduce you to some great music. That's whay Aunt Devon used to do. I'll tell you about her while you're here. I miss her.

Love always,
Aunt Kitty

* * *

Dot sat in a large, dark, leather-upholstered chair opposite Dr. Vivian

Frye. Dr. Frye had her legs crossed, fingers interlaced over her knee. Her brow creased as Dot finished recounting recent events.

"Sounds like you've had an exhausting few days."

Dot nodded. Her eyes were red. She hadn't slept well the night before, and now here she was telling the story, from the beginning, of her relationship with Kat.

Dr. Frye assessed her with an inquisitive stare. "Now, from what you've told me over the phone these past few years, you've generally been doing very well, right? No major hiccups until now."

"Yeah. I mean I have my moments, but I catch myself." Dot leaned back into the cushioned seat. "I don't usually have to think about it. It's mostly second nature now."

Dr. Frye pursed her lips and glanced down at the clipboard on her lap, then returned her gaze to Dot. "Dot, I want you to know, I'm gonna ask some hard questions today. If you need a break at any point, that's totally fine."

Dot raised a hesitant eyebrow. "Uh . . . that sounds ominous."

"I just don't want you to be caught off guard. I think you'll do fine. You came here today to work, right?"

"Yes." Dot answered assertively.

"Okay." Dr. Frye sat back and leaned on the arm of her chair. "Then tell me, how's life been going outside of derby and Kat? Before this weekend, I mean. How's the business going?"

Dot snorted. "*Business* . . . if you can call it that." She looked down at her hands and played with her fingernails. "I don't know. Okay, I guess, for what it is. We made a little profit at MAD. I don't see us making a real living off of it, though."

Dr. Frye nodded. "And how are things with your mom?"

"Not great." Dot answered quickly, then paused. Her eyes occasionally flicked up to Dr. Frye as she explained. "When . . . when I go up there to see her, she lavishes attention on me. Always wants to do stuff together, which is fine and all, but"—she shook her head—"she just doesn't get it. Not the way Dad does. The shit I've been through to get this far—she wasn't there for it, so she doesn't know. And then she rides me for still living at home. She wants me to be *her*, and I'm clearly not, which just . . . I don't know, it makes me feel like I'm failing at life or something. It's exhausting."

Dot folded her arms. "And I know you're gonna ask me about my art. Kat loves that shit for some reason. I don't know why. I hate it." She stopped and glanced off to the side, at Dr. Frye's bookshelf. She sighed. "That's not always true. Sometimes I feel proud of it, just because . . . ya know . . . I made something that wasn't there before. And it felt good the first time Kat came to the studio and I watched her jaw drop. For a minute, I felt like a real artist."

"But that feeling didn't last."

Dot shook her head.

"Things are good with Dad, though?"

A brief grin flashed across Dot's face. "Yeah. He's . . . pretty dope." She swallowed, remembering that exchange with Kat. It felt like years had passed since that day at the market. She let the twinge of sadness hit her but tried not to dwell on it. She planted her feet on the floor and focused on the immediate present—the smell of the leather chair, the way she sank into it. The feel of Dr. Frye's stare. She sniffed. "Sorry, I . . ."

"Take your time, Dot."

Dot breathed in slowly. She exhaled. "Anyway, yes. Dad's awesome. He's my rock."

"Do you have any other rocks in addition to him? What about Lynn?"

"Yeah, I guess she's one. She's always there to talk shit through. She doesn't know I'm borderline though."

"Okay." Dr. Frye shifted to the other arm of her chair. There was reservation in her tone. "I think that's a testament to how well you've been managing these past several years . . ."

"But?"

Dr. Frye gave a side nod. "Well, you two are very close, if I understand correctly."

"Yeah, she's my best friend."

"And you're going through a lot right now. I know I've said it a thousand times, but a support network is very important. Especially at times of stress."

"Mmh." Dot half-frowned. "I know I should fill her in. It's . . . hard."

"It's just something to think about. You don't have to decide right now." Dr. Frye sat back. "Let's talk about something else."

"Mkay."

"What are your goals, Dot? What do you want out of life?"

Dot laughed. "I don't fuckin' know! I guess . . . I want my art not to suck, for one. And I . . . well I don't even know if I want my own place or if that's just what I'm *supposed* to want. I don't know. I'm just taking things one day at a time, now that the season's over."

Dr. Frye squinted at that. "The season. The derby season, right?"

"Yeah."

"Because you didn't get into playoffs."

"Yes."

Dr. Frye leaned forward, her forearm resting across her knee. "So you'd say derby was your main focus prior to this weekend?"

Enthusiasm shone in Dot's eyes now. She looked directly at Dr. Frye. "Definitely! That's the one place I felt like I was accomplishing anything. I told you how Coach had me in there leading the pack. Derby just makes sense to me. The strategies, the whole metagame . . ."

"So if you *had* gotten into playoffs . . ."

"Oh my god, that'd be the furthest we'd ever gotten! And we were *that close!*" Dot held up her thumb and forefinger, indicating a hair's breadth. "Don't get me wrong—I don't think we're gonna beat Empire or Thorn any time soon. But just making the bracket is an accomplishment."

"So that's a goal of yours, making playoffs."

"Yes. Definitely."

Dr. Frye made a note on her clipboard. "Okay, Dot. We're coming up on one of those hard questions." She eyed Dot expectantly.

"Okay."

Dr. Frye nodded. "I'm gonna ask you to do some self-reflecting here. You don't have to answer yes or no." She held Dot's gaze. "I'm wondering . . . if it's possible that derby has become a bit of a blind spot for you."

Dot contorted her face, puzzled. "A blind spot?"

Dr. Frye searched Dot's expression before continuing. "Here's what has me concerned. Derby's obviously very important to you. But from what you told me earlier it also sounds like the one place where you haven't been managing so well when things turn south."

Dot's eyes fell.

Dr. Frye went on, "That tells me there might be a correlation between those two things."

Dot could see where this was leading. "You think I'm in the wrong here and can't admit to it."

Dr. Frye took on a generous tone. "Dot, I know you can admit when you're wrong. I think in this case it's more likely you can't even see it to admit to it."

"Pfft." Dot gave a confidently skeptical smile. "You really think that's true?"

"I'm just speculating. Looking at the information I have. If being successful at derby is such an integral part of your identity, it's possible you can't *afford* to let yourself be wrong. 'Cause then who would you be?"

Dot's mind instantly railed against this idea. Her pulse quickened. It suddenly felt very claustrophobic in this office. "No. No, that's bullshit. How could I not even see it?" Why was Dr. Frye putting this on *her?* She was supposed to be helping! "Why would you say that?" Dot spat the question, her smile now having flipped into a scowl.

"Dot." Dr. Frye extended a hand to her. "Dot, look at me. You can do this. Swim."

Swim. Dot's old code word from her teenage years. A reminder that she was capable of keeping her head above water by using the coping skills she'd learned. Dr. Frye used to say it to her at the first sign that she was being swept out to sea.

Dot reflexively took Dr. Frye's hand. She inhaled deeply. Exhaled. Focused on the present. The touch of Dr. Frye's fingers. The sound of her gentle voice.

"You're safe, Dot. We're just talking. You got this."

Though her heart raced, Dot took slow, deliberate breaths, letting herself feel the wave of emotion. The rage, the fear. Allowing it to run its course. "I'm . . . I'm okay. I'll be okay." The words came shakily from her lips.

"Breathe. Take your time." Dr. Frye held fast until Dot loosened her grip. Then she withdrew her hand and eased back into her chair. "Now, I could be wrong. I know that. I just want to keep you informed of my thought process."

"Transparency." Dot blinked. It took a little effort for her to stay in the moment, to listen and respond, but she was doing it.

"Exactly. *You're* ultimately in charge of your recovery. I'm just here to assist you. I don't want to keep anything from you."

Dot nodded. She could feel her fingers trembling. "Why is it so hard? I thought I was past this."

Dr. Frye smiled sympathetically. "Everybody stumbles, Dot." She paused, giving Dot another moment to breathe. "Are you okay to keep talking? No more hard questions, I promise."

"Mmhm." Dot pulled a tissue from the box on the side table and wiped her nose.

"Just some basic check-in." Dr. Frye clicked her pen. "Any excessive drinking? Drugs? I know that's never been an issue for you before."

Dot shook her head. "No. No drugs at all. And never more than two beers—or one if it's strong."

"Good girl." Dr. Frye made a note on her clipboard. She looked up. "I'm going to suggest, for now, no drinking at all. Does that sound reasonable?"

"Yeah. I haven't since . . . everything happened."

"Excellent." Another note. "And Dad's gonna be around for a while, right?"

"Yeah, he, uh, he took off from work for a couple weeks, and he's not traveling for a couple months."

"Good." Dr. Frye was still writing. "You have a good dad." She glanced at Dot and smirked. "But you know that."

Dot smiled.

Dr. Frye finished her note and placed her clipboard on the side table. She interlaced her fingers over her knee and looked to Dot. "So, my dear, I have some homework for you. A little unconventional, maybe, but I would like you to try it."

"What is it?"

"You said you're cleared to skate, right?"

"Right, but no contact yet." Dot squinted. "Why?"

"Well, your coach asked you to ref."

Dot's face went stark. "Oh no."

Dr. Frye fixed her with a knowing stare. "You know the rules of the game, right?"

"Well . . . yeah."

"And your fellow skaters need someone to do it."

Dot let out a defeated sigh.

Dr. Frye lowered her voice to a soothing murmur. "I know it's daunting. There's gonna be a learning curve. But I want you to give it a shot. Challenge yourself to change gears and get a different perspective."

Dot closed her eyes and groaned. "This is gonna suck."

"Maybe at first. But I know you, Dot. You can do anything you put your mind to. Plus I think it'll be healthy for you."

Dot pressed her lips together in consternation. She really didn't want to do it, but she also didn't want to disappoint Dr. Frye. And Dr. Frye did have a point about the need for refs. The Powder Kegs had a bout coming up, and it would really help them to have a full ref crew at scrim. Dot didn't want to let them down either.

"Just consider it." Dr. Frye stood up. "You have until, what, Tuesday to decide?"

"Yes, Tuesday." Dot rose as well and strapped her purse across her torso.

"You or your dad will call me if there's an emergency?"

Dot nodded.

"Otherwise I'll see you a week from today and we'll see where you are then." Dr. Frye walked Dot to the office door and held it open for her.

"Thank you . . . Dr. Frye."

"Take care, Dot."

* * *

Knock-knock-knock.

"Kat, wake up."

Hm? Kat's eyes cracked open, just barely. She squinted hard. The light from the window was painful. The cream-yellow ceiling shifted to pink and back again, in time with her pulse. She turned her head—AHH!—and stopped immediately. Upon moving, the world seemed to jump, like a record skipping—if a skipping record came with a jolting pain behind the eyes.

Knock-knock.

"Kat, seriously." Lonnie. "I'm worried here. The door's locked, but I'm coming in anyway if you don't answer."

Kat tried to swallow. Her throat was parched. A hoarse whisper emerged from her lips. "Don't—" She wasn't audible. Shit.

Kat rolled onto her side, and the whole world tilted like a ship in a storm. The skipping record became a blinding streak of lightning strobing in her brain. Her hand was visibly shaking as she reached for the half-empty bottle of Kickback on the nightstand, next to which stood three empty bottles. On her desk were two empty sauvignon blanc bottles. More bottles sat atop the other trash in her wastebasket.

Kat closed her hand around the Kickback and reeled it in toward her mouth. She hastily poured it down her throat. As quickly as she swallowed, she started coughing.

"Kat? You alright?"

"Wrong—" The word got caught. Kat coughed again and cleared her throat. "Wrong pipe." Her voice was haggard. Raspy.

"Can we talk?"

Kat laid back, head propped against the headboard. Sound was grating to her ears, whether Lonnie's voice or her own. She wanted the talking to stop. Her skull was going to burst. "Not now."

"Kat, you've been in there all week. The only way I know you've been eating anything is 'cause food disappears from the kitchen when I'm not home."

Kat didn't answer. Maybe he would leave her alone if she didn't engage.

"What if I make you my hangover remedy?"

Oh god, anything to ease this pain. "'Kay."

"Okay?"

Kat nodded. Please no more talking.

"How about I go make that, and you unlock the door while I'm gone?"

Kat cringed. "'Kay."

Lonnie's footsteps could be heard descending the stairs. Kat took a gulp of Kickback, then rolled over and set the bottle on the nightstand.

Moving was nauseating, but she was going to have to muscle through this. She dragged herself to the edge of the mattress, then pushed herself up into a sitting position, hunched over with her head hanging. Finally, she scooted her butt and slid off the bed, planting her feet on the ground. Slowly—very, very slowly—she leaned forward and stood up.

Her brain did flips inside her head as she raised it. The floor shifted beneath her. She reached out to the wall for support. Now she could see the light at the end of the tunnel. The door was only several feet away.

She shuffled along the wall to her desk and dropped her hands onto its surface.

Her ungraceful landing jostled the mouse and woke the screen on her laptop. Patti Smith's "Pissing in a River" was still open and playing on repeat, but the volume was set to zero. Kat kicked the chair to turn it toward her, then twisted around and fell into it. She rolled the last foot or so to the door and unlocked it.

Mission accomplished. Exhausted and sweating, Kat folded her arms on the desk and laid her head down on top of them.

She dozed briefly. Minutes later, footsteps approached up the stairs. Lonnie opened the door.

"Here, si—" He stopped and grudgingly corrected himself. "Kat." He was speaking more quietly now, at least. It didn't hurt as much.

Kat sat up and blearily eyed the drink Lonnie offered. "Does'iss have booze innit?"

"Yeah. A little."

She reached out to take it with unsteady hands. The first sip alone brought a degree of relief. The cold fizz was a major improvement over the lingering taste of warm, stale beer.

Lonnie stepped into the room, closed the door, and leaned back against the wall opposite Kat. He looked at her with sad eyes. "Kat, listen. I know you're hurting, but I can't watch you do this to yourself. Drinking yourself into oblivion every night for a week . . ."

Kat swallowed a sip and looked up at him. "What day is it?"

Lonnie sighed. "It's Saturday, Kat."

She didn't have a response to that. Lonnie watched as she took another sip.

He folded his arms. "You've only left the house to go pick up more alcohol. I don't even know if you've been driving sober."

Kat glanced at him but couldn't maintain eye contact. She didn't know either. Everything ran together. Honestly, she probably hadn't been sober enough to drive.

Lonnie slid down the wall to a crouching position and looked up at her. "Can we at least break part of this cycle? Maybe get you out of the house? With people?"

Kat closed her eyes. "I don't want to see anyone from derby."

"Fine, you don't have to." He touched her knee. She opened her eyes enough to see him. "Look, I've been invited to a house party tonight by some of my work friends. It's near West Chester. You can drink, I'll drive. No derby people. Just come out and be around other humans for a night."

Kat frowned. She wanted to say no, but she knew he was right. She needed to start pulling out of this nose dive. She just . . . didn't want to start living again. Socializing, working, being a person. Doing so would mean accepting that her life with Dot was over. That it had been a fleeting illusion. That *this* was real life. Her life.

She just wanted to be numb. To forget the pain.

Lonnie tilted his head and caught her eyes with his. "I could really use a good flip-cup teammate."

"I can still drink as much as I want?"

Disappointment pulled at Lonnie's brow, but he nodded. "I'm not gonna let you give yourself alcohol poisoning, but yes, you can get drunk. Again. If that's what you really want."

Kat sipped slowly. She swallowed, staring down at the softly hissing orange liquid.

"'Kay."

* * *

With a hollow *tap*, Lonnie's empty red cup landed face-down on the table. Kat, the final team member, immediately picked up her own cup and gulped down the small quantity of beer therein. She balanced the empty vessel on the table's edge, put a finger underneath it, and flipped it over. It bounced and rolled. She caught it and replaced it. The woman across from her had just finished drinking and was placing her own cup. Kat attempted another flip.

Tap.

And with that, her side of the table erupted into cheers.

"Nicely done, Kat!" Lonnie went for a high-five. Kat obliged.

She didn't feel the rush of the win, though. She didn't revel in the playful gloating and ribbing being thrown across the table between teams. She didn't much care. She wished Dot were here.

Fuck! No, she didn't. No.

"How 'bout another round?" One of the guys on the other side of the table held up a bottle of beer, ready to refill the cups.

Kat turned to Lonnie. "I need a break. Gonna find a bathroom."

"Okay. There's one upstairs, I know."

"Cool."

Kat left the dining room and made her way through the crowded living room. This house was pretty big, as was the party. People were gathered in every room on the expansive first floor, whether playing games, dancing, or just talking. Lonnie had introduced Kat to his work friends, who in turn had introduced her to some other folks. Names had been fired at her in rapid succession, and she didn't remember most of them.

As she walked to the main staircase in the foyer, Kat started to realize just how inebriated she was. The floor tilted ever so gently this way and that. She had to focus on putting one foot in front of the other.

The second floor proved as crowded as the first. The bedrooms were occupied by groups in quiet conversation, or couples getting frisky. Partygoers practically lined the hallway. Kat had really been hoping for a little solitude. Even in the bathroom, she'd know people were right outside. She wanted room to breathe. Around the corner, another flight of stairs waited. Kat continued up.

The third floor was quieter. Most of the rooms were dark. Kat strolled through this hallway until she found a bathroom on her left. She turned on the light and closed the door.

While sitting, she checked her phone. It was habit. There was nothing new. The notifications were still showing from Dot's attempts to contact her. Kat didn't want to deal with them.

She missed Dot. Missed her so much that it had eaten a hole inside of her. Every second that she was conscious, she ached for Dot's touch, Dot's scent, the sound of Dot's voice. She couldn't escape it. The alcohol wasn't helping. She'd drink until she blacked out, and the next morning it would be the same.

After all the accusations, all the rage Dot had thrown at her—god, the hatred that could flicker in those eyes—and after all the blatant disrespect, why did Kat miss her *so much?*

Worst of all was that final image of Dot. It was burned in her memory. That desperate, tearful creature. Screaming. Begging. Who *was* that?

Tears dripped from Kat's cheeks onto her lap. She tore off a few squares of toilet tissue and dried her face. Dammit. She shouldn't have left the crowd. Sitting alone with her thoughts had been a bad idea. Pull it together, Kat.

She cleaned up, washed her hands, and lingered for a moment in front of the mirror, dabbing at her eye makeup. She pulled several tissues from the box on the counter, folded them, and stuffed them in her pocket. Just in case.

Partway back to the stairs, Kat passed a bedroom door and stopped. She'd only caught a glimpse, but something in there had seemed . . . off. She backed up slowly and peered inside.

The scene in the room was something out of a movie. A young woman in black pants and a white button-down blouse appeared passed out on the bed. A young man in similar dress sat in a chair in the corner. He stared vacantly as another guy, sitting on the edge of the bed in a tee shirt and jeans, used a credit card to arrange a line of white powder on a mirror.

Tee shirt guy took notice of Kat's presence and looked up. "Hey, girl. You good? Need a hit?"

"Uh . . ." Kat was taken off guard by the directness of the question. "No. Thanks." Were these people doing actual hard drugs? Right here?

"You sure? I mean, I don't wanna pry, but you look like you're goin' through some shit."

"Yeah. I . . . I am, but . . ." Kat didn't know why she was looking for a polite response. She could just keep walking. Maybe she was grateful for the unusual distraction. "Not really looking for 'n upper right now. I jus' kinda wanna be numb." A reasonable excuse—and true.

Tee shirt guy flashed a friendly grin, a glint in his eye. "Oh, well this is perfect, then. Did you think this was coke?"

"Well . . ." How many powdery white narcotics *were* there? "Yeah . . . or somethin' like that."

"Nah, girl, this is oxy. And it sounds like just what the doctor ordered."

At that statement, Kat's gut told her to walk away. But to what? Back to the party that she was totally disengaged from? At least this was interesting in its surrealness. Curiosity got the better of her. "What's oxy do?"

Tee shirt guy gave her a sympathetic smile. "It makes the pain go away. No matter what's going on in your life, it makes you feel good, like everything's gonna be okay."

A drug could actually do that? Just make all the pain stop? *Any* pain? "So . . . if the pain was a broken heart . . ."

"Cured. For a few hours, anyway."

Kat settled herself against the door frame. "Like . . . I would forget about'er?"

Tee shirt guy chuckled. "No, you'd remember her. It just wouldn't hurt anymore. It's like being wrapped in a blanket of perfect—"

"No, Kitten." A hand closed around Kat's wrist and pulled her away, down the hall. "Come with me."

Kat turned to look as she stumbled to keep up. That voice sounded familiar. And those bouncy red curls . . . "Mags?"

* * *

"I'm sorry, Kat. I didn'know."

Maggie sat cross-legged on a queen size bed, facing Kat. Kat had her back against the headboard, legs stretched out in front of her, one foot crossed over the other. They'd left the lights off and closed the door. Artificial light shone through the window from outside, offering them just enough illumination to make out one another's faces. They spoke in hushed tones amid the quiet of the third floor.

Maggie held up a mostly-empty bottle of pinot grigio. "You wan'any more?"

"Not right now." Kat sniffed. She wiped her nose with a tissue retrieved from her pocket.

Maggie took a swig. She swallowed softly and paused for a breath before speaking again. "I feel like a jerk. I should'a warned you from the start."

"Warned me?"

"Yeah. I knew Dot had baggage. Serious emotional problems. Her reputation preceded her in my case." Light glinted off Maggie's eyes and earrings. "Why d'you think I turned down her advances?"

"I thought because'a Ricky."

Maggie shook her head. "No. Rick and I weren't together yet when I met Dot."

Kat narrowed her eyes. "But you flirt with'er all the time. I thought—"

"Well, there's a little story behind that. See, when we first met, she came on strong right from the get-go. Like *really* strong. But after I said no, she backed off." Maggie shrugged. "I was surprised, honestly. We ended up talking. She felt really bad, so I told'er hey, I can take it, 'n I can dish it out too! And we've been sparring ever since."

Kat laughed. "Flirt-sparring?"

Maggie smiled. She swayed in place as she stared at Kat. "I like that sound."

"What sound?"

"You. Laughing." Maggie brought the bottle to her lips again. "It's pretty." She took a sip.

Kat found herself blushing. She was silent.

Maggie planted the bottle on the bed, leaning on it. "I dunno. Maybe

I would'a been better off saying yes to Blue back then instead of endin' up with Ricky. At least she didn'cheat on you."

Kat's eyes fell. "As far as I know."

Maggie snorted. "She'd be crazy to cheat on you."

"She *is* crazy."

"Mm." Maggie nodded. "Fair point."

Kat eyed the wine bottle. Maggie passed it to her. Kat took a gulp from it. When she lowered it again, she felt a tear roll down her cheek.

"Kat."

"Mmhm?" And a lump had formed in her throat.

"You know you don'need those drugs to get through this . . . right?"

Kat sniffed. There was an awkwardly long silence.

"Kitten." Maggie put a hand on Kat's boot-covered shin. "There are other ways to lose yourself for a while if that's what you wanna do."

Kat swallowed the lump and found her voice, shaky as it was. "Like what? Alcohol isn'really doing the trick."

"I can . . . show you a way." Maggie's lidded green eyes shimmered as they settled on Kat's face. "If you want me to."

Kat remained quiet, unsure what Maggie was talking about. Her focus was on trying not to fall apart again.

"Here." Maggie leaned forward and crawled to Kat. As she got close, her face became obscured by shadow. In her denim short shorts, she lifted a knee and straddled Kat's legs.

"What . . . ?"

Wordlessly, Maggie took hold of the headboard, with a hand on either side of Kat, and lowered herself onto Kat's lap.

"Mags . . ."

Maggie's dark figure drew closer still. Warm breath brushed Kat's face. It smelled of grapes and alcohol, but with an underlying crisp coolness. Maggie's nose grazed Kat's. Cleaving through Kat's drunken haze came an acute awareness of her own heartbeat pounding in her chest.

Maggie hesitated. "Is this okay?"

Kat inhaled the words. Her mouth watered. Her lips begged to be touched. She'd never been this close to Maggie before. Never considered this. But here they were. And just like that, Kat's mind was flooded with a primal urge. She didn't know the answer to Maggie's question, but the question alone was mercifully drowning out all other thought.

Kat closed the gap. She pressed her mouth to Maggie's. She didn't want to think. She wanted to taste and touch and fill her senses with Mags. Maggie received her readily, parting her soft, pouty lips against Kat's.

"Huh—!" In a flash of self-awareness, Kat pulled back, vague implications of attachment pouring into her mind. What was she *doing?* Words spilled from her in protest. "Mags, wait, look, I'm not—I'm still—I don'wanna get involved in—"

"Shhh. Involved?" Maggie lowered her hands to Kat's shoulders and locked eyes with her. "Kitten, this doesn'have to *mean* anything. Jus' get lost with me for a little while. That's all."

Just get lost. Surrender to the moment. Could it really be that simple? Did it matter? Kat could already feel a void where Maggie had been during that brief connection. Now, memories of Dot threatened to rush in and fill it again.

Run.

Impulse drove her forward. She found Maggie's lips in the darkness. Clung to them with a desperate need. Maggie cupped Kat's face and pressed her back against the headboard. Kat wrapped her arms around Maggie's middle and pulled her close. She opened her jaw wider, inviting Maggie's tongue to explore.

"Mmmh," Mags moaned as she deepened the kiss, feeding herself to Kat.

Saltiness mingled with the sweet taste of Maggie's saliva. She began to move in Kat's arms, wriggling in place, rubbing the backs of her thighs on Kat's lap. The motion jostled Kat's bra against her breasts, her nipples soon crying out for attention.

When Maggie came up for air, Kat released her embrace and slid her hands down to seek the bottom of Maggie's camisole. Mags raised her arms as Kat pulled the garment over her head. Without any ceremony, Maggie proceeded to reach behind and unfasten her bra, sliding it down her arms and revealing her generous teardrop breasts.

"Now you." Maggie reached for Kat's waist and peeled the fitted Ramones tank top up her torso and off, tossing it to the floor. Kat wasted no time sending her sports bra flying after it.

Kat hooked an arm around Maggie and rolled her down onto her back. She lowered her face to Maggie's left breast. Gathering the supple flesh in her hand, she eagerly closed her lips over the pink areola and sucked gently. She flicked her tongue against the stiffened peak.

"Ahh!" Maggie's breath hitched with each lick. She ran fingers into Kat's hair, messing it about.

With her left hand, Kat cupped Maggie's other breast. Pinching Maggie's nipple between her thumb and finger, she twisted and pulled, softly at first, then a bit harder.

"Ahh . . . Kat . . . Mmm!" Maggie purred.

Kat raised her head and sought Maggie's mouth again. Mags met her lips and hungrily devoured her slick, probing tongue. She ran fingernails from Kat's shoulders down her back and around her sides.

Maggie gripped the front of Kat's belt and deftly unbuckled it. As her hands ventured further, unbuttoning and unzipping, Kat pushed her hips forward to allow easier access. Her clit jumped at the promise of Maggie's touch. Anticipation shot waves of heat through her.

"Mags," she breathed, "please, yes."

Maggie wore a fevered grin as she slipped her fingers down the front of Kat's panties, through her curly hair. Kat shuddered as Maggie's middle finger slipped between her labia.

"Mm, Kat, you're already wet for m—"

Knock-knock.

Who the fu—

"Kat? You in there?" Lonnie!

Kat and Maggie froze.

Maggie snickered. "Who's that?"

Kat glanced toward the door. "I'm, uh, a little busy in here, Lon!"

"Should we ask him to join us?"

Kat snorted audibly and tried to stifle laughter. She lowered her voice to a whisper. "No! Shut up!"

Lonnie persisted. "You alright?"

Maggie slid the length of her finger over Kat's swollen clit.

"*Awhaw!* Ahh!" Kat shivered and inhaled through her teeth. "Mmmhmm. Just—*oh god*—fine!"

Lonnie's laugh could be heard through the door. "Sorry, my bad! Carry on!" His footsteps creaked down the hall with a final "Go Kat!" echoing back.

Maggie's keen eyes once again focused on Kat's. "Now . . . where were we?"

CHAPTER 17

Start

Kat opened her eyes. Something was different about this morning. Her head wasn't *pounding*, for one thing. And the sunlight shining in between the blinds wasn't unbearable.

She propped herself up on her elbows. No skipping record today. No storm-tossed ship. Just a dull headache and an unsettled belly.

She pushed herself back and sat up against the headboard, noting how sore her legs and abs were—depleted from the workout they'd gotten the night before. Maggie's scent still lingered on her. Ah, yes, and that explained the relatively mild hangover. Kat had stopped drinking after that encounter. All she'd wanted was water, she'd been so thirsty.

On her nightstand, Kat found a tall glass of Lonnie's signature remedy, along with two ibuprofen. The glass was still cold. Lonnie must have snuck in and delivered it while she slept. She scooped up the pills and threw them back, chasing them with a sip of the drink.

Also on the nightstand was her phone, plugged in and

charging—another favor from Lonnie, no doubt. She unlocked it and was greeted with a multitude of notifications.

To begin with, there was a text from Jake, asking her to work a couple of shifts this week. Pretty standard.

Next, emails. There were four of interest. Two of them related to freelance jobs. The first was simply confirming Wednesday's appointment—Kat would be doing a shoot for the new indie gym around the corner. Second, an inquiry from a potential client—would she be available for a "Christmas in July" party on the twenty-eighth?

She put mental pins in both of those while she moved on. She'd saved the more personally important emails for last. One from Eli:

Aunt Kitty,

Are you okay? Your last email contained a lot of typos, which seems unlike you.

I don't know that I can do a whole week. I've got to pull this off without mom and dad knowing, remember. They have to think I'm just going to school a few days early to get oriented. It was hard enough convincing them not to drive me there themselves. Anyway, I can probably get to Crosscannon Wed the 22nd at the earliest. That would give us a solid 3+ days. How's that sound?

With so much love,
Eli

P.S. – This is really freaking exciting!

And one from Verona:

Ms. Brooks,

My apologies for the delayed reply. It has been a busy summer thus far, but I find myself at last with a little time to catch up. As promised, included below is a schedule of my availability throughout July. I can meet with you at any of those times.

I have reserved the main gallery from September 6th through the 12th for your exhibition. The Warfield will cover all costs to print and prepare your photos. All I ask of you is that you put forth your best work. I will gladly help you determine which pieces make the cut, though you shall have the final say.

Warmest regards,

Verona Fairchild
Owner/Director, Warfield Gallery

So. It seemed life was determined to go on after all, despite Kat's protestations. She had business to take care of this very week. The camera shop needed her. Clients were depending on her. Verona was waiting for her.

And on the other side of things, Eli was worried about her. Lonnie too—despite her attempts to push him away, he kept looking out for her. And then there was Maggie. Whatever her motivations were, and whatever complications might come of it, Kat couldn't help but feel Mags had saved her from herself the night before. In more ways than one.

This wasn't the way Kat wanted to live. Entanglements. Reliance on others. These were recipes for getting hurt again and again. She needed to stand on her own. She was done giving her heart away. Done trusting. Done leaving herself vulnerable for someone to pull the rug out from under her.

She was angry at herself for her behavior over the past week. The fact was, she'd been trying to run and had only succeeded in falling down. Well, maybe it was time she pushed herself up off the ground and got moving for real. Let the past be the past. The future was calling, and she had work to do.

* * *

Lynn reached the top of the stairs and stepped into the Mausers' living room. Ben was seated at the end of the couch. Dot was pacing. She stopped when she saw Lynn.

> Can you come over a couple hours before scrim tonight? There's something I need to tell you. In person. Something I should have told you a long time ago.

Dot had sent the text that morning. From that point on, she'd known there would be no going back.

Lynn's brow wrinkled curiously. "Hey, Dot. I'm here, so . . . what's this about?"

Dot's was a face of pure dread. She swallowed hard.

In contrast, Ben seemed calm as ever. "Lizard, why don't you come have a seat? I'll get you something to drink." He rose from the couch. "Iced tea? Water?"

"Water would be fine. Thanks, Mr. M." Lynn claimed the lounge chair in the corner. She sat forward, elbows on her knees.

While Ben was in the kitchen, Dot found her voice. The dam broke in a rapid flood of words. "Lynn, I have to tell you something, and I'm sorry I never told you. I was afraid it would change what you thought of me, but I should have trusted y—"

"Whoa! Dot!" Lynn's eyes widened in surprise, then eased into sympathy. "Slow down. *Sit* down. What's going on?"

"Uh . . ." Dot crept to the couch and sat sideways at the far end, facing Lynn. At this point, she realized she was breathing rapidly and her heart was racing. She started taking slow, deliberate breaths.

"Easy." Lynn put on her calming tone. "Breathe, Dot. It's me. Whatever you have to tell me, I'm not gonna jump to any conclusions here. Does this have to do with . . . ya know . . . last weekend?"

After a beat, Dot nodded.

"Here you go, Lynn." Ben handed Lynn a plastic mug with the CRD logo on it. "Dottie, do you want me to stick around?"

"I can . . . um . . ." Dot looked down, blinking a few times. "Maybe don't go too far?"

Ben pressed his lips together and nodded. "I'll be in the kitchen, starting dinner. How's that?"

"Yeah."

He flashed a reassuring smile before leaving the room.

Dot tried again. "Okay, so . . . I guess I'll start at the beginning." She was unable to look at Lynn apart from brief glances. "When I was a teenager . . . I started having serious problems."

Lynn's eyebrows rose. "A teenager?"

"Like fourteen-fifteen-ish."

"Mmkay. What kind of problems?"

"Um . . ." Dot winced, ashamed of what she was about to say. "The same kind I've been having recently. Anger. Emotions out of control. And . . . other things. Only a lot worse."

"A lot worse? Than last weekend?"

Dot nodded. "I was paranoid. Delusional. I used to start fights. I got in trouble a few times for hurting people. I didn't have any friends . . . 'cause . . . I . . ." She trailed off. "Look, long story short, I was impossible to be around. I spent so much time feeling completely overwhelmed by my emotions. The only way I knew how to get control was to . . . uh—" she swallowed "—hurt myself."

Concern etched Lynn's face.

Dot held up her splinted hand. "This . . . wasn't an accident. And it isn't the first time."

Lynn covered her mouth. "Oh, Dot."

"Yeah. I know. Anyway, the point . . . of the story . . ." Dot found herself gasping for air. The admission of self-harm had knocked the wind out of her, and the follow-up to that wasn't any easier for her to say. "I ended up . . . uh . . . hospitalized . . ." She kept trying to push through. "On the . . . psych ward."

"Kiddo? You okay?" Ben was in the doorway. Just the sound of his voice started to pull her back.

Dot nodded. She stared at him with glassy eyes and focused on her breathing.

Lynn left her chair and sat down beside Dot. "Would it help to hold my hand?" She offered one.

"Yeah." Dot took it. "I'm sorry. I need a second."

"Of course."

Dot held onto Lynn's fingers. They were rough, calloused in places. The room was quiet except for the sizzle of beef searing in the kitchen. The savory aroma filled Dot's nose. Gradually, she came back to the present. "Okay. I'm okay." A half-truth. The acute moment of panic had passed, at least.

"So . . . did they find out what the issue was?"

"Heh." Dot attempted a smile. "What the issue *is*, you mean. And yeah . . . after a while."

Lynn watched her, patiently but clearly expecting more.

Dot's smile twisted into a frown. She sighed and muttered to herself, "Fuck me. Here goes." She met Lynn's eyes. "Do you know what borderline personality disorder is?"

Lynn was silent for a moment, but her eyes went wide with realization. "That . . . kinda makes sense, actually."

Not the response Dot had been expecting. "It does?"

"Yeah." Lynn pursed her lips. "Mm . . . shit. Now that I said that, how do I explain it without sounding like an asshole?"

Dot snorted. "Story of my fucking life. Speak first, think later."

"Pff." A chuckle snuck out of Lynn. She quickly composed herself. "But really, listen. You know I'm into psychology and stuff. And I know you, Dot. You seem to take things so hard sometimes. And you can get so stubborn. I figured you must be dealing with something, but I didn't wanna make any assumptions. If you wanted me to know, you'd tell me, right? And hey, here we are!"

"So it doesn't scare you that I'm borderline?"

Lynn shook her head. "Dot, you're still the same Dot. And for as long as I've known you, you've mostly had your shit together. I'm no expert, but from what I know of this illness—sorry, do you call it an illness? A condition? I don't know . . ."

A relieved smile was already creeping onto Dot's face. "Whatever, it doesn't matter to me."

"Okay, anyway. It's a lot to overcome. More than I would have guessed if you hadn't told me." Lynn paused to wipe tears from her eyes before they could fall. "I . . . I don't know where I'm going here. I'm just glad you decided to trust me with this. It helps me understand."

Dot was too choked up to respond. Instead, she leaned in and wrapped her arms around Lynn.

Lynn reciprocated. "I love you, Dot. Just let me know what I can do to help."

Dot pulled back and sniffed. "That's kinda why I picked tonight to finally tell you."

"Whaddya mean?"

Dot shrugged. "I don't know what's gonna happen at scrim. I'm gonna be reffing, and—"

"You *are?*" Lynn beamed.

Dot smirked hesitantly. "Yeah, don't get too excited. It's new territory for me. So like I said, I don't know what's gonna happen. If I start to lose my shit, I might need to rely on you to help reel me back in."

Lynn squeezed Dot's hand and looked her in the eye. "No problem. I got you. What do I need to know?"

At those words, a seed of hope sprouted in Dot. Her anxiety relented and allowed a degree of relief to wash over her. There was more to explain, but the hard part was done. Lynn was in the know. Dr. Frye would be proud. And Dot just might survive her first night of reffing. While this didn't bring Kat back, it was a victory nonetheless—the first since her breakdown more than a week before. And that was a start.

* * *

TWEEET!

"White four-six, multiplayer block!"

Polly Dactyl made the call. Dot watched across the track as he performed the proper hand signal and confidently directed Jocelyn to the box.

Dot was skating as the lone outside pack ref tonight. Coach was covering inside pack. Dac and a visiting official named Jason Mimosa were the jammer refs. Four refs made a decent crew for scrimmage—or *would* have, if Dot had known what the hell she was doing.

They were nearing the end of the first period, and Dot hadn't called a single penalty. How had Dac even seen that multiplayer happen? There was so much going on at any given moment, how had he known where to look? How did *any* of them know where to look?

Then again, maybe Dot wasn't being entirely fair with herself. She had *seen* a couple of penalties—a back block early on, and then a clockwise block a few jams later. She just hadn't been quick enough to call either of them before the other refs. But really, if the other refs were seeing all this stuff anyway, why did they even need—

WHOA! Just then, the black jammer's feet slipped out from under her, and she took out Kara's legs! That was a definite . . . uh . . .

TWEEET!

Dot was the first to whistle it! What was the next thing? "Black, uh . . . new girl—what's your number?" She leaned forward to read Julie's arm. "Zero! Black zero! Low block!"

While picking herself up off the floor, Julie addressed Kara. "I'm so sorry! Are you okay?"

"Yeah! Fine! Don't worry!" Kara was all smiles, as usual.

Julie glanced at Dot. "Sorry! I'm going!" She hurried off the track to the box.

Well, that was one for Dot. Still, it seemed pointless. She'd been the first to whistle, but all the refs had seen it happen. If she hadn't been there, it wouldn't have made a difference. Oh, and she'd forgotten to do the hand signals! Dammit!

The final minutes of the period wound down uneventfully, penalty-wise. The jam timer whistled intermission. Dot skated to the rink wall and grabbed her water bottle.

Coach rolled up beside her. "How're you feeling out there?"

"Hm! Kinda useless, honestly. How do you guys catch all these penalties? I'm not seeing anything!"

"I know." Coach gave her an optimistic smile. "It's a learned skill. It takes time, but you'll get it."

Dot folded her arms. "Yeah, well . . . it's frustrating. I feel lost, like I don't even know where to start."

Coach looked out over the rink. A few skaters were doing leisurely laps. "You want a place to start?" She dropped her gaze to the outside line of the track. "Watch for cuts. One thing that's tough for us to see from the inside is track cuts on the outside. We need you to be our eyes out here."

Track cuts. Of course. Now that Coach had pointed it out, it made perfect sense.

Dot nodded. "I can do that."

"And if it's close, but good, give us a thumbs-up so we know it's not a cut. Does that help?"

"Yeah, definitely."

"Good!" Coach started to roll away backwards. "Now, let me go talk to the Kegs before we get started again." She turned and headed toward the bench area, calling for the B-team skaters to gather.

Okay. Now Dot felt like she had a purpose. Watch for track cuts. She could totally do that.

* * *

TWEEET!

"White one-eight-one! Cut!" Dot made the appropriate "X" gesture with her arms, then signaled for Siren to leave the track. Siren gave her a look of utter surprise, which quickly hardened into skepticism.

Midway through the second period, Dot was starting to feel like she had a handle on this track cut thing. She felt useful . . . if unappreciated.

While the skaters complied with her penalty calls, half of them had reactions like Siren's—shock, disbelief, suspicion. As though Dot had something to gain by making up these penalties. Like, really? Was Siren not aware she'd just stepped out of bounds as she passed Lynn? Everyone had seen it. Hadn't they?

Honestly, the more negative reactions she perceived, the more Dot started to doubt herself, even on straightforward calls like that. And things weren't always as simple.

Case in point: Fiend, now on a power jam, came around for a scoring pass. She juked to the outside, where she was clipped by Lynn and knocked out of bounds. *Jocelyn* then immediately skated back about twenty feet, arms in the air, obviously trying to force a run-back or a cut. But hadn't Fiend been in front of her already? Dot was relatively sure of it. Sort of. Fiend quickly jumped back in play behind Lynn, ignoring Jocelyn. Dot let it go.

Jocelyn scowled. "What was *that?*"

"She was already past you!" Dot countered, glancing at her only briefly.

"She was not!"

Coach stepped in. "Joss. Chill."

TWEET-TWEET-TWEET-TWEET!

Fiend called it with Siren standing in the box, giving black a power start for the next jam.

During the thirty second break, Coach crossed the track to visit Dot. "Don't let them draw you into an argument, Mouse. Just stay focused. You're doing fine." She gave Dot a pat on the arm before rolling back to the infield.

Stay focused. Right. Easier said than done, Coach.

Dot returned to her starting position. A new set of skaters took the track. Reggie lined up to jam for black.

"Five seconds!"

Dot rolled back slowly, looking for a good vantage.

TWEEET!

Reggie hit the pack center-track. Peaches and Julie tried to pry Lynn away from the inside line to open a lane for Reggie, but Lynn was having none of it. She held fast, forcing Reggie to seek an alternate route. Reggie continued to drive into the white defense, slowly moving it forward.

Nothing was happening near the outside line. Dot scanned the pack, hoping to catch and recognize anything illegal. Multiplayers? Forearms? What else should she be looking for?

Reggie pulled back for a second, and the white defenders rolled backwards to stay on her. Kara's butt bumped her, seemingly pushing Reggie back further. Reggie put her hands up and looked to Dot with wide, expectant eyes. What? Had that been a clockwise block? It hadn't seemed clear to Dot. She wasn't sure. She glanced at Dac, who was tracking Reggie. If it had been a legitimate penalty, he would have called it, right?

Reggie stepped forward again and continued looking for openings. Meanwhile, Siren re-entered the track.

"White jammer!" Peaches cried. The black blockers abandoned their attempts at offense and coalesced in the front, setting up a three-and-one defense.

Siren slipped past her white teammates and engaged the black blockers. Now there was twice as much going on. Where should Dot be looking? Her eyes darted back and forth between the action up front and that in the rear.

Reggie juked in, then out, finally finding a gap and darting through it. The white blockers scrambled to catch her again. Siren moved to intercept Reggie, delaying her while Lynn and Kara went up ahead.

Reggie made it past Siren before Lynn and Kara could get in position. Kara turned sharply and, flailing a bit in the attempt, managed to get a piece of Reggie. She just barely pushed Reggie out of bounds, but also stepped out herself.

Reggie wailed, "Aw, come on! Forearm!"

"She went out!" Peaches called to her. "Just go!"

Lynn skated back on the inside, now putting herself behind Reggie's position. Reggie didn't seem to notice and jumped back in-bounds, taking off around the turn. Dot chased after her in the ref lane.

TWEEET!

"Black nine-nine-nine! Cut!"

Reggie kept skating. "It wasn't a cut! She went out!"

"Y—mmff." Don't argue, Dot. Just, um . . . what now? Oh, right. "Black nine-nine-nine! Cut!" She repeated the hand signals.

"Aw *god!* Come on, Mouse!" Reggie slumped her shoulders, hung her head back, and rolled her eyes as she exited the track.

That was too much for Dot. "What do you want from me? I'm doing my job here!"

"Mouse!" Coach.

Dot whipped around to face her. "*What!* This is ridiculous!"

"Save it."

Save it, she says! Urrrgh. Dot's blood boiled. She watched Reggie take a seat in the box. The jam was still going. Dot drifted back into step with the pack and ran her eyes over the skaters, but the action was getting harder to follow. Her train of thought kept going off the rails. She started second-guessing that call, questioning her memory of the situation. Reggie had been so defiant, could she have been right? Had Dot been watching from a bad angle or something?

But no! 'Cause at the time, Dot had been certain of that call! Hadn't she? And regardless, that was only one of several track cuts she'd called over the course of the night, and even if she *had* made some mistakes, she couldn't possibly have made as many as the skaters seemed to think!

Plus, most of these penalties were easily avoidable! How did so many cuts even happen? Shouldn't these skaters know better? Have better track awareness?

And mistakes or not, this was Dot's first night reffing! That's what really rubbed her the wrong way. The disrespect. The lack of appreciation. She didn't even have to be here! She'd volunteered to help, and she was doing her best, goddammit! Could somebody cut her some *fucking slack?*

"Cut! Cut!" Peaches pointed at Siren.

"Huh?" Dot's heart jumped as she realized she hadn't been watching. She'd been facing that direction, but she'd been so preoccupied. Now Coach and Jason were looking to her, questioning.

Reggie yelled from the box. "That was a cut!"

"Uh . . ." Dot was stricken with panic. She had no idea what had happened right in front of her. "I don't . . ."

"Come *on!*"

"I DIDN'T SEE IT, *OKAY?*" The switch flipped like lightning streaking across the sky. "I'M TRYING HERE!"

"Whaddya mean you didn—?"

"Domme, shut the fuck up." Lynn's words sliced through the air, clear and bold. She rolled off the track toward Dot. Reggie went silent, as did most of the rink.

Dot's eyes, full of fire, flicked in Lynn's direction. Now what the fuck did *she* want? Everyone was ganging—

"Dot." Lynn reached out and touched Dot's upper arm. Gripped it gently. "Swim."

Swim? Dammit, Lynn! Dot had told her to reserve that word for . . . for . . . when . . .

And then the reality of it started to hit her. Her pulse echoing in her head like rolling thunder. Her quick breaths like wind whipping up the waves. The storm raged, and she was drowning. In front of everyone. How had it gotten this far?

Dot muttered through clenched teeth. "Fuck."

"Breathe." Lynn offered her other hand. Dot took it.

TWEET-TWEET-TWEET-TWEET!

Coach Rex whistled the jam officially dead.

Kara approached cautiously. "What's up? Is she okay? Are you okay, Mouse?"

Lynn glanced back at Kara. "Just an anxiety attack. She'll be fine."
She looked Dot in the eye. "Let's get some air, huh?"

* * *

"The first time I really talked to her was out here in the parking lot." Dot
released the wistful reminiscence into the warm night breeze.

She and Lynn lay on the hood of Jet's Camaro, staring up at the clear,
starry sky. They'd exited the rink maybe half an hour earlier, though it
felt to Dot like much more time had passed.

Dot had spent the first ten minutes griping about the skaters, getting
her frustration off her chest. Lynn had proven once again to be a good
listener. A good friend. Now that Dot had found a bit of calm, other
thoughts were bubbling to the surface.

"I remember," Lynn said. "The night you returned her pin."

"Did I tell you she said she loved me?"

Lynn turned to look at Dot. "Not that night, right?"

"No. At MAD. In the middle of my . . . my tantrum." Dot tensed
at the thought, a sudden chill flashing through her. "I was practically
breathing fire, and she came right at me. She always surprised me like
that."

"She always said your bark was worse than your bite."

"Heh." The hazy memory replayed in Dot's mind for the umpteenth
time. "Anyway, she got right in my face. She was so angry with me. And
then the first thing she says is 'I love you.'"

"Did you say it back?"

Dot sneered in regret. "I don't think I said anything. I was so far gone.
It didn't even register that she'd said it until the next day."

Lynn found Dot's left hand and gave it a squeeze.

Dot groaned. "Why couldn't I have just kept the peace? It's only a
game."

Lynn snorted. "Never thought I'd hear you say *that*."

"Yeah. I guess I couldn't see before—"

Dot cut herself off as the rink doors opened and voices carried out into the parking lot. Practice had ended. Before long, the wheels of a rolling skate bag could be heard approaching on the concrete. Jet? Dot turned to look. No, it was Coach!

Coach Rex stepped close to the car, haloed by the moonlight as it glistened in the thin layer of sweat on her ebony skin. She eyed Dot with concern. "How're you feeling, Mouse?"

"Better. Thanks."

"Good." Coach hesitated a second. "Listen. You don't have to ref if you don't want to. We're grateful for the help, but if it's too much . . ."

"Why *did* you ask me to ref, Coach?" There was a sorrowful sincerity in Dot's tone.

Coach frowned, clearly surprised at the question. "Well, because we need refs. We're down two."

"Yeah, but I mean, any of the Heavies could do it." Dot waved her splinted hand. "Just 'cause I can't play right now doesn't mean I'm cut out to ref."

Coach fixed Dot with a stern gaze. "I didn't ask you just because you're injured, Mouse. I asked you because you're capable and you really know the game. Same reason I wanted you to step up and lead the team on the track."

Dot's expression turned sour. "Yeah, well, I fucked that up too."

"You—" Coach folded her arms. "Things fell apart a little bit, that's true. So what?"

"A *little bit?* All it took was one bad call to totally throw me off my game, and . . . then . . ." Dot's argument lost some steam as she debated how much to reveal about her state of mind that day. "It was all downhill." Not much, she decided. "So if I wasn't capable of that, what makes you think I'm capable of this?"

Coach's firmness became tempered with compassion. "Mouse, you *are* capable. Capable doesn't mean perfect. We all fuck up."

Dot considered this. She turned away and cast a doubtful glare at the stars. Maybe everybody did fuck up, but nobody could fuck up as epically as she could.

Coach lingered for a moment. "Does that answer your question?"

"I guess so." Dot figured it was the clearest answer she was gonna get.

Puzzlement overtook Coach's face, as if she were stumped by some evasive bit of trivia. "If I may ask, what was the bad call?"

"Hmh!" Dot looked smug. "Do you remember, in the second half, when I hit the jammer out on turn one and Kat called it a no pass no penalty?"

"Yeah . . . and?"

"That was it. Should'a been a cut."

"Mmm, no." Coach squinted an eye at Dot. "You stepped out."

"Pfft! Yeah, okay. We're clearly remembering different moments here. It was—"

"Vee was in the box. Green forty-seven was the jammer. You caught her with your hip about fifteen feet out from the pack."

Now it was Dot whose face twisted in perplexity. She gaped at Coach.

Coach Rex held a finger pensively in front of her lips. "I know which call you're talking about. Nice hit, but it was a good call on Kat's part. You stepped out."

"Coach, I did not!" Dot sat bolt upright and turned, dangling her legs over the side of the car. "And anyway, how do you even remember all those details?"

"Well, that was just about the time my star blocker started getting into penalty trouble, for one thing." Coach smirked. "But I've also rewatched that bout like ten times."

Dot blinked. "Wait. Rewatched it?"

"Yeah, it was live streamed. You can watch the archives online." Coach was so matter-of-fact in her answer . . .

"You . . . but . . . so . . ." Dot stumbled, trying to formulate her thought through the haze of shock. Her tone grew almost accusatory. "You're saying there's hard evidence out there that Kat was right and I was wrong?"

Lynn interjected gently, "Dot."

Coach shrugged at the implication. "Wrong?" She shook her head. "You made a mistake, that's all."

Dot's jaw had already tightened. She closed her eyes and balled her hands into fists, pressing her knuckles down against the hood. "Mistake." Her voice trembled. It felt like she'd just been broadsided—the same as when Dr. Frye had suggested her inability to see the truth. But there was proof now. There was hard proof. She had no reason to doubt Coach's honesty.

Memories flooded Dot's mind. The sound of her own voice, roaring at Kat in childish denial. Images of Kat's face, torn between tears and broken-hearted fury. The touch of Kat's lips. The feel of her hand in Dot's. The sight of her walking away for the last time. Dot felt sick. Faint. Anger sparked fresh, but it was turned inward now.

"Mistake," Dot repeated, her stomach coiling into knots. She hung her head as Lynn's arms closed around her from behind. "You . . . you have no idea."

* * *

"I was up all night, watching the footage over and over." Dot found herself once again red-eyed and exhausted in the big leather chair. She stared off at the wall behind Dr. Frye. "It's all there, in full HD. I hit the jammer out, and then I stepped out for a split second while balancing myself. Kat was right."

Dr. Frye listened attentively, her questioning gaze fixed on Dot.

Dot was distant as she went on, "I don't understand how I could be so blind. For so long. All those times I shouted at her. Demonized her. God, the looks I got from skaters last night. To think I was ten times worse . . ."

Dr. Frye put her elbow on the arm of her chair and rested her index and middle fingers just behind her ear. "You say you demonized her. What do you mean, exactly? Do you think you started to slip back into black-and-white thinking?"

"I . . ." Dot's mouth hung open a moment. "Maybe. It's complicated."

She looked at Dr. Frye. "Honestly, I feel like I split on Kat *the ref* ages ago. Consciously on her part or not, I really thought she had it in for me. So in that sense, yeah." She bit her lip momentarily before continuing. "But then this other Kat came along out of nowhere. This amazing person. And I couldn't totally reconcile that she was the *same* person." She looked down at her hands. "After that first fight we had, I just resolved to keep the two separate."

"Hence the agreement."

"Yeah. I guess that was never really gonna work, was it?"

Dr. Frye watched Dot. Gave her time to process.

Dot sighed, frustrated with herself. "I feel like I've been sleepwalking or something. Why couldn't I have just trusted her, Dr. Frye? Why did I need to see proof before I could wake up?"

Dr. Frye pursed her lips in thought. "Well, you were under prolonged stress, Dot." She proceeded cautiously. "You told me last time how important derby is to you, right? How it was the only place you felt successful."

Dot shifted in her seat, her jaw introspectively offset. "Mmhm."

"So, anything that contradicted that success probably felt like an attack. And being, as you were, stressed . . . you reacted in unhealthy ways."

"Yeah, unhealthy is putting it lightly." Dot shook her head. "I fucking relapsed. Raged out, cast Kat as the bad guy, and projected my shit onto her." She rested her brow on the heel of her hand. "I destroyed everything, Dr. Frye! How did it get this bad? I feel like I'm back at square one!"

Dr. Frye sat forward and brought her hands together over her knee. She spoke reassuringly. "Dot, I remember what square one looked like for you. This is not square one."

Fine. So Dot hadn't physically assaulted anyone or destroyed any property besides her own. Somehow that was small comfort. "I don't know, I feel like it might as well be. I don't know what to do now. I hurt

Kat. Badly. And I drove her away from derby." She blinked away the first threatening tears. "I hurt a lot of people."

"What do you mean by a lot of people?"

Dot released a stilted breath. "CRD needs her more than it needs me. I robbed the league of its best ref."

Dr. Frye furrowed her brow and pressed her lips together. She settled patiently on the arm of her chair again.

Dot sniffed. She wiped her eyes. "This is my fault. I have to fix it."

Dr. Frye nodded slowly. "Fair enough. I get that you want to make amends. But let's do it right, okay? Let's start by getting you back on track."

Back on track. Yeah. And how long would *that* take? All Dot could see was Kat walking away from her, ever further with each second that passed. A lump in her throat threatened to turn into more. She swallowed it down, waiting to respond until she was certain she could do so without sobbing.

"What is it, Dot?"

Dot's mouth twisted into a frown. She couldn't fight it. Tears started streaming. "I'm afraid by the time I do that, there won't be anything left to salvage."

Dr. Frye handed her the box of tissues. "It pays to be patient. You know from experience."

"But it took me *years* to get on track the first time!"

"This isn't the first time, Dot. You're older now. You're wiser. You know what you're doing. And believe it or not, you're not that far *off*-track."

Dot looked away. "How am I not that far? I broke my fucking hand on a tree."

"Granted. But what you took away from that incident was that you needed help, and I'm proud of you for realizing that." Dr. Frye leaned in conversationally. "I'm looking at the big picture here, Dot. Look at where you are now. Thinking clearly. Accepting responsibility. Remember how I said derby seemed to be a blind spot?"

Dot nodded.

"Outside of that, you've still been doing well this whole time, haven't you?"

"Yeah . . . I guess." Dot wiped her nose with a tissue. Then realization hit. She narrowed her eyes at Dr. Frye. "So what are you saying? I should quit derby?"

"Not at all." Dr. Frye blinked slowly and shook her head. "I still think derby has been a good thing for you. You always struggled to believe in yourself, and derby helped you with that, big time. It helped you make friends, find your confidence. We're not gonna throw the baby out with the bathwater here, my dear. We're going to address the problem."

Dot untensed a bit, still wary. "How?"

"From a couple of angles." Dr. Frye sat up and glanced at the clipboard on her lap, then back at Dot. "Number one, we're gonna work on basic skills. Specifically at derby practice."

"At practice . . . So I take it you want me to keep reffing?"

"That's entirely up to you. I know the first time was rough. Participate at whatever level you're able. Go to scrimmage, go to regular practice. Just be there. The important thing is that you're present in that context and consciously practicing your skills. Can you do that?"

Dot nodded.

"Do you still have your DBT workbook?"

Dot's workbook? She hadn't opened that thing in ages. Dialectical Behavior Therapy had taught her the coping skills she still used today, but it had been years since she last sat down and worked through the exercises in the book.

Dot cringed. "It's . . . somewhere."

"If you can't find it, we can get you a new one. But I want you to use it with regard to your experiences at derby."

Dot groaned. "Do I really need to fill out the worksheets?"

Dr. Frye smiled. "I'm not gonna collect your homework, Dot. But you know the more you put into this, the more you get out of it—and the faster you make progress."

There was that image again, of Kat walking away. "I'll fill out the worksheets."

Dr. Frye made a note on her clipboard. "I have some blank ones I can give you. Remind me before you leave today." She set the clipboard on the side table and returned her gaze to Dot. "So that's thing one."

"And thing two?"

Dr. Frye cleared her throat. She lowered her voice. "Thing two is maybe the harder part. And I think it's probably the real root issue here."

A deep, sudden sense of shame overcame Dot like a cold void opening to swallow her. Her eyes fell.

Dr. Frye sat back in her chair. "You know what that is, don't you? We touched on it already."

Dot nearly mumbled her response. "My sense of self."

"Smart girl."

Dot blew out a breath. "So yeah . . . I guess you were right. Derby's where I saw . . . Derby was *everything*. So I had to be perfect, 'cause that's all I was worth. And that meant Kat had to be the bad guy." Her glassy-eyed stare drifted up to Dr. Frye. "I even clung to it after I shit the bed at MAD. I blamed it all on her."

Dr. Frye nodded once. "And where do you see your worth now?"

"I *don't*." The admission fell from Dot's lips without thought. She covered her mouth. Tears started anew. "Without derby and . . . without Kat . . . I feel like nothing, like . . . just hollow. I *tried*, Dr. Frye. I went through the motions. I held onto my art all this time, but I still don't see it. I can't go in the studio, 'cause I just feel it all looking at me. All my wasted time. I *feel* like a waste of time."

Dr. Frye extended a hand, and Dot gripped it tightly, as though holding on for dear life. The doctor's next words came with a gentle strength and certainty.

"We're gonna talk about this a lot, you and I, okay? We're gonna find you again, Dot. That's thing two."

* * *

My name is Dorothy Mauser. I am not my diagnosis. I create (crappy) art, therefore I am an artist. I own half of a (failing) small business, therefore I am a small business owner. I play roller derby (badly), therefore I am a derby skater. I hate this exercise.

The more you put into this, the more you get out of it.

Dot tore off the sheet of college-ruled paper, crumbled it up, and tossed it in the wastebasket next to her bed.

This was Dot's "Declaration of Dot"—a freeform exercise she used to do as a teenager. Something she and Dr. Frye had come up with together. It could start with simple facts, but by the end it had to contain at least one definitive "I believe in . . ." statement. She could qualify her statements if she felt she had to, but no negative talk—even in parentheses. The Declaration was about defining and *affirming* herself as an individual. She started again.

My name is Dorothy Mauser. I am not my diagnosis. I am a human being. My favorite color is blue. My favorite food is Nonna's giambotta the way Dad makes it. I make sculptures out of trash. I am a sculptor. I own half of a very small business. I am a very small business owner. I have friends. I like to cook. I am a pretty good cook. I like EDM. I like Iggy Pop, apparently. I love my dad. I love roller derby. I love Kat's photography. I love Kat. I am in love with Kat.

Dot paused. She might be wandering outside the intent of the exercise at this point. But she was supposed to be defining herself, and that last sentence felt relevant.

It also felt awful. She didn't deserve Kat. And Kat probably really did hate her now anyway. As she ought to.

Regardless, Dot still needed to find a way to set things right, to somehow undo the pain she'd caused. She would quit derby in a heartbeat if it would bring Kat back to CRD. But no one had heard from

Kat in a week, and she certainly wasn't reading any messages from Dot. So things weren't going to be that simple.

For the time being, Dot figured she'd better commit to reffing. She could never replace Kat, but it was on her to try to fill that void the best she could. Much as she dreaded it, it seemed like the right thing to do.

Wait, yeah . . . she would do it because it was *the right thing to do*. That was relevant.

She put pen to paper again, adding a final line to her Declaration.

I believe in trying to do the right thing.

There. That felt real. Dot who believed in doing the right thing. It was authentically *her*, and something no one could take from her. Something she could build on.

Dot tore off the sheet of paper and carried it with her as she jumped off the bed and crossed the hall into the bathroom. She stood in front of the mirror and read the Declaration again, silently. It was no great work of literature, but it wasn't meant to be. For its intended purpose, she actually felt okay with the things she'd written. But it was that last line especially. That was *worth* something, wasn't it?

She looked up from the paper and studied herself in the mirror. She ran her eyes over the details of her own face—the soft curves of her lips and cheeks, her naturally long eyelashes, her unkempt electric blue hair with its overgrown brown roots—searching for the person she'd just written about.

But Dot didn't feel okay about the person in the mirror. That was the sleepwalking Dot. The blind Dot. The Dot who'd brought everything crashing down on herself. She didn't want to be that Dot anymore. She *wasn't* that Dot anymore. Today represented a fresh start, and something needed to change to reflect that.

In the closet across from the sink, behind rolls of toilet paper and the first-aid kit, Dot discovered the case containing her electric hair clipper. She opened it on the counter. Inside, she found the clipper itself, some cleaning brushes, lubricating oil, and an assortment of guide comb attachments for cutting at varying lengths.

She ran her fingers over the guide combs, settling on the longest one—the one-and-a-half-inch comb. She picked up the clipper and fastened the comb over the blades. She uncoiled the power cord and plugged it into the outlet above the counter. She assessed the tile floor, deciding it would be pretty easy to clean up afterward.

She put the clipper on the counter and took one last lingering look in the mirror—at the Dot who had torn out Kat's heart and stomped on it.

Goodbye, old Dot. Good riddance.

Dot turned and leaned forward, hanging her head upside down over the tile, and brushed her hair out with her fingers. She reached up and grabbed the clippers.

Just as she was about to hit the "on" switch, Dot could hear the faintest crackle of the neighbors' fireworks going off outside. Happy Independence Day.

BZZZZZZZZZZZZZZZ!

CHAPTER 18

Pick Up

Hey Aunt K! Arriving in CC @ 4:15pm tmrw. See you at the station!
xoxo E

* * *

Bzzzt. Bzzzt. Bzzzt. Bzzzt.

Maggie was calling. Again. Kat hit "ignore."

So much for their little arrangement. Mutual pleasure, no strings. Simple. But Mags was obviously getting attached now, which meant it was time to stop.

Kat didn't need her anymore anyway. Just about two months had passed since MAD, at this point. Time heals, and Kat's wounds had hardened into scars—reminders of the price of attachment.

She silenced her phone and shoved it back into her purse just as Verona entered from the main gallery.

"Have you made a decision, Ms. Brooks?"

"Not yet." Kat stood before a large, wooden table, on which there lay five prints. She had room for one more piece in her show, and the choices had been narrowed down to these five. She folded her arms, took a deep breath through her nose, and let it out between tight lips.

Verona put a hand on her shoulder. "There's nothing to be nervous about, my girl."

The reassurance did little to stop Kat's mind from racing, comparing each photo to the next. Which looked most expertly composed? Which had the best lighting balance? Which, in short, made her look the most competent as a photographer?

Verona stepped forward and spread her fingertips on the edge of the table. "There's no wrong choice here. Each one has its strengths. This is one of those situations where you just need to listen to your gut."

"I know." Kat shifted her jaw back and forth. "It's hard to hear my gut over everything else."

"Hm! Very well. What if help you narrow it down?"

Kat's eyebrows rose. "Please do!" She stepped forward beside Verona.

"Right." Verona pointed. "The apothecary scene or the snow maiden statue."

Those two? Upon its omission, Kat felt an instantaneous pull toward another photo—a shot inside the candlelit living quarters of an old lighthouse. "Not this one?"

"Ahh." Verona grinned. "Now it becomes apparent, doesn't it?"

"What do you mean?"

"I just picked two at random. Narrowing the options always prompts the gut to speak up."

Kat gave her a sly smile. "Tricky."

Verona chuckled. "Indeed. So, the lighthouse it is." She turned around and leaned back against the table. "Now, we're just about two weeks out from opening night. We'll have the large format prints made up next week, so if any last minute changes come up, let me know by . . . let's say a week from today?"

"Sure. And otherwise, what else should I do?"

Verona leaned closer. "Pick out a nice outfit. Something a little formal. You want to look your best on opening night."

"That's . . . that's it? You don't need anything else from me?"

Verona shook her head. "We've done all the paperwork. I have your bio, right? We've got the feature pieces chosen. From here on out, my staff will handle the labor. Promotion is already underway, online and in print."

"Promotion?" The Warfield was known to advertise across the Philadelphia metropolitan area and beyond. How far were they going for this little pro bono exhibition?

"Of course! This is a big opportunity for you. And for us, if I'm being honest. As I told you at our first meeting, you are a rare talent." Concern wrinkled Verona's forehead. "I see that lip quivering, dear. There's nothing to fear. It's my choice to take chances on unknown artists like yourself. And I will play hostess and be at your side throughout the opening night gala." She took Kat's hands in her own. "Be nervous, as I know you will. But also let yourself enjoy this. You've earned it."

"Right." Kat stood up straight and nodded, her countenance of cold determination a stark contrast against Verona's warmth. "I will."

* * *

Kat arrived at the bus station around four. She waited in the car for a few minutes, anxiously checking her phone. She opened the photo Eli had sent her. They'd exchanged current-day pics of themselves ahead of today's meeting.

A shot of Eli from the waist up appeared on screen. He had the same dark brown hair and light skin as Kat. He was built broader than Kat's brother—as she remembered him, at least. Same smile, though.

Kat's heart raced. She was really doing this. A Jacobs was going to arrive here any minute. After ten years.

Time to get out and walk around. She would go stir crazy sitting in this car. She took a long drink from her water bottle, then grabbed her purse, turned off the car, and opened the door. She crossed the parking lot, under the oppressively hot sun, in her cutoff denim shorts and a tank top. She'd decided to forgo the Docs in today's heat, opting for sneakers. And shades, of course.

The only one present, she didn't have to wait long in the open-air station. The bus pulled in at 4:16. Her stomach did flips as the brakes screeched and the vehicle came to a stop. She stood several feet back from the doors, unconsciously clutching her purse strap over her chest.

Pictures could not have prepared her for the sight that came around the corner and down the stairs. A young man, as tall as she was, stepped down onto the pavement. Same dark brown hair, yes, and same pale complexion. But also beard stubble. Arm and leg hair. Muscled shoulders protruding from his cutoff tee. Big, rugged hands. He could have been a football player.

Eli lifted his shades. Those blue eyes. He had Kat's father's eyes, but... he wore them differently. Warmly. He was unmistakably a Jacobs, but Kat's little Eli was still in there.

"Aunt Kitty." That deep voice. He had Kat's father's voice as well. How bizarre to hear those words spoken in that voice. Kat was momentarily frozen. A smile tugged at the corner of Eli's mouth.

Kat lifted her own shades, still in shock. "Hey, buddy."

Eli beamed. "You look the same."

"You—" Kat swallowed "—grew up."

A laugh bellowed forth from Eli, shattering the tension. Kat's expression melted into joy. They stepped together into a hug.

"I missed you." In his whisper, Eli hadn't aged a day. He smelled so familiar.

"I missed you too, buddy." A tear escaped Kat's eye.

While they embraced, the driver came down and opened the underbelly of the bus.

"Oh yeah, my stuff." Eli stepped back, flashed a grin at Kat, and hastened to help the driver unload his luggage—two rolling suitcases, a large duffel bag, and a loaded backpack.

Kat hefted the backpack and strapped it onto her shoulders. "Holy cow. What's in this thing, Eli?"

He turned. "Oh, uh, books mostly."

"Don't you get your books at school?"

"Well, yeah. These aren't for class. What's in there is my Bible and some related stuff. History and scholarly texts, like."

Kat shifted under the weight. "Feels like a whole library."

"Ha! Almost!" Eli extended a hand. "I can carry it. You don't have to—"

"I got it, young man." Kat tucked her thumbs under the straps. "Your aunt's stronger than she looks."

Eli smirked. "Actually, you look pretty strong." He took her in from head to toe. "Cool tattoos, by the way."

"Aw, thanks!" Kat bent sideways and peered down at the ink on her legs. On the outside of her right thigh were two "female" symbols linked together, surrounded by flame-like shading embellishments. On her left thigh, a ragged garter, held together with safety pins. She'd had them for so long, she rarely thought about them anymore, but they were brand new to Eli.

Eli lifted the duffel over his shoulder with ease, and they each took a rolling suitcase. As the bus drove off, Kat pulled her shades down and led the way to the car.

She glanced at Eli. "You hungry?"

He cocked an eye at her. "You kidding? I'm always hungry."

"We can grab something on the way to my house." After a moment's thought, an idea struck Kat, and she whirled around to face Eli. Speaking of brand new—"Ever had a real cheesesteak?"

* * *

Wednesday night and Thursday were largely spent talking and catching up. Eli had his portfolio with him and was eager to show Kat the work which had landed him his scholarship. He gave her the rundown of this semester's classes and the things he was most excited about.

At Eli's request, Kat showed him some of her freelance work—material he wouldn't have seen on her website. Not just the finished photos she'd sent to the clients, but also some of those she'd opted to omit. She explained her editing process and how the whole business worked. Eli was enthralled. The look of wonder she caught in his eyes mirrored his reaction to the Canon Sure Shot all those years before.

Later, they got into some philosophical religious talk. Eli opened his backpack and they cracked the books. He'd brought some on the history of the Bible and the science behind it, as well as a comparative survey of religions. He was fascinated by the common threads which ran through many faiths and ideologies, finding himself drawn especially to concepts in Buddhism and Humanism. His insightfulness regarding his faith proved impressive, especially considering his age.

As promised, Kat introduced Eli to some of her favorite music. They listened to album after album while they talked. Now and then, a break in conversation would prompt a "Who's this?" or "What's the title of this song?" from an interested Eli. Sometimes these inquiries led Kat to reminisce about Aunt Devon. After a while, Eli began asking more questions about Devon than about the music, and she became the main topic of discussion—or perhaps not so much discussion as story time.

Kat explained how a young Aunt Devon—younger than Eli was now—would often babysit her as a child. Devon would put on a CD or vinyl record and give pre-teen Kat a musical history lesson. They would sit in candlelight and listen together. The subject matter of the songs wouldn't all make sense to her until she grew older, but little Kat would treasure those sessions all the same.

Of course, this had all been back before Devon was outed. Before her "therapy." Before they'd stopped allowing Kat and Devon to spend time together unsupervised. Even then, the two of them had found ways to communicate covertly, but it was never the same. Devon was never the same.

Teenage Kat would see Devon's life fall apart, and watch her wither away, helpless to intervene. Kat told Eli about Devon's warning to her—to run. It had been as though Devon herself knew she wouldn't be around much longer. Here was the person who'd been, to Kat, the mother she should have had, driven to an early grave by her own family.

Kat tried to convey to Eli how lost she'd felt in the following years. How trapped and afraid. Even away from home, at college, Kat lived in fear of discovery. She would explore, tentatively—drunkenly kiss girls at parties, sometimes venture a little further in the relative privacy of a sorority house bedroom. But not until junior year would she build up the courage to date her first real girlfriend—Maxine.

Looking back now, Kat wondered if some part of her had been daring her parents to learn the truth. She'd so grown to resent having to hide who she was. But when the time came, the idea of running—of leaving behind all her flesh and blood, of leaving school and facing the world alone—would prove too daunting. In light of that, she'd find herself agreeing to a phone consultation with Devon's old "therapist."

In the end, the consultation would turn out to be the last straw, as it made fresh the memory of Devon's fate. Caught between the unthinkable and the unlivable, Kat's desperation would ultimately drive her toward survival.

Kat had never told anyone that entire story. Not one person. Not even Dot. By the time she finished the telling, it was late. The music had stopped. She and Eli were both exhausted, mentally and emotionally.

As they began to doze off, side by side on top of the covers, Kat rolled over to face Eli.

"I love you, buddy," she said. "I'm sorry I left you."

Eli responded in a sleepy mumble, "It's okay, Aunt Kitty. I love you too. I'm glad you stayed alive."

* * *

Friday morning. While Eli remained fast asleep upstairs, a bleary-eyed Kat wandered into the kitchen in search of coffee. Her heart sank as she rounded the corner of the fridge and laid eyes on an empty pot.

Groaning, she grabbed the pot from beneath the filter basket, put it in the sink, and started it filling. Then she opened the cabinet above the coffee maker and pulled out the grounds and filters.

Not even an entire minute later, Kat watched as the first drops of coffee dripped into the pot. It never really took all that long, but somehow this process felt like an eternity every time. She put her elbows on the counter and stared at the thin stream of dark liquid, as though her impatience could intimidate it into brewing faster.

"Kid still sleeping?"

Kat jumped. "Jesus, Lonnie!"

Lonnie snickered. "Sorry!" He opened the fridge and retrieved a carton of almond milk.

Kat settled back against the counter. "Yeah, he'll probably be out for a couple hours yet."

"You guys got plans today?" Lonnie grabbed a bowl from the drying rack. He set the bowl and the milk on the table.

"We were gonna check out the local United Church of Christ, and maybe the Unitarian Universalists. He's never been to either."

Lonnie perused the cereal selection in the far cabinet. "Have *you* ever been to either?"

"A couple times, yeah. Unitarian, anyway. I've never gone to the normal services, but they hold a vigil for the Trans Day of Remembrance each year. I've gone to that with Siren—Leah. So I'm at least acquainted with the place."

Lonnie pulled down the raisin bran. "Well that sounds interesting." He turned to Kat. "Your plans for the day, I mean."

"Yeah, we might stop at Jake's too. Check out camera gear." The coffee finished brewing. Kat grabbed a mug from the rack.

"Cool, cool." Lonnie filled his bowl with cereal. "What about tomorrow? Any chance you're gonna come to the Kegs' bout?"

Kat was silent as she poured her coffee.

Lonnie closed the box. "Everyone there misses you. And it's a prime opportunity to show Eli derby."

"No." Kat's tone was stone cold. "He's here to hang out with me and see what I do. I don't do derby anymore." She scooped sugar into her mug.

"Kat . . ." Lonnie had started to pour the milk, but he stopped and put it down. "You can't just run from this forever. Derby's been your life for . . . god, years and years. And now I get why!"

Kat heaved a sigh as she stirred her drink.

Lonnie stepped away from the table, toward her. He softened his voice. "Look, you haven't been the same since—"

"Since MAD?" Kat whipped around. "Yeah. I know. I'm not the same. I'm smarter. I got burned, and I learned from it." She picked up her mug. "I'm real glad you and Leah are happy and you've got your whole NSO thing going on now, but leave me out of it. I'm done." She strode toward the stairs.

"Ya know, Dot's reffing."

Kat froze in the kitchen doorway. Had she heard that right? Dot was trying to ref? What kind of nonsense . . .

"Tomorrow." Lonnie stood stock still, eyes on Kat. "And she's not half bad."

There was a strained pause. Kat said nothing.

"You didn't know, did you?"

Kat shook her head.

"Have you read any of her messages? She—"

"Drop it, Lonnie. I'm not going." Kat disappeared around the corner and took the stairs up, two at a time.

* * *

Kat and Eli spent much of Friday driving around, doing a mini tour of Crosscannon. She took him to visit the liberal churches and the camera shop, and they went on to stop by the Warfield, the park, and one of Kat's favorite little cafes for a late lunch.

They were finding their groove together as . . . well, family—relearning each other's idiosyncrasies as they'd evolved over the past decade, getting a feel for one another's sense of humor. The bond between Aunt Kitty and her no-longer-little buddy was evident, just forty-eight hours into their reunion.

* * *

Saturday afternoon found Kat sitting cross-legged on her bed with Eli's Bible open in her lap.

"You sure do have a lot of notes in these margins, kiddo."

Eli laughed. "Yeah, the most recent ones are in orange pen. Not to be confused with the red, which are kinda old." He glanced at Kat. "I don't want you thinking the red ones represent my views *now*."

Eli was seated at the desk, making use of Kat's laptop. He had a gallery of photos open in Lightroom—specifically a batch from one of Kat's statue shoots. Several memory cards were lined up on the desk. Eli was working his way through them, studying Kat's technique over time.

"Aunt Kitty, how do you even pick which shots are the keepers here? Most of these look flawless. I mean, you don't have nearly this many on the website."

Kat looked up. "Oh, you should have seen the full original batch. What's on those cards has been pruned down already." She stepped off the bed and moseyed up behind Eli, looking over his shoulder. "But yeah, it's not easy to decide which are the best, especially when it's your own work. That's one of the things that gets more frustrating the better you get as a photographer. You end up with so many usable shots. But here . . ." Kat stepped over to the foot locker and knelt in front of it. "I've got a memory card in here somewhere, from ages ago, that'll show you what my stuff *used* to look like. If I can find it."

Kat went about rummaging through the nooks and crannies of the padding inside the locker, searching for the same lost card she'd been seeking months prior. Meanwhile, Eli ejected the current card and inserted another. As the new photos loaded, his eyes went wide.

"Oh dang! Aunt Kitty, where are *these* from? You've got some of these in the show, I'm sure, right?"

Kat continued digging. "You still looking at the snow maiden? She got cut from the show, actually."

"No, this is something else. There's like a horse . . . thing."

Kat was puzzled. Where the hell had that old memory card gone? "Horse thing? Lady Godiva? She's in the show."

"No, it's got, like . . . spaceship wings."

"What?" Kat popped up and nicked her head on the edge of the shelf above her.

"Oh no! Are you okay?" Eli turned with a start, half leaving the chair.

"Ahahh. Owww, fffuck." Kat waved him back down, holding her head. She sat on the edge of the bed, wincing. "Yeah, yeah, I'm fine. No damage, it just smarts. What . . . where did you find that photo?"

Eli turned back to the laptop. "On one of these cards. It said 'D-O-T.'" He pointed to the screen. "Who's this girl?"

At those words, Kat suddenly found herself rather aware of her own heartbeat, the throbbing on the top of her head becoming but a background echo of the thumping in her chest. She stood slowly and moved behind Eli again for a clear look.

Dot was mid-stroke at the screen printing press. Colorful ink speckled the olive skin of her forearms. Her powerful biceps and shoulders flexed as she pulled the squeegee toward her. The overhead light shimmered on her perspiration. It traced with shadow the curves of her cheeks, the corners of her lips, the weight of her focused brow over her shining brown eyes. Stray strands of blue hair cut down the side of her face to her jawline, rounded and soft but capable of tightening with terrible strength.

Eli moved to advance to the next photo.

"No." Kat put a hand on his shoulder. It was an automatic response. She hadn't seen that face in nine weeks. Her heart tugged against her will, begging her to linger—to recall that moment of supreme desire, standing so close to Dot, aching to reach out and touch her. That fateful step which had landed Kat on the floor, Dot rushing forward to save her. The warmth of Dot's hands and the sweet scent of her breath as they'd stood face to face. The magnetic pull of her lips.

"Who is that, Aunt Kitty?"

The answer came as a soft utterance from a thousand yards away. "That's Dot."

Eli looked up at Kat, his eyebrows raised in inquiry.

Kat's eyes didn't leave the screen. "I haven't spoken to her since we broke up."

"She was your girlfriend?"

Kat nodded.

"How long ago was that?"

"Two months." Kat folded her arms and bit her lip. Her brow wrinkled as she stared, almost unblinking.

Eli observed her for a moment before gently breaking the silence. "You still care about her, don't you?"

No.

No, not after ... that day. Not after everything. The total lack of respect. The blame. The misdirected rage. Kat recalled brief glimpses of Dot shouting at her like a petulant child. Tried to hold that image in her mind.

But it wouldn't stick. Kat's heart still tugged at her. Why? Why was Dot like that? And why did Kat still care?

She didn't know what to tell Eli, so she let that stretch of silence be her answer.

He pressed further. "Why haven't you spoken? What happened?"

Kat sighed. "It's complicated, Eli. It was a—it wasn't an amicable breakup."

Eli turned back to the screen and studied the photo of Dot. "I'm sorry."

"Yeah."

He hovered the mouse pointer over the "next" button and glanced back at Kat.

She nodded. "Go ahead."

He clicked through the photos one by one—photos of Dot working, smiling at the camera, blushing. Photos of the sculptures. Kat couldn't tear her gaze away.

"Aunt Kitty, these are unbelievable." Eli swiveled the chair around to face her. "It's your best work. Tell me it's in the show."

Kat shook her head wordlessly, fixed on the photo that was showing—the mask.

"You probably need permission from Dot, right? And you aren't talking." Eli pursed his lips in thought. "There's gotta be a way. Do you know where to find her?"

"She's at the bout right now," Kat answered absentmindedly. It didn't matter anyway. Dot had already given her explicit permission to use the photos.

"The bout? What's a bout?"

"Hm?" Kat snapped back to the present. Eli looked perplexed. "Oh . . . a roller derby game. Lonnie said she's reffing. I'll believe that when I see it."

Eli's eyes went wide with excitement. "Well, let's go see it, then! It's happening now?"

Great. Kat hadn't been thinking, and she'd . . . let the cat out of the bag, as it were. Now she had to let Eli down. "Actually . . ." How was she gonna do that, exactly?

Eli eyed her hopefully. The mask watched her from the screen. Kat closed her eyes. Just tell him no. Just say it.

Urrgh. She didn't want to disappoint him! But what was the other option? Go to the bout? Ha! Right! There was no way. No.

Then why was it still so hard to say it aloud? Why did it ache to think about squelching the idea again, now that it had been given a little room to breathe? Was it even feasible, going to the bout? They'd be late, for one thing. But . . . that meant fewer people would notice them coming in. They could stay toward the back and watch from a distance. And leave before the end, before Dot even knew they were there. Maybe.

Then again, maybe it wouldn't work. Maybe the whole thing would blow up in Kat's face. But dammit, why did a feeling of relief accompany the possibility of going? She couldn't deny it. Part of her *wanted* to go. Part of her was really curious to see Dot ref. And part of her just . . . really wanted to see Dot. One more time. Maybe seeing her in present day, instead of these old photos, would bring some closure.

Yeah, maybe that was it. And then she wouldn't have to say no to Eli.

"Aunt Kitty?"

"Fine." She exhaled. A weight was lifted. "Let's go to the bout."

CHAPTER 19

Farewells

"Fine, I won't say anything if you don't want me to, but I'm not happy about it." Annoyance tinged Leah's voice as she slid two ticket stubs under the window to Kat. "Anyway, there's no way you're gonna stay hidden the whole bout."

"We'll see. Thank you, Si." Kat took Eli by the hand and, with haste, led the way through the open double doors to the venue proper.

A couple of freshies were on wristband duty and didn't recognize Kat. She presented the pair of stubs while she scanned the area. Spectators were either sitting trackside—on the floor or in chairs—or standing outside the rink wall. Most eyes were on the track.

Once banded, Kat pulled Eli along into the crowd. She had them moving like two shadows, avoiding the places she knew league members would be—the merch table, the side door, the entrance to the rink floor. When a familiar face came into view, she made sure to pass on the opposite side of another person, so as to block line of sight.

Finally, she arrived at an agreeable spot in the corner, where a group of tall gentlemen effectively hid her from most angles. Still, she glanced around them, nervous that she might have been seen.

"So, the ones with the stars score points, right?" Eli was decidedly less concerned. He was already watching the action with interest. There were about fifteen minutes left in the first period.

"Yes. They're called jammers."

"Can they hit people too? Or are they just avoiding being hit?"

Kat still hadn't looked at the track. "They can hit people." She'd spotted Domme several yards away. Domme would blow Kat's cover for sure, if she saw. Kat inched forward, hiding behind Eli.

"Okay, and which ref is Dot?"

Dot! Kat's head instantly swiveled to face the track, locating Dot in seconds. She pointed. "There." She'd know that figure anywhere. Though something was missing. No blue.

Dot was one of two OPRs. God, it was surreal to see her in stripes. But then, it was surreal to even see her in the flesh. Kat watched her take leisurely strides, keeping pace with the pack. Watched her legs flex and extend. Dot's jaw was tense as she held her whistle in her teeth.

"I *thought* I recognized that voice!"

Kat whipped around.

Jet was right behind her, wearing a wicked grin. "Thought you could hide, eh?"

"I-I . . ." Kat's mouth fell agape. Her heart raced. This was it. Jet was going to chew her out and reveal her to everyone. Dammit, this had been such a stupid move, coming to the bout! What had Kat been thinking?

Jet's grin fell away, her features drooping into a look of concerned dejection. "I didn't think you'd show. We haven't heard from you since MAD."

Kat swallowed.

Jet went on, "Good thing Si's dating Lonnie. He kept us updated, let us know you were okay."

"He . . . he did?"

"Of course he did! You weren't responding to me or Lynn, and we got worried."

Kat's eyes fell. She didn't know what to say, how to explain.

"Dammit, Kat. Come 'ere." Jet closed the distance and wrapped her arms around Kat. "We've missed you *so much*."

Kat hesitantly returned the embrace. Fear at being caught still had her stomach twisted. "Jet . . ."

"Yeah?"

"Please. Please don't tell everyone I'm here."

Jet backed off, gripped Kat's arms, and looked her in the eye. "Is that what you're worried about?"

"It's just . . . I'm not ready to—" Kat's voice caught.

"See Dot, right?" Jet finished. "I get it. I won't say a word. But you must have read her email if you're here."

Kat shook her head.

"You *haven't?*" Jet's eyes went wide. "Girl, you gotta read what she sent you!"

"She's been sending me stuff off and on since the breakup. I've been ignoring it."

"*All of it?*"

Kat nodded.

Jet's brow creased. Her tone became dire. "Listen. I won't tell anyone you're here, but you gotta read her last email as soon as you get home, okay?"

It was rare to see Jet appear so stern. Kat's answer came timidly. "Okay."

"Hey." Eli's gentle baritone interrupted the tension. "Aunt Kitty, this guy—"

"*Aunt?*" Jet turned to him with a start. She looked at Kat. "Is he . . . ?" Then back at him. "Are you Eli?"

"Heh." Eli grinned. "Yeah. How did you know?"

"Wait, what . . . ?" Kat's face contorted. "How *did* you know?"

A voice answered from the other side of Eli. It was warm and familiar. "Did you think Dot wouldn't tell us about Eli?"

Kat turned slowly, a mix of emotions swirling. That was . . . "Ben?"

Eli backed out of the way. "Yeah, this dude said he knows you. That's what I was gonna—well, there ya go."

Ben smiled with a kind of sad sympathy. "Hey, kiddo."

"Ben . . ." Kat had been dreading the possibility of this moment. How could she face this man, who loved his daughter more than anything in the world? Who'd been so gratified to see her happy with Kat, only to have it all go to shit. But now that the moment was here, Ben's mere presence seemed to make dread the furthest thing from Kat's mind.

"She talks about you all the time." Ben's eyes wandered to the track. To Dot. His tone was so easy, as if he'd just spoken to Kat yesterday.

"She does?"

He turned back to Kat, his brow rising with a hint of optimism. "I'm glad you're here. It's really good to see your face."

Somehow that smile was just as comforting as ever. Just as welcoming. A beacon of safety. Before she knew what she was doing, Kat propelled herself forward, reaching for a hug. Ben caught her in his arms with natural ease. They stood wordless for a long moment, tears welling in Kat's eyes. She inhaled sharply. Ben smelled like . . . home.

Kat rested her brow on his shoulder, hiding her face from the world around them. Her voice creaked as she bit back the urge to cry. "I'm sorry things didn't work out . . . between Dot 'n me."

"Shhh. It's okay." Ben spoke in a soothing whisper. "If it wasn't meant to be, it wasn't meant to be."

He was still so kind. So patient. From his perspective, Kat had broken his daughter's heart and walked away. Yet here he was, comforting her, glad to see her. How was that possible?

"Why are you being so nice to me, Ben?"

"Hmh." Ben rested his temple against Kat's head. "'Cause you're a good kid, Kat. I'm glad you're in our lives, and that you gave Dottie a chance."

"I'd hardly say I'm in your lives anymore." A touch a cynicism coated Kat's response.

"What, 'cause you needed some time?"

Some time? How much time would Kat have taken if events had unfolded differently today? She might never have come back at all. She'd even considered moving away and starting fresh after the gallery show. She might yet.

Ben continued, "Two months is nothing, kiddo. You're here now. And I know, when you're ready, Dot will be happy to see you."

TWEEET!

"Black two-eight-nine, direction!" Dot was just audible, as she was on the nearest stretch of track.

"Really?" The skater threw her hands up.

The sounds of derby rushed back into Kat's consciousness. It was sobering. Her breathing calmed as she lifted her head and turned out of the embrace. "What's going on?" She sniffed.

The visiting team's bench coach was shouting something.

Ben squinted at the situation on the track. "Dottie's getting flack for a penalty call."

Kat smirked humorlessly. "Sounds familiar."

Dot calmly repeated the call.

The skater cast a resentful glare at her, then yelled at the coach, "It's fuckin' bullshit!"

Kat's eyebrows rose. "Well *that's* an insub."

TWEEET!

"Black two-eight-nine, insubordination!"

Wow. Dot had been right on top of that. And with the same even-toned delivery.

Wait—*Dot* had just been antagonized, called into question, and hadn't reacted at all. What witchery was this?

Kat flicked a curious glance at Ben. "Did she take a Valium before she went out there?"

Ben chuckled. "Impressive, right? She's been working hard. No Valium needed."

After that little incident—or non-incident, on Dot's part—Kat settled into watching the bout. She tried not to think about the impending repercussions of the past few minutes, or the fact that her plan to stay hidden had immediately crashed and burned. Right now, in this moment, things were comfortable. Surrounded by Eli, Jet, and Ben, there was a sense of belonging. Kat had been working hard too—working to forget this feeling. She hadn't realized until now how much she'd missed it.

* * *

Come halftime, Eli had countless questions—about the rules, individual skaters, the way the league operated, and so on. While Kat fielded his queries, Jet took a walk around the venue to make sure all was running smoothly.

With five minutes left in intermission, Ben showed Eli to the restroom. Left without much of a crowd to hide her, Kat crouched with her back against the rink wall. Trying to appear nonchalant, she busied herself on her phone. When, at last, Ben and Eli returned, they came carrying drinks—lemonade for Eli and beers for Kat and Ben.

When the second period started, all eyes returned to the track. While most were focused on the skaters, Kat consistently found hers following Dot. She did keep an eye on the action, but with specific attention paid to the areas Dot should be watching.

And Dot held her own out there, to be sure. Her positioning relative to the pack was always good. She communicated well with the inside refs. She didn't miss any calls as far as Kat could tell, but that was hard to judge from this distance. All in all, Dot seemed to be making a decent referee.

Now and then, though, Kat would find her critical observation slipping. An entire jam would pass, only for Kat to then realize her gaze had been glued wistfully to Dot the entire time. Admiring the way her short-sleeved, low-cut ref shirt hugged her torso. Wondering if her blue hair was somehow tucked up under her helmet. Remembering the feel of those smooth, muscular legs, intertwined with her own.

It seemed to happen more and more as the period went on. Old memories came back of Dot catching her staring across the track. Some subconscious piece of Kat longed for Dot to turn right now and meet her eyes. Dared her to. *Willed* her to. Even as she mentally fought the desire, her heart leapt at the prospect.

TWEEeeeEET!

End of the bout.

Wait, what? *End of the bout?* A sudden adrenaline surge hit Kat. Her leaping heart plunged into a thunderous pounding. She'd meant to leave early. This was bad.

Amid the excitement and applause, she grabbed Eli's hand. "We gotta go."

"But—"

"Now."

* * *

Dac rolled into the locker room, his eyes going straight to Dot. "Excellent work out there, Mouse."

"I'll say!" Jason sat across from her, unstrapping his elbow pads. "Especially for your first bout. You can be on *my* crew anytime."

"Jeez." Dot looked down and blushed, a proud grin overtaking her face. "Thanks, guys."

"First drink's on me." Dac patted her on the shoulder as he passed. "You earned it."

Dot had her wristguards and elbow pads off. She'd been free of the splint for a week at this point. She'd just removed her helmet and set it down when she heard her name being shouted.

"MOUSE!" It came from down the hall. "Outta the way! MOUSE!" Sounded like Reggie, and she was getting closer.

Dot stood up just as Reggie reached the door. "What's—"

"Kat's here!" Reggie delivered the news with wide-eyed urgency.

Dot's expression now mirrored hers. "She's . . . *Where?*"

"Parking lot! Right now! She just left!"

Dot froze. Her pulse had just gone into overdrive. She slowed her breathing. She'd known the day would come when she would see Kat again, and she'd known it would be overwhelming. She'd been planning, preparing herself. Okay—one step at a time, Dot.

Reggie frowned and motioned for Dot to hurry. "Go! Get 'er!"

Dot put up an index finger. "Wait." She reached into the side pocket of her skate bag and retrieved a white envelope. She looked down. She was still wearing her skates, without full gear. She weighed the options. There was no time. It had to be now. "Scoot." She made for the door, and Reggie stepped aside.

Dot barreled out of the hallway and began weaving through the sparse crowd. "Sorry. Pardon me." She made a conscious effort to ignore the rapid drum beat in her chest and focus on her task. Get to the exit. Don't run anyone over. She could do this.

She began to shoulder her way through the bottleneck at the door. "I'm so sorry. Please. It's an emergency." Her voice quivered, but she kept her composure as the exiting guests parted, a few at a time, to let her by.

Dot stepped out onto the blacktop and surveyed the parking lot by the light of the setting sun. A red car in the distance. Two figures running toward it. She didn't recognize the figure on the right, but the one on the left was unmistakably Kat.

Dot got a running start on her toestops and took off like a rocket, her hard indoor wheels rattling on the blacktop. God, that sight—Kat running away again. Please let this be the last time. After today, she wouldn't have to run anymore.

"Kat!"

Kat didn't look back. She kept running. Dot kept skating. She was closing the distance, but she didn't want to catch up. She didn't want to force this.

"Kat, please!"

The guy with Kat glanced back. He slowed to a walk and said something to her. She turned and looked back at him. Walking backwards toward the car now, just a few yards from it, she waved for him to come. But he stopped where he was.

"Just see what she wants, Aunt Kitty."

Dot slid to a stop several feet from him, her pleading eyes fixed on Kat. "Please. This is the last time you'll ever have to see or hear from me, I promise. I'll disappear."

At that, Kat stopped dead and shifted her gaze to Dot. Their eyes locked. There was a long stretch of silence. The young man glanced back and forth between them. Dot battled the urge to cover the remaining distance. She ran herself through mental grounding exercises as her heart hollered ruinous impulses in her ear.

"Eli… get in the car." Kat clicked her key fob and the Corolla beeped, unlocking. Eli did as she asked, casting one last, long look in Dot's direction.

After Eli reached the car, Kat took her first hesitant step back toward Dot. Then another.

Dot rolled slowly, non-threateningly, holding the envelope with both hands. She stopped a few feet from Kat. Kat stood with her arms at her sides, fingers half-curled.

Neither spoke, though both seemed about to. Dot had rehearsed this moment an untold number of times in her head, but the words escaped her now. Unsure how to start, she held out the envelope. Kat didn't move to take it.

Dot looked at the envelope, then back at Kat. "I'm sorry."

Kat's expression was stony—not uncaring, just restrained. It was a relief, in a way. Dot had expected anger. She *deserved* anger.

Kat glanced down at Dot's skates. "You're gonna ruin your good wheels that way."

A threat of a smile just barely flickered at the corner of Dot's mouth. It was quickly buried. "I don't care."

Kat's jaw tensed. A crack in the stone. Was she fighting to hold herself together? Dot didn't want to put her through any more pain.

"Please read it." Dot's voice faltered. "I know you stopped reading my messages. Just read this one. It's the last one."

Kat's brow creased. She reached out and pulled the envelope from Dot's hand. She didn't look at it, but held it at her side, eyes on Dot. "Is that all?"

Dot swallowed. She nodded. That was it. The deed was done. Now she could leave Kat in peace.

Dot lowered her eyes and started to roll away backwards. She turned toward the rink.

"Dot."

She stopped and looked back.

Kat hadn't moved. "I . . . I like your hair."

Dot had let it grow out a little. She'd kept a streak of blue on top, just off-center to the right. "Uh—thank you." At this moment, the shaggy mop was partially matted to her head with sweat. She self-consciously reached up with both hands and ran her fingers through it. "That . . . means a lot."

Kat nodded. With a slow blink, she tore her eyes from Dot, turned back toward the car, and resumed walking. Seconds later, she was opening the door.

"Goodbye, Kat." But the words came as a stifled whisper under the crushing weight of the lump in Dot's throat.

It was just as well. Let her go.

Lynn burst out of the rink doors and came sprinting across the blacktop.

Kat's Corolla pulled out of the parking spot. It accelerated around the edge of the lot, to the exit, and turned onto the main road. When it was out of sight, Dot fell onto her knee pads and let the tears come.

* * *

"So we'll do something around New Year's?"

"Absolutely, buddy." Kat gave Eli a squeeze before ending the embrace. She held his hands and took one last mental snapshot of his smiling face. They'd taken tons of photos together over these past few days, but no photo could really capture the bittersweet experience of this parting moment. "And I'll see about coming to visit before then."

Eli's eyes brightened. "I'd really like that!" He glanced back at the bus. The driver was closing the underbelly. Eli turned back to Kat. "And let me know how the show goes! And what happens with Dot!"

Kat nodded. "I'll tell you about all the things, I promise."

"Good." Eli grinned. The driver climbed onto the bus. "I think it's time. I love you, Aunt Kitty."

Kat stole a final, quick hug. "I love you too, buddy. Have an awesome time at school."

She backed away as Eli ascended the steps. He disappeared around the corner, behind the tinted windows. Kat stayed put and watched the bus pull away. As it exited the station, she pivoted on the sole of her sneaker and began walking back to the car.

She took her time traversing the short distance, in no hurry to go anywhere now. It was strange to be without Eli after three days of constant companionship. Kat had expected to feel some relief at having time to herself—and there *was* a touch of that—but what struck her most right now was a kind of gnawing loneliness.

She'd tried to swear off family, but Eli had to be the exception. He believed in her. Loved her for who she was. Even after she'd abandoned him all those years ago, he'd kept the faith and put in serious effort to reconnect. That was worth something. Wherever she might go after this show, she would never disappear from his life again. They'd lost too much time already.

As Kat arrived at the car, her fingers automatically fished in her purse for keys. She opened the door and planted herself in the driver's seat. Soon enough, she was pulling out onto the road.

It was quiet in the car. Kat imagined that coach bus hitting the highway, carrying her only family off to Baltimore. Except . . . "only family" didn't sound right. Not after yesterday. She'd tried to run. She'd cut herself off from everyone. But they'd never stopped thinking of her as family. Lonnie was still looking out for her. Jet and Lynn too. Hell, Ben still called her "kiddo." Talk about defying her expectations. Kat did feel lonely with Eli gone, but she didn't feel *alone*.

There was no relief in that, by the way. She'd fucked up the whole plan by showing up at the bout. And for what? One last look at Dot? "Closure"? Right. Looking Dot in the eye had been the opposite of closure. It had only made the pain fresh. Made it that much harder to look away again.

When Kat got back to the house, no one else was home. It was hot on the first floor. She headed for the kitchen, opened the fridge and grabbed a cold Kickback. She popped the cap using the nearby wall-mounted bottle opener, then carried the beer up the stairs with her.

As Kat opened the door to her room, a burst of cool air hit her face. The AC had been left running. She put her purse down on the desk—next to the envelope.

Despite her promise to Jet, Kat still hadn't read any of Dot's messages, including this one. She'd told herself she wanted to focus on Eli for the last hours of his visit. But now he was gone, and she stood alone, staring down at the flowing script that read simply "Kat."

The last time you'll ever have to see or hear from me, Dot had said. So . . . if Kat wanted closure, supposedly this was meant to be it. But what was Dot's idea of closure? She could still see the trembling hand offering the envelope. The defeated expression. The sad eyes. *Please read it.*

Kat's jaw tensed. She snatched the envelope off the desk and tore it open. Inside, she found a series of handwritten pages on college-ruled paper. As she unfolded them, she lowered herself into the desk chair.

Kat,

The word apology doesn't begin to describe what I owe you, but an apology is a place to start. I'm sorry. I'm sorry for hurting you. I'm sorry for blaming you. I'm sorry for doubting you. I'm sorry for shouting at you, taking out my anger on you, projecting my shit onto you. I'm sorry for everything. I don't deserve forgiveness, and I'm not asking for it.

You were right to walk away from me. But please don't walk away from derby because of me. CRD is your home, and I took that from you. You're a phenomenal ref. I never gave you credit for that. I've been filling in, poorly, in your absence, but CRD needs you. I shouldn't be the one who's still here. I was in the wrong. Worse than just being wrong, I was abusive to you. If you're reading this, then by now I've already retired from the league, so I won't be there when you return.

There are things I should have told you about myself a long time ago. You offered me a chance to do so at MAD, but I was already too far gone. I'm going to tell you now, because I owe you an explanation. As I write this, I fear you might think it's meant to be an excuse for my behavior. Please understand that it is not.

Here, the script seemed to lose the ease of its flow, becoming shakier and more deliberate.

When I was a teenager, I was diagnosed with a condition called borderline personality disorder. It's a complicated mental disorder. I won't try to define it all here, but in short, I was an unholy terror. My emotions were out of control, especially my anger. I didn't know what was wrong with me or how to cope.

But I'm not a teenager anymore. I've been working towards recovery for twelve years now. I have the ability to recognize my symptoms and control my actions. I started to relapse in some ways because I got lazy and thought I was doing fine. I wasn't being mindful. I let fear get the better of me, and that's on me. But I took it out on you, and that's unacceptable.

I'm trying to make things right. I can't undo what I did, so I'm doing the best I can. I'm still a work in progress, and I might be that way forever. But I'm doing the work now that I should have been doing already—seeing my psychiatrist regularly and getting back to basics.

So I heard you have a thing going with Mags now. I'm glad. She's pretty awesome. You're an amazing person, and I want you to be happy.

Lastly, if you ever need anything, you know how to find me. Anything. Day or night, whatever it is, I'll be there in a heartbeat. I know I would be the last resort, but sometimes in an emergency it comes to that. So the offer is there, always.

Otherwise, I promise this is goodbye. Please take care.

Dot

Tears dripped onto the paper. Kat barely moved except to flip the pages as she read and reread the letter.

"Goodbye." Kat had tried so hard to disappear without even saying it. Why was it tearing her apart now to see it written in Dot's neat cursive hand?

Kat pulled her phone from her purse and opened her email. She filtered by Dot's address and began going back through the messages she'd left unread. The contents were more or less the same as the letter, or parts of it. For nearly as long as Kat had been running from her, Dot had been trying to apologize. Trying to explain. Trying to do exactly as Kat had asked at MAD. But Dot's efforts had been falling on deaf ears.

Kat's stomach twisted. It felt like the world had just shifted beneath her. Suddenly, she was the asshole here. The further back she read, the heavier the weight of her guilt grew.

The Dot who'd written these messages was rational, self-effacing—such a far cry from the tantrum-throwing loose-cannon she was capable of becoming. This was the person Kat had fallen in love with. But how? How could Dot shift so dramatically?

"A complicated mental disorder," the letter said. Kat wanted to understand. More than anything, she wanted to reach out to this rational Dot and beg her forgiveness for not listening, but how would

Dot even react? Which Dot would she get? Kat *needed* to understand more first.

She opened her laptop with every intention of Googling "borderline personality disorder." But the screen awoke still showing Lightroom with the "Dot" gallery loaded, and Kat's train of thought hit an unexpected junction.

Eli had been right. She'd known it the moment he'd said it. This was her best work. And none of it was in the show. The one thing Verona had asked of her, and Kat had failed to deliver. Well, she could remedy that, but there was no time to waste. She picked up the phone, found Verona in her recent contacts, and hit "call."

CHAPTER 20

A Portrait of the Artist

Dot cut the steering wheel and backed the van in nice and tight against the curb—a parallel parking job to be proud of, just about a block from the Warfield Gallery.

The sun was setting, and the opening night gala was getting underway. From here, Dot could see guests arriving, many of them her leaguemates. They were turning out in impressive numbers, considering Kat's recent absence from the derby scene.

Dot was dressed in her best—a perfectly tailored black pantsuit with a dark blue shirt and thin black tie. She'd coiffed her hair and even applied some subtle lip and eye color.

She looked down at her phone.

You should come to the gala tonight. Your work is in the show.

A text from Kat, received that morning. Dot had leapt into action without a second thought and spent the day preparing.

Now that she was here, however, a troubling realization was dawning on her. This text had been the only communication between them since the bout. The last minute invitation seemed curt. To the point. And so she had to wonder—did Kat really want to see her? Or had Kat felt *obligated* to invite her?

Dot wanted more than anything to walk into that gallery and see Kat in her glory. To see her photography getting the recognition it deserved. To watch as everyone else discovered what Dot already knew—the incredible artistic genius of Katrina Brooks.

And simply to see Kat again. In her heart of hearts, that was the number one reason Dot had come. But if Kat didn't feel the same, then wasn't this just a selfish endeavor? Dot had promised not to push herself on Kat. She'd promised *goodbye*. A courtesy invitation seemed a poor reason to break that promise—if, indeed, this was only a courtesy invitation.

Dot loosened her collar and cracked the windows. She sat and watched the door from a distance, racked with indecision. She'd come this far . . .

* * *

"I can't believe you came." Kat stood in the main gallery, dressed in a long, black, off-the-shoulder evening gown. Rose red lips, smoky eyes. She had Verona at her side, and Lynn and Jet across from her. "I can't believe *everyone* came." She peered around the room at all the CRD members who'd gotten dressed up to come see her photography.

Jet grinned. "Did you think we would miss this? Your first gallery show?"

"Yeah, this is incredible." Lynn stared with wonder at one of the larger pieces nearby. "I wanna look around again, actually."

"Me too." Jet took her hand, shooting an excited glance at Kat. "We'll be back!"

Guests had been congratulating Kat all night. It was hard to accept as real, seeing her own work on the walls of the Warfield. Seeing faces she didn't recognize admiring said work—serious art critics and collectors, interspersed among her . . . friends. She kept waiting for someone to wake her up from this dream.

But apart from all that, something else had Kat distracted, mentally absent from her own party. Blown away as she was by the attendance at tonight's event, there was one person missing. One who should really be here.

"I do believe this is the first time we've ever played electronic dance music in the gallery." Verona's words carried a hint of amusement.

Kat listened closely. Beneath the ambient sounds of conversation, she could hear it—the steady beat of "Polaris" by Deadmau5, the artist that had inspired Dot's derby name.

Verona looked to Kat with gentle, questioning eyes. "Do you think she'll come?"

"I . . ." Kat realized now that she'd been watching the main doors. She continued to do so. "I don't know."

"You did invite her, no?"

Kat nodded hesitantly.

"What's wrong, my girl? You're shaking."

Kat swallowed. "I'm not sure I'm ready, Verona."

She still didn't know what to think. She'd been researching BPD like crazy for the past week, hoping to find some kind of guidance. She'd found countless success stories claiming that it's highly treatable with the right motivation and support. But she'd come across just as many cautionary tales telling her to run for the hills and never look back. Dot's letter had made it sound like she was putting in the work, but . . . to still be struggling after twelve years of recovery—what did that say?

Despite the celebration all around her, *for* her, worry etched Kat's face.

Verona put an arm around her shoulders. "Relax. You don't need to have all the answers tonight."

Kat folded her arms. "But what do I say if she shows up?"

"Oh, my dear Ms. Brooks. That's simple." Verona smiled and shook her head. "Say, 'Hello.'"

Kat's brow relaxed a bit. *Hello.* She could do *hello.* That definitely helped. Because for all her uncertainty, Kat knew one thing for sure. She didn't feel right about celebrating tonight without Dot here. Now she could let herself hope. Hope to see those brown eyes and that blue streak appear in the doorway. And she would say *hello.*

* * *

Bzzz-bzzz.

"Hm?" Dot woke with a start and raised her head. She was hunched over the steering wheel. She blinked the bleariness from her eyes. The shops along the street had all gone dark.

She checked her phone. What the—how many notifications ... ? *Fifteen* texts and *twenty-four* new Facebook messages? From ... well, from everyone! Lynn, Jet, Reggie, Siren, Coach, and more.

Mouse, where are you??

Dude. Get. Here. Now. Trust me.

Are you coming to the gala or what? You're the freaking guest of honor!

Guest of honor? What the heck did that mean? The messages went on like this, ending with the most recent one, from Kat herself.

I'm really sorry you missed the gala. I should have invited you sooner. Please come and see the exhibition though. It would mean a lot to me.

Dot practically fell out of the van. She sprinted the length of the block to the Warfield, skidding to a stop in her shiny black Oxfords. The lights were still on inside. She tried one of the doors. Locked. Fuck! She tried each of the four doors in succession. All locked.

A door inside the foyer opened, and a woman emerged in black pants and a tux shirt. She furrowed her brow at Dot and came to the front door. As she approached, her eyes widened. She pushed the door open.

"You're . . . you're *her*, aren't you?"

Dot squinted, puzzled. "I'm who?"

"Ms. Mauser, please, come in."

"How do you—?"

"I'm sorry, the opening night gala is over, but I'm certain Ms. Fairchild won't mind." The woman crossed the foyer to the massive main gallery doors.

Dot's eyes went to the "Now Showing" placard on the wall to the left. There was a picture. It took her a moment to register what she was looking at, but as she stepped closer, her jaw dropped.

She'd expected to see one of Kat's photos, but not this one. It was a photo of Dot, vigorously stirring a tub of plastisol ink with a metal spatula. She was silhouetted against the light of the window, arms and shoulders flexed with exertion. She exuded strength, and one could feel the potential of creation. It was a flattering shot, but why make this the face of the exhibition?

The answer would come in the caption beneath the photo:

The Warfield Art Gallery presents

"A Portrait of the Artist"

Featuring the work and likeness of local sculptor Dorothy Mauser, as seen through the lens of photographer Katrina Brooks

The show—it was all about Dot? How could that . . . ?

"I-is Kat still here?"

The woman pulled the gallery door open. "I believe everyone's gone, but see for yourself."

Dot took the cue and ran through the open doorway, into the main gallery. "Kat?" She hurried to the far end of the central hall, peering into the side rooms. She ignored the art on the walls, her eyes searching feverishly for one thing. "Kat!"

But there was no answer. No sign of anyone else, save for the few gallery employees picking up used napkins and leftover champagne glasses.

Frustrated with herself, Dot balled her hands into fists. She'd missed her chance. If only she hadn't doubted Kat's original text. She wanted to scream, but she choked back the urge. Instead, she breathed deep and took a seat on the nearby bench, facing the back wall. She buried her face in her hands as the first muffled sobs pushed their way out.

Minutes passed in silence, until at last the slow tap of hard-soled footsteps echoed through the hall.

"Chin up, Ms. Mauser." The warm-yet-commanding voice came from Dot's left. She turned to see a woman approaching in a flowing, green chiffon dress, carrying two glasses of champagne.

"I thought everyone left."

"Everyone but me. I own the place, you know. Champagne?" The woman arrived at Dot's side, offering a glass.

"Thank you, but I don't drink. At least, not for now." Dot wiped the tears from her eyes, smearing what little blue shadow she had applied. "So you're Verona, then, right? Sorry—Ms. Fairchild, I mean."

"'Verona' is fine." She set the glasses down on a side table and took a seat beside Dot. "Literally, though. Chin up, my girl. Look at what's in front of you."

Dot lifted her head and raised her eyes to the huge, framed print on the wall opposite her. It must have been five feet tall, in vivid green, against that black backdrop—the mask.

It loomed, seeming to project out from the frame. The play of light and shadow brought to life the tiny figures of the army men—the agony of the lost, each flowing into the next, never knowing where one ended and another began. And the void behind those eyes. The hollowness. The horror of being no one, hidden under an ever-shifting facade. A reality Dot knew too well.

For the first time, Dot was really *seeing* the thing. Seeing it the way it had appeared in her mind as a concept. Seeing the expression of her own personal experience manifested physically.

She stood up, gaping in disbelief. "She made it real." She glanced back at Verona, who just smiled.

Dot moved closer and looked down the wall. Not far away, there hung another, smaller picture of the mask—a shot of it mounted to the oak tree in the light of the setting sun. The effect was twofold. On one hand, the objects blended visually to create a thing fantastic—Kat's dryad, fully realized. On the other hand, the shadow in the eyes and mouth remained. The sorrowful, mutable nothingness of the mask stood juxtaposed against the eternal, unyielding power of the ancient oak. Or perhaps that was only apparent to Dot, whose hands ached as she looked upon the image.

There were photos of Dot's smaller sculptures—what she thought of as her lesser efforts. But Kat treated them here with no less reverence. A disembodied human arm, built out of artificial foliage and floral wire, reached forth lazily as if to crawl from its frame. A violent tornado, made of broken glass and shredded teen girl magazines, swirled with the power to raze cities.

These smaller pieces went on, leading into a side room, where Dot encountered another large print—the waterfall. Kat had placed it off-center in the photo, shining light through it from the side. The resultant shattered patterns cast upon the wall were as much a feature of the shot as the sculpture itself, which seemed to shimmer and flow. Kat had found an ingenious way to demonstrate the chaos beyond the tranquility. The warped world on the other side of a fractured mind.

Verona followed, keeping her distance and observing as Dot explored.

The next room was dominated by the pegasus—a piece which had begun as a joke, constructed mainly from two large toys Dot had found at a yard sale. Once they'd been combined, she'd started to see a reflection of herself in the result—the noble creature, reduced to a fearful, twisted thing, adrift at the mercy of wings that were not its own. By the time it was done, she'd invested countless hours trying to transform it, to palpably demonstrate the terror. But in her perception, it would always remain simply two toys mashed together. Until now.

Set under dark, rolling clouds, and illuminated with a harshness like lightning, all the pain Dot had poured into the thing came back to strike the eye and leave the viewer reeling. Now, at last, the pegasus screamed.

Mixed in among the depictions of her work, Dot came across the occasional photo of herself. Some at the screen press, from that first day in the studio. Some candid shots she didn't even know Kat had taken—hoisting the mask into position, or diligently working on the eyes of the dragon. Dot didn't generally like seeing pictures of herself, but she couldn't help blushing at these. She appeared . . . powerful. And beautiful. And graceful. Was this really what she looked like to Kat?

Back in the main hall, Dot's gaze was drawn immediately to the opposite wall. She froze, transfixed. There, in the center of it all, the dragon lorded over the room. It roared in blazing firelight, scales shimmering red—no longer a thing of discarded metal and hobby paint, but of muscle, claw, fang, pride, and blind rage. The beast, in the flesh. Just as she'd envisioned it. This was her ruinous temper given form.

"Unbelievable."

Verona appeared at Dot's side. "It's certainly otherworldly."

Dot was silent for a moment. Entranced. Overwhelmed. Finally, she blinked and turned to Verona, voice cracking as she spoke. "I mean all of it, though. She told me she was gonna show me my own work through her eyes. I didn't think it was possible . . . ya know, that it could look like . . . *this*."

Verona's brow creased with a sort of pity. "All the years it must have taken you to create these pieces, and it's only now that you're really seeing them, isn't it?"

Dot shook her head. "I could never make them come alive like this."

"Oh, but Ms. Mauser, I think you did." Verona pivoted slowly, surveying the gallery. "Every detail was crafted by your hand, after all. Katrina merely revealed the life that was already there. That's her gift."

Dot studied the print of the dragon again. She couldn't deny that the physical structure was just as she had built it. The sight of it here called to mind the visceral feel of the materials under her fingers. "Maybe." While she contemplated the nature of her own work, a different question began to tug at her. She scanned the hall, looking for another side room, but there was no apparent continuation beyond what she'd seen. "Ms.—uh, Verona . . . where's the rest of Kat's stuff? Why is the whole show about me?"

"Ah. Yes." Verona turned back around to face Dot. "Katrina was rather insistent that you be the focus."

"She was?"

"Mm. She fed me some guff about how this is her best work, and that she didn't want the exhibition watered down with her older pieces." Verona chuckled softly. "While it's true that her best is represented here, I saw through her little story."

Dot's face twisted in puzzlement. This didn't make sense. Kat's older work was amazing. It deserved to be included here. "What do you mean you saw through her story?"

Verona stepped closer. She put a hand on Dot's shoulder and looked her in the eye. "My dear, I gave her the spotlight, and she shifted it to *you*. It was a big opportunity for her, and she decided to put your name first on the marquee. I've never had any artist do that, much less one of my unknowns. It tells me you must be quite important to her. Can you imagine what would make you so important?"

In the space of a breath, realization began to show in Dot's eyes, but confusion too. Her mouth hung open.

Verona smirked. "I don't know if she's completely admitted it to herself, but she still cares for you a great deal."

Dot found her voice. "But . . . she's with someone else now."

"Someone else?" Verona arched an eyebrow. "My dear, where Ms. Brooks is concerned, you're the only someone I'm aware of."

Dot squinted, hesitant to let herself believe what Verona was telling her. "But Maggie. I thought . . . they were . . ."

Verona put a finger to her cheek, pensively. "Come to think of it, there *was* a pretty young redheaded thing here tonight. Hovered around our girl rather like a hummingbird might a flower."

Dot nodded.

"Hmh! Was that the alleged *someone else*, then? Funny. Dear Katrina could hardly be bothered to give her the time of day. Too busy watching the door, I think—waiting for *you*."

"W-waiting for me?" Dot's face went stark. Her pulse quickened. Her thoughts began to race. "I . . . I should have come in. Why didn't I come in?" She turned toward the door. "I was parked out there all night, afraid she didn't want to see me. God, I fucked up."

That was it. Tonight had been the night. All dressed up at the ball. All of their friends gathered. Kat's moment of triumph. Dot had been meant to walk in here and share it with her. Reunite with her. It had been the perfect night, and she'd blown it. Ruined—

"Dorothy."

Dot's head swiveled back to Verona, eyes wide. Desperate.

"Easy, my girl." Verona touched Dot's arm. "Look around you. Look at these walls. Do you really think you've missed your chance?"

"I . . ." Dot's eyes darted around the hall. Frame to frame, portrait and sculpture—all her. *All* her. And all of this Kat's doing.

Slow down, Dot. Breathe. Think. Look at the facts.

Verona was right. Kat had made her entire show an homage to Dot. What a ridiculous thing to do. But if she still cared this much, then maybe it wasn't over.

"Okay . . ." Dot stared into the middle distance, in the direction of the mask. "Okay, so . . . what should I do?"

A satisfied grin spread across Verona's face. She gripped Dot's arm gently, pulling her attention back. "If I were in your shoes, dear girl, I would follow my heart."

Dot's heart was beating like a drum at this point. "Follow my . . .

Heh." She smiled wryly. "You don't know me very well. My heart's like a bull in a china shop."

Verona burst out laughing, her cool demeanor shattered. Her cackle echoed through the gallery. "Oh. My goodness." She paused to catch her breath. "Young lady, you are something."

Dot blushed.

"'Mouse' they call you, don't they? A mouse with the heart of a bull." Verona beamed, her voice still ringing with humor. She reached up and, with maternal care, brushed Dot's hair back behind her ear. "I am truly glad to have met you tonight. I'm starting to see what all the fuss is about, I think."

Glad to have met you? That sounded like a subtle prelude to a goodbye. What time was it, anyway? "I guess it's, uh, getting pretty late, right? I'm sorry I've been keeping you."

"Oh, not at all. It was my pleasure to be kept." Verona clasped Dot's left hand between both of her own. Her fingers were cool. "You're a brilliant artist, Ms. Mauser. I hope one day to see your sculptures firsthand."

"Eh heh." Dot laughed nervously and scratched the back of her neck. "I hope they live up to your expectations after this."

"Now, don't start worrying over that." Verona patted Dot's hand. "You've got more pressing matters."

"Yeah. I, uh . . ." Dot glanced at the door. "I guess I better go follow my heart before it runs off without me. Thank you. For everything."

Verona nodded graciously. "Good night, my dear. And good luck to you."

She watched with a contented smile as Dot withdrew her hand, turned, and made her way out through the foyer. Dot waved back at Verona, then pushed open one of the outer doors.

As she strode purposefully back to the van, Dot pulled out her phone and checked the time. 1:35 AM. Good lord, it *was* late. But her adrenaline was up and her hopes were high. She needed to *do* something.

She pulled open the driver-side door and stepped up into the seat, then thrust the key into the ignition. But what to do? Raw impulse urged her to go straight to Kat's house, throw pebbles at her third floor window, hold up a boombox playing Peter Gabriel. Something. Anything! Just go to her now!

But Dot knew better than to trust her impulses, especially after everything that had happened between them. Anyway, where would she find a boombox and a Peter Gabriel tape at 1:30 in the morning?

No, she would take a gentle approach, be an adult about it. She would do something right now, but something which wouldn't scare the shit out of a sleeping Kat or cause her housemates to call the cops. A text would do. If Kat was indeed sleeping, she'd see it first thing in the morning. If she was still awake, all the better.

Dot brought up Kat's number and started a new message. Now—what to say?

I love you

No. No! Idiot. That may be the truth, but it assumes way too much. Delete.

I'm sorry

Ghaa. No. Apologizing again sounds so pathetic. Delete. Hmm . . . Keep it simple. Respond to her last text. Talk about the show.

Leaving the gallery now. So much to say, but words can't do it justice. I'm so proud of you. And humbled by you. You made me believe. Thank you.

Five minutes later, Dot had crafted this message. She read it several times over. It seemed appropriately restrained while managing to say a lot—didn't it? It felt that way to her, at least. She hovered her finger over the screen. Held her breath. Swallowed. And hit "send."

But there was still a question. Still a burning uncertainty, despite Verona's confidence. Dot needed to know for sure.

Would you want to see me?

Send.

There. Now what? Go home? Sleep certainly wasn't an option. She needed something to occupy her mind.

Dot started the engine. Shifted into drive. Ignoring the desire to show up at Kat's house, one other place called to her. She still hadn't been in the studio since *that day*. After tonight, maybe it was time.

CHAPTER 21

Home

Daybreak.

Kat glanced at her phone again. At the texts. She hadn't replied. There was too much to say, and not all of it could be said in words. So she'd gotten in the car and made the short drive here instead.

Now, with trembling fingers, she reached out. The knob turned readily. The door cracked, and music bled out—the rhythmic thumping of EDM, just as loud as Dot liked it. Kat's heart pounded in response. Her breath escaped her.

Soaked in sound, she moved forward, unable to hear her own footsteps. The door shut silently behind her. She floated through the short hall and stopped at the step-down.

There, kneeling on the drop cloth, facing the far corner. There she was. Dot.

Kat's stomach twisted to think of the way she'd treated Dot at their last meeting. Her mind raced with fears and unanswered questions. She pushed these things away. Tried to focus on *hello*. Just start with *hello*.

She descended to the main floor of the studio and peered over the screen press table. Dot was working intently. The sleeves of her blue dress shirt were rolled up to her elbows. Safety glasses on. Soldering iron in hand. Her shoes and tie lay several feet away. In front of her, bridged across two wooden blocks, was the circuit board she'd purchased at Third Saturday Market. About a foot and a half long and a foot wide—the TR-808 drum machine board.

Kat stepped closer hesitantly. Waves of heat could be seen in the air around the soldering iron. She dared not startle Dot at this moment. She could be patient. Neither of them was going anywhere.

She looked around the room. Very little had changed. The old, heavy table remained by the windows. No new sculptures were prese—

The mask! Kat gasped. She covered her mouth. The mask lay in pieces on the small table, its place on the wall a conspicuously empty space. Why? What had happened to it? She crossed the open floor and bent over the broken sculpture, inspecting the fragments. They'd been arranged like puzzle pieces, loosely reforming the fractured face. Numerous tiny, unplaceable shards littered the tabletop as well.

Beside the mask, Kat discovered a pad of college-ruled paper—the same the letter had been written on. She flipped through the pages, at first just giving each a casual glance. But she soon slowed down, her expression growing solemn as she read.

There were drafts of the letter. Many drafts. God, the care Dot had put into getting the wording right. It must have taken her days. Weeks. This had been a major project.

There was also . . . something else—a piece of writing, rewritten over and over. Each draft was dated, and each one unique, except that all of them began, "My name is Dorothy Mauser. I am not my diagnosis." There was one for nearly every day, starting in early July. Page after page, Kat scanned the contents—"I am a sculptor," "I am a derby skater," "I believe in human rights," "I believe in my friends"—simple statements describing Dot. Several major themes repeated in every iteration, but one in particular always caught Kat's eye—"I am in love with Katrina

Brooks," or some variation thereof, appeared in each entry without fail. Dot did love her, and had never stopped thinking about her.

The corners of Kat's mouth pulled into a frown. She wiped away tears before they could drip. Dammit, she knew she probably shouldn't be reading these. They weren't meant for her eyes. But she couldn't help her curiosity. She flipped to the most recent page, dated today.

My name is Dorothy Mauser. I am not my diagnosis. I am a capable sculptor. I believe that my work has value, even though I needed help seeing it. I was a skilled skater, a capable leader, and a pretty okay ref. I believe my contributions to derby had value, even though I sometimes fucked up. Derby will always be part of who I am. I am still in love with Kat. I believe in Kat's vision as an artist. I believe in Kat as a person. I believe in Kat because she made me believe in myself. She will always be part of who I am.

Kat sniffed, and pressed a fist to her lips. She couldn't stand it—the way it sounded like Dot might never see her again. She walked back and turned to face Dot, willing her to put the iron down and look behind her. Kat was right there!

She watched over Dot's shoulder. Dot appeared to be removing all of the little buttons, knobs, capacitors and things from the board. A pile of such parts lay to her left on the drop cloth. Next to that was a spool of thick craft wire. A length of this had been carefully coiled to resemble a giant spring, and another had been straightened and folded into a large, square U-shape. On the floor to Dot's right were spread three sheets of paper displaying pictures and diagrams . . . of old-fashioned mouse traps. Mouse traps? Is that what she was building? A giant mouse trap?

Written in pen on one of the papers, surrounded by markings and notes, were the words "Katbot9000 Mau5 Trap." That was . . . adorably silly. Kat couldn't help but giggle.

The music track ended. No fade-out, just a final beat and then nothing. Kat's laugh reverberated in the silence. Dot went stock-still.

Surprised, Kat stepped back. By the time her foot touched the floor, the next track had begun. It was an atmospheric, downtempo vocal piece—"Beneath With Me," version four. Kat remembered. She'd always liked this one.

Dot switched off the iron and placed it back on its stand. In seeming slow motion, she lifted her safety glasses and twisted her torso. Kat's breath caught as Dot's eyes came around to meet hers. Dot opened her mouth as if to speak, but she seemed to think better of it in the music-saturated space. She got up on a knee and rose to her feet, never breaking eye contact.

Once standing, Dot shot a quick glance down at her project, then returned her gaze to Kat. After a brief hesitation, she mouthed three words.

"You caught me."

Kat didn't have a response. She'd forgotten the questions. She couldn't even remember *hello*. It was just as well they couldn't hear one another. She knew only that the person she wanted more than anything, despite all the time and effort she'd put into denying it, stood mere feet away. Driven by instinct, Kat broke the stillness. She stepped forward and reached out.

Dot raised her hand to meet Kat's. Contact. Fingers interlaced. Dot's grip was warm. Sweaty. The space between the two of them narrowed until they were inches apart. Face to face. Sharing the same air.

The sweet, sharp aroma of Dot's breath filled Kat's nose. Kat's gaze wandered to Dot's full, parted lips, then back up to her eyes—and a brow heavy with thought. Or with worry.

"I . . ." Dot was inaudible, even at this distance. She leaned in, bringing her mouth to Kat's ear, and the words spilled forth desperately. "I love you too. I love you so much. I'm sorry I never said—"

And then Kat's lips were on hers.

They stood unmoving, locked in that initial kiss. Kat savored it, her mouth pressed to Dot's, eyes tightly shut, exhaling through her nose in stilted breaths. She could cry at the relief of this moment. The joy of it.

Her heart thundered in her chest, aching for more. She parted her lips and closed the gap between their bodies. Dot's right hand landed on Kat's denim-clad hip and slid up to the small of her back, fingers exploring the bare skin beneath her tee shirt. Dot coiled her arm around, pulling Kat tight against her.

Kat cupped the corner of Dot's jaw. Nibbled at her lower lip. Teasing. Begging. Dot opened her mouth invitingly. Kat slipped inside and greeted her tongue with a gentle caress. She brought her other hand up and ran her fingers into Dot's hair. Dot closed her left arm around Kat's torso, wrapping her up completely.

With that, Kat surrendered the last of her fear. Her heart soared, unfettered. *This* was happiness. This was where she belonged. And god, did she want to belong. To be one with Dot, just as they were right now.

She laughed to herself, breaking the kiss. Lips still touching, she felt a grin spread across Dot's face. Dot widened her stance, got a careful grip around Kat's torso, and lifted her a couple of inches off the ground. She carried Kat the few feet to the old table by the windows and set her back down. Kat played along with the apparent intent and hopped up to sit on the table's edge in her cutoff shorts. She shifted forward and parted her legs.

All concern had fled from Dot's eyes. She stood before Kat with a look of pure, longing hunger. Her shirt had already been partially unbuttoned. Now disheveled, the blue cotton was parted, exposing her cleavage. Kat grabbed the two sides of the collar and pulled Dot into the space between her knees. She worked her fingers down, parting buttons from their holes. When she had done that, she ran her hands up and pushed the fabric back over Dot's shoulders. Biting her lip, Dot finished the job, dropping the shirt from her arms and tossing it behind her.

Dot's hands were quickly on Kat's waist, pushing up the sides of her tee. Impatient now, Kat tore the shirt off herself and dropped it on the table. Dot leaned in, her practiced fingers locating the clasp of Kat's bra and sliding it down her arms. As soon as that was done, Kat's mouth found Dot's once again, this time with animal desire.

They fed from one another. Gave to one another. Moved in unison, tasting and touching, until at last Dot put a hand to Kat's shoulder. Licking her lips, she pushed Kat backwards. That look—those lidded eyes and that knowing smile. Her body language was as familiar as ever. Kat didn't need words to understand.

She settled onto her elbows while Dot ran a fingertip across her collarbone, down her sternum, between her breasts, over her belly. With reverence, Dot moved down each of Kat's legs and removed her boots. Her socks. Slid her hands up behind Kat's calves, around to the tops of her thighs, and to the front of her shorts. Kat felt the release of her button fly, and the *click-click* of the zipper teeth separating one by one. She lifted her pelvis as Dot finished disrobing her, deftly sliding shorts and panties down and off.

Dot's muscled arms arose beneath Kat's bare thighs and snaked around them, placing her calves over Dot's shoulders. Dot pulled her to the edge and knelt on the floor before her, eyes just visible over Kat's tuft of curly pubic hair. She planted kisses along the insides of Kat's thighs, approaching her center with patience, allowing the anticipation to build.

When at last it came, the touch of Dot's tongue brought with it a wave of visceral memory. Kat's breath hitched. She'd forgotten just how much she'd missed this—the way Dot, with long, steady strokes, eased Kat into the warmth of her mouth. The way she anticipated Kat's responses. Dot knew Kat's body—knew her like no one else.

When Kat began to move with her, Dot probed deeper. She slid her tongue up between Kat's labia, pushing ever so slightly inside her. Again and again, the powerful licks teased Kat's entrance until she began to push back, aching to be filled.

And that's when she felt the touch of fingertips on her inner thigh, creeping closer as she writhed in torturous wanting. Kat spread herself before Dot in desperation, and Dot obliged. She slipped her long middle finger inside and pressed up against Kat's inner wall. Kat's head dropped back. She worked herself against Dot's hand, needing more.

Dot turned her wrist and slid a second finger in. Her adoring eyes watched attentively as Kat's chest heaved with satisfaction. At that, Dot lowered her head once again and closed her lips around Kat's swollen clit. She sucked gently.

The sensation drove all thought from Kat's mind. Waves of heat pulsed through her. She felt herself laid open to Dot, an offering crying out to be consumed. She involuntarily pressed up against Dot's mouth, and Dot moved with her, never missing a beat.

Dot flicked her tongue, slowly at first. Kat shuddered with each touch, an exquisite tension building in her core. Her hands opened and closed. Her toes curled. Her breaths grew quick and shallow. Before long, her body was screaming for release. She raised her head and locked eyes with Dot, pleading. Dot increased her speed, holding tight with one arm as Kat quivered and shifted on the table.

A serenity overcame Kat as she lay panting at Dot's mercy. She lowered her back onto the smooth wood, then reached down and grasped Dot's hand, squeezing as Dot sent her over the edge. She throbbed uncontrollably in the warm safety of Dot's mouth while wave after wave of pure sunlight flooded her entire being. For a brief time, she floated high above the clouds, and all the world fell away, save for Dot.

It had never been like this before. In all the times she and Dot had done this—or she and anyone, for that matter—she had never felt so . . . free. So completely free to let go. She had never let herself trust like this. She had never *believed* in someone like this.

Kat breathed deep. Her muscles untensed as she fell gradually back to reality. The waves relaxed into gentle echoes. Dot softened her ministrations, eventually planting a final kiss before rising from her position. She crept forward, placing her hands on the table, and gazed down upon Kat.

In the sobering afterglow, thought returned to Kat in sharp detail. As she looked up at those deep brown eyes, full of both gratitude and relief, the questions came back to her. But not the fear. There was much to be said, yes. There were a lot of unknowns. But whatever happened, she was done running. She was home.

* * *

Dot opened her eyes. Kat was sitting with her back against the headboard and her knees up, naked but for the sheet covering her legs. She was looking through Dot's DBT book by the light of her phone.

From where she lay, Dot could see the digital clock on her dresser. 5:12 PM. After their morning escapades, they'd come into the house and passed out without talking. Dot had fallen asleep full of hope, but she might have been getting ahead of herself.

There was so much Kat didn't know. Dot had already resolved that if she were ever to get another chance with Kat, she would keep no secrets. Not like last time. She would tell Kat everything there was to tell. But where to even begin?

"Kat."

"Hm?" Kat turned, a smile beaming on her shadowed face. "Good morning, baby."

"I . . . I broke the mask, Kat. The night I got home from MAD. You should know."

Kat pressed her lips together in concern. She closed the book and placed it on the nightstand, with her phone on top of it. Then she wormed her way under the covers with Dot, settling beside her, face to face. Dot could see only Kat's eyes, sparkling faintly in the dark.

"I wondered." Kat's fingers came searching for Dot and found her arm. They followed it down and took hold of her hand.

When Dot spoke again, her voice had a hint of hoarseness to it. "I broke my right hand too."

A sharp intake of breath. "Baby . . ."

"Punching the oak tree."

Kat was silent for a moment. She delicately caressed Dot's knuckles. "Do you mind if I turn the light on? I want to see."

"No, go ahead."

Seconds later, the warm glow of the bedside lamp filled the room. Kat turned back to Dot, squinting.

Dot shifted her right arm out from under her and presented the back of her hand. "Metacarpal fracture, right here." She pointed just behind the middle finger. "It's hard to tell now."

Kat took the hand between hers and ran her thumbs over the years of scars. "I never asked you about all these marks."

Dot cleared her throat. "Most people don't notice them." She watched Kat's expression. Those gentle eyes were full of care and curiosity. No sign of shock or disgust.

Kat looked up to meet Dot's woeful gaze. Her brow creased. "What's wrong?"

Dot took a deep breath and held it a moment before answering. "I'm afraid, Kat. Are you . . . are you sure you want to do this again? With me?"

An easy smile emerged on Kat's face. "I'm certain."

Dot began speaking quickly, as if trying to get everything out at once. "But I mean, what if I hurt you again? What happened in June, that's the worst I've been in years. I thought I was okay, and it crept up on me. What happens if—"

"Dot, breathe." Kat squeezed her hand. "I'm here. I'm not going anywhere."

Dot closed her fingers around Kat's. Slowed her breathing. She stared into those blue eyes and found focus. "Kat . . . listen. Being with me . . . it's not easy. It's, uh . . . it's kind of an emotional roller coaster sometimes. Just ask my dad."

"Hmh." Kat smirked. "Baby, I've ridden your roller coaster myself. At the worst, like you said."

Dot's eyes fell. "Well? Doesn't that scare you?"

"It did." Kat slid a hand around Dot's ear and cradled her face. "It scared me *more* when I didn't know what it was." She brushed Dot's cheek with her thumb. "After you told me, in your letter, I looked up

BPD and started reading everything I could. And yeah, it scared me then too."

Dot met Kat's eyes again. "It doesn't scare you now?"

Kat shook her head subtly. She wore a look of peaceful clarity.

"But how can you be so confident?"

Kat's mouth curved into a sympathetic frown. "Dot... I *know* it's a lot, getting involved with someone who has BPD. I've read a lot of horror stories. But I've also read a lot of success stories." She shifted an inch closer to Dot, so that their knees came into contact under the covers. "You showed me, through your words and your actions, that the person I fell in love with is the real you. That I wasn't just chasing a ghost. And besides..." She lowered her eyes. "You're not the only one who has issues."

Now Dot frowned. "What do you mean?"

"Dot, I..." Kat winced as she contemplated her response. "When everything went down at MAD... I got hurt, and I ran. Not just from you, but from everybody."

Dot grimaced. "Yeah, you kinda disappeared."

"I shut everyone out. And I did some things I'm not proud of, to try and forget how I felt. I've been so afraid to let myself depend on anyone—to let myself *believe* in anyone—for so long. I finally started to let my guard down with you, and then... you know. And after that, I said never again, and I ran."

Dot covered Kat's hand with her own. "I'm so sorry."

"No, baby, you've apologized enough. *I'm* sorry. I'm sorry I wasn't listening when you tried to explain and make things right. I'm sorry I tried to forget." Kat turned her hand and gripped Dot's. "But I *couldn't* forget. And when I finally turned around, you were there. You showed me this is where I'm supposed to be."

Dot's welling eyes shimmered in the lamplight.

Kat went on, "Not just with CRD, but with *you*. You make me happy, Dot. So no, I'm not afraid. I want this. I want to be with you. If you want to be with me."

Dot swallowed the lump in her throat and nodded eagerly.

"And if things get bad for you, I want to know what I can do to help you through it."

Dot could hardly believe her ears. Kat really did seem to be walking into this with eyes open. And despite everything that had happened, and everything that might come, she wanted to stay—to face it together.

"Swim." Dot sniffed, grinning through tears. "To start. Try telling me to swim."

* * *

Dot fished around in the dark corners of Kat's mostly-empty skate bag. "Got it!" She pulled her hand out, the backing to Kat's catnip pin clutched between her fingers. She proceeded to fasten the pin back onto the front of the bag.

"Thank you, baby." Kat finished strapping on her elbow pads and reached for her wristguards.

"We really gotta find a way to secure that better. Maybe a different backing."

"I know, I can't believe it fell off again. I'm lucky you have good eyes. I'd never find it on this carpet."

Lynn rolled off the rink floor and came to a stop in front of them. "Come on, guys! Warmups are about to start!"

"Okay, we're almost ready!" Dot hastily pulled her own wristguards on and donned her helmet.

Kat stood up, fully geared. "I'll be out in a minute. Just wanna check in with the ref crew." She flashed a smile at Dot and was off toward the refs' changing area.

Lynn rolled her skates back and forth in place. "So, we all hitting the diner after this? It's been forever."

"Uh . . ." Dot rose from her seat with her face scrunched in apprehension. "That could be weird. Ya know—Mags?"

"Nah, Mags got that job at Upstarts. She's not at the diner anymore."

Dot's eyes widened. "Oh! I didn't realize! Well, good for her, I suppose."

"Yeah, better pay, better hours. The diner won't be the same without her, but... I mean... I guess it wouldn't anyway." Lynn cringed. "Sorry, I'll stop talking about it."

Dot chuckled. "It's okay. I think Kat feels weirder about the Mags thing than I do." She took a stride and rolled past Lynn. "Anyway, warmups!"

Lynn followed her out onto the wood floor. Coach Rex whistled to get everyone on the track. Warmups carried on as usual until about halfway through, when Kat snuck into the pace line behind Dot. She stuck around for the remainder of the exercises, much to the delight of many skaters.

When warmups had finished, Kat took to the infield with the other refs. Dot headed for the black team's bench area. She arrived to find Reggie already wearing the stripe helmet cover and twirling the star on her finger.

"Who wants to jam first?" Reggie called over the ambient noise. "I'm your pivot. You can pass the star if you need to." She cast an intimidating glare at each of her teammates in succession. "Any takers? Or am I picking someone?"

"*I* got it." Dot's bold answer drew all eyes. She reached out to receive the star cover.

"*Mouse?*" Reggie froze in shock.

Dot pulled the cover from her hand. "Yup!"

"But . . . you *hate* jamming."

Dot gave a side nod. "Meh. I don't *hate* it. I'm just not great at it." She grinned and patted Reggie on the upper arm. "But hey, that's why I have you! Come on, let's go!" She led the way onto the track.

Reggie shook her head, blinking away the disbelief, then turned to the rest of the team. "You heard the woman! Let's go! Three more blockers! Who's with me?"

Jet rolled up to the jammer line with an air of casual indifference. But a broad smile broke across her face when Dot took up the position to her right. The two exchanged warm glances.

Number Scruncher, the jam timer, was still busy over by the rink wall, helping a newer NSO get situated. It would be a minute before this jam got under way.

"'Scuse me, Pol." Dot rolled around Jet to the inside line. "Need to start this off right."

Kat stood watching her from the infield. "What's up, babe?"

"Question for my jam ref." Dot's cheeks went rosy. She arched an eyebrow at Kat. "Fancy a shift on the inside line?"

A blush instantly began to tinge Kat's face. She bit her lip in giddy contemplation, then rolled to the line, eyes locked on Dot's. The skaters within earshot watched expectantly.

Dot slipped her arms around Kat's waist and captured Kat's mouth with her own.

The rink erupted with a chorus of "Wooooooooo!" as skater and ref stood joined in a tender embrace. Time seemed to slow down in that moment. Their kiss went on, long and passionate, both parties seemingly oblivious to happenings around them.

"Okay, you two!" Scrunch finally called from several feet away. "Next whistle starts the jam!"

Dot and Kat broke the kiss and hurried to their positions, still making amorous eyes at one another.

"Good to have you back," Jet said as Dot got settled beside her. Jet looked to Kat, then back to Dot. "Both of you."

"Five seconds!" Scrunch cried.

Dot grinned. Adrenaline surged. Her heart raced, but she was able to take the rush of excitement to a good place. It was her first jam in months—and win or lose, it was gonna be fun.

"It's good to *be* back."

TWEEET!

Epilogue: Moving Day

December 31st

"She cancels her plans to visit in July, and I barely hear from her until *I* come *here* for Thanksgiving." Dot's mother sat at the table with her legs crossed, her chair turned to face across the kitchen. She was tall, thin, with Dot's olive skin and dark features, wearing tan dress pants and a flowing white blouse. Her speech rang with an almost royal affect—cordial, polite, not especially warm.

Ben glanced at her from his place in front of the stove, only briefly taking his eyes off the simmering pots and saucepans. "Diane, we talked about this."

"Yes, I know. It was her *borderline* thing again." She sipped her scotch on the rocks, crunching a piece of ice with her teeth before continuing. "This has been going on since she was a teenager, Benjamin. She's not going to grow out of it until you stop coddling her."

Ben didn't respond. He took a deep breath and blinked slowly. Kat imagined his thoughts must be mirroring her own—*God, grant me the serenity.* For her part, Kat was finding serenity hard to hold onto. She stood at the sink, catty-corner from Ben and, mercifully, facing away from Diane, who couldn't see her clenched jaw and intense expression. She tried to focus her anger into scrubbing potatoes.

Diane went on, "She'll be twenty-nine next month. She should be working for a living and taking care of herself, not playing with junk in her father's garage all day." From the purse hanging on her chair, she produced a pack of Davidoff Slims cigarettes and proceeded to slap the top of the box against her palm. "She should have her own place by now. Instead, you're letting her girlfriend move in here *with* her." She looked up as she pulled a cigarette from the pack. "No offense to you,

Kat. But what kind of message does that send? I mean really? By the time I was her age—"

"Do you *ever stop?*" Kat's fingers tensed. She dropped the potato and brush into the sink and turned around, embers smoldering in her eyes.

Diane appeared unfazed, her brow bent in condescending sympathy. "Oh, I'm sorry sweetie. I didn't mean to imply that *you* were—"

"It's not about *me*, Diane. It's the way you talk about Dot. I can't stand here and listen to you belittle her." Kat's tone was forceful, but controlled.

Ben ventured a conspiratorial glance at Kat, lips pursed as he tried to suppress a smile.

Diane tilted her head. "I'm not trying to belittle her, honey. She's a smart girl with so much potential. I just want to see her succeed in life."

"*Succeed?*" Kat rolled her eyes. She inhaled sharply and bit back the urge to raise her voice. "You don't think she—Jesus Christ..." She didn't know where to begin. "You don't take her art seriously at all, do you? Even though you know she just sold a piece for six *thousand* dollars. To a discerning collector. She's not *playing with junk*, Diane. She's a creative genius. And you would have her stifle that in favor of some stuffed-shirt job in an office, like a soulless schlub. No offense, by the way."

Diane's jaw dropped. "Did you just call me—"

"And on top of that"—Kat threw a hand up—"you just write off her BPD as though she's making it up! You don't have a clue what she's been through! You have no idea how amazing your own daughter is, because you don't see *her!* You just see—"

"Don't you lecture me about my parenting." Diane's plastic smile had melted into a scowl. "I don't have to take this from a girl who cut her own parents off completely. What would you know about any of it?"

Ben extended a cautious hand into the crossfire. "Diane . . ."

Diane shifted her death glare to Ben, where it eased into an annoyed sneer. "You're gonna let her talk to me like this?"

"Diane, we have this argument every time we see each other." The soothing calm of Ben's voice sliced through the tension. "I know you disapprove of the way I do things. But it's my house, and they're welcome to live here as long as they want." He offered an open palm. "And I've told you before, you're always welcome here if you decide you actually want to spend more time with Dot."

"Ben, you *know* I can't—" Diane cut herself off and blew out a frustrated breath. "Never mind. I'm not going to get anywhere with you two. I'm going out to have a smoke." She put the cigarette between her lips and grabbed her drink and phone off the table. She pulled open the door to the back deck, shaking her head as she exited.

Ben shut the door behind her, then turned to Kat with a satisfied grin. "Bravo, Kat! That kind of arguing is what got me divorced!"

Kat released a strained laugh, still on edge. "I can't see you getting that worked up."

"Oh, believe me, I used to lose my cool with her regularly. Over the past few decades, I've learned to tune her out." His grin became subdued, and his eyes fell momentarily before rising back up to meet Kat's. "I'm sorry, I should have chimed in sooner. You didn't need to hear all that toxic nonsense."

"She's fucking insufferable." Kat leaned back against the counter, staring at the empty chair. "Is she ever like this with Dot?"

Ben had already returned his attention to the stove and was diligently stirring a bubbling sauce. "She's ... more tactful with Dot. But Dot definitely feels the pressure from her, which is unfortunate. Lately I think it's getting to her less, though." He peered back over his shoulder. "*You're* partly responsible for that."

Kat looked at the floor, a blush creeping up. "Yeah, well, I hope my little outburst didn't make things worse."

"I wouldn't worry." Ben opened the oven and peeked inside. Aromas wafted forth—of roasting beef, garlic, thyme, and carrots. "This is nothing new. Diane'll cool off and pretend like it never happened, and we'll get to do that all over again next time she visits."

"Oh joy." Kat pivoted back around to face the sink and picked up her brush again.

Ben reached out and put a hand on her shoulder. "Welcome to the family, kiddo."

Kat smiled to herself and grabbed another potato. She went about scrubbing the dirt off. "Speaking of family . . ." She hesitated.

"Mmhm?" Ben took a taste of the sauce from his wooden spoon.

"I've been thinking . . . about maybe letting Eli give me an update on the Jacobses. People evolve over ten years, right?"

Ben tapped the spoon on the edge of the pan and set it down on the counter. "I'd like to think so. Why the change of heart now?"

"I guess . . . I'm not as afraid anymore of what I'll find? I mean, I *hope* they've come around. I wouldn't put money on it. But either way, I have Dot and you." Kat placed the potato on a paper towel to dry with the others. One more to go. "And Lonnie. Lynn and Jet. And Eli, of course. So if the rest of the Jacobses still don't want to accept me as I am, then that's too bad for them. 'Cause I have a family that does, right here." The potato dirt washed away under the running water, leaving a shiny skin. "When I'm done with this one, do you want me to start grating them?"

She turned to look at Ben. He was speechless, beaming, with watery eyes. He moved closer and opened his arms. Kat dropped what she was doing and stepped into his embrace, hugging him tightly.

Ben answered softly, "We can hold off on that until we're ready to make the latkes. And you know we have your back, whatever you decide."

* * *

Lonnie put his end of the foot locker down on the floor in the back of the van, and Dot slid it into place next to Kat's box of vinyls and CDs.

"Well . . ." Lonnie exhaled, his breath billowing in the cold air. "It's official now. I mean sure, she hasn't slept here in months, but when her camera stuff goes, you know it's for real." He eyed the vanload of boxes wistfully. When he spoke again, his voice had lost its jovial luster. "I'm gonna miss her."

"Aw, come on." Dot backhanded him playfully on the arm. "It's not like you're never gonna see her."

"I know." Lonnie sat down on the floor of the van, laying an arm over the nearest box. "It's just gonna be different, not having the room next-door belong to her." He narrowed his eyes at Dot. "Are you *sure* you don't just want to move in here? Split the rent with Kat?"

Dot smiled and shook her head. "Neither of us has, like, regular income, and we're trying to build up a savings. Also, the studio's right there—"

"Yeah, okay, okay. Kat gave me the same speech. Thought I'd give it a shot anyway. It's my last chance."

Dot shrugged. "Plus, Domme already claimed the room. So hey, at least you know it's not some weirdo moving in."

Lonnie cringed. "Ehh . . ."

Dot conceded a side nod. "Okay, she's a little weird. But the good kind of weird."

"Between you and me? She kinda scares me."

Dot burst out laughing. "Don't worry, she'll grow on you. She's good people, I promise!" She took a seat next to Lonnie. "Get to know her a little at dinner tonight. You're coming, right?"

"Wouldn't miss it!"

"My dad's making his brisket. That's an all-day affair. Not to be taken for granted!"

Lonnie met her stare and raised his eyebrows assuringly. "I know! Again, I'm vegan. But I'm coming. I promise."

"'Kay, good." Dot folded her arms, satisfied. "You bringing Si?"

At that, a bright smile crept onto Lonnie's face. "Yeah, I'm picking her up on the way over." He jutted a thumb in the general direction of Leah's apartment.

Dot grinned. "So things are going well with you two?"

"Yeah! Yeah, things are great." Lonnie answered quickly, then took a moment before continuing. He looked off into the distance, squinting in the sun. "It's easy being with her. Comfortable, ya know?" He turned back to Dot. "I mean, it's not all fireworks like with you and Kat, but not everybody can have that kind of love story, right?"

Dot laughed. "What are you talking about? Fireworks?"

"Oh please. We can all see it in your faces." Lonnie smirked and shook his head. "Whenever you two lock eyes, it's like *boom*. Sparks. Electricity. Fireworks. You just know it's something special."

Dot could feel heat flushing her skin, pushing back the chill of the air. "I *guess*." She knew exactly what he meant. "So . . . you don't have that with Siren?"

"Nah. Not like that." Lonnie shrugged. "But not everybody finds that. Sometimes it's just . . ."

"Comfortable."

"Right."

Dot felt as though she and Kat had both fireworks *and* comfort—in spades—but she didn't have the heart to burst his bubble by mentioning that. Anyway, maybe he was right. Maybe some people didn't have those sparks, but it worked out great regardless.

She patted him on the shoulder. "Well, if you're happy, I'm happy for you."

Lonnie brandished a casual grin. "Thanks."

"Last one!" Eli came around the back of the van with a sealed-up cardboard box in his arms.

"Oh, here!" Dot jumped out of the way, Lonnie following suit.

Eli eased the package up on top of the foot locker, then stood back and observed the loaded vehicle. "Wow, it all fit!"

Lonnie put a hand on the door. "Yeah, she doesn't really have that much stuff without the furniture." He looked to Dot. "Nice of her to leave it for Domme."

"Like we have anywhere to put it anyway." Dot shut her door and turned to Eli. "Ready to hit the road, E? It's freezing out here."

Eli nodded. "Ready when you are, D."

Lonnie shut the other door and exchanged quick hugs with each of them. "Alright, see you guys tonight!"

Dot and Eli hopped in the van. Lonnie watched from the house as they backed out of the driveway. Moments later, the pair sped off down the road with all of Kat's earthly possessions in cargo.

* * *

The sun had just finished setting. Margaret MacKenzie carried a case of beer up the driveway and followed the walkway to the front door. She was still wearing her work outfit—black button-down shirt, black flared skirt, glittery black leggings, and black sneakers—with a black pea coat to match.

She perched the case on her hip while she reached up and rang the doorbell. Seconds later, the inner door opened and Dot peered out.

Dot pushed open the outer door, eyes wide with excitement. "Mags! You made it! Lynn told us you might come."

Maggie's mouth fell agape at Dot's enthusiasm. She blinked and found her voice as her eyes were drawn to Dot's most vibrant feature. "Blue! You went blue again!"

"Oh! Yeah." Dot delicately touched her hair. It looked purposefully styled tonight, all swept to one side, with bangs just barely obscuring her left eye. She'd grown it out and once again dyed it entirely electric blue. "Kat missed it, and it was my favorite look. I figured, you know what, hair doesn't define you—anyway, it's a long story. Come in out of the cold!" She held the door and motioned for Maggie to enter.

Maggie hefted the beer and stepped inside.

Dot shut the door behind her, then reached for the case. "I'll take this. And Lynn said you wanted to talk to us about something?"

Maggie nodded. "Yeah. In private, preferably."

"Sure, lemme find Kat. Be right back." Dot disappeared into the kitchen with the beer.

Maggie stood by the door and surveyed the living room, which buzzed with music and conversation. Just to her right, two familiar faces—Lynn and Jet—were seated on the near end of the couch. A cute, green-haired girl occupied the far end, and a tall-dark-and-handsome guy had claimed the chair next to her, in the corner. The two of them were talking to a hot, scantily-clad goth girl on the loveseat across the way.

"Mags. Hey." Kat's voice drew Maggie's attention. The greeting was somewhat cool, especially compared to Dot's warm reception.

"Kat . . ." Maggie glanced between Kat and Dot. "I hope this is okay."

"Yeah, it's fine. Come on, we can talk downstairs." Kat led the way down two half-flights of stairs to the hallway outside Dot's room.

Dot leaned back against the wall next to the bedroom door. "Is this private enough?"

"Sure, yeah." Maggie folded her arms, tucking her gloved hands underneath. She shifted nervously from one leg to the other, searching the two expectant faces that now watched her. "Hey, so . . . I haven't seen you two in ages, and there are a couple things I wanted to say." She met Dot's eyes. "First—Dot, I . . . I wanted to apologize to you specifically."

Dot's brow creased. "To me? For what?"

"Well, a long time ago, I think I took some bad advice." Maggie winced. "Your, uh . . . your old classmates . . . warned me about you."

Dot's face went stark. "Ohhh."

"Yeah. And that's why I never even gave you a chance, back when we met. Which wasn't fair of me. And I see now that I would have been lucky—that Kat *is* lucky—to have you." Maggie's eyes fell. "Anyway, I hope that's not a weird thing to bring up. It's just, I've been doing a lot of soul-searching, and I feel pretty shitty about the way I handled things then."

Dot exchanged glances with Kat, then gave Maggie a sympathetic smile. "Hey."

Maggie looked up.

"Don't sweat it. It's water under the bridge, okay?"

Maggie brightened some, answering with a half-smile and a nod.

"Thank you, Dot. Really." She took a deep breath. "So . . . that's one thing." Then she turned her attention to Kat. "And then there's you, Tiger."

Kat rolled her eyes.

"Yeah. Exactly." Maggie grimaced as she contemplated her next words. "I feel like I took advantage of you, that night at the party. I'm sorry for that. The fact is, I always really liked you. But I was with Ricky, and you were chasing after Dot. Then when I saw you that night, and both of us were single, I . . . I thought that was my chance—and I leapt at it." She shook her head. "It was dumb, and I shouldn't have." She put a hand up. "Not that I regret *you* . . . I mean . . . urgh." She covered her face. "I hope you understand what I'm getting at. It was a bad move on my part. And then to top it off, I got attached. You two should have been getting back together, and I was in the way. I feel awful about that. I . . . I guess I'm asking if you can forgive me."

Kat sighed, and her stony countenance softened. "Mags, you were never in the way. I was in my own way. Is that all you came here for? Forgiveness?"

"Well . . ." Maggie looked questioningly at Dot, then back to Kat. "Yeah. Why?"

Kat smiled. "Honestly? I was a little worried you were gonna make some grand gesture and try to win my affection."

"Eh heh—no, I just brought beer, for both of you." Maggie pointed back up the stairs. "I made a mixed pack at work. Half Kickback, and the other half is some Triticum and some Brazen Tart. Lynn said those are your favorites."

"Then look"—Kat gently gripped Maggie's arm—"if it's forgiveness you want, you got it. As far as I'm concerned, like Dot said, it's water under the bridge."

Maggie's brow rose in disbelief. "Really?"

Kat gave a sincere nod.

A relieved grin overtook Maggie's face. Her voice cracked. "Alright. Thank you so much. That's a major load off my mind." She blinked back a few threatening tears. "I hope you'll come see me at work sometimes. I've really missed that." She offered a hand to Kat.

Kat looked at it and chuckled. "What are you doing?" She opened her arms and hugged Maggie instead.

"Oh . . ." After a beat, Maggie reciprocated.

Dot narrowed her eyes. "And I hope you don't think you're leaving already."

"Well, I was gonna get out of your hair. I'm interrupting the party."

"No, no," Kat said as she broke the embrace. "You gotta stay for dinner! Ben's making his brisket! I mean, unless you already have other plans."

"Not really. I was just—"

Then Dot threw her arms around Maggie. "It's settled, then!"

"Okay."

"Okay!" Dot gave her a good squeeze, then backed off. "Let's get you something to drink! Lonnie's making some kind of pomegranate sparkler cocktail. It's really good." She breezed past Maggie and up the stairs. "Lonnie!"

Still feeling uneasy about all of this, Maggie turned to Kat. "You sure?"

Kat now wore a carefree smirk. It was a radical shift from her initial standoffishness. "Mags . . ." She folded her arms. "Even though I think you're being a little hard on yourself, it means a lot that you care this much. And yeah, things got a bit messy back in the summer, but they turned out okay in the end." She looked Maggie up and down, as if assessing her overall state. "Anyway, you were the one who caught feelings, so if it's awkward for you to be around me, I get it. But otherwise—you're a *friend*. Stay for New Year's!"

With that, Maggie finally relaxed and exhaled. She'd been so nervous coming here, but so far the night was defying her expectations. "Alright. I will."

* * *

"So she says someone's interested in the waterfall, based on Kat's photos alone, and can he come look at it." Five minutes later, Dot was telling Maggie and Lynn about her recent art sale. Her *first* art sale, as it were.

Maggie was on the couch between the two of them, each of the three with a beverage in hand. She sipped her bubbly, rose-colored cocktail. It went down easy. These could be dangerous.

The stereo system was playing a mix of things, mostly from the eighties and nineties. Mellow rock and pop. Music that wasn't boring, but was still easy to have a conversation over. Duran Duran's "Hungry Like the Wolf" ended, and The Pretenders' "I'll Stand By You" began.

Kat came running in from the kitchen before the vocals even hit. In her socks, on the hardwood floor, she slid to a stop in front of Dot and extended a hand. "Dance with me." She was beaming. "Please, I love this song."

"Of course!" Dot took her hand and rose from the couch.

Kat led Dot into the open area between the kitchen and the front door. There, they came together and began to sway in one another's arms. That's when Maggie noticed the matching rainbow bracelets. They really did make such a sweet couple.

"So . . ." Maggie turned to Lynn, but Lynn was already halfway out of her seat, on her way to the dance floor with Jet.

Ah. Oh well. Maggie sat back and sipped her drink, taking in the room. There was a palpable feeling of holiday warmth in the air. A Christmas tree occupied the far corner, adorned primarily with handmade ornaments. An electric menorah flickered on the mantle above the stereo. Mouth-watering aromas drifted in from the kitchen—roasting meats and veggies, frying potatoes, herbs of all kinds.

"Vee's in Ireland for the holidays." The goth girl—Domme?—was talking to Lonnie, who appeared to be listening intently. "I told her she'd better take me with her next time."

Were these all derby people? Maggie wondered. She didn't know any derby people outside of the diner crew—at least, not that she was aware of. She'd never even been to a game. Maybe she ought to get on that, see what it's all about.

As she mused on this, a rich, soothing sound entered her consciousness. *"And when . . . when the night falls on ya, baby . . ."* Just to Maggie's right, the green-haired girl was singing along with The Pretenders, an octave below Chrissie Hynde. She had a voice like silk. Smooth and sultry. It surrounded and enveloped Maggie, calling her closer.

Maggie hesitated a moment, then shifted herself over, next to the source. "That's beautiful."

"Uh—!" The girl's eyes went wide, and she quickly looked down at her drink. Emerald locks cascaded across her cheek.

"Sorry, I didn't mean to startle you." Maggie leaned forward slightly, searching for the face behind the veil of green. "I'm Maggie."

"Leah." She just barely glanced at Maggie, offering a reluctant, fleeting smile. "It's okay. I didn't realize I was singing."

"Don't let me stop you. I came over here to listen."

"Heh." Leah's cheeks turned pink. "Yeah—I don't like to sing in front of people."

"I can . . . go back over there." Maggie pointed to the other end of the couch. "If that helps."

Leah chuckled. "It's not that. It's just . . ." She ventured another brief glance at Maggie. "I have a guy's singing voice. My natural range. I hate it."

Maggie's brow furrowed. "A guy's . . . ? No." She put a hand on Leah's, on the cushion between them. "That's not a guy's voice. It's *your* voice."

The color in Leah's cheeks intensified. Biting her lip, she stared down at Maggie's hand overlapping her own.

"Oh!" Maggie removed it. "Sorry, I . . ."

"S'okay."

Maggie paused, worried that she'd just overstepped a boundary. She bowed her head and looked at their hands, resting side by side. Seconds passed.

"What were you gonna say?" Leah reached up and brushed her hair behind her ear as she turned to face Maggie.

"Just, uh—so what if it's deep? It belongs to a woman, so it's a woman's voice." Maggie could feel Leah's gaze on her—and a blush rising. "Anyway . . . that's what I think. If you wanna sing, you should. 'Cause it's really"—she raised her head and was greeted with freckled cheeks, shapely lips—"really beautiful." Their eyes met. Time seemed to slow down.

The Pretenders ended. The Cars' "Drive" came on.

"Thank you." Leah put her hand back down. Her fingers fell partly over Maggie's with a feather-light touch. She didn't move them.

Maggie ran out of words. She'd become lost in those big, soft brown irises. There was a pull like she'd never felt before. A magnetism. A spark, igniting the air between them. She swallowed. Her heart pounded.

Boom . . . boom . . . boom . . .

Afterword

(contains spoilers)

When I set out to write this book, it was on the heels of my short story "Wrapped Up with a Bow"—a light, erotic romp introducing Lynn and Jet. I certainly didn't expect *Kat & Mouse* to become as heavy as it did. But as I built the story, Kat and Dot began telling me who they were, and I had a lot of learning to do to keep up—especially with Dot.

It was a conscious decision on my part to avoid naming Dot's diagnosis early on, largely due to the stigma surrounding it. I wanted to let you get to know Dot without preconceptions, so your understanding of her BPD would be based on your understanding of *her*, and not the other way around.

Please note that Dot cannot be—and isn't meant to be—representative of anyone but herself. As she mentions in her letter, BPD is a complicated condition. Symptoms and coping mechanisms can vary widely from person to person, and treatment plans are highly individual. Dot's experiences, perspective, and journey of recovery are specific to her.

That said, it is my hope that readers—both with and without BPD—are able to connect with aspects of Dot's experience. It's often easy to view those with a mental illness as "other." But such things are far more common than many people realize, and we are often far more alike on the inside than our outward actions might suggest.

If you would like more information on BPD (also called emotionally unstable personality disorder, or EUPD), a couple of good places to start are nami.org and borderlinepersonalitydisorder.org. Additionally, at themighty.com you'll find many firsthand stories about living with BPD, which can give unparalleled insight.

Acknowledgements

Mom and Dad, who believed from page one (literally and figuratively). Bex, who taught me the value of accountability by always calling out suspected bullshit. Foley, Charlie, and Hoffenson, to whose wit and wordplay I owe much of my appreciation for linguistics.

Ren, Ash, Art, and Jae H., who've been steadfast supports and confidants. Liz and Jae B., whose enthusiasm inspired me to revive this whole Crosscannon mess. Buffie, Cathy, Amanda, Tracy, and Vince, for all their time and thoughtful feedback.

My entire derby family, which consists of far too many names to list here. Everyone in Philly Roller Derby who inspired me to keep getting back up and trying again. Everyone in Brandywine Roller Derby who made me proud to call it home. Shout out to Shore Points for those wild two months we had together (and for introducing me to picklebacks).

All the folks who let me talk their ears off and think aloud throughout this process.

All the people whose shared stories provided windows into understanding Dot better.

Shirley, Duke, Steve, and Butch, who pulled me to the surface and kept me swimming long before I could even see land.

And Isabel the iguana, who was my constant companion through the ups and downs of the past eleven years.

About the Author

Jacquelyn Heat is the derby moniker of one Rita Kelly. Rita has been involved in derby since 2009, starting with Philly Roller Derby and later moving to Brandywine Roller Derby. She was a bit of a pioneer as the first openly transgender member of each league.

In addition to playing as a skater, Rita has been an official, held positions on BRD's leadership board, occasionally filled the roles of bench manager and bench coach, and served as captain of the 2015 Brandywine Brawlers. In 2017, Rita reduced her direct involvement in derby to focus on music and writing.

Outside of derby, Rita is a rock vocalist, songwriter, and author. In addition to working on her own original songs, she can be seen performing regularly with the "Grad School" group at her local School of Rock. *Kat & Mouse* is Rita's first major work of fiction.

By day, Rita works in a clerical support role at a psychiatric facility. Rita herself lives with depression and anxiety and believes strongly in visibility as a means of fighting the stigmas surrounding mental illness.

New Recruit FAQ

THANK YOU FOR YOUR INTEREST IN CROSSCANNON ROLLER DERBY! IF YOU ARE NEW TO THE SPORT, YOU UNDOUBTEDLY HAVE MANY QUESTIONS, ESPECIALLY IF YOU HAVE YET TO SEE ACTUAL GAMEPLAY. IN THIS FAQ, WE BREAK DOWN SOME OF THE RULES, STRATEGY, AND TERMINOLOGY WITHOUT GETTING TOO TECHNICAL. WHILE THERE IS MUCH TO LEARN BEYOND THIS, WE HOPE TO PROVIDE YOU WITH A SOLID FOUNDATION IN UNDERSTANDING THE GAME WE SO LOVE.

– Coach Train Rex and the CRD Training Committee

WHAT IS FLAT TRACK ROLLER DERBY?

Flat track roller derby is a full-contact sport played between two teams on quad roller skates. Each team fields five skaters at a time—one "jammer" and four "blockers." Players skate counter-clockwise on an oval track. The job of each jammer is to score points for their team, which they accomplish by lapping opponents. The blockers' job is twofold; they must work to impede the opposing jammer, but they must also try to clear a path for their own jammer.

BUT ISN'T ROLLER DERBY PLAYED ON A BANKED TRACK?

A little history: In the mid-twentieth century, professional derby was played on a banked track. In 2001, the sport was revived at a grassroots, amateur level, and the building and storing of a banked track proved cost prohibitive. To overcome this dilemma, the game was redesigned to be played on a flat surface. This allowed leagues to lay down track outlines with little more than paint or tape. The flexibility of the flat-track design made derby far more accessible.

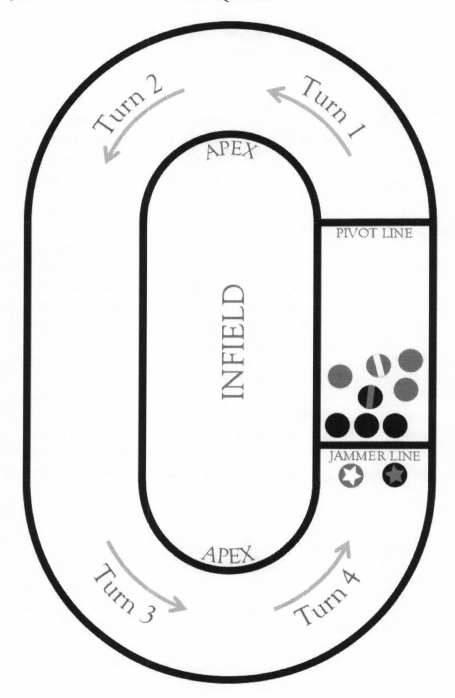

News spread, and flat track derby grew from a single league in Austin, TX into a worldwide phenomenon.

THE TRACK

The track is about 14 feet wide, from the inner boundary line to the outer. The distance traveled in a single lap is around 200 feet. The out-of-bounds space inside the oval is known as the **infield**. Team benches and the penalty box are located off to the side of the track.

JAMS AND PERIODS

Roller derby is played in a series of short rounds known as **jams**. Jams vary in duration, but never go longer than two minutes. There is a break of thirty seconds between jams, during which teams may switch out players. A single game (often called a "**bout**") is divided into two thirty-minute **periods**. If a jam is still in progress when the period clock reaches 0:00, gameplay continues until the jam is over.

SKATER POSITIONS

Jammer

Each team fields one jammer per jam. Each jammer wears a helmet cover displaying a star. Jammers begin each jam behind the jammer line. Jammers score points for their teams by lapping opposing skaters.

Blocker

Each team fields four blockers per jam. Blockers begin each jam just ahead of the jammers, in the area between the jammer line and the pivot line. Blockers work together to stop the opposing jammer from scoring. Blockers also help their own jammer by interfering with the opponents' defense.

Pivot

One of the blockers on each team may be designated as a pivot. The pivot wears a helmet cover displaying a stripe down the middle. During a jam, the jammer may **pass the star** to the pivot, who would then take over as jammer.

WHAT IS THE "PACK"?

Blockers must remain within a certain distance of one another. This grouping is known as the **pack**. The pack may expand and contract to a certain degree. But if a blocker gets too far away from the rest, that blocker is considered out-of-play and may not hit anyone until she returns to the pack. Under certain circumstances, skaters might be separated in such a way that there is "no pack." If this happens, none of them may hit each other until the pack is reformed.

WHAT IS "LEAD JAMMER"?

Each jam, the jammers start behind the pack. The first jammer to make it through the pack is declared **lead jammer**. The lead jammer may choose to end the jam at any time by touching her hips twice. This is known as "calling off the jam." There are a number of strategic reasons that one might call off the jam.

WHAT KINDS OF HITS ARE ALLOWED?

Skaters primarily use their hips, shoulders, butts, and chests to check opponents. A skater may NOT use the following body parts against an opponent: elbows, forearms, hands, knees, shins, feet, or head.

Additionally, a skater must hit the opponent in a legal target zone. This means no tripping, no head shots, and no hitting directly in the back.

Jump shots are NOT allowed, though a jumping skater may *be* hit by an opponent. Downed skaters are off-limits entirely.

WHAT HAPPENS IF SKATERS STOP OR SKATE IN THE WRONG DIRECTION?

A skater is allowed to stop or skate clockwise on the track, but **may** not hit or impede an opponent while doing so. That would result in a penalty call of "stop block" or "direction."

PENALTIES: HOW DO THEY WORK?

A referee issues a penalty by whistling once, then calling out the player's jersey color, number, and the type of penalty. (*TWEEET!* "White five, stop block!")

A penalty is **thirty seconds** long. If the skater is still in the box when the jam ends, the penalty time is paused until the next jam starts. That skater can't be switched out between jams.

Most penalties are self-explanatory—forearm, high block, low block, etc. However, some are less intuitive.

WHAT IS A "MULTIPLAYER" PENALTY?

A multiplayer block happens when two teammates hold onto one another while holding an opponent back, creating a defensive wall that is *impossible* to break through. Teammates may press themselves together to keep an opponent from pushing between them, but they may not link arms or grip each other for this purpose.

WHAT IS A "TRACK CUT" PENALTY?

Put *very* simply, a track cut happens when a skater goes out-of-bounds behind someone, then comes back in-bounds ahead of them, thereby "cutting" in front of them. But that's just the tip of the iceberg. Track cuts can become complicated and confusing to the untrained eye.

Here's a scenario: Siren is on the red team. Vee and Fiend are on the blue team. Fiend is up ahead of Siren. Vee comes alongside Siren and hits her, sending her out-of-bounds. Now, Siren must return in-bounds *behind* both Vee and Fiend.

Simple enough, right? However, what happens if Vee suddenly starts skating back the other way while Siren is out-of-bounds? Siren must still come in behind Vee, which means Siren must also backtrack before returning in-bounds. Vee is doing this to delay Siren. It's a strategy known as a "runback."

But let's say Vee gets knocked out-of-bounds herself while Siren is still out-of-bounds. In that case, Vee's position becomes void. Siren may now legally cut in front of her. This situation is known as "no pass, no penalty."

Track cuts are tricky, but they play a major role in strategy at all skill levels.

WHAT IS AN "INSUBORDINATION" PENALTY?

Penalties like "insubordination" and "misconduct" refer to issues of protocol and sportsmanship. Actions like cussing at the refs or failing to obey a penalty call would be considered insubordination.

WHAT DO THE DIFFERENT WHISTLE SIGNALS MEAN?

TWEEET!
   A single whistle blast signals the start of a jam. If the jam is already underway, then a single whistle blast indicates that a penalty is being called.

TWEET-TWEET!
   A double whistle blast indicates that a lead jammer has been declared.

TWEET-TWEET-TWEET-TWEET!
   Four whistle blasts signal the end of a jam.

TWEEeeeEET!
   A rolling whistle signals the end of a timeout. It can also be used to signal the end of halftime or the end of the bout.

WHAT IS AN "APEX JUMP"?

The apex is the tip of the infield (see track diagram). Normally, a jammer would need to fight her way through the pack on each lap. But when the pack is on the curve of the track, you may see the jammer try to bypass the pack entirely by jumping over the apex. This is a daring move, flying over that small out-of-bounds area. But as long as the jammer takes off in-bounds and lands in-bounds, it's perfectly legal and very effective.

WHAT DOES IT MEAN WHEN SKATERS SHOUT "ONE," "TWO," "THREE," OR "FOUR"?

For communication's sake, we divide the track into **four imaginary lanes.** "One" refers to the innermost lane, then "two" and "three," with "four" being the outermost lane. This shorthand lets teammates quickly and concisely communicate the position of the opposing jammer.

WHAT IS A "WALL" IN DERBY?

A wall is a defensive formation intended to hold back the opposing jammer. A "four-wall," for example, refers to four skaters standing side by side across the track. More commonly, you'll see something like a "three-wall with a brace," in which case three skaters would form the wall itself, facing forward. A fourth skater—the brace—would be positioned in front of them, facing backwards. The skaters in the wall can reach out and lean on the brace for support. The brace has a clear view of what's happening behind the wall and communicates this information to her teammates.

WHAT DO THE DIFFERENT REFEREE POSITIONS MEAN?

All referees watch for rules infractions and issue penalties when necessary.

Pack Refs primarily keep an eye on the pack. They signal warnings when skaters are out-of-play. **Inside Pack Refs** (IPRs) skate in the infield, and **Outside Pack Refs** (OPRs) skate along the outside of the track.

Jammer Refs also skate in the infield. Their job is to track the jammers. Jammer refs tally points and communicate them to the scorekeepers via hand signals.

WRAP-UP

Much of the information here has been simplified or generalized, as this FAQ is only meant to help you get the gist of what's going on. Should you wish to dig in and learn more about specific rules or advanced strategy, a wealth of information is available online. Stop by the CRD website (crosscannonrollerderby.com) or use your favorite search engine!